Gunning for the

FINISH

Also by Jim Overturf

The Kurt Maxxon Series

Masonville

Kings Rapids

Carpentier Falls

Gunning for the
FINISH

A Kurt Maxxon Mystery

Jim Overturf

Three Cords Publishing Co
Lincoln, NE 68521

Gunning for the Finish

A Kurt Maxxon Mystery

© 2012 by James L Overturf

ISBN 978-0-9839117-2-2

LCCN: 2011961986

Follow Kurt at: www.KurtMaxxonRacing.com

Three Cords Publishing Co
5100 No 27th St., Ste., A-2
PMB-306
Lincoln, NE 68521
www.ThreeCordsPublishing.com

Printed in the United States of America

Dedicated to *Karen Lee, with*

All the love I can share!

CHAPTER ONE
Friday Afternoon, August 24

Kurt Maxxon

It seemed like the main gate into the racetrack got narrower each time I arrived. However, since my rig was two feet longer than the last time might help explain it. My tow vehicle was a new Ford F-350 with a 6.7 liter V-8 diesel engine—enough heft to carry and pull whatever I needed. A full sized cab-over camper was tucked into the bed behind the cab, and I was towing an enclosed car carrier. With only inches to spare, I made it through the gate, and shut the rig down in the driveway in front of the admin building. My bladder felt ready to burst.

I looked at Christina, who shook her head and said, "You go ahead, I'm okay for right now." Beau, our Beagle-Schnauzer mix, bounced over the console from the backseat onto Christina's lap. He eagerly pawed at the door to be let out, wagging his tail wildly. "I'll take him for a walk before we unload Nikki," Christina said, nodding toward Doggy Do Field, the grassy area between garage row and the racetrack. Several drivers brought their pets to the races, so every track provided accommodations.

As soon as I got out of the truck I noticed the cacophony of noise from the fairgrounds adjacent to the track. Greene County owns and operates both the fairgrounds and the racetrack with a minimum of fencing separating the two. I walked quickly toward the driver's lounge door. The August weather was cooler than normal due to overnight rains that swept across the valley. The driver's lounge door was usually wide open on Fridays, Saturday and especially race day—Sunday. As I reached for the handle, the door flew open stinging my hand. I stopped. What the devil?

A man stood in the doorway, one blue eye looking at me,

the other—a brown eye—stared wildly off in a slightly different direction. He hadn't shaved for months. His dirty gray hair looked like it had been cropped by a dull knife. His torn jeans and T-shirt were filthy. His sneakers were black from dirt. In his left hand, he held a wad of money; the right hand pointed a huge pistol at me.

We stared at each other for an eternity. My heart was trying to beat its way out of my chest. "Ummm, may I help you?" I asked.

"Get back," the man croaked and stepped toward me, moving the gun within inches of my face. I backed up and stared at the canon-sized barrel. "Get down on your stomach," the man croaked louder. I heard Beau bark as he warned Christina.

"Take—take it easy, partner," I stammered, hoping my voice didn't betray my fear. I let myself down onto one knee. Before I could get all the way down, the man turned and ran toward the main gate. He hesitated for a moment, then turned right and ran into the fair parking lot. I got up and trotted to the gate, looking to see where he'd gone, but he'd vanished into the sea of cars and the crowds of people.

I turned around and nearly knocked Christina off her feet. I grabbed her by the arm to keep her from falling. Fortunately, she's a light woman at about 135 pounds and easy for me to handle with one hand. Her blue eyes shot wide open, her mouth shaped in an "o", and a stiff breeze ruffled her blond hair from behind. Beau barked wildly at the end of his leash pulled taut toward where the man had disappeared.

"Where'd he come from?" she gasped, fighting to catch her breath. She swept her hair back from her face with both hands.

"He must have robbed the office," I said. "He had a wad of cash in his hand." I reached into the cell phone pocket of my cargo pants, but my cell phone still sat on the dash of the truck. "Call 9-1-1," I said to Christina.

Christina dug her cell phone out of its holster and dialed. I listened as she went through the grilling only 9-1-1 operators are trained to give. I checked the door into the admin office and confirmed it was locked. Where was Helen Tobias—the racetrack's secretary? I hope she took a long lunch, but then how did that guy get in there?

As I followed Christina toward the driver's lounge, I

glanced at my rig, standing alone in the driveway. On the side of the car carrier was a stylized drawing of Nikki, my number 27 Ford Taurus racecar. Along the bottom of the trailer was red lettering: Kurt Maxxon Racing.

I'm Kurt Maxxon; five-foot-eleven and 192 pounds with balding gray hair and brown eyes. At least that's what my driver's license said. The height and weight were true a dozen years ago. I retired from the U.S. Marine Corps as a Lt. Colonel after twenty-six years in aviation, flying all-weather fighter aircraft. When I retired, I moved back to my boyhood hometown, bought an auto parts store, and took up stock car racing.

Christina was still talking to the 9-1-1 operator as we entered the driver's lounge adjacent to the admin building. Nature, who had called earlier, now screamed at me. I saw Christina sniffing the air, and then it dawned on me. "That guy must have shot that pistol in here," I said.

Christina nodded agreement. "It smells like firecrackers," she said, holding her cell phone close to her chest.

I moved toward the men's facilities. As I walked past the locker area, I noticed a man's hand under a bench and turned into the area to check it out. A few steps in, and I bent down to look under the wood bench and saw Melvyn Hightower, a local driver.

Melvyn had pulled his boxer shorts on before someone put a bullet into his chest, at close enough range to slam the body against the row of lockers. He was lying on his back with his right leg crumpled under him at an odd angle. His right arm was also askew. The blood spatter told me he had been shot standing in front of his open locker, a few feet from where he was lying now. I made a quick survey. A brown leather wallet was on the floor in front of Melvyn's open locker with several credit cards scattered around it on the floor. Damn, that's where that dude got the wad of cash! Is a handful of cash enough to shoot a man for?

I walked quickly back into the kitchen area and heard Christina saying, "The man had a gun and a wad of cash in his hand." I waved to get Christina's attention. When she saw me, she spoke into the phone, "Hold on a minute." She mouthed "what" to me.

I said, "Tell them there's a dead body in the locker room."

"A—what?" Christina's eyebrows went up, and her mouth

made another "o".

"That guy robbed Melvyn Hightower and shot him to death."

"Operator," Christina shouted. "Operator, there's a dead body in the locker room here, apparently shot during the robbery."

I nearly trotted toward the restroom—Mother Nature was near the end of her patience. "I need to go." As I moved toward the facilities, I shouted to Christina over my shoulder, "Would you dig out the coffee pot and get it started?" I heard Christina rattling the fifty-cup coffee maker out from under the sink. Feeling a whole lot better after taking care of nature's call, I walked back into the kitchen area.

Christina still held her phone to her ear. She had slipped a filter into the basket, scooped coffee into the filter with one hand, and was filling a quart Mason jar with water. I walked over, took the jar from her hand, and finished filling the pot. Christina nodded and walked to sit down at the dinette table in the kitchen corner of the driver's lounge, her cell phone still at her ear.

The racetrack was used by five regional racing associations, four of which raced on Saturday afternoons. I was the president of the Swift River Valley Stock Car Racing Association, or the SRVSCRA, or "Shrev-Scraw" for the brave of heart who tried to verbalize it. We were the largest of the racing leagues competing at the track which we did twice a year on Sunday afternoons. There was a high interest in stockcar racing in the valley so all the racing leagues garnered a lot of fan support.

I made a quick survey of the driver's lounge to see if anything was out of order. The driver's lounge was ostensibly for drivers to relax in, but during a race weekend it functioned mainly as a meeting room. We had a pre-qualifying meeting each Saturday afternoon before the qualifying runs, and then there was a pre-race driver's meeting each Sunday before the race. The lounge had two pool tables and kitchen cabinets in a corner with a sink and a refrigerator. We used folding chairs for the meetings, and they were lined along the wall next to the pool tables. The wall between the kitchen corner and the entrance door contained two white boards, and there was a bulletin board at the kitchen end of the wall. The rest of the lounge building was made up of a Men's Locker/Shower room and a smaller Women's Locker/Shower room.

The coffee pot had settled into a rhythmic gurgling. No matter what time of day, the aroma of freshly brewed coffee enchanted me, capturing my total attention. In the distance I heard several sirens approaching the fairgrounds. Here we go again, Maxxon.

I felt sorry for the cops. Getting all the vehicles to the crime scene was going to be difficult. The streets surrounding the fairgrounds—through which the cops had to negotiate—were established in the days when horse-drawn wagons were the principal means of travel and were very narrow. Today the fair crowd made them even more difficult. The Centralia race was run the Sunday after the state fair closed on Saturday night. Friday and Saturday the streets and parking lots were always wall-to-wall people and cars. I had just driven through the mess.

Davy Westlake, the father of another local driver, crashed through the door. He was panting heavily, so he must have run on foot from Security Central to the driver's lounge. He was a retired cop from the Centralia Police Department who worked for a Rent-A-Cop agency now. I've seen him each year since he worked the fair and then the Sunday race.

"Hey, Colonel," he said, leaning over with his hands on his knees, gasping for breath. When his breathing was back to near normal, he said, "Tell me about this guy with the gun."

I described the man as best I could remember and stood by as Davy radioed everything to Security Central, nodding agreement with his transmissions. All the local fair security people were monitoring Davy on their radio frequency, as were the local police on their mutual-aid frequencies, so if they saw the guy they could keep track of him.

"We'll be watching all the gates," Davy said. "Are you okay?"

"I'm fine," I said.

Davy looked around the room and saw Christina sitting at a table in the kitchen area. "Hey, Christina, how you doing?" he said, and walked to give her a hug. A siren grew louder, and then trailed off to silence. Two uniformed police officers came through the door. The cavalry had arrived.

*   *   *

The incident commander came up to introduce himself.

"Masterson," he said. "I'll be in charge until the detectives take over."

"Kurt Maxxon," I replied.

"I know you, Colonel," Masterson said. "I root for Drew Westlake, normally. You know, Davy's boy and all."

"That's fine." I shrugged. "Drew is a very good driver." I would like for every man, woman, and child in the world to root for me. I knew that wasn't going to happen, so I was just happy there were so many race fans.

"Do you know the person who was killed?" Masterson asked.

"Yes. His name is Melvyn Hightower," I answered. "He's a local driver."

Masterson scribbled in his notebook, and then said, "I know who he is. Didn't remember his name. He owns the carpet store out east of town. Can you stand by and give the detectives a preliminary ID?"

"Sure."

"While you're waiting for that, we need a statement about the shooter. You ran into him when you got here, I understand."

"Yes, smack-dab face-to-face."

The coffee gurgled itself done, and I motioned toward it. Masterson led me to it, and we both drew a cup of coffee, and then I led him to the kitchenette table in the kitchen area. Christina took Beau for a walk and then put him into the truck. The temperature was in the mid-eighties, the truck was parked in the shade of the building, and we could leave all the windows down. She strolled into the driver's lounge, nearly being denied entrance by a cop Masterson had stationed to guard the door.

"She brewed the coffee," I yelled to the cop, who was obviously enjoying a cup of her coffee.

"She was in here before?" he asked, looking to Masterson who waved okay and the cop allowed Christina to enter.

To show there were no hard feelings, Christina phoned Rodger's Diner and asked them to bring a two-gallon jar of iced tea, two gallons of lemonade, three dozen finger sandwiches, and potato chips to the track. Rodger's Diner had catered several meetings and get-togethers at the track for me over the years. After I gave Masterson my description and statement, he left, and

Christina and I stayed in the kitchen area of the driver's lounge in order to stay out of the way.

Even before the tea and lemonade arrived, the driver's lounge was crowded with at least twenty people—cops, EMS personnel, crime scene technicians, medical examiner personnel and the medical examiner herself. The driver's lounge held forty people comfortably for the driver's meeting, even with two pool tables, a TV set, a dinette table and two chairs. We moved the pool tables aside to allow for the setting up of the rows of folding chairs.

Masterson walked up to me and said, "Do you have a key to that door into the admin offices? We'd like to check it out. We're about to call in a locksmith."

"I don't have a key," I said. "But I can get to it from the admin side, since I have a key card into the track's auxiliary office. I'll go around and open the door from the other side." I nodded toward the locked door.

Christina excused herself and followed me out of the lounge, saying she would wait in the truck with Beau. I walked around the building and let myself into a small auxiliary office. It was used by the track's bookkeeper, track officials, and other racing association officers like me. It held a desk, a table and a waste basket, all empty.

I moved out into the open bullpen and made another quick survey. Nothing seemed out of order. I gazed down the hallway formed between a restroom and a storage room that led to the locked driver's lounge door and walked to the door that led into the driver's lounge. I twisted the deadbolt knob unlocked, opened the door and motioned to one of the uniformed cops nearby.

"Nick is here," the cop said. "He just got here."

"Nick Boynton?" I asked.

"You know him?"

"Yes I do," I said. Nick was the oldest detective on Centralia's force. When he donned his blue uniform, he had more stripes and chevrons than any other cop on the CPD. He had more merit awards on his trophy wall than any other cop in the valley. He was two inches shorter than me and was growing a pot belly a quarter inch per year. If you envisioned a full head of black, unkempt hair instead of the white wisps on his head, Nick would be the perfect look alike for Peter Falk's Columbo character. His suit jacket was always rumpled and askew, and he often wore a trench coat when the weather demanded. He always talked with his hands just like Falk's character—but denied he did it intentionally.

I turned and walked back into the office area and went to my mailbox on the wall. There was a folded note in my box, and I unfolded it. Helen Tobias had handwritten the note telling me she had been called to Maplewood because her father had had a massive heart attack, and she wasn't sure how long she would be there. "Call me on my cell," she wrote.

I was reading the note when Nick Boynton walked up to me. He stuck out his hand. "You at it again, Colonel Maxxon?"

I gave him a wan smile. "My bad luck," I said.

"Ahhh, but my good luck," Nick said, his dark blue eyes twinkling. "When Kurt Maxxon finds a dead body, Kurt Maxxon usually finds out who made that body dead."

I grimaced and shook my head. The first time I became involved with a murder was in Masonville a few years ago. My lifelong buddy, Brad Langley, was very upset with me about my involvement, which nearly got Christina killed.

The next murder I helped solve was in Kings Rapids and, after it was over, Brad called me to thank me for my help but warned me not to be playing cop again. The third time was just last year when I helped solve two separate murders in Carpentier Falls. Brad begrudgingly told me I was good at it. I always worried about what Brad was going to say because his friendship was too important to me for me to screw up again.

Nick sat down in one of the steno chairs. "So, you found the body in the locker room. Bat says you can identify the guy in the locker room." Nick pointed with his chin toward the driver's lounge.

"That cop's name is Bat Masterson?" I said. "Like the wild west gambler and gunfighter?"

"Nah. His real name is Timothy." Nick chuckled. "But, we all call him Bat."

I shrugged.

"You know where the track secretary is?" Nick asked.

I handed the note to Nick. He read it and handed it back. "Okay. Can you call her?"

I twisted around and dialed Helen's cell phone number, using the phone on a nearby desk, and pressed the SPEAKER button.

"The track manager is still Karl Albertson?" Nick asked as we listened to the dial buzz.

"Yes," I said. "He's rarely here except on race days."

Helen answered, "Hello."

"Helen, this is Kurt Maxxon," I said.

"Oh, hi Kurt," Helen said. "I wondered who was calling on the track's phone. I'm glad you called me. My dad died Wednesday night. I've hardly been here, and now he's gone. We're going to have the funeral Monday morning."

"I'm sorry," I said.

"Thanks. I couldn't get hold of Karl," Helen said. "I left him a message."

"Don't worry about anything over here. We'll get by."

"If it was any of the other associations, I'd be worried. You're there, though, and you've been through this many times. I'm sorry to desert you, but I know you can do it yourself, Kurt."

"You've been in Maplewood since Wednesday?" I asked.

"Yeah. I left the track about two in the afternoon. Got here at four. Dad died about six-thirty. What's up?"

"There's been a homicide here in the locker room," I said.

"Who?" Helen asked.

I glanced at Nick. He nodded okay. "Melvyn Hightower," I said. "I found him dead about an hour ago."

"Shag!" Helen gasped. "My God! Someone killed Shag?"

Hearing Melvyn's nickname—Shag—gave me a pause. I'd trained myself to ignore nicknames, while an officer in the Marine Corps, and now over all the years I've been the president of the SRVSCRA. Nearly every person involved with the SRVSCRA had a nickname. Mine was "The Colonel," and Christina's was "The School Marm."

"How'd they kill him?" Helen asked.

I glanced at Nick again, and he wobbled his head. "I can't tell you that, Helen," I answered.

"I'll have to watch the news, huh?"

"Right! Has anything happened lately dealing with Melvyn that you know of?" I stared at Nick who was now bobbing his head.

"Nothing unusual that I know about," Helen said.

"Anybody unusual been hanging around the track?"

"No."

"You take care of things over there and don't worry about this place." She thanked me again, and we rang off.

"The stud in the locker room is Melvyn Hightower?" Nick asked.

"Yes. Melvyn Hightower. He's a local driver—owns Economy Carpet out on the east edge of town."

"Looks like he took a shower," Nick said. "What was he doing here at this time of day?"

"He probably ran practice laps," I said. "Finished and showered so he could go back to work."

Nick swiped at his forehead with his left hand, another similarity to Columbo. "I didn't pay any attention to whose truck is parked outside. Is that yours?"

"Yes, it is," I said. "I can move it out of the way."

"Where's Melvyn Hightower's car?"

"He rents garage number thirty-five. That's the number of his car. He was sort of superstitious. Number thirty-five is in the second batch of garages near the north end or garage row."

Nick pursed his lips. "Which garage do you use?"

"Number one, of course" I said. "I've rented that garage for years now. And I park my camper right next to it in the first space in the RV lot."

"You staying in your camper for the race weekend?" Nick asked.

Before I married Christina, Beau and I stayed in my camper for race weekend, even though the racetrack was only twelve miles from our house. It was easier being in the middle of the action. "No. I've got a new driver for my car," I said. "She and her boyfriend will be staying in the camper for the weekend."

"She?"

"Her name is Angie Prescotte," I said.

"I'll be snookered," Nick said, raising his eyebrows and dipping his head. "Is she as good a driver as you are?" He screwed up his face and looked at me in a questioning way.

"She's probably better—more patience. You know how I

am."

"Okay." Nick stood. "We'll be setting up a grid to search the area immediately around this building. My people will go over the tires on your rig with a fine toothed comb to see if they picked up anything when you drove through the crime scene area. Then I'd appreciate it if you would move it out of the grid area. Where can we find a key to Melvyn's garage?"

"They're probably in his clothes. If not, all of us are required to leave a key to the padlocks we use here with Helen. Those keys are in a locked key box in Karl's office." I nodded toward the corner office.

"You got a key to that lockbox?"

"No. But, I know where it is." I gave Nick my knowing smile. He doesn't need to know that Karl's office is typically not locked.

Nick said, "I'll have one of my people check out Melvyn's garage. Would you go with him, identify the car, see if there's anything unusual about it?"

"Sure. After you do my truck, I'll move it and unload Nikki."

"You don't leave Nikki here in your garage?"

"She's been over to Maurey's shop getting a new set of brakes. I'm just bringing her back."

Nick stood and stretched his lower back muscles. "It's hell to get old," he said, turned and smiled at me and continued, "but the alternative is worse."

"You're preaching to the choir, my friend," I said, and stretched my back by wiggling side to side.

Nick started to walk down the hall, stopped, and turned back to me. "I'll get the M.E. and you can give us a preliminary ID on the guy in the locker room."

"Okay," I said. "I hope they catch the guy with the gun before anybody gets hurt. He didn't look very stable, if you know what I mean."

"We'll get him," Nick said confidently. "We placed our people at every gate into the fairgrounds as fast as possible. Each gate has surveillance cameras, so we should be able to see which direction he went. A guy with a gun in one hand and a wad of cash in the other tends to stand out from the crowd."

"That's good," I said. "The fairgrounds are not a good place for a shootout."

*   *   *

A team of crime scene techs inspected the tires of my truck and trailer, and looked under both vehicles with mirrors. Christina and I took Beau to the Doggy Do area and walked with him on his leash. He kept looking back at the team inspecting the rig. "It's okay, Beau," I said. "They aren't going to hurt your truck."

"Angie and Tugs should be showing up anytime," Christina said. "Angie said they would leave Carpentier Falls right after lunch. Tugs had to work until noon."

I knelt down and scratched Beau's ears while he stood on his hind feet and pawed at my knees. Beau gave a low growl, and I swung around to look at what was upsetting him. "I should have known Kurt Maxxon was in town," I heard a gruff but familiar voice say behind me. Raeffert Komminski hobbled toward me using his matching ebony canes with ivory hand-carved handles.

"A dead body at the racetrack," he said as he shook my hand. "The stuff the Kurt Maxxon legend is made of."

Raeffert was the Editor-in-Chief of the Valley Voice & Reporter newspaper. He was eighty-one years old, six foot eight and weighed about 250 pounds; completely bald with just a few wisps of white hair around the ears. His gunmetal blue eyes always made me feel like he was X-raying my brain. A large bulbous nose dominated his face and he wore a perpetual frown, from a rather hard life, I supposed.

Rafe, as Raeffert was affectionately known, walked to Christina and patted her on the arm. Being an old-line European male in America, Rafe was rather patronizing toward women.

I've known two of Raeffert's four wives since I met him. Three of them died. Fortunately, his current wife was much younger, in very good health, and she took very good care of Rafe. In 1994, two years after I met him, his third wife, Ruth, died from some disease contracted while on one of her missionary trips to Central America. Rafe swore off marriage, since he was sixty-eight years old.

"Nick told me you were here," Rafe said. "We had a hell of a time getting in, what with all the fair traffic and people. But, that gives us rag guys an advantage."

"An advantage?" I said, glancing toward the rubberneckers at the perimeter.

"The TV people won't be able to get their trucks back here," Rafe said, smiling. He stood hunched forward braced against his two canes.

In January 1997, at age seventy-one, Rafe slipped on an icy sidewalk and shattered his pelvis so badly, some of the doctors questioned whether he would ever walk again. The doubters, however, didn't know Rafe. He underwent several surgeries and then went to a rehab nursing home for nine weeks. After his release, Rafe returned to his home in the Woodlawn area of Centralia, since his youngest daughter, Deborah, lived five blocks away. There was also a great visiting nurse system from a nearby hospital. One of the visiting nurses was Katarina (Mendoza) Muire, a divorced woman in her mid-thirties at the time. Katarina and Rafe were married in September of 1998.

"The TV people have their trucks over in the infield of the racetrack," I said.

"Yeah, I know," Rafe said. "They're broadcasting from there now. But they won't be able to get those trucks over here. They're just out of range to use their cameras over here."

I always marveled at how little of Rafe's background came out in his speech. You could just barely detect a faint English Cockney accent, not the Swiss German or the Polish dialect of his father.

"For Christ's sake, Maxxon," Rafe said as if he needed to talk. "You come to town, and we've got a murder on our hands."

"My auto parts store is in Centralia," I said. "So I didn't just come to town today. I come to town every day." Christina and I lived in Albertstown. Most people ignore the Albertstown City Limits signs.

"Oh, yeah," Rafe said. "That's right. Albertstown is still a separate suburb." He pointed a cane toward the driver's lounge door. "Have you figured out who the killer is yet?"

"No, I'm not officially involved."

"Bullshit, Maxxon. You, Kurt Maxxon, found the body. That always means you, Kurt Maxxon, are going to figure out who the killer is."

"I hate to disappoint you, Rafe, but I'm not involved with

this case."

"Alright, yeah, okay," Rafe said. "Just because you're working undercover, would you keep me informed about what the hell is going on? I mean, let me have the scoop of who killed the guy, just as soon as you figure out who did it."

"If I can help you scoop the other media, I surely will," I said, and spread a wide grin. "We are partners, right?"

"You're already getting all the discounts we give for your advertising, Maxxon. Do it for me as an old friend," Rafe said. "You found the body. Did you get here in time to see the guy with the gun?" Rafe asked.

"Yes, I did," I said. "In fact he pointed the gun at me and then took off running."

"You saw the guy?" Rafe said, his eyebrows rising. "You can identify him?"

"I think so," I said, not sure if I could or not. "He rattled me a little bit, pointing that gun at me."

"Kurt Maxxon was rattled by a gun toting crook?" Rafe said, screwing up his mouth and pulling his head back in disbelief. "If he rattled you, that would be a first—a first that would make front-page headline news. I can see the headline now: INCIDENT RATTLES KURT MAXXON."

"He rattled me," I said.

"Amazing," Rafe said. "Kurt Maxxon can be rattled."

I looked around. "Where's your chauffeur?" I knew they couldn't get very close because of the patrol cars blocking the entrance to the garage/admin area. "I forgot her name; what is it again?" I asked.

"Roberta," Rafe said. "She's parked south of the admin building, unloading my golf cart. Will you open the gates so she can drive around through the driver's storage area over there?"

"Sure," I said. "And I'll turn on the electrical hookup in RV space number two so you can charge it."

"Thanks," Rafe said.

I left to unlock the gates. I decided to leave the gates unlocked, the padlock open and hanging on the chains. The fairgoers, hopefully, would not try them. While I waited for Roberta to drive the golf cart through the gate, a photographer arrived, ran to jump into the seat next to her and rode in with her. I couldn't remember his name, either, which set me to worrying about me having early onset Alzheimer's.

I heard a noise and looked to see Bat Masterson waving me toward him. I walked back to my rig. "Nick wants to see you," he said, throwing a thumb toward the driver's lounge.

I went to find Nick. He was in the driver's lounge, sitting at the kitchenette table, and talking on his cell phone. I hung back waiting for him to finish his conversation.

Nick hung up and folded his cell phone. When he saw me, he walked to me and handed me a business card. "I wrote my cell number on it. You're the only non-law enforcement guy in the valley that has it."

I gave him one of my KurtMaxxonRacing.com cards. "Mine's on there."

"Good," Nick said. "We'll be done with your truck in a minute. I'm serious about wanting your help on this case. Off the record, of course."

"I'll do whatever I can," I said. "Off the record is good enough for me."

CHAPTER TWO
Friday Late Afternoon, August 24

Kurt Maxxon
When the cops cleared my truck and trailer, I moved my rig to the front of garage number one; where Christina and I prepared to unload Nikki. I ran the stabilizing jacks down to level the trailer while Christina pulled the ramps into position. As I locked the levelizers, Christina opened the rear doors. We both stood looking at Nikki's rear end, gleaming from the polish Maurey had applied.

As I climbed into the trailer with Nikki, I noticed Rafe Komminski sitting in his golf cart and chatting with Officer Masterson. Since Rafe was making notes, Masterson must be answering questions. The photographer was shooting pictures of the area, waiting for access to the driver's lounge to get shots of the actual murder scenes. The afternoon was still pleasantly cool with a breeze rustling the edges of the golf cart's canvas roof, wrinkling the lettering that read: The Valley Voice & Reporter.

In 1989 the Valley Voice, the oldest newspaper in the entire valley, merged with the Greene County Reporter, the second oldest newspaper in the valley, to form The Valley Voice & Reporter newspaper. Rafe has been the top man at the newspaper since the merger.

Nikki creaked slightly as we eased her down the ramps. We had just rolled Nikki off the ramps when a female uniformed cop walked toward us and said, "Detective Boynton wants you to get a key and go with me to check out the number thirty-five garage."

The brass name badge over her left pocket read: OFR: K. Lacy. She was moderate height and slim waisted, probably mid-thirties. Dark brown hair cut easy-to-manage short framed her oval face. She had a hook nose that might have been broken once or twice; brown eyes with penciled on eyebrows. Her smile was disarming even with the butt of a huge Glock 9 mm weapon sticking out of a holster on her left hip.

I left Christina and Officer Lacy talking, walked around to the visitor's office door, and used my key-card to let myself in. I moved to the filing cabinet next to Helen Tobias's desk and pulled the bottom drawer open. I fingered through the files to a file marked MISC TAGS and took out the key to the key lockbox, on the wall in Karl Albertson's office, usually unseen behind the open door. I opened the lockbox and took out the garage key hanging on the number thirty-five peg. A spare car key also hung on the peg, so I grabbed it to prevent another trip.

I walked back to Officer Lacy and Christina and led them toward the number 35 garage. While we walked, I listened to Christina explaining her involvement with the school system, and that she knew several Lacy children. Officer Lacy recognized all the names Christina mentioned as cousins. When we arrived at the garage, Lacy pulled evidence bags from her pocket, carefully grasped the padlock inside the bag, and unlocked it. She repeated the process with the padlock on the other side, stepped back and as she sealed the evidence bags, said, "Can you lift the door using just the end of that rope? Hemp rope like that doesn't take on fingerprints very well, but we always check."

I nodded acceptance and bent down to grip the rope. I was careful not to grip more than was necessary. Lacy walked to the outside garage wall and wrote on the evidence bags with a permanent marker.

I was so focused on lifting the door without leaving any of my fingerprints, that I didn't pay attention to the room inside until the door was fully open. We stood looking into an empty room. A pair of tool boxes occupied the metal work bench across the front of the room surrounded by air tools and test gear neatly arranged for easy use.

"That's strange," I said.

"No car," Lacy observed, a puzzled look on her face.

"I wonder where his car is?" I said. "If Melvyn hadn't run practice laps, why would he shower?"

"Good question," Lacy said as she walked toward the

workbench. "Is all this stuff normal? Anything missing or out of place?"

I walked slowly around the room, surveying the clean floor, the array of stuff on the workbench, and the nude calendar on the wall above the bench. "Other than no car, the garage is pretty much what I expect," I said. "Typical driver's garage."

"You better not have a calendar like that one in your garage," Christina said.

I grinned at her. "I think it adds a nice touch." When Christina grimaced, I moved to hug her shoulders and said, "You know I don't have anything like that."

"My husband has them, too," Officer Lacy said. "It's a man thing."

Two technicians came up to the entrance to the garage, pushing a flatbed cart loaded with equipment and cans. They looked around and frowned. "Boss said we should come dust a car," one said. "Where's the car?" the second one asked.

"There is no car," Lacy said. She pointed to the door knob on the side door and a key on a nail next to the door. "Dust those, please." she said to the technicians.

"Melvyn's car may be somewhere around the track," I said. "Not many drivers would leave their car unattended with all the fairgoers in the area. I'll make a fast tour to see if I can spot it. I've got spare padlocks in my rig. When I get back from looking around the track, I'll lock this door with a pair of spare padlocks, so no one steals the tools and equipment. I'll give you the key."

"That'll work," Lacy said.

Rafe drove his golf cart to the area in front of the garage. "Where's the guy's car?"

I walked toward Rafe and sat down next to him in the cart. "I have no idea," I said. "You can drive me over to the grandstand so I can look around. Maybe he left it over there."

"Worth a look," Rafe said and he punched the throttle hard. We leaped forward, leaving Christina, Lacy and the technicians in the dust. I've only got a little more hair than Rafe, and it was whipping around tickling my ears.

"I didn't realize you have a secret desire to be a race driver," I said.

"Stow it, Maxxon," Rafe said. "This damn thing will only

do twenty miles per hour. Takes me forever to get anywhere. Besides, I do not have a desire to be a race driver. I do, however, sometimes think about writing mystery stories about a hero who is a race car driver. I have been looking for a good driver to model my sleuth after, but I haven't found one yet. Soon as I do, I'll start writing."

As we bumped toward the racetrack area, I studied Rafe's twin canes in their special tube holders. They were crafted from ebony wood with hand-carved ivory handles. The carving in the handles represented everything important in Rafe's life: seven grown children, his Polish and Czech heritage, his escape after Nazi Germany invaded Poland, and his journey to the United States via Switzerland and England.

Rafe drove to the elevators, and we rode up to the concession level. Rafe steered me to the center of the grandstand and stopped. I stepped out and made a quick survey. From the higher vantage point, I scanned the track area and pit rows on both sides of the infield littered with TV trailers and other communications vehicles. There was no black and gold car. I walked out onto the stair landing opposite the track and looked over the parking lot, looking for Melvyn's black and gold number 35 car. The track's parking lot was littered with people because there was a Ferris wheel and a Tilt-a-whirl set up in it. There was a fair parking lot across the street, and I studied the cars in it for several minutes. There was no sign of the black and gold number thirty-five car, so I returned to Rafe waiting for me in his golf cart.

"No number thirty-five car?" Rafe asked.

"I didn't see a black and gold anything." I shrugged and wobbled my head.

"The plot thickens," Rafe said, as we lurched forward and drove back toward my truck in the garage area. Christina and Beau were sitting in the truck. As I climbed out of Rafe's cart, I saw Lacy and the technicians coming toward me.

"You can put your padlocks on the door now," Lacy said. "The techs lifted a couple of latents off the door knob, the key, and the door. They look to be old and the same person. They'll know more after they get to the lab and can work with AFIS. Maybe these padlocks will have better prints on them."

I walked to the junk box built into the side of Nikki's

transporter and dug out a package of two matching padlocks. I unlocked the padlocks, kept one key, and handed the other keys to Lacy. "Thanks for your help," she said as she took a business card from her breast pocket and handed it to Christina. "You can call me or Detective Boynton if you remember anything else. If you spot the car, please let us know." She left to go report to Nick.

I walked to Melvyn's garage, installed the locks, and returned. For the next several minutes Christina and I watched a dozen people search the grid they had laid out, marking locations, picking up and bagging bits of evidence, and making notes of everything. Beau stood with his paws on the dashboard to watch occasionally, but lost interest quickly and hopped into the back seat to curl up and sleep.

About 3:30 Angie and her boyfriend, Tugs Matthews, arrived at the main gate. Tugs parked his Ford Explorer in a space outside the main fence, and I watched as Angie led him in a circuitous route through the main gates into the driver's storage area, through to the track, and then back into the garage area.

At the end of last year's racing season, after much deliberation, I decided my body, at sixty-something plus, had had enough of driving, and called it quits. I was tired. I had thought about just parking Nikki and walking away, but my competitive spirit wouldn't allow that. Christina prodded me to find a driver to keep Nikki roaring around the SRVSCRA tracks. Maurey Kennedy, who builds my race-winning engines, said, "You can't quit now. You're at the top of your game, winning every third race."

"I'm getting tired of it, Maurey," I'd said.

Christina and Maurey teamed up on me.

"Do you really want to quit racing?" Maurey asked me. "Or just the driving?"

"Just the driving," I'd said after several moments of reflection.

"Then let's find a driver to drive our car," Christina said. "If Dukes Ford won't continue as a sponsor, we'll sponsor the car ourselves."

In one of the more convoluted events to occur in my life, we eventually found a driver in an unexpected way. I tried to help a young fellow by getting him interested in racing. He had been in the youth correction facility near Farmer's City for dealing drugs.

He dug his life deeper into a hole when he ran away and was sentenced to some serious time in spite of the promise of a good career. His girlfriend had a sister, Angie, who he said, "… is an avid racing fan."

Angelica Prescotte had lettered in volleyball all four years at Carpentier Falls West High School. She won a scholarship to Centralia College in volleyball, and helped lead her college team to three state championships over four years, all the while carrying a GPA of 3.6. She was and still is an amateur weight lifter of considerable merit. She went to the gym religiously each day to work out for three hours.

When Christina convinced me to go talk to Angie, I reluctantly went along just to keep the peace.

"I've got a degree in Education Theory," Angie lamented. "But the best job I can find is stocking shelves at the Walmart store."

Angie had impressed us with her reasoning abilities, her drive to succeed, her knowledge of racing, and her upper body strength.

"Driving a one-hundred and fifty mile race is grueling," Christina told Angie. "Your arms and shoulders will ache for a week after each race."

"It's important to exercise, stretch and stay in shape," I said.

"I haven't been doing it for a few months," Angie said. "In the past I've gone to the gym every morning, seven days a week. I can start doing that again."

I arranged with the racetracks at Carpentier Falls and Centralia to let us train Angie during the off season. When she was ready, we sent her to a six-week professional driving school in Daytona, Florida. True to her word, Angie had spent long hours each day—seven days a week—in the gym lifting weights and working out. At her May debut at Masonville, Angie had performed admirably, finishing the race in twelfth position.

"I didn't even finish my first race," I said, hoping it didn't sound like I was whining. In the five races since, Angie has finished every race fourteenth or better and finished seventh at Ford Junction two weeks ago.

Our agreement with Angie was that for the first two years,

I would keep and maintain Nikki in Centralia, at Maurey's shop, and deliver her to each racetrack no later than Friday twelve o'clock, noon, before each race. That would allow Angie to drive to the track and practice for each race. I coached Angie on the characteristics of the racetrack—its ins and outs. That allowed me to keep my finger on the pulse, but not have to deal with the ordeal of driving the races.

At this time, Angie was kind of restrained; she had her driver's license revoked for too many speeding tickets. Her last speeding ticket was written on the way back from the Florida driving school. "Ol' Tugs chauffeurs me or I take a bus," Angie said.

To help her as much as we could, Christina and I hauled my old camper to each racetrack and set it up for Angie and Tugs to use for the weekend. Christina never cared for the camper, preferring motels "with good solid floor underfoot."

Angie had gone into the camper to change clothes. "I'll never get used to changing clothes in the garage, even with all the doors locked and no windows," Angie told us more than once.

"Use the women's locker room in the lounge," Tugs suggested once.

"Too much of a hassle," Angie replied.

While Angie changed, Tugs and I were leaning against Nikki and chatting. I saw Nick Boynton coming towards me, talking on his cell phone. He flipped it shut and slipped it into his jacket pocket. "We sent a car to notify the guy's wife. She told us Melvyn took his car to a body shop on the west side last night to get it cleaned and waxed. She doesn't know the name of it."

"He probably brought his car here and ran practice laps," I said. "Not much other reason to be at the track and taking a shower. His truck and car hauler are both black and gold with the number 35 on them. "They must be somewhere around the fair parking lot."

"Maybe he left his car parked where some kid could climb in and steal it," Nick said absently.

"It's not a car you can drive around town in," I said.

"Unless the kid's trying to impress his girlfriend," Rafe said.

"You have to know how to start the damn beast," Tugs

said. "That's not all that easy."

"You don't just turn the key?" Nick asked.

I wobbled my head. "The key just turns on the electrical system. Next, you have to get the fuel pressure up, and then you turn on the oil pump. Since these engines are carbureted, you depress the foot feed a couple of times before you push the start button."

"I'm glad my old brain doesn't need to remember all that," Nick said, spreading a broad grin on his face. I looked over my shoulder. Rafe was sitting in his cart in the shade of the eave.

"It does help keep aging drivers out of the game," I said, looking at Rafe, who glowered at me.

"Stow it, Maxxon," he said.

I smiled and looked around the track. I stopped to focus on the miscellaneous storage area adjacent to garage row. Suddenly it registered. There was a black and gold car transporter parked in one corner. I walked to the fence—so I could see it better—and saw the number 35 on each side. It definitely was Melvyn's. I turned to the crowd of people looking at me. "That's Melvyn's car hauler over there," I said, pointing toward the trailer. "When I went looking before, I was looking for a car—I didn't think about his truck or car hauler."

Rafe maneuvered his cart closer to the fence.

Nick whistled for attention and then waved to one of the uniformed cops standing near the driver's lounge door. "Let me get that thing impounded and checked out," he said. "What does the trailer parked there mean?" Nick asked me as he waited for the uniformed cop to arrive.

"Well, it means he brought his car back to the track after getting it cleaned and waxed, unloaded it, and parked the trailer there in storage. He probably didn't put the car in the garage before he practiced. I would suppose he parked his pickup truck out somewhere in the fair parking lot." I pointed to the lot south of the admin building.

"Do you know the make and model of his truck?" Nick asked.

"No. I don't," I said. "Maybe it's in his records." I watched as Christina led Beau on his leash from another trip to the Doggy Do area. I walked to open the truck door for her. Nick stood nearby watching, waiting for me to continue. Nick's cell phone rang and he walked further away as he answered it. I looked at Christina. "Can you pull up Melvyn's records?" I asked. Since she and I married, I've been better organized than any time since I left the Marine Corps. The main reason, of course, was that Christina was not only computer literate, but, more importantly, patient enough to make computers serve her. In one weekend she loaded all my SRVSCRA records and information into her laptop and from then on, if Christina was close, I had all the data I needed to operate the association efficiently and effectively.

Christina put Beau in the truck and opened the rear door to pull her computer. She climbed up into the front seat and opened the computer. "What do you want?"

"The usual. Address. Wife's name. I know where he works."

Christina clicked keys and sat watching the screen, then finally responded. "His address is 59 Hidden Harbor Trail. Wife's name is Lorianne. He was born January sixteenth, nineteen sixty one. He's five-ten and weighs one hundred and ninety two pounds. Black hair and brown eyes. Two children."

Melvyn had joined the SRVSCRA the first year I was president, and I approved his application. I remembered the interview we did as part of the membership process, and Melvyn mentioned his two children adopted from orphanages in Mexico. "Does it list anything under team members?"

"Mechanic is Steven Cosburn," she said.

"Oh, sure," I said, patting my forehead. "I know Steve; he owns Reliable Auto Repair over on 55th Street. He buys a lot of parts from us for his garage. I've got his number in my cell phone."

I dug out my cell phone and looked up Steve's number in my Contacts List and dialed the number. After he answered we exchanged small talk until I felt comfortable to break the news about Melvyn being dead.

"Damn," Steve said. "She was serious about it."

"Who was serious about what?"

"His wife," Steve said. "A few weeks ago I was working on his car in the garage at the track, and I heard him and Lori arguing, and she yelled something like, 'I could kill you.' I ignored it. Shag never said anything to me about what it was about, but I suspected old Shag might be involved with other women."

"Damn," I said, looking around to see where Nick was—hoping he couldn't overhear the conversation. Christina gave me a talk-nice look. "It wasn't Lori who pulled the trigger," I said. "I saw the gunman when I arrived at the track."

"She may not have pulled the trigger," Steve said. "But, she's got the money to have it done." Then he paused. "You're not working with the cops, are you?"

"No."

"Good," he said. "I don't want to get anybody into trouble by me talking out of church."

I remembered why I'd called Steve. "Do you have any idea where Melvyn's car is?"

"Where his car is?" Steve repeated. "It's not at the track?"

"No. The transporter is here. But the car isn't."

"I know he was going to have the car cleaned and waxed like he does before every race," Steve said.

"What kind of tow vehicle did he use?"

"He has ... had ... an F-350 Ford crew cab, just like yours except his was black and had a gold number 35 on each side door."

"I'll see if we can find it," I said.

"He drove it back and forth to work," Steve said. I heard him talking to someone else and he said, "I've got to go. Let me know what's going on."

I tuned to see where Nick was and spotted him, cell phone to his ear and waving his free hand in the air. I realized the cops had opened the main gate to foot traffic. The medical examiner's hearse was gone. Rafe's golf cart was parked just outside the driver's lounge, so he and the photographer were probably inside the driver's lounge doing their thing. I saw Horace Knottingham walking toward me from the main gate.

Horace lived in one of the upper-story tenements across the street from the fair grounds and was the only person I knew who absolutely detested car racing. He hated the noise generated by the cars. He hated the smell of gasoline, oil and burnt rubber. He complained to the Greene County commissioners regularly, and tried to get injunctions against racing several times but had yet to find a sympathetic judge. I was the diplomat selected by the SRVSCRA board of directors to deal with Horace, and when he wanted to complain to someone in racing—about racing—he usually sought me out.

"Hello, Horace," I said. "How have you been?"

"I've been fine, Mr. Maxxon," Horace said. He always addressed me very formally. I think it helped to make him hate racing but not me. "Now I'll have to suffer through another weekend of racket. It already started this morning. The fair is quiet by comparison." He paused to wave to Christina. "I saw you and Miss Christina over here unloading your car. Can't you make these drivers put mufflers on their cars?"

"We've been through this a dozen times before, Horace," I said. "You know I can't do that—in the SRVSCRA or any of the other racing associations."

"None of the other cars have mufflers either; Saturday and Sunday afternoons are always hell around here." Horace gave me his typical blank look. Horace had never impressed me as being on a mission—over the dozen years he complained about racing. Why he bought one of the upscale condos across the street was a question I could never find a reasonable answer for. He claimed he bought it during the off season when there was no racing.

"You heard someone this morning, running around the track?" I asked.

"Yep. That number thirty-five guy. The black and yellow car," Horace said.

"The black and gold number thirty-five car was running around the track earlier?"

"Yep. He may be the loudest of them all," Horace said. "What were all the cops over here for?"

"A driver was found dead in the driver's lounge," I said matter of factly.

"Dead?" Horace's face took on a fearful look. He looked toward his building. "Who?"

"His name hasn't been officially released, so I can't say."

Horace stood for a long time, his tongue swiping across his lips. Then, having posted his complaint, he turned and walked back toward the gate. If a can had been available, I imagined him kicking it in frustration.

So Melvyn Hightower had been here running practice laps in his car. His car was definitely here somewhere. Where was it now?

The man with the gun popped into my head. He'd apparently taken Melvyn's cash. He definitely had not taken Melvyn's car!

*   *   *

Christina and I were sitting in the first row of seats watching Angie going into her fifth practice lap. Tugs was timing her laps. As I watched, my mind wandered back to when I was just starting to compete in races. The adrenalin rushes, the thrill of it all, the noise, but most important, the speed. Watching her, I could see Angie's driving skills improve with every lap she ran—in both practice laps and racing laps.

"She's doing great," Christina said.

"I agree. She's a natural at driving."

We both were looking to our left, waiting for Angie to emerge from the banked corners, and didn't notice Nick Boynton walk up to us.

"You got a minute?" Nick asked.

Both Christina and I shook off the startled feeling that spread over us. "Sure," I said. "What do you need?"

Nick sat down in the row of seats behind us to our left. "Somebody to bounce a few things off of."

"We're both good listeners," I said, and smiled, "especially Christina."

"We talked to Steve Cosburn," Nick said. "He told us Melvyn used a black Ford F-350 to pull that trailer. We found his truck parked in the fair parking across from the admin building. So we have the truck and trailer. The CSIs are going over both of them now. My question is: How could a person get the number thirty five car out of here without using the truck and trailer?"

I shook my head. "They might have called a tow truck to come haul it off," I said. "That's about the only way to get it out of here. On the other hand, if it wasn't hauled off—maybe another driver drove it away."

"You think the car could still be here at the track?" Nick asked, absently looking toward the garage area. "In another garage?"

"That's a possibility," I said, shrugging. That didn't sound terribly plausible. However, nothing was making sense.

Nick's eyes followed Angie as she roared past on the track. Neither Christina nor I turned to look that way. We continued to study Nick.

"I kind of wonder—" I started to say.

"All but twelve garages have padlocks on them," Nick interrupted me. "Out of how many?"

"Four buildings with sixteen garages in each," I said. "Sixty-four garages, total."

"The padlocks mean they're rented?" Nick said absently.

"If they're padlocked, they're being used. Helen Tobias does an exceptionally good job of keeping track of them."

"How many of your people rent garages?" Nick asked.

"Only a dozen or so," I said. "Five different racing associations use this track. Local drivers in each association rent garages year round, including me. Then there are drivers who rent a garage for race weekends only—maybe six to eight other drivers. We rent garages when we send in our entry forms and fees. Helen would often put a set of padlocks on the garages she assigned to us and send a key with the driver's gate keycard. There will be three or four drivers coming in tonight who find an empty garage and put their car in it, padlock it, and pay the rent tomorrow morning."

"Here's my dilemma," Nick pursed his lips and supported his chin on his cupped right hand. "I'm trying to decide if it's worth opening every locked garage," Nick said, "in case someone stole the car and parked it in one of the empty garages and locked it up." He studied the garage area from this distance. "But, the counter question is: How important is it that we find the car? If the car is still here, I doubt it will provide much evidence about who shot Melvyn in the locker room. A smart crook would wipe everything down for fingerprints, or at least try hard enough to make it difficult for us to find anything useful. Hell, he might've worn gloves."

"That's your call," I said, suddenly realizing Nick's predicament. "You can't get a blanket search warrant?" I asked.

"Not a chance," Nick growled. "No judge in this town is going to sign a blanket search warrant for all the locked garages." Nick let his gaze roam around the racetrack and said. "I'd have to get a warrant for each garage."

"Sixty-four total less the twelve we've already looked into.

Fifty-two search warrants will take four people all night to get ready for a judge to sign," Nick said. "Then, since tomorrow is Saturday, I'll have to send them to a golf course somewhere to find a judge who would agree to take the time to sign fifty-two warrants. Christ, they bitch and moan and groan about signing just one document on the golf cart dash. 'You know you are violating these people's right to be secure in their person and property? Yeah, but we're trying to solve a murder. Yeah, but there is only one murderer, and you're rousting fifty-two different people.'" Nick paused as he thought of something. "Is there any way to check Helen's garage rental receipts?"

"Sure," I said and stood up. I led Christina and Nick back to the admin building and into the auxiliary office area using my keycard into the auxiliary office. We walked to Helen's desk and I sat down on her steno chair, dug out her receipt book from the desk drawer where I knew she kept it. Nick and I leafed through it. The last receipt written was from the Saturday before to one of the SRVSCRA drivers I recognized—for garage number twelve. The next receipt was two weeks old. "Not too much to go on," I said as I held the book out to Nick. He took it and leafed back a few more pages then handed it back.

Nick straddled a second steno chair. "I got to thinking that if someone planned this, they might have rented another garage to stash the car in a day or two before it happened. But if it was a spur of the moment thing, well, if they stashed the car in another garage, they would have had to know a little about the track and then come up with a pair of padlocks."

I nodded agreement with Nick's logic. "Helen might have left a pair of padlocks unlocked on the door of a vacant garage for a driver to use before she left to go to Maplewood. If the killer knew she often did that, he might just go looking for a pair of open padlocks to steal and use on another vacant garage. If he was planning on shooting Melvyn, the killer might have brought his own padlocks with him."

Nick stood and paced around the small open bullpen area. "Can you help me with an exact description of the number thirty-five car? You know: make, model, any distinguishing features, etc. Anything that'll help my people identify it if it's been modified?"

"I can do that," I said. "After Angie finishes practicing, I'll write something for you."

"Good," Nick said. "There'll be cops around this area all afternoon. Just give it to any one of them and tell them it's for me. I really appreciate your help. Both of you."

"If someone had the car towed from the track, wouldn't the security cameras show that?" Christina asked.

"We've taken all the security camera tapes we can find to the lab," Nick said. "Only a couple of cameras were aimed at this area, however."

"There used to be security cameras on each end of the admin building," I said. "But they quit working, and the county didn't want to spend the money to replace them."

"Tell me about it," Nick growled. "Half the damn cameras around town don't work."

"One camera on Gate Two," Nick said, pointing a thumb over his shoulder, "showed during a preliminary viewing what looks like a car being towed out of the parking lot. The camera is so far away we can't tell much about the car. We've got the boys downtown magnifying the frames; hopefully we can get a name off the tow truck."

"This is really getting strange," I said. "The guy with the gun, he shot Melvyn during the robbery, but he didn't leave in the car, and—"

Nick stood, stretched his lower back, and walked toward the front door of the office. "Can I get out this way?"

"Yes, just open the deadbolt. I'll relock it behind you."

"Thanks for your help, Maxxon. And you too, Christina. I really appreciate it." Nick opened the door and left.

Christina and I walked back to the track to watch Angie practice. The infield TV trucks were busy, probably broadcasting the latest on Melvyn's murder.

"Whoa," Tugs yelled, and swung to look at me from the pit stall. "That was a thirty-six second lap. Man, she's flying low."

"That's over one hundred miles per hour," I yelled to Tugs. "That's great." Christina's puzzled look made me remember she was not yet thoroughly initiated into the world of stock car racing. "At this track," I said to her, "a thirty-seven point five second lap is one hundred miles per hour."

"Anybody ever done it faster?" Christina asked.

"One of the Indy car guys did it in twenty nine and a half seconds," I said.

"Well, I'll tell you what, Mr. Maxxon," Christina said, letting a smile spread across her face. "If I want to travel one hundred and twenty miles per hour, I'll book a flight on an airplane, thank you very much."

Angie ran four more practice laps and then pulled into the pit area. Christina and I crossed the track and watched as she climbed out of Nikki.

"I've got some questions about turns two and four," Angie said. "Let me think them through, and I'll call you later."

"Okay." I looked at Christina. "We'll be at home. Call us on the land line."

"Will do," Angie said. "After I get rehydrated and take care of this terrible hungry feeling."

I nodded, "I know the feeling,"

CHAPTER THREE
Friday Evening, August 24

Kurt Maxxon

We all helped tuck Nikki into her garage for the night. Once we were in normal traffic, after an agonizing exit through the fair parking lot, I said, "I'll call and order pizza delivered," hoping Christina was too tired to think about my diet. She thought I should eat the same way she did, but that was just not in the cards. I saw Christina out of the corner of my eye turning to look at Beau curled up on the back seat. When I mentioned pizza his ears probably perked up. He loved pizza nights. "We have smoked salmon in the fridge that I can do something with," she countered. I looked at her face—her smug expression made me decide against invoking the terrible deprivation Beau's been suffering not having pizza regularly.

I drove toward the clouds gathering on the western sky, hungry for pizza, but happy there were no storms on the way. The weather forecast for Sunday was "cloudy and dry," which helped to lift my mood.

*　　*　　*

True to her word, Christina had dinner on the table within twenty minutes of getting home. Beau and I had taken our evening walk around the block and returned home to a leisurely meal.

"That was a great salad," I said to Christina as I stood to carry my plate to the sink. "Was that wild Alaskan Sockeye salmon?"

"Yes, I bought it yesterday at the fish market over on Central Avenue," Christina said. "Baxter has the freshest seafood in town. He said to tell you hello. He's not happy that you've given up driving."

"A lot of people have said that," I said. "I feel much better, though." I stood and walked to the living room to read the mail and the newspaper while Christina cleaned the kitchen.

Our recliner chairs sat side by side where I once had a sofa. We each kept our favorite recliner chair after we married and she moved into my house. Even though they were both the same brand, they were much different in color and appearance. Hers was dark blue clothe and looked new. Mine was maroon leather, and obviously well worn, but still very comfortable. Both were older designs with high arms that helped both of us hoist ourselves out of them. Christina and I stayed in pretty good condition, but as we grew older, our knees and hips started to bother us.

I picked up the newspaper. The recent stock market collapse was the main feature of the nightly news. Now I could read the gory details in the business section of the newspaper.

"Are you worried about the stock market?" Christina asked as she came from the kitchen to sit down in her recliner.

"Not really," I said. "Our portfolio is in good shape."

Christina sat eyeing me for a long time. "You're thinking about Melvyn's murder, aren't you?"

"Yes. I guess I am."

"What's on your agenda for tomorrow morning?" I asked. Christina volunteered at the animal shelter on the weekends, although usually not on race weekends.

"I have to dust the Doll Room," she said.

"Okay," I said. "I need to get up and be at the track at five thirty to let the cleaning crew in. Then I'll go over to help the Kiwanis Club cook pancakes for their fundraiser."

"Oh, that's right. That's this weekend, too, isn't it? I'll come and help for awhile," Christina said. "I can do the Doll Room after."

Christina had a collection of Raggedy Ann and Andy dolls totaling one hundred and eight dolls. I had my late wife's collection of Raggedy Ann and Andy dolls totaling fifty five dolls. We kept the two collections separate because we both hoped our daughters would take them over and keep the collections going in the future. In the meantime, we displayed the dolls in the third bedroom of our house, and Christina was meticulous about their cleanliness.

"The dolls are fine," I said. "They'll get along."

After a long pause, Christina looked at me, and said, "Angie has a problem."

"She does? What's her problem?"

She's having problems with her bladder. She's concerned about it becoming a problem while she's running the race."

"She can go to the restrooms during the breaks between heats," I said. As I thought about it, I remembered that Angie had been quick to get out of the car at each break and head for the port-a-potties in pit row. "All the drivers do."

"She says it's getting harder and harder to hold it to the break," Christina said. "She's really concerned about it affecting her concentration."

"If she's worried about the heats being too long, we can get her a piddle-pack."

"A what?"

"A piddle-pack," I said, and realized they might not be common knowledge to people. It's a plastic bag she can strap to her leg with a catheter. We used them all the time in the military— for long missions."

"That's interesting," Christina said. She paused to think it over. "That's probably what we need to look into. Can you get them locally?"

"Isn't there a war surplus store over on Main Street?" I said.

Christina's frown made me wish I hadn't tried for the levity.

"Seriously, can you get them locally?"

"I'm sure one of the medical supply stores has them. We can check tomorrow."

"Are those places open on Saturday?"

"If they aren't, then I'll have to pull some strings."

Christina sat back. "Angie said she would be calling. We can talk to her about it."

When Angie called, I said, "Speaking of the devil," and turned on our speaker phone.

Christina said, "Hi Angie. I was just telling Kurt about your problem, and it sounds like he has a solution for it."

"I hope not the same solution as ol' Tugs," Angie said.

"He said, 'just get a big cork.'"

Christina winced and I hoped for her sake, the conversation didn't go any further downhill. "No," Christina said, "Kurt told me about piddle-packs they used in the military for long flights. A plastic bag that you strap to your leg."

"I'll be damned," Angie said. "But, there's a catheter, right?"

"Yes, there is." Christina said.

"I hate those damn catheters, but if that's what it takes, I'll get used to wearing one."

"You'll get used to them," I said, remembering my experience with piddle packs for a number of years.

"I just can't seem to get it right coming off the banking from turns two and four," Angie blurted. "I tried the high line and then the low line and then the middle line—at different speeds. But each time I felt Nikki getting loose, and way too damn close to the wall. Should I be learning about the suspension system?"

"No, you don't need to worry about the suspension system at this point in your racing career."

"I do need to ask a lot more questions, I can see that," Angie said.

"You're doing just fine," I said. "Turns two and four are physically identical, the radius and angle of banking. That gives your body identical sensations as far as gravitation is concerned. However, those two turns give the driver very different visual sensations because of the sunlight, and the sunlight affects the track's surface temperature."

"Oh, yeah!" Angie said. "Is that what it is?"

"As you come off of turn two, you are in the sun, the track is hotter, and slicker, your tires won't have as good of grip. Turn four is in the shadows so the track is cooler, and your tires will grab better."

"Yeah, that makes sense," Angie said. "I've also noticed this track is harder on tires than others?"

"Yes, they used a coarser blacktop than the others, and it chews up tires bad."

"Okay, boss, what do you think I should do?"

"Coming off of turn two, I recommend you use the middle line and scale back to about fifty-five hundred RPMs," I advised from memory. "That way—"

"I don't like letting my torque drop that low," Angie said. "Especially if I have to accelerate to the Start/Finish line."

"Coming off turn two you will never be dashing for the finish line," I chided her.

"Yeah, you're right," Angie conceded. "I'll try that on two."

"For turn four," I continued, "I'd hold six thousand RPMs in the middle line. That way you'd be ready to dash to the finish line."

"Anything else I need to know?"

"A lot," I said. "At this track you just have to chill out and take each turn and each straightaway as they are," I said with conviction. "Bottom line, you've always got to think about your tires."

"I try to remember the tires. But, there's so much—"

"I know," I said, "I've been there, done that."

"Did you know that guy killed at the track?" Angie asked.

"Yes. Yes, I did."

"Bummer," she said. "Do you think the killer will target other racecar drivers?"

"I don't think so," I said absently. I hadn't thought about that angle until now.

"Where do I get a piddle pack?"

"I'll track one down for you."

"Okay, boss." Angie hung up.

Christina dug out our ancient phone book and looked for medical supply stores. Most of those have been around for years, so their addresses and phone numbers were current. Looking at the yellow pages I remembered that I knew one of the store owners from the Kiwanis club. I decided to give him a call. It was only seven thirty. He answered, and after a few minutes of small talk, I asked about piddle packs. He assured me he had several brands and he would meet Angie at his store the next morning to get her started. I thanked him and hung up.

My cell phone jangled. The caller ID indicated it was restricted, so I answered it on speaker phone.

It was Nick Boynton.

"We got the guy who pointed the gun at you," Nick said,

without preamble.

"Good. Who is he?"

"A drifter named Angelo Pavalino. He says he went into the lounge looking for anything he could find, and saw Melvyn lying on the floor, dead. He checked the open locker and saw Melvyn's wallet and grabbed the cash. He says he damned near tripped over the gun. So he grabbed it, figuring he could hock it for more cash." Nick paused. "They rounded him up over on west 91st Street. He went into a Liquor Store to buy a jug of wine. Pocket full of cash and a revolver jammed into his waistband, which the clerk saw when he came in, and the clerk sent a silent alarm downtown. Damn good thing all seven slugs had been fired or he might've shot himself female." Nick chuckled. "We got him about five minutes after he left the store. It all went down pretty easy. When we started talking to him about shooting Melvyn, he broke into a cold sweat and swore to help us all he could."

"How big a weapon was it?" I asked.

"A thirty-eight caliber Saturday night special," Nick said.

"I thought it was a bigger bore than that," I said.

"Yeah, well, it depends which end you're looking at it from," Nick said. "Like I said, no live ammo; so he couldn't have shot you with it; if that's any consolation."

"Not a lot," I said. "I'm glad you're concerned about my health. Where did the weapon come from?"

"Stolen during a burglary five months ago," Nick said.

"Anyone else's prints on it?" I asked.

"Don't know. The only good prints on it were Angelo's."

"What's going to happen to Angelo?"

"I'd bet big money he'll wind up being turned loose," Nick said. "Sorry about that, old buddy, since he pointed that big ol' gun at you. But the DA isn't really chomping at the bit to charge him with anything. He was just taking advantage of the situation. He didn't break and enter, since the door was unlocked. You and I know that. He saw a dead body, emptied the dead man's wallet of cash, picked up the murder weapon, and ran into you on the way out. All that amounts to is unlawful theft. We recovered five hundred and forty five dollars and the murder weapon. All he'd spent was nine bucks for a jug of wine. Even though we're pretty sure the weapon Angelo Pavalino had on him when we arrested him is the murder weapon, we know for sure he wasn't the shooter. All he did was smear hell out of the other fingerprints on the weapon. Major question is who really pulled the trigger on Melvyn Hightower?"

"You're positive he didn't kill Melvyn?" I asked.

"We did a GSR test on his hands," Nick said. "He hadn't fired that weapon, or any other weapon. What little residue he had on his hands was from him handling the weapon—not firing it. We were right on the edge of the window when the test is effective, but it was still real negative."

"What does GSR stand for?" I asked.

"Gunshot Residue. It's a forensic thing developed by the FBI labs."

I remembered reading about the nitrate residue left on a person's hand when they fire a weapon and how they could test for it.

"We got a lot of partials off the gun," Nick said. "The one good print on the trigger doesn't match him and none of the partials had a match in IAFIS. Angelo doesn't fit the profile of a guy who takes a gun and goes looking to kill someone for money."

"Anything on the car yet?" I asked.

"Nothing," Nick said. "I decided against doing a search warrant for all the garages; didn't figure it would be worth the effort. I can put the resources to better work. If they stashed the car there at the track, they'll not get it out of there without us knowing about it. We're going to monitor that track twenty-four seven." Nick paused. "I appreciate the information you sent me about the car. I've updated the BOLO we put out earlier. Great help."

"I suppose the car could be in one of the locked garages," I said. "So far, I don't see a clear connection between the car and the murder of Melvyn."

"There may not be a connection," Nick said. "But we are handling the missing car as part of the murder investigation."

"They may be waiting for the fair and the Sunday race to be over," I said. Come back sometime next week to get the car."

"We've got just as much time as they do," Nick said. "Now, the reason I called you. I've got my lead investigators with me, and we'd like to pick your brain about some stuff. If you don't mind, I want to put you on speaker phone and answer their questions. That okay with you?"

"That's okay," I said, looking at Christina who smiled encouragement. Suddenly I heard a noise in the background.

"You there?" Nick asked.

"I'm still here," I said. Christina got up and led Beau down the hall to the bedroom.

"Okay, boys, ask away," Nick said.

A disconnected voice said, "Is there a market for cars like that or the parts? You know, someone stole the car to strip it down and fence the parts?"

"I suppose it's a possibility," I said. "There are not that many parts, really. The body, fenders, doors, etcetera, are welded together and there is a cage welded inside the body. The fenders, doors and other parts would be difficult to cut up to use on another car. The seat is usually specially made, molded to the driver's body. So that wouldn't be comfortable to other people. The engine and drive train would be the most valuable parts of the car, but they are also the most unique."

"What would an engine like that be worth?" another voice asked.

"Anywhere from five thousand to about twenty thousand dollars," I said. "It's way too much engine to put into a street car. Some kid might think he could stuff it into his Camaro, but he wouldn't be able to reinstall the steering system or the mufflers. Neighbors would complain about the noise and call the cops."

"What if someone stole the car hoping to repaint it, put a new number on it and start racing it?" another voice asked.

"That might work," I said. "But, they would have to take it several hundred miles away from here and get into a new racing association."

"Why?"

"The SRVSCRA, like most racing associations, owns all the car numbers. The SRVSCRA leases the numbers to the car owners on an annual basis. A buck a year. Nothing outrageous, more formality than anything else. If someone stole Melvyn's car, repainted it and then applied for a new SRVACRA number, we'd figure out pretty fast where the car came from, because we have the VIN numbers from the cars in our records."

"What about titles?" Nick asked.

"Race cars usually don't have titles, per se," I said. "If we start with the fact that cars made over the last several years have the vehicle identification number, or VIN, stamped into several different parts in the car—"

"Oh, yeah," a voice said. "That's the way they identified the van carrying the explosives under the trade center back in the early nineties."

"Right," I said. "So if a driver builds a car from junkyard parts, he'll be buying parts from several different cars whose titles have been terminated. He buys a chassis from one car, an engine block from another car, a radiator from another, a drive shaft from yet another, and so forth. Chances are pretty good that by the time he gets a car built and ready to race, there's a half-dozen VINs in the car. Since the titles to those cars have been discontinued, the only way a person could sell a car like that is with a Bill of Sale. What we do in SRVSCRA is ask each driver to list on the entry form for each race at least two of the VINs in his or her car that are clearly accessible. That way, theoretically, and as terrible as it sounds, if the car crashes and burns, we would be able to tell whose car it was."

"And ID the charred remains," a voice said.

"That too," I said.

"How do you do Nikki?" Nick asked.

"Well, I start with a used Ford Taurus, two or three years old. So most of the parts will have the same VIN stamped into them. However, Maurey and I lift the body off of the chassis and cut it into pieces. We beef up the chassis and build the tubular structure you see when you look inside Nikki. We add a bigger radiator, with no VIN. We add a manufactured transmission, again no VIN. The engine block would be the first major disconnect, since we build our engines from small Ford truck blocks with a truck VIN. When we finish adding all that, we weld the body pieces back together to the tube structure."

"If you wreck your car, how do you rebuild it for the next race?" a new voice asked.

"Normally I have two bodies and three engines available. Right now, however, we're switching from the Taurus body to the Ford Fusion body. The second car is just now getting put back together. If need be, we could get it all welded up in four or five days. If Nikki gets wrecked, we'd see if we could repair it first. If not, then we'd replace it."

Do you have a title to Nikki?" Nick asked.

"Well, yes, I do. But it would be useless if I tried to sell Nikki. Like I mentioned, the engine, transmission, and drive train don't have the same VINs. The state DOT inspects all cars when the registration is changed and there are so many different VINs in Nikki, they would arrest anyone trying to register it."

"Including you?"

"Including me, no doubt," I said.

"What does a stockcar weigh?" the last voice asked.

"Anywhere between twenty-five hundred and thirty-five hundred pounds," I said. "Give or take a couple hundred pounds depending on the brand and model."

"Are they easy to tow?" Nick asked.

"Most drivers add tow hooks on all four corners of the body," I said. "That way you can get a tow strap on it after a wreck, no matter what end or side is damaged."

"Okay," Nick said. "We've taken enough of your time, Colonel Maxxon. We all thank you for your help." I could hear chairs scraping and commotion as they must have left the conference room. Nick picked up the handset and the background noise diminished. "I want to thank you for your time, Kurt," Nick said before he ended the call.

I glanced down the hallway and saw a light on in the bedroom. I walked to the bedroom door and looked in. Christina was propped on pillows against the headboard reading a novel; Beau was curled up in his bed with his old pillow in the corner next to the bed. Everyone was settled for the night. I considered climbing in next to Christina, but decided I wasn't ready for bed yet. So I walked back to the living room and turned on the TV. The ten o'clock news would be coming on in a few minutes. I muted the sound and punched in closed captioning using the remote.

The news started and I read the closed captioning. After a few minutes the station went to advertising. My cell phone rang. I said," Hello."

There was nothing on the other end. "Hello!" I said again,

and listened. I heard traffic noise in the background. "Hello, this is Kurt Maxxon," I said again.

"Maxxon," a distorted voice said. I could tell the man was filtering his voice through some cloth, maybe a towel.

"Yes."

"I know you found Melvyn's body; I heard that from a friend," the voice said. "I know who you are. I also know you always get involved in solving the murder."

"Who is this?" I asked.

"Yeah, right. You think I'm going to give you my name, rank and serial number?" The voice laughed. "I know you, but you don't know who I am."

"What do you want?" I asked.

"It would be a damn good idea if you just forgot about this case, you know what I mean? If you don't, you won't like what I'll do to you. I took out that double dealing Melvyn Hightower, so I can do the same to you. Won't bother me at all."

"So you shot Melvyn Hightower."

"That lying, cheating, stealing sonofabitch."

"How did he cheat you?" I asked, but the line had gone dead. I looked at my cell phone screen and wrote the number on a magazine cover. I went into the office and sat down at my desk. I took a small note pad out of the top drawer and sat scribbling all I could remember about the conversation I'd just had. After I wrote three sheets of information, I realized my heart was pounding against my chest wall and I was breathing heavily.

After I calmed down a little, I dialed Nick's cell phone. When he answered, I told him about my phone call and gave him the phone number.

"That's a payphone," Nick said. "The 392 prefix tells me that."

"Damn," I said. "That figures. He's smart."

"Sounds like it," Nick said. "I'll have someone track its exact location, check the phone for fingerprints, talk to anyone who might have seen the guy using it, and check out any surveillance cameras that might be working in the area. In the meantime, you better lay low for awhile. Don't stop thinking about the case."

"Another thing of interest," I said. "I think the guy is our age or so."

"How's that?" Nick asked.

"He made reference to name, rank, and serial number. The way he used it made me think he might have been in the military when they still used serial numbers as ID number rather than Social Security numbers."

"I got that down," Nick said. "Good work, Maxxon." The phone went to a dial tone.

As I entered the bedroom, Christina said, "I heard your phone ring again. Who else called you at this hour?"

"The guy who killed Melvyn Hightower," I said.

"What?" Christina's eyes jerked wide open as she flew into a sitting position. She eyed me for a long time.

I told her about the conversation with the voice.

"You're going to have to be more careful," Christina said.

As I tried to fall asleep, I replayed a special TV program I'd watched about sniper cops, how they could take out a criminal at 500 yards. What if the voice I'd just talked with became the sniper? I mentally calculated the distance from various locations around the racetrack to where I might be sitting or standing; especially those locations where a man with a sniper rifle could be lurking in the shadows. My mind was overwhelmed with all the spots I could visualize, and there were probably more.

"Lord," I prayed. "Give me the strength to deal with this mess."

Sleep eventually won out, albeit fitful.

CHAPTER FOUR
Saturday Morning, August 25

Kurt Maxxon

The cops and technicians always leave a major mess of a crime scene: the blood, fingerprint dust, and other residues. I'd arranged to have a special cleanup crew take care of the driver's lounge, locker room, and shower. The cleanup company had asked if they could get their trucks and equipment into the track area before the crowds arrived for the final day of the fair, and I had assured them I would be there to let them in at 5:30 A.M.

Since I was scheduled to help with the annual pancake breakfast put on by my Kiwanis Chapter, starting that early was not a problem. For the last twelve years I've volunteered to work on the first wave, which meant I normally arrived about five o'clock. This morning I'd opened the gates and the driver's lounge for the cleanup crew and then walked over to the big tent to start mixing pancake batter even though I had less than four hours of sleep. Other volunteers straggled in and stoked the propane fired griddles. After mixing gallons of pancake batter, I moved to one of the massive griddles and started cooking pancakes and sausages. The air temperature was in the seventies, and dew covered the tents and grass. I quickly worked up a sweat.

Christina arrived shortly before seven and gave me a "good morning" kiss. "I'll cook for awhile," she said. More volunteers arrived, and it looked like we would have enough people to cover the operation. Just after eight o'clock, I grabbed a cup of coffee and sat down at the nearest table.

"I read you quit driving," another Kiwanis member said as she sat down across from me. "And I see you hired a woman to drive your car."

I couldn't remember the woman's name, but I knew she owned a beauty supply store on the north side of town. She was short and a little "chunky around the middle," as Christina would say. Her hair was a platinum blonde rinse that needed redone soon, and she wore enough makeup to cover her sixty plus years. "Her name is Angie," I said. "Angelica Prescotte; she's an exceptionally talented young lady."

"All women are exceptionally talented," she said. "I'm glad you finally realized women can drive those racecars."

Even though she was smiling, I worried where this conversation was going. Christina walked toward us, stripping off her apron.

"Hello Maxine," Christina said as she sat down next to me.

That jogged my memory. The woman's name was Maxine Jarvis—Jarvis Beauty Supply.

We chatted for a while, and then Maxine got up to go back to cooking pancakes. I finished my coffee, and then Christina and I started cleaning tables as the first wave of pancake eaters left the big tent.

At one table a young woman and her three children were just finishing their pancakes and sausages. The little girl watched Christina and I approach the table next to theirs. "Momma, Momma," the girl shouted, "There's Mr. Kurt Maxxon." She pointed her tiny finger toward me. I smiled at the little girl, sure she knew me from having seen my picture in the newspaper. I guessed her to be seven or eight years old, with a head full of reddish, Shirley Temple curls bouncing in all directions. I couldn't ignore her intense hazel eyes. Her mother swung around to see who the girl was pointing to and her eyes widened. As the woman stared at Christina, I saw recognition spread across her face. "Mrs. Zouhn?" the woman said.

Christina paused, looked, and then smiled. "Hello. I'm sorry I don't remember your name, but I remember you from high school."

"I was Kimberly Hinds back then," the woman said, as she stood and walked into Christina's embrace.

"Oh, sure," Christina purred. "Your mother worked at the dry cleaners across the street from the school."

"That's right," Kimberly said. "Mom works for Henderson Uniforms east of town now."

"Well, you look good," Christina said. "And you certainly have a delightful family."

"There's one more," Kimberly said, "Madison Jane. She's at the neighbor's house this morning. She's two and the neighbor has a two-year-old also. So they watch cartoons together most mornings."

"And what is your name?" Christina asked, turning to the little girl.

"Brittany Grenwahl," the girl said proudly, smiling at the attention. "This is Daniel." She pointed to the boy sitting outside the group. "And, this is Mikie," Brittany said, pointing the boy sitting next to her.

Kimberly smiled at Christina and said, "Would you mind watching the kids for a couple of minutes so I can go the restroom?"

"I would love to watch them," Christina said.

We all watched Kimberly walk around tables and groups of people standing in the aisles chatting. Brittany turned to look me in the eye. "I love you, Mr. Maxxon. Uncle Chuck told me you are the best race driver in the world. He roots for you all the time, and when he takes me to the races with him, I always yell for you, too. Uncle Chuck said you have the best engines in racing." She paused to remember. "He said ... He said you use big block Ford engines that are over four hundred horses, I think. Is that what you're running?"

Brittany's smile melted my heart; her words were like milk chocolate poured over strawberry shortcakes. "Yes, my engines are big block Ford truck engines. Does your Uncle Chuck like Fords?"

Brittany scrunched her face, and a tiny frown creased her forehead. "Is a Mustang a Ford?"

"Yes, it is."

"Yep, Uncle Chuck likes Fords." She beamed. "He loves his Mustang."

I wondered why Brittany seemed so close to her Uncle Chuck instead of her father. However, I didn't want to ask her since I might be nosing into something personal—like a frequent late-night visitor of Kimberly's. If he took this little girl to car races, he couldn't be the worst guy in the world. Still, I wondered where Brittany's father was. "So Uncle Chuck has a Mustang?" I asked.

"Yep. He's out of town this weekend," Brittany said, her face clouding. "He's taking care of impor'ant business in Birmingham, Alabama. I won't get to see the race tomorrow."

"Oh, I think we can fix it so you can come to the race tomorrow," Christina said. "Don't you think so, Kurt?"

"I'm sure of it," I said.

Brittany's face brightened considerably. "Uncle Chuck roots for you because … he said you used to race Mustangs."

"That's right, I did," I said. "When I first started racing in the SRVSCRA I drove Ford Mustangs. That was before you were born. So that was a long time ago. What else did Uncle Chuck tell you?"

"Well … he's been telling me about dis … displacement, is that what it is?" She frowned as she searched her memory.

"Yes, displacement is an important number we use to describe engines," I said, marveling at her knowledge.

"Displacement is in cubic inches, right?" she said.

"That's right," I smiled. I could tell she was very smart for a seven or eight year old.

"How old are you Brittany?" Christina asked.

"I'll be nine next January," she said, shaking her head for emphasis.

"You probably won't be able to understand displacement completely until after you take high school algebra," I said. "In the meantime—."

"I can't start high school for a long time," Brittany blurted.

"That's okay," I said. "The displacement of an engine is the area of the piston times the stroke the piston travels. Areas of circles and all that stuff are hard for me to remember. For now, we'll just say—"

"Displacement is the area of the piston times the stroke?" Brittany repeated. "What is stroke?"

"Stroke is the distance the piston travels in the cylinder from low to high." I looked at Christina, hoping she, being an old school teacher type and all, might jump in to help; she gave me a "you're on your own, here, buddy," look with her eyes going skyward.

"Uncle Chuck told me about the pistons moving up and down in the cylinder," Brittany said. "I think I understand that part. So the distance the piston travels is impor'ant?"

"Yes."

"That's complicated, huh?"

"It is very complicated. Like I said, I have trouble remembering it all."

"I have to wait until high school to understand it?" Brittany said. "What size pistons do you use, Mr. Kurt?"

"Nikki has pistons that are four and one quarter inches in diameter," I said.

"Who is Nikki?"

"That's my car's name," I said.

"I did not know that," Brittany said and frowned again.

"Your Uncle Chuck might not know that either," I said and smiled. "So you can teach him something."

Brittany focused her intense eyes on me and said, "Would you help Momma, Mr. Maxxon, please?"

I didn't react to the quick change of subject, since I remembered keeping up with Vanessa at the same age. I said, "I'll do whatever you want me to, Brittany. If I can."

"Call me Brit," she said, matter-of-factly. "Everyone else does."

"Okay, Brit, what do you want me to do?"

"Well … I'm not sure," Brittany said. Her forehead wrinkled into a deep unnatural frown. "But Momma cries every night. I can hear her after we go to bed. Daddy left last year. Then Mikie got sick. And then Momma got fired from her job. I know we don't have money like we used to. Could you talk to Momma? Find out why she's crying every night? Is something hurting her? And then fix it. Would you do that for me?"

My throat constricted, and I had to look away to hide the moisture welling up in my eyes. "What's wrong with Mikie?" I whispered, hoping my voice was stronger than it felt, talking through a constricted voice box. I didn't want to upset Mikie if he felt betrayed.

"He has epi—epilepsy," Brittany said slowly. "He has seizures 'bout every day. Sometimes they are bad, and they really scare me."

I looked at Christina, who nodded and said, "He just went into what they call an Absence Seizure."

Brittany looked at Mikie. "Yeah, that's what they call it. I can't remember that one too well. Other times he has a grand mal. I remember that one because I just remember Grandmomma." She held Mikie in a cuddling movement and reached around to pull his tongue out to keep him from swallowing it. "It's okay, Mikie. You're alright. It will be better in a minute."

I saw Kimberly winding her way back toward our table. She saw what Brittany was doing and immediately moved to sit down and take Mikie onto her lap.

"Mikie is having one of his problems, Momma," Brittany said, as she released Mikie into the arms of their mother.

"You did the right thing," Kimberly told Brittany. "You are so much help."

"Do you know what model of Mustang your Uncle Chuck drives?" I asked Brittany to take the subject away from Mikie's "problem."

"What's the most expensive?" Brittany asked.

"I'm not sure. I'd guess it would be one of the Shelby Cobra models, something like the GT500. They may cost even more than one hundred thousand dollars."

"I don't know for sure," Brittany said slowly. "He's got a fancy one, though. My daddy had a Mustang, too. But it was not as fancy as Uncle Chuck's."

Kimberly looked at me and said, "Uncle Chuck has what he calls "The Boss," whatever that is. Brit's daddy, Jim, was a dreamer. He had a beat up regular old Mustang, but he pretended it was one of those hundred thousand dollar editions, like you just talked about."

I nodded acceptance, not wanting to pursue the matter. I could sense that Uncle Chuck may not be a shadow in the night.

"Uncle Chuck is Jim's twin brother," Kimberly offered. "They are alike in a few ways—both like Mustangs—and as different as day and night in most ways. Jim was always competing with his brother—and losing, I might add. Chuck is a lot better off simply because he never married and didn't have four kids to raise. Jim could never understand that, besides getting involved with another woman."

"Daddy never took me to the races," Brittany said. "But Uncle Chuck always does. Well almost always. I always yell for you. You are the best race driver ever. I love you."

"Thank you, Brittany, I love you, too," I said, looking at Christina. She was smiling at Brittany's talkativeness, too.

Christina sat on the bench across from the children. She looked back at Mikie. "You have medication to control this?" she asked Kimberly.

"No. I don't have the money to take Mikie to the doctor." Kimberly put her chin in her palm and looked away.

Christina gave me a "you're up" look, stood up, and said, "I know where we can get some syrup coated waffle cakes. Would you guys like some of them?" she asked Brittany and Daniel. Daniel was immediately interested, and Brittany only agreed reluctantly. Christina led the two toward the cooking area.

I scooted on the bench to where I was sitting directly across from Kimberly and studied her as she watched her children disappear. She was a pretty woman, five foot five, heavy bosom, probably the product of having borne four children. Her round face was framed by black hair in a page boy cut, her eyes were dark brown. A couple of worry lines seemed permanently etched between her eyes. She wore a smile, though. "Brittany is worried about you," I said. "Because she hears you crying every night, after you go to bed."

Kimberly jerked her eyes back to me, and the worry lines deepened. She sat for several moments, and then said, "That girl. I didn't realize she could hear me."

"I have no intention of prying into your life," I said, "but maybe you need someone to talk to."

She sat silently for a long time, and then said. "I don't mind telling you." She dipped her head, and I knew she was fighting down emotion. "It's hard, damn hard," she continued with a shaky voice. "I'm supposed to be getting child support, but in twelve months Jim has sent only three checks. My unemployment benefits ran out last week." Her voice had grown stronger; now it trailed off.

"You can't find a job?" I said.

"About all I know what to do is clerk work. Every clerk's job that comes available, they have two, three dozen "twentysomethings" applying for them. One of them always gets the job. I've applied at eleven places and not got one interview."

"I assume you graduated high school," I said.

"Oh—yes, I did." Kimberly said. "I went three years to Centralia College toward a teaching certificate. I had to drop out during the first semester of my senior year because I was pregnant with Brittany. She was born in January. After Brittany was born, I got a job as a clerk at Hempshaw Rope. Worked there in between having kids until last September, when they closed the plant here and moved it to Mexico. I've been unemployed ever since. My unemployment checks ran out last week."

"You and Jim are divorced?"

"Oh, yeah. Hell, Jim was screwing another CPA at the firm who was a rising star. When the firm transferred her to the Washington, D.C. office, he wanted to be with her, even though he had to essentially start all over at the bottom of the ladder. So he told me and the kids, 'Adios' and left. He comes to town every few months, whenever his sweet thing has to come to Centralia. He takes the kids out for pizza."

"You've got four children. That has to be expensive," I said.

"Tell me about it," Kimberly said. "Brittany is eight, Daniel is six, Mikie is four and Madison Jane is two. Yeah, they are my pride and joy, but expensive to raise, especially now that Mikie has been diagnosed with epilepsy. It seems like the epilepsy is getting worse all the time. But I can't take him to a doctor since I don't have insurance."

"You didn't get COBRA from the rope company?" I asked.

"Hell no. They didn't give us insurance. I had to buy my own. Now, I simply can't afford it."

I hoped my frown wasn't as deep as it felt. "Your doctor shouldn't refuse to treat Mikie just because you don't have insurance," I said.

"I just don't like to beg."

"That is not begging, young lady," I said, adding a fatherly sternness to my voice. "Anyway, I can use another clerk at my auto repair shop. You can start Monday. Your new boss will be at the track this afternoon about three. Can you come back then?"

Kimberly sat staring at me. Finally she said, "Are you serious?"

"Yes, I am. I provide insurance and scholarships for my employees. In the meantime, I want you to schedule an appointment with Mikie's doctor as soon as you can get him in next week, Okay? Either Christina or I will take you both and get your family enrolled in our insurance plan." I took one of my KurtMaxxonRacing.com business cards from my shirt pocket and scribbled the address of Maurey's repair shop on the back, along with his name; Maurey Kennedy.

Kimberly sat for a long time, cuddling Mikie and staring into the space above my head. "Good Lord. Am I going to wake up and find this is all a wonderful dream?" She paused, and then made direct eye contact with me. "I sure do thank you, Mr. Maxxon. Uncle Chuck rooted for you, and he taught Brittany to root for you because you are the best. She loves you."

"She told me that," I said.

There were only a few females who owned a piece of my heart. Christina, my new wife, who shared a spot next to my late wife, Vicki, was first and foremost. Then there was my daughter, Vanessa Louise, after that there was my granddaughter, Ashley Renee, and of course Christina's daughter, Tabitha Faye, and her new baby girl, Isabella. Now, all of sudden, Brittany Grenwahl had just become a special addition to the list, bringing her mother along with her.

I looked at Kimberly, who sat studying me. Tears were leaking down her cheeks, and I looked away to avoid dealing with them. I saw Christina leading Brittany and Daniel toward our table. Christina helped the children up onto the bench seats. Then she came around to sit down next to me. "Did you two have a good chat?" she said, and I knew she was studying the tear streaks Kimberly had used the wet towel on in a futile attempt to wipe away.

"We did," I said. "I told Kimberly we needed a clerk to help Maurey at his shop. She said she would accept the job."

"That's wonderful," Christina said. She looked at Kimberly. "So you are part of the family now. That means we'll be seeing more of you and these charming children." Christina winked at Brittany, who smiled broadly.

"You got a job, Momma," Brittany said.

"Thanks to you." Kimberly took Brittany into her one free arm and hugged her, letting her tears flow freely. "God blessed me when He gave me you, my wonderful daughter."

How long has Mikie been sick?" I asked Brittany.

"Just since, like—around my birthday." Brittany looked at her mother for support.

"When is your birthday?" Christina asked, taking the lead.

"January fifth," Brittany said. "It's so close to Christmas that I hardly ever get birthday presents."

Kimberly shook her head. "That's right, darling, you don't get many birthday presents. We'll have to change that. I promise we'll do better in the future."

"Brittany mentioned that Uncle Chuck had to go out of town, so she's worried about not getting to come to the race tomorrow," I said.

"Yes, Chuck had to make a special trip to Alabama. Brittany is very disappointed about not getting to come to the race."

"Well, we'll be happy to bring her to the race," Christina said. "I can come get her, or you can come and bring her."

"How much are the tickets?" Kimberly asked. "Good Lord, I think Chuck said they were thirty-five dollars each."

"For you and Brittany, they are free," I said. "I have tickets for both of you. Since you work for Kurt Maxxon Racing, one of your benefits is free passes to all the races here at the track. We'll throw Uncle Chuck in too, if you'd like, Brit."

"Yeah," Brittany yelled. "He'll like that."

"You can tell him it's your gift to him for being such a good Uncle," I said. "We'll get him a permanent Pit Pass."

"Cool," Brittany said. "That's cool, huh, Momma?"

Kimberly was only able to nod. Her eyes and voice were lost to emotion.

I heard the roar of a race car echoing from the garage area over to the racetrack. I glanced at my wristwatch, eight forty five. "That's probably Angie," I said to Christina.

"That girl would practice every minute of daylight in the two weeks between races, if we could afford the gas," Christina said.

"If you want to come back this afternoon, you can meet Maurey," I said.

"That's a good idea," Christina said.

"I'll come back," Kimberly said.

"Can I come, too?" Brittany asked.

"Maybe," Kimberly said, looking at me.

"It's okay, bring the kids with you rather than pay a baby sitter," I said.

"Yes, please do," Christina said. "I'll help with the children."

"I'm pretty sure I can get Joanna next door to watch them. I'll bring Brittany with me. She loves car racing as much as her uncle does."

"I love Mr. Maxxon," Brittany said, and her smile would have melted Scrooge's heart. My heart felt kind of mushy, and I hoped it would keep pumping.

*　　*　　*

After the breakfast crowd died down, Christina and I walked with Kimberly and the children to Kimberly's car parked in the fair parking lot. We helped load them into their safety seats and waved them goodbye.

"I should go home and dust the doll room," Christina said. "On the other hand, I can do that Monday morning after the race."

We walked to the track and sat in the grandstand three rows up from Tugs, who was timing Angie's laps. The sun was warming the air nicely, and the temperature would be into the mid-nineties by afternoon. I listened to Nikki's roar and looked around the track. There were communications trailers set up to cover the fair and the race in the racetrack's infield. Thick black cables snaked from trailer to trailer and then to satellite dishes aimed toward the heavens.

I saw Nick Boynton coming toward us and stood to greet him.

"Sit down," Nick said. "Hell, you may be a couple of years younger than I am, but you don't have to get up every time I approach out of respect for your elders."

"Okay," I said. "What are you doing out here at this time of the morning?"

Nick grinned. "Came by to walk the scene again. I do that

several times. Helps me pick up the spirits hovering around."

"The Chindi," I said, smiling.

"The what?"

"The Chindi, the spirits of the dead that hang around after their last breath."

Nick looked at me and frowned. "I've never heard of chin—whatever before."

"Haven't you read any of Tony Hillerman's mysteries?"

"No. I get all the mystery I need in this job. Who is Tony Hillerman?"

"In my estimation he's one of the greatest mystery writers who ever lived. He wrote a series of novels about two Navajo Nation police officers, Lt. Joe Leaphorn and Sgt. Jim Chee. Chee was studying to be a Navajo shaman, so Tony always had him talk about the elaborate spiritual system the Navajo believe in, and how they avoid the Chindi of the departed."

"Huh. That's interesting," Nick said. "So, here I am, trying to communicate with the... what'd you call them?"

"The Chindi," I said. "Pronounced chin-dee."

"The ghosts of the victims are chindee," Nick said.

"Well, actually, the Navajo Chindi represented only the bad parts of the deceased person's life, the parts the person hadn't been able to bring into harmony before they died. That's probably what's hanging around inside the driver's lounge." I watched Nick's eyes move back and forth.

"You think?" Nick asked.

I laughed. "Anything new?"

Nick pulled out his notebook and skimmed the pages. "The M.E. did Melvyn's autopsy earlier this morning," he said. "I swear she suffers from severe insomnia worse that I do. Anyway, I didn't read all of her report, but it looks to me that the cause of death boils down to a thirty-eight caliber slug in the chest. That usually isn't real healthy for anyone."

"I heard Melvyn and his wife Lorianne might be having marital problems," I said, hoping it sounded spur-of-the-moment. "I suppose because Melvyn was fooling around with other women. I also heard Lorianne might have hired the hit man to take out Melvyn."

"Yeah. Well, we've talked to her. The wife is always the

first person who comes to mind in these kinds of cases. She's got a pretty solid alibi. She was at her beauty salon working all morning, ate lunch in the lunch room, full roster of clients. So far the clients verify she did their hair, and we haven't found anything out of the ordinary moneywise—no large insurance policy at all. She could've hired it done. Hell, she might have latched onto the car—maybe had a buyer for it."

"So you're watching Lori Hightower?"

"You betcha, Kimosabe," Nick said with a wide grin. "I got a warrant last night to put a GPS bug on Mrs. Hightower's car. Judge signed it without a whimper. That bug will be on her car this morning which will let us know where her car is at all times, and where it's been in between."

"I'll sleep better tonight," I said, "knowing Nick Boynton and his sidekick, Tonto, are on duty. Oh, and there's Bat Masterson, too."

"That's okay, Maxxon. Just keep me up to date on what other things pop into your head," Nick said, still skimming pages of notes. "Melvyn was shot at fairly close range—there was considerable tattooing around the wound. The techs dug a spent bullet out of the wall. The shot threw Melvyn a couple of feet from where he was standing."

"Did you find the phone booth where the guy called me from?"

"Yeah, it's down on a hundred and twenty first and McKinley," Nick said. "The lab guys picked up a couple of prints off it, but nothing we can fly with yet."

Nick's cell phone rang and he walked away to answer it. He paced in his usual circle for several minutes and then hung up. He started to come back to my seat when his phone rang again. As he studied the Caller ID, he waved goodbye to me and walked toward the Admin Building. I decided it was time to look in on the cleanup folks.

"I need to go check on the cleanup crew," I said to Christina. "You want to walk along?"

"I'll stay here and watch Angie," she said.

As I walked toward the admin building, I saw Nick leaning against his car talking on his cell phone. Inside the driver's lounge I went to get a cup of coffee. Two drivers sat at the dinette table in the kitchen area chatting. The cleanup crew was noisily working in the locker room and shower area. I walked through the locker room area to peek around into the shower area and was pleased at how clean the place looked. I glanced through the open lounge door and saw Nick still out of his car pacing in a circle. I stepped outside the door and watched Nick for a few minutes. He saw me and walked toward me.

"One thing I forgot to tell you from the reports I read this morning," he said as he approached, putting his cell phone away, "whoever shot Melvyn was shooting left-handed. That's not for general dissemination."

"Good to know," I said. I knew the lab people were good at determining a lot of things about a killing from the angle the bullets strike the body and other factors. It always mystified me, however.

Nick waved goodbye again, walked to his car and ducked down into it.

CHAPTER FIVE
Saturday Noon August 25

Kurt Maxxon

I wasn't focused on the racket emanating from the track—Nikki's roar—until I heard an awful sounding "whoomp," a loud bang, and the crunching of metal. Nikki went silent. In an instant I ran headlong toward the racetrack. Christina was climbing through the access gate when I came into the track area. I stopped, gasping for air, and looked for Nikki. I saw her sitting against the inside wall near the entrance to pit row. My lungs burned. Angie! Is Angie okay? In a move I'd never be able to repeat, I leaped over the concrete barrier and ran to the driver's side just as Tugs was helping Angie out of the car through the passenger's window. "Are you hurt?" I gasped.

"No. Dammit," Angie growled. "Dammit, dammit, dammit. We were running so good. And now this."

"Don't—worry—about—it," I said, gulping air between each word. "Just so—you're okay."

"Dammit, dammit, dammit," Angie wailed and pulled away from Tugs grasp and walked in a pacing circle. "I'm sorry, boss."

I surveyed the crunched fender. "Nikki, you look like you could use some makeup," I said. Angie stopped pacing and looked at me, just like my daughter, Vanessa, had done a thousand times, with that "I didn't mean to do it, Daddy," look. I grinned at her and said, "You look like you could use a beer. It wasn't your fault, so chill out."

"She was decelerating to come down pit row," Tugs offered.

"We'll have to do something with her fender," I said.

"Pound it out or put a new one on. New tire and wheel, and realign the front end. Hopefully, her steering system isn't damaged."

Christina came running up and, even though she was gasping for breath, took Angie by the elbow and led her to the concrete barrier and made her sit on it. She quickly surveyed Angie's eyes, complexion, and breathing. Satisfied that Angie was no worse for the wear, Christina, sat down next to Angie and let her breath return to normal. "How do you feel?" Christina asked.

"I'm okay, dammit," Angie said with a heavy sigh.

I dug out my cell phone and punched in Maurey Kennedy's speed dial number. I walked away from the scene far enough to be out of earshot. When Maurey realized it was me, he said, "What's up?"

"Angie hit the wall," I said.

"How bad?" Maurey asked.

"Not too bad. But we need to fix or replace Nikki's left front fender, check her alignment, and get her a new wheel to show off."

"I'm on my way," Maurey assured me. I walked back to the car. Christina hovered over Angie, and I could see Angie was still upset about hitting the wall. Her pride was the only thing bruised.

"Can we get it fixed in time for qualifying?" she asked me.

"Oh, sure," I said. "Maurey's rounding up a couple of guys to do the fender and alignment. He's bringing a new wheel and tire along, too."

"I'm sorry," Angie said, and I hoped she didn't start crying. I have a tough time dealing with weeping women. "I didn't mean to crash."

"The tire blew out," Tugs said. "I heard it from the pits there."

"I heard it over in garage row. It's still not your fault, Angie," I said.

Christina wrapped her arm around Angie's shoulders and gave her a quick hug. Angie's face relaxed a little.

I saw Nick coming toward us. "You want me to call the Highway Patrol?" he asked, and spread a wide grin.

"Humph, this is not a public highway," I said. "Even your cops don't have jurisdiction here. I thought you'd left."

"I went over to get a hot dog. I heard the crash and wondered what had happened," Nick said. "Does this knock you out of the race tomorrow?"

"No. We'll have this fixed later this afternoon." My confidence in Maurey and the mechanics was making me bold.

"I'm glad everyone is okay," Nick said. He turned to leave.

"I appreciate your interest," I said to his back.

Maurey's repair truck came through the passageway followed by a flatbed tow truck. They drove toward us. Maurey parked and walked around Nikki, surveying the damage even as the driver of the tow truck lined up to load the car. When Nikki was securely settled on the tow truck's bed, I motioned Angie into the shotgun side of Maurey's repair truck and Tugs climbed in beside her. "Christina and I will walk over," I said and patted the door twice to let Maurey know it was clear to leave.

They unloaded and parked Nikki in front of the garage. Maurey and the mechanics had sprung into action. There was a flurry of activity that I knew better than to get in the way of. Angie and Tugs sat in Maurey's truck watching.

Christina said, "I'm going home to check on Beau now. I was planning to leave an hour ago."

I nodded acceptance and watched her walk toward the fair parking lot. I climbed into the driver's seat of Maurey's truck and watched the action around Nikki with Angie and Tugs. Maurey's repair truck held all the tools needed to do anything to a car, including an air compressor to drive heavy duty air tools. It was best to stay out of the way of hammers, wrenches, and other tools flying around. There was action at the front of Nikki, action on both sides. The words "poetry in motion" came to mind, and then evaporated. Maurey wandered around in supervisory mode, occasionally pointing out something to one of the repairmen; other times answering questions from the workers. Angie and Tugs eventually got out of the truck and wandered around the edges, dodging the action while staying close and personal.

Maurey and I built a new Nikki every three or four years from the chassis up. A couple of the repairmen had helped build the latest version of Nikki. Nearly everyone knew exactly what had to be done at each step along the way. Angie and Tugs were getting a good education. In the hands of the best mechanical team in the state, Nikki was ready for a test run in two hours and twenty minutes. The team followed Maurey as he walked around Nikki, in the inspection mode, looking at their handiwork. I got out of the truck and walked around after them. Maurey and his crew would be the only ones who could tell the fender had been pounded out. We would spray paint it later for tomorrow's race. The tire and wheel looked nice and straight.

Maurey motioned for Angie to climb into the cockpit. The team pushed her to start the engine, and she roared off toward the track. The repair team and Tugs hopped into Maurey's truck. I walked to the track. I needed some time to calm my nerves.

Angie made five laps and stopped in the first pit. I watched as she climbed out of the cockpit. I walked to Nikki. "How's she running?" I asked Angie.

"She's running great," Angie shrieked, doing a half turn jump and bringing her hands to her knees. "I told her I was sorry for wrecking her."

"Put that out of your mind," I advised Angie again, with good reason.

"She accepted my apology," Angie said, with a wide grin. "We're friends again. We both just forgot about it, and shared a Saturday drive."

"That's great. I'm glad you're taking Nikki seriously," I said with a twinkle in my eye. I looked at Maurey. "Do you need to do anything else before the qualifying runs?"

Maurey wrinkled his face and said, "No. She's running better than before."

"You going home?" I asked Maurey.

"No. I'll hang around for the qualifying runs," Maurey said, "make sure everything is okay."

"Good. I want you to meet your new clerk," I said.

"My new clerk?" Maurey said. "Do I need a new clerk?" He had a quizzical look on his face.

"Yes, you do," I said. "To order parts, keep track of parts ordered, inventory, and all the other paperwork you have to do."

"Okay, boss," Maurey said. "I don't know what's going on, but I'll go with it."

"She's a hard working woman who needs a job," I said. "And, she's a single mother with four children."

"Okay, I get the picture," Maurey said. He looked at me. "Is she pretty?"

"She's very attractive," I said. "But it was her eight-year-old daughter, Brittany, who introduced herself as a fan and owns a chunk of my heart."

"I see," Maurey said. "To keep the fan happy, you're gonna keep the momma happy."

"You know me pretty well, Mr. Kennedy," I said.

"Can I make a few more laps?" Angie asked after she returned from the ladies room.

"Sure," I said, looking to Maurey for agreement.

Maurey nodded. "Go ahead, then bring her back here to the garage. I want to check some things."

Angie roared away. I saw Rafe Komminski sitting in his golf cart across the track on the grandstand ramp. I dashed to meet him. "Hello, Rafe. What are you doing here today?"

"I wanted to talk to you about covering the driver's meeting before qualifying this afternoon," Rafe said. "I'd like to get Manchester back out here to take some pictures. Do a feature article on the SRVSCRA."

"We have a rule that doesn't allow the press at driver's meetings," I said, uncertain of the exact wording of the rule. "The question would be whether the rule also covers the pre-qualifying meeting. It's never come up before."

"I think it would be good for everyone involved," Rafe said.

"Okay," I said. "We'll have to let the drivers decide. If you want to gamble, go ahead and get your guy out here. The meeting starts at four o'clock."

"You got it," Rafe said as he dug his cell phone out of its holster. "And thanks."

*   *   *

I'd finished setting up the chairs for the meeting: two rows of nine for today's qualifying meeting. Rafe Komminski came clomping into the lounge. He walked to the dinette and sat down in one of the chairs. He looked at the two rows of nine chairs. "Are there enough chairs?" he asked.

"Yes. We usually have fifteen or sixteen drivers for the qualifying," I said. "For tomorrow's pre-race meeting we'll need three rows of eleven." The sun brightened the room and the air conditioner was beginning to knock the edge off of the ninety-three degree temperature outside. The drivers never want it cold, eighty to eighty five degrees is comfortable to them.

Whenever the air conditioner paused, the fair noise seeped in. There were at least five public address systems competing with each other along with the noise from muffled engines driving the Ferris wheel and other nearby rides. Today was the last full day of the fair, and most of the PA noise was from the animal sale barns where the auctions of the ribbon-winners were being held.

I noticed Rafe glance up at a particularly loud moment. "It's always noisy the last Saturday with the animal auctions," I said. "But nothing compared to our cars on Sunday."

The clock on the wall was an old 12 hour/24 hour model that chirped loudly, which drew my attention. There was one hour until the meeting to draw qualifying order started, so I walked over and plugged in the coffee pot.

"That's true," Rafe said.

The roar of a racecar engine made Rafe and I pay attention. I walked to the window to see which driver was headed for the track. "It's Eugenios Christofides, the Greek," I said as I watched the number 114 Buick Century move toward the track. Eugenios' car is blue over white with the blue and white Greek flag emblazoned on each side door.

"He'll drown out the fair noise for a while," I said.

A loud click drew my attention toward the admin office, the door opened, and Karl Albertson came into the driver's lounge. He saw Rafe first and said, "Hello, Rafe, how have you been?"

Rafe stayed seated but stretched his hand to greet Karl. "I'm good, how about you?"

"I've been better," Karl said, shaking hands. Then he walked to me and shook my hand.

Karl sat down in the first folding chair in the back row. "Helen called me and told me she had to go to Maplewood. I haven't heard from her since."

"Her father passed away," I said.

"That's too bad," Karl said, letting his face go blank. "I'll call her in a few minutes to offer my condolences."

"I think the funeral is going to be Monday."

"I'll verify the date. The track will send flowers and a memorial."

"Helen will like that," I said. "She's more than just an employee, isn't she?"

"A lot more," Karl said. "Are the cops close to solving the case?" Karl asked. "I assume you're involved, since you found Melvyn's body."

"Not really," I said. "Nick Boynton is the lead detective. I think he's good and that he'll have the case wrapped up pretty quickly."

"I know Nick and I don't think he's all that good," Karl said. "He's just been around longer than any of the other cops." Karl swung around to look at the entire driver's lounge. "I'm glad you had this place cleaned up. It looks good. Like nothing ever happened. Just send me the bill; the racetrack will pay it"

"How well did you know Melvyn Hightower?" Karl asked me.

"About the same as most of the other drivers. Some I know better. If I remember right, the Hightower family was one of the first families in Greene's Ferry. I'll have to look it up."

"Oh, yeah?" Karl nodded interest. "Well, you're the history buff."

Rafe shuffled his chair back and hobbled toward us. "I already looked it up," he said. "The Hightower family was the second family in Greene's Ferry. The ferry capsized while they were crossing the river, and Desmond Greene helped them build a log cabin to live in. The Hightowers decided to stay here."

"That's interesting," Karl said. "There are other Hightowers in the area, aren't there?"

"There are several," I said. "They all claim to be related."

Rafe went to the door to wait for Manchester to arrive.

"Confidentially, Helen told me she and Jason are getting a divorce," Karl said in a low voice. "Surprised the hell out of me. She told me I could tell you. I'm going to tell her to take a couple of weeks off to deal with everything."

"Okay," I said. "Thanks for sharing with me."

Karl stood and said, "I assume you're handling the qualifying runs this afternoon for Helen?"

"I was planning on it."

"Good," Karl said. "I heard Melvyn's car is missing, is that true?"

"Yes, we can't locate it."

"Where could it go?" Karl spread his hands palms up.

"I don't know. I can't figure it out."

"I know Nick checked all the legal tow trucks in town," Rafe yelled from the door. "And none of them was called out here to pick up a car. Charlie Blackwell came out for a no-start in the parking lot. That's all Nick found."

"Why doesn't Nick just start looking in the garages?" Karl said. "There should be keys to all the padlocks hanging on my wall in my office. Hell, Kurt, you know where they are."

"Nick needs a search warrant for each garage," I said. "That's a lot of paperwork he wants to avoid, if possible, especially since the car might not tell him much about who the killer is."

"You and I can look in all the garages, just checking the track," Karl said. "If we find the car, Nick only needs to get one search warrant."

"We can do that tomorrow afternoon after the race," I said. "There'll be a half dozen fewer locked garages then, and it would be interesting to see who has cars here."

"I'll get with you tomorrow after the race," Karl promised. "In the meantime, I'm going to make a couple of phone calls and then go home. I've been out of town and just got back. I know you can handle the race and all this weekend, and thank you for doing it."

"You're more than welcome," I said. I watched Karl walk toward the admin office, bidding Rafe goodbye as he passed him.

Rafe answered his cell phone, spoke a few words and closed it. "Ernie Manchester is on his way back. Do we have time to get some shots of this room before the meeting," Rafe asked, "in case the drivers don't want us in the meeting?"

"Go for it," I said. I ignored Rafe while I tidied the kitchen area and straightened the chairs Karl and Rafe had used.

When the photographer arrived, Rafe showed him which shots he wanted of the inside of the driver's lounge. Manchester blasted away. I turned to realize he was aimed at me. He snapped a picture, the flash catching me off guard. It also made me wish I'd worn better clothes than my faded blue jeans and a twenty year-old

United States Marine Corps T-shirt that was nearly unreadable.

I met Rafe in 1993, right after I retired from the Marine Corps. My mentor, Brian Jeevers, introduced me to Rafe. "More people read The Voice than the morning thing," Brian counseled me, "and their ad rates are a bargain." Rafe introduced me to the advertising manager, Sara Devereaux, and since then, most of my advertising has been in The Voice.

From that day forward Rafe and I have been friends, meeting often for lunch, and attending many civic group meetings and dinners. Whenever The Voice needed inside information about the racing business, Rafe sent his reporters to interview me.

"How are those two boys you found in Carpentier Falls doing?" Rafe asked as I sat down in a chair beside him.

"They're doing great," I said.

"I want to meet them sometime," Rafe said.

"Your wish will be granted, Herr Komminski." I grinned. "They'll be arriving sometime this afternoon. "Do you know Marguerite Grossman?"

"Why, hell yes," Rafe said. "What's she got to do with it?"

"She and Terry took legal guardianship of the boys to preserve their names of Joshua and Jacob Wallace. The boys settled into life with Marguerite and Terry in Kings Rapids and have been very happy ever since."

Rafe wrinkled his lips into a knowing smile. "I'll be damned," he said. "When a kid wins your heart, you take care of them in grand style, Maxxon."

"Wait'll you meet the little girl who stole my heart this morning."

"What's her name?"

"Brittany Grenwahl," I said. "She'll also be here this afternoon."

"I'll wait to meet this girl," Rafe said. "How old is she?"

"Eight."

"What did she do to draw your attention?" Rafe asked.

"She said, 'I love you, Mr. Maxxon. My Uncle Chuck said you are the best driver, ever.'"

"That's all?"

"What else do you need?"

"Damn, you are getting easy, Maxxon."

"It's genetic," I said.

*   *   *

Kimberly Grenwahl

She finished the laundry, folding all the children's clothes and stuffing them into a rickety chest of drawers, and hanging her own clothes on hangers. If she was going to go to work, she would have to dress up better than her normal slouchy cut off jeans and tank tops. Kurt Maxxon had told her to plan on wearing jeans and casual shirts. He would order her some company shirts. She stopped frequently to ponder on her good fortune—meeting Kurt Maxxon this morning. Fate was finally looking down on her.

She heard Brittany yell from the kitchen, "Mommy, Mommy, Mikie's having another problem."

Kimberly stopped what she was doing and ran to the kitchen. Mikie was sitting at the table, on the pillows she used to boost him up, staring into space. She moved and knelt down next to him. She gently took him in her arms. "Oh, Mikie, Mikie, we're going to fix this. I promise you we are going to get you well."

When she and the kids returned home from the pancake breakfast, she'd remembered that Dr. Wright's office was open Saturday mornings until noon, so she called to make an appointment for Mikie. The next available opening was Wednesday morning at ten o'clock. Satisfied at taking care of Mikie, she wondered about her future. A job with the Maxxon Auto Parts and Repair organization was the most wonderful thing that ever happened to her. Should I go ahead and do what I promised to do tomorrow night? Is it worth it now?

Mikie stirred while Brittany placed a cold cloth against his neck.

If you need medicine, maybe I can get an advance against my paycheck to pay for it from Kurt Maxxon. He's such a nice man. Hell, I didn't even ask him about pay. Good Lord. Oh, well; I'll worry about that later.

When Mikie started swallowing rapidly, Brittany made sure he didn't swallow his tongue, as Kimberly had taught her to do. "Thank you, Brit," she said to the girl. "You are such a good help to me. Especially talking Kurt Maxxon into giving me a job."

"I love Mr. Maxxon as much as Uncle Chuck does," Brittany said. "He is such a nice man."

"He sure is." Kimberly let her stare blur on the far wall. Do I need to go through with it? It's easy money. It would be enough money to get us by for several weeks. But there's risk. If you get caught…

Once again the impact of this morning's meeting with Kurt Maxxon overwhelmed her. I don't want to blow this opportunity. She glanced at Brittany, helping Mikie in his recovery from the seizure. Was I dreaming? Would Joan watch the kids?

Kimberly walked back to the bedroom. Her cell phone was lying on top of the chest of drawers. She fished the business card from her shirt pocket and studied the phone number for several minutes. Then she punched in the number, listened as it rang, and then relaxed when she heard Kurt Maxxon's voice answer on the other end. "Oh, hi Mr. Maxxon, this is Kimberly Grenwahl. I was just wondering if you still wanted me to come back to the track later."

"I sure do," she heard him say. "Maurey is anxious to meet you."

She smiled. "Thank you, Mr. Maxxon," she said, and hung up.

It's not worth it. She leaned forward to look down the hall. All four children were watching old cartoons on the Vintage Channel. The TV was blaring. She dialed another number. Listened while it rang and then a voice mail message said, "Please leave your name and a brief message."

She said, "This is Kay Hinds. Something has come up, so I won't be able to deliver that package tomorrow night. Thanks. Good-bye." She pushed the END button. That's the end of that.

CHAPTER SIX
Saturday Afternoon, August 25

Kurt Maxxon

Rafe and the photographer were both outside the driver's lounge on their cell phones, waiting to learn their fate. Both are dealing with the heat rather well. Angie and Tugs had gone for a sandwich at the fair midway. I decided I wanted to scribble a few lines on what to say about Melvyn Hightower's death—since nearly everyone in the SRVSCRA knew Melvyn, I wanted to handle his passing gently. I needed to let everyone know why Helen wasn't here. I also wanted to write down some of the things rattling around in my head.

I walked out to my truck to get a writing pad out of my briefcase. While I was digging around the back seat, I heard car doors slamming and a pair of voices saying, "Hey, Mr. Kurt." I looked to see Joshua and Jacob Wallace rushing toward me. I braced myself and leaned to let them crash into me, a boy in each arm. "Mr. Kurt," Joshua yelled into my ear, "Where's Beau?" In the other ear, Jacob yelled "See our new car?"

I gave each boy a hug and a formal handshake, then stepped back to look them over. I saw the boys about every three or four months, and never ceased to marvel at how they grew in between visits. Joshua is fourteen now, and Jacob is twelve. "What are you guys up to?" I asked.

"We came to see the race," Jacob yelled.

"Is that girl still driving your car?" Joshua asked.

"Yes, she is," I said and watched Marguerite and Terry Grossman approach. I hugged Marguerite and shook Terry's hand. "Those two are growing like weeds," I said.

"Both are going to be tall and lanky," Marguerite said.

"Their father is taller than Terry by a couple of inches."

Marguerite was the chief of police in Kings Rapids. She was an elegant, statuesque African-American. The boys were also African-American. Marguerite and her husband Terry Grossman took custody of the boys after I rescued them in Carpentier Falls a couple of years ago. Then Marguerite and Terry filed for legal guardianship of them so the boys could keep their given surname of Wallace.

"Where's Beau?" Joshua asked again.

"He's at home," I answered. "He's better off at home in this heat."

"We got a new car," Jacob said again. "It's cool, man, see." He turned to point to a new white Mercedes GL-Class. Terry stepped aside to allow a clearer view.

"Three-Fifty or Four-Fifty?" I asked.

"A Four-Fifty, naturally," Marguerite said. "Terry Grossman never buys anything that's practical and economical."

Terry grinned. "It'll do one hundred and twenty miles per hour."

"Hurrrmp," Marguerite growled.

"Won't be but a couple of years before these guys will be driving it," I said, looking from Terry to Joshua and then Jacob. "You want them doing a hundred miles an hour on the streets of Kings Rapids?"

Marguerite smiled widely and said, "Bravo, Kurt Maxxon! But, don't try to confuse Mr. Terry Grossman with logic."

"When Joshua starts driving," Terry said, "we'll get him an old Volkswagen." Terry's grin outshone Marguerite's natural smile.

Jacob beamed. "Mr. Kurt used to fly an old Volkswagen."

He was referring to my standard reply about what it was like to fly the A-6E Intruder with a navigator sitting next to me—in side-by-side seats. The cockpit of the A-6E was wide enough for about one and a half people, but there were two of us stuffed into it. "It felt like I was flying an old Volkswagen," I responded.

Rafe came into the lounge and moved toward Marguerite. "Hello, Chief Grossman. It's good to see you again."

"You're looking good, Mr. Komminski," Marguerite said. "Are you covering the homicide here at the track last Friday?"

"I am, yes," Rafe said. "But, mainly, I'm trying to stay

close to Colonel Maxxon. I figure he'll be the one to solve the crime."

"Not a bad plan," Marguerite said, turning to smile at me. "I wish he'd come to work for me in the homicide division."

Not my idea of a pleasant job. I shook my head and gave Marguerite a hard look. "It's a lot cooler in here, too," I said. "I need to nudge the temperature up a bit, though. Most of the drivers don't like it this cold."

Joshua and Jacob went to the refrigerator to get a bottle of water each. "You want one?" Joshua asked Terry.

"No, thanks," Terry said.

"I'll have one," Marguerite said.

From my observations over the last couple of years, I knew that the boys were happy, well adjusted, and getting educated. Terry and Marguerite were happy to have the boys as family. Christina had commented many times on how great a family the four had become.

I heard Eugene's car wind down and went to the window to watch him return to the garage area. Something's wrong! He only ran a half dozen laps. Only the fair noise remained. We re-arranged chairs so we could sit in a circle to chat. Rafe sat down for a few minutes, but soon got up and excused himself. He went outside. I had moved one of the pool tables into the corner out of the way, but left one so the boys could use it until the last minute before the start of the meeting.

"Where're we going for supper?" Jacob asked after missing a shot.

"Are you hungry already?" Marguerite asked.

"No. Just wonderin'," Jacob said, and moved his footstool out of the way so Joshua could line up for a shot.

"I thought we'd go to Romanov's," I said.

"Where's that?" Jacob said.

"North of here about five miles," I said.

"Have we been there before?" Joshua asked as he moved to make a second shot, having sunk one of the pool balls.

"I don't think you guys have," I said, glancing toward Terry. Terry shook his head.

"What they got to eat?" Jacob asked, watching Joshua sink yet another ball.

"What have they got to eat?" Marguerite corrected.

"Ok, Mom," Jacob said. "Mr. Kurt, what have they got to eat, please?"

"It's really like Italian," I said, feeling my eyes sparkle as I tried for a straight face. "The owners are Russian, so they do some foods a little different, but you'll like it."

"Do they have filet mignon?" Jacob asked.

"They sure do," I answered. "A six ounce, an eight ounce, and a ten ounce."

Marguerite smiled. "I know a few guys who'll order the ten ouncers. Jacob will order one, but Terry will help him finish it."

"How soon are we going?" Jacob asked. I concluded he was tired of playing pool with Joshua, who was running the table.

"We have to wait for Mrs. Christina," Marguerite said. "Do you want to go eat or watch the qualifying runs?"

The boys looked at each other, then to me. "It'll be three or four hours before we can go," I said. Their faces clouded a bit, but Joshua took on a brave look. "We can wait, Jake. We want to watch the races and see Mr. Kurt's lady driver run."

"Can we help with the timers?" Jacob asked.

"Sure," I said. "That's what I planned."

I glanced at the clock on the wall. Three-fifty. Meeting in ten minutes. Drivers started coming into the lounge. I'd heard them arriving as they unloaded their cars, shouting to each other in greetings and friendly banter.

Terry said, "Come on, guys, let's go over to the fair and walk around a bit." Everybody knew the rule in the SRVSCRA that forbid children at any driver's meetings.

"Can we ride the Ferris wheel?" Jacob asked.

"Sure," Terry said. "Josh, you can ride with Mom, and Jake, you can ride with me."

"We're big enough to ride it alone," Jacob said sharply. "Me and Josh can do it by ourselves."

"Joshua and I can do it …," Marguerite corrected.

"That's what I meant." Jacob grinned. Marguerite let him off the hook.

"You guys can ride once," Terry said. "But we don't have a lot of time if you want to watch Angie run."

"Okay," the boys said in unison. "Can we get a corndog?"

Jacob asked.

"Are corndogs good nutrition?" Marguerite asked. "If they are, then you can have one."

"They're good to eat," Jacob said.

"But not very nutritious," Joshua said. Marguerite gave him an encouraging nod.

Jacob didn't give up easily. He looked to Terry. "Can't we cheat once in a while, Dad?"

Suddenly I realized the boys were calling Terry or Marguerite "Dad" and "Mom." It was so natural; it had been sliding past me.

Terry smiled and screwed up his face. "Yeah, let's cheat once in a while." He glanced at Marguerite and winked. Marguerite wasn't ready to concede, but I imagined she would before it was all over.

"Cool," Jacob said.

Terry, Marguerite and the boys left as the room started to fill with drivers. "Hey, Jake," I heard someone yell.

"Hey, Mr. Dave," Jacob responded. I turned to see Dave Kellogg shaking hands with the boys as Terry and Marguerite watched. Dave Kellogg had formed a special relationship with the boys at the Carpentier Falls racetrack the year I took them under my wing. Now every time Dave saw the boys, or the boys saw Mr. Dave, they had a happy reunion.

*   *   *

The drivers came in and some sat down while others moved to buy water or soda pop out of the machines in the corner. I counted thirteen drivers, including myself, and wondered if they would let me start the meeting with that superstitious number in the room. I delayed opening the meeting until Eugenios Christofides wandered into the room, wearing a sweat soaked T-shirt and soggy jogging pants. He made fourteen, which took care of the superstitious members. Eugenios headed to the machine and bought a can of Diet Dr Pepper. He opened the can and drank about half in one swig and then walked to a chair and sat down. The other drivers continued to mill around.

"You didn't run very many laps," I said to Eugenios. "Something wrong?"

"Too damn hot," he said.

"Oh! Okay," I said. "Let's start the meeting, everyone." The drivers slowly quieted down and found chairs. Rafe came through the door and stood inconspicuously near the door. Another driver strode through the door, saw what was happening, and quickly moved to a chair. Ah, we had fifteen. The group quieted completely. The moment they realized Helen Tobias wasn't running the meeting they wanted to know where she was. I told them about Helen's father passing, and all expressed sympathy.

I said, "Reverend, would you do the honors, please." The Reverend was the nickname of Kerry Atkins who drove the number 123 Ford Taurus sponsored by Martin's Marina in Troy. He was an ordained minister in one of the evangelical churches cropping up around the valley.

Kerry led us in prayer, offered up a brief memorial for Helen's father, and then Melvyn Hightower.

I thanked Kerry and added a few words about Melvyn as the representative of the SRVSCRA. Being president of the association made me the spokesperson for all manner of occasions, some of which I enjoyed. Today wasn't something I wanted to repeat.

Other drivers stood near their seats and offered eulogies for Melvyn. I waited a respectable amount of time until another stood, then I said, "I have a request from the Valley Voice and Reporter to be allowed to cover this meeting for a feature story next Wednesday. As you all know, we generally don't allow the press to cover the pre-race driver's meeting. I decided to put it to a vote during this meeting. If you don't mind letting them cover this meeting, raise your hand now."

All but one driver threw a hand into the air. I looked from driver to driver to see if there were any other dissenters. When I finished that survey, I realized Angie wasn't in the room. Tugs stood next to the door. I gave Tugs a questioning look.

"We were running late," Tugs said. "So Angie went to the camper to change, and I'll draw her number if you don't mind."

I looked around the group with the same questioning expression. "Go for it, Tugs," someone said. "Yeah, hell, go for it," someone else yelled from the back row.

"Anybody opposed?" I asked. No one said anything. "Okay," I continued. "We have approved letting the newspaper cover the meeting, and to let Tugs draw for Angie."

Everyone moved their heads in a way I interpreted to mean "okay."

Rafe walked out to wave to his photographer. He and the photographer came into the room, and I introduced them to the drivers and rapidly pointed to each driver giving their name. With Rafe and I standing to one side, the photographer walked to the front of the room and blasted us with his flash.

"When he gets that picture ready, I'll have you identify the drivers. That will be my road map for the rest of the pictures."

I nodded agreement, and Rafe set up a recording device and started it. I walked back to the front of the room and said, "I want you all to welcome, Mr. Komminski and Mr. Manchester from the Valley Voice and Reporter."

I retrieved the wood cigar box from its hallowed place on top of the refrigerator, hoping it would hold together long enough for another drawing. The paper covering the wood had worn off years ago and I noticed that the wood was wearing thin in spots. For Rafe's recorder I said, "All the racing leagues that use the River Flats International Speedway use this wood cigar box for any drawings." I held it so the photographer could get a picture of it. Then I walked around the group, letting each driver extract one of the fifty numbered cubes. When I shoved the box toward Tugs, he drew the cube marked with a "1" on all six sides.

Behind me I heard, "He's lucky for her." Without looking I knew it was Eugenios Christofides, The Greek.

"You going to demand a recount?" Someone quipped.

"I was just hoping to get this over with and back in the shade," Rocky Balloossah said. "Hell, I drew number thirty six. Anyone got a higher number?"

No one spoke up.

"Looks like I go last," Rocky groaned.

The drivers scuffled out of their chairs and out of the lounge, headed for their cars and garages. For qualifying, there were four cars on the track at a time, each starting so they were running a quarter of a lap apart. Since Helen wasn't available, it was up to me to control that part of the runs, plus be the official timer. The drivers weren't racing against each other, but racing against the clock. The starting positions for tomorrow's race were determined by the fastest qualifying times.

I walked to Rafe. "Not much of a meeting," I said.

"Would you see if the drivers will let me sit in on their pre-race meeting tomorrow?" Rafe asked.

"I can do that," I said. "Do you want to take the chance?"

"It'll just be me. I've got enough photographs to use," Rafe said. "What's the significance of that cigar box? Christ, I haven't seen one of those in decades."

"Legend has it that when the first car races were held, the only thing they could find to use was that very cigar box. The track manager smoked the cigars and typically threw the boxes in the trash. The drivers found it in the trash can out back. It's been used ever since. It's getting a little ragged around the edges, however."

"You are a walking encyclopedia of valley history, Mr. Maxxon," Rafe said. "And I'm glad you're my friend. If you need a new cigar box, I know someone who has dozens of them."

"When this one goes for good, I'll call you."

He and the photographer packed up and left.

When I walked out of the lounge, I saw Angie follow Tugs into garage number one, and then I saw the rear end of Nikki come slowly out of the garage, Angie inside steering, Tugs pushing. As I walked toward them, Angie started Nikki's engine and the roar made me cringe. I quickly dug out the ear plugs from my shirt pocket and pushed them into my ears. You're getting lax, old man, a voice in my head said. You know better than to be next to a running engine without ear protection. I hoped Terry or Marguerite had remembered to bring ear plugs for the boys.

With my ears ringing. I walked to the track. The drivers followed Angie in procession and passed me in the passageway between garage row and the track. It wasn't until I arrived at the timer's station on the track that I realized I'd forgotten to bring the electronic timing equipment. I'd have to walk back to get it.

"Where you going?" Jacob asked as I walked past them toward the admin building.

"To get the timer," I said.

"It's on your wrist," Jacob shot back at me.

I laughed heartily. I wanted to stop and enjoy the levity, but I didn't have time. I waved as I walked back to the driver's lounge, dug the electronic timer out of the closet and doubled my pace back to the track. When I got back with the timer, most of the drivers were looking at me with less than friendly smiles. The air temperature was now reading ninety five, so their cockpits would be 110 plus degrees.

It took me about two minutes to align the timing device to the mirror on the far wall. If their cars had horns, I could imagine the blare of horns that would be going up as I worked.

"The instant the beam stops being reflected back to the instrument here, the timer stops," I explained to the boys. "So, here's what we're going to do. Joshua, you run the chronometer. Jacob, you write down the times. Can you hear me with your ear plugs in?"

Jacob looked at me as if I had never asked the question before. "I can hear you, if you yell," he replied.

I positioned the boys on either side of me and gave Joshua my wrist chronometer and Jacob the clipboard. "Okay," I said loudly, "we're going to time five laps for each driver, and then we divide their total time by five to get an average time. The electronic timer will time each car separately, so Jacob, you write the times on those sheets right there as I tell you." I pointed to the sheets where I'd scribbled each driver's name and car number on a sheet and stacked the sheets in the order they would be running the qualifying runs.

"Joshua, you time the cars I tell you," I said. "Then we'll compare our numbers after." I could time all the cars electronically, the timer would time up to fifty different cars with the right programming. But just in case the cars got too close to each other, Joshua would be my backup.

*   *   *

All in all, the qualifying runs went well. There were only three instances where I was overwhelmed by the events. In each case, Joshua, my back up, saved the day. We wound up with good times for every car. By the time Rocky finished his qualifying laps, I was as wet as if I had run the laps in Nikki myself. The boys and I adjourned to the air conditioned driver's lounge to do the calculations.

The drivers either put their cars away or prepared them to run practice laps. I hoped they could all work out who followed who and realized all they had to do was go in the same order as used for the qualifying runs. Those who rented garages parked in front of their garages while they waited. Other drivers would keep their cars in the storage area where they would leave them overnight. However, before anyone left the admin area, they wanted to know the results of the qualifying runs—the starting order for tomorrow's race.

Jacob ran the calculator faster than Joshua or I, so we let him do the averages. We had the results ready in about fifteen minutes. I wrote the results on the white board as Jacob read them off to me.

No one had ever questioned Helen's timing numbers. I hoped they wouldn't start challenging the results today, especially since it looked like Angie had the second-best time. When Angie finished her run, she and Tugs had left the track area, put Nikki in her garage, and were waiting in the driver's lounge.

I was writing the numbers on the white board when Christina came through the door. She stopped to let her eyes adjust, then read the list. "Angie's starting in second place?"

I nodded.

"That's great," Christina said. She looked around the room and saw Angie playing pool with Joshua and Jacob. Tugs leaned against the far wall, chatting with Jimmie Davison, who was also from Carpentier Falls. The two knew each other well. When the boys saw Christina, they dropped their cue sticks and ran to her. She greeted them with her exaggerated hug and a kiss on top of the head.

"Angie came in second," Jacob said. "Did you see?" He pointed to the big white board.

"I saw that," Christina said. Then she moved toward Angie. "Congratulations, Girl," she said.

"Thank you," Angie purred.

"Where's Beau?" Jacob yelled.

"I left him home," Christina said. "It's so hot out, and I figured we would be going to supper right after the qualifying runs. We'll go to Mr. Kurt's house after supper, and you can see him then."

"That's a good idea," Jacob said. He didn't hide his disappointment very well. He returned to the pool table, but Joshua had lost interest and Angie was talking to Tugs.

Some of the drivers started straggling into the lounge around the room; the rest were mingling around outside the lounge. After I had recorded the last number, I motioned to the drivers in the room. They stood and nodded acceptance and walked to the door.

One driver shouted "They're up."

A gaggle of drivers pushed through the door and stood studying the white board. I waited.

Eventually, each driver turned and walked out of the lounge.

No challenges.

I sat in one of the meeting chairs. Christina walked up to me. I stood up to kiss her.

Terry and Marguerite came into the room. The boys were sitting on the edge of the pool table.

"Are we going to eat now?" Jacob asked.

We all smiled. "I just need to take a quick shower," I said. Christina left to get a change of clothes out of her car for me.

When she returned she handed me the clothes on hangers and said, "I'll ride with the boys and take them to the restaurant. We'll meet you at Romanov's."

I showered and dressed in near record time. Before I left for the restaurant, I checked to make sure the admin office was locked. The driver's lounge was left unlocked for the other drivers who would be arriving during the evening, overnight, and early tomorrow morning. I climbed into my truck and navigated through the fair traffic. The fair officially ended at 8:00 p.m. tonight. The rides, trailers, and carnival people would pack up overnight and travel somewhere down the road.

*   *   *

Lorianne Hightower

She'd waited until after dark to come to the salon. It had been closed for hours, and the other hairdressers had left for the day. She had been thankful that the other girls had covered all her appointments today so she could stay home and answer calls from friends, relatives, and neighbors. Her thoughts today had been disconnected, maybe even disoriented.

Melvyn is dead. Gone!

What am I going to do now?

She replayed the conversation with their accountant that afternoon. He had called to give her advice on what to expect in the next few days. Melvyn's sister had called to say she would take charge of the funeral since she was the family member who watched the family plots in the cemetery. Melvyn's body was still under police control at the hospital.

The sixteen boxes of paperwork that lined the wall under the stairway brought her back to the present. Those records are a major problem. I've got to get rid of them.

But how?

Figure out a way. And do it fast.

"Why the hell didn't you haul them off a long time ago?" she asked herself aloud. Now they are a problem. My life is under the microscope. I'm being watched. The sound of a creak made her look up the stairs. What was that? Damn, if the cops find them ... you ... do ... not ... want ... the ... cops ... finding this stuff.

"You've got to get rid of these boxes," she mumbled as she climbed slowly up the stairs and peeked around the doorway. Nothing. She slipped into the room and moved to look into the main salon room. The street lights outside and nightlights inside cast shadows in a confusion of directions. Six empty chairs. Four empty dryer chairs with their hoods poised. Nothing else. The creak again. She saw the cabinet door at one of the operator's stations open and moving gently in the breeze from a floor fan left running. She walked over and slammed the door shut and turned the fan off, and then returned to the stairway.

As she descended the stairs, a plan started to form in her mind. She stopped in front of the pile of boxes again, and let her thoughts gel in her mind. That'll work! She lifted one of the boxes, tested its weight, and without stopping carried it to the top of the stairs and to the back door. She went back down for another. Several exhaustive minutes later, she had four boxes near the back door of her salon. She went out to get her car. At four boxes per trip, it would take four trips, but she would get those damn boxes of paper out of her salon. Can I do it fast enough?

* * *

Kurt Maxxon

The maitre d' had seated the group at a large round table in a quiet corner. When I arrived, Terry was sipping on a cold Budweiser,

Marguerite and Christina were nursing glasses of white wine and the boys each had a soda glass with a straw in front of them. Menus were laid open at each place. Joshua and Jacob were sitting on either side of Christina. I sat down between Joshua and Terry.

The maitre d' waited after leading me to the table and said to the group, "Our Special tonight is Beef Stroganoff with Russian noodles."

"Do you have filet mignon?" Jacob asked.

"We do," the maitre d' said, smiling. "We offer very nice six or eight ounce steaks. And for a young gourmet like yourself, we can cook you a special ten ounce steak if you desire."

Jacob beamed. "Are they wrapped in bacon?"

"Indeed they are," the maitre d' said, obviously enjoying the exchange.

A smiling waitress stood off to the side while the maitre d' finished his duties. The maitre d' looked at the waitress and said. "Sally, this young gentleman must be given special treatment."

Sally grinned and nodded. "I'll do my very best," she said and smiled at Jacob. She was a pretty girl with black curls on top of her head and straight black hair hanging down over her shoulders. Her smiling face was round with a pug nose and dark brown eyes hooded by black eyebrows. Her cheeks were a little pudgy with dimples on both sides. She wore a pastel lip blush that enhanced her smile.

Her eyebrows rose slightly when I ordered iced tea. She hustled off and returned with a tall glass of iced tea. She stood ready to take our meal order, and looked toward Jacob to lead off.

"I want the special ten ounce steak, medium rare, with mushroom/onion sauce, please."

"What kind of potatoes do you want: mashed, baked or French fries?"

"Baked," Jacob said. "With sour cream, butter and chives."

The waitress was enjoying Jacob. "And what kind of salad dressing would you like?"

"Bleu cheese, please."

The rest of us marveled at Jacob's gourmet knowledge. He must be practicing someplace.

Joshua ordered the Stroganoff Special with French fries, salad with French dressing and said he would want dessert later.

I remembered when Little Kurt ate so voraciously. That thought made me think of Vicki, my late wife who passed away a few years ago from ovarian cancer. I glanced at Christina, busy with Jacob and Joshua. Suddenly I was feeling extremely thankful for her friendship over the years and thankful for the chance to be her husband. I swung my gaze to the ceiling. Thanks, Big Guy. Thank you so much for making me such a lucky man.

Christina and Marguerite ordered small steak dinners. I ordered the same dinner as Jacob. When Terry ordered the small steak dinner, I looked at him quizzically.

"I'll have to help one of our gourmets finish his steak," Terry said with a grin. "I'll get enough to eat before it's all over with."

I noted that Jacob no longer needed a booster seat. Yes, the boys were growing up fast.

"Are Alisa and Mutt coming over tomorrow morning?" I asked Terry.

"They're coming over this evening," Terry said. "Alisa just wrapped up an important case and said she wanted to finalize it today. I told her to leave it, but you know Alisa. They might be at your house when we get there from here."

"Where are you staying tonight?" I asked.

Marguerite said, "We're at the Downtown Marriott. They have a lovely family suite we found out about last year when we came to the race."

"It's a neat place," Joshua said. "We have our own game station in our bedroom."

"Yeah, and they got the Car Racing Extreme game on it," Jacob said.

"They have the Car Racing Extreme game on the play station," Marguerite corrected.

Jacob stared at her for a long moment. "What did I do wrong?" he asked.

Marguerite smiled and patiently explained: "You don't say 'They got.' You say "They have the game on the machine."

"Okay," Jacob said. "They have the Car Racing Extreme game on the machine and we got to play it."

CHAPTER SEVEN
Saturday Evening, August 25

Kurt Maxxon

After dinner at Romanov's, the Grossman family followed us to our house. The boys were anxious to see Beau, and Beau was happy to see them. In typical boy fashion, Joshua and Jacob scattered Beau's toys around the house and played with them more than Beau. The adults sat in the kitchen, chatting, drinking decaf coffee, and catching up on what and how the boys were doing. "Jacob is working on a science exhibit and getting a jump on starting back to school week after next," Marguerite reported.

"Yeah, Mr. Kurt," Jacob yelled from the living room. "You oughta see the thing I'm making of the planet's orbits around the sun."

"You should see the thing I'm making ...," Marguerite corrected Jacob.

"Okay," Jacob said, politely turning toward me. "I'll show you how it works when you come to see us."

"Joshua is playing basketball at the YMCA just about every evening," Terry said. "I play with him as often as I can."

"Joshua is going to be the athlete," Marguerite said. "And Jacob will be the scientist."

For a fleeting moment, I remembered my days in school and the science projects I'd completed.

Christina dug around in the freezer and pulled out an apple strudel she'd made. She put it in the microwave oven and in a few minutes we were oohhing and aahhing over the succulent treat. Marguerite had to exert all her motherly finesse to keep the boys from having third helpings. Beau got a tiny piece in his bowl.

After the strudel, Beau sauntered down the hall to his bed.

The boys came into the kitchen and sat down on the floor, leaning against the wall. "You guys ready for school?" I asked them.

"Yeah!" Jacob said quickly. "I can't wait! Mom and Dad got me into the planetarium summer camps."

Joshua acted like he hadn't heard the question.

"All the other kids thought I was a genius last year." Jacob beamed. "When I told them the rhyme you taught me about keeping the names of the planets straight; you know, My Very Elegant Mother Just Served Us New Potatoes."

I remembered the incident very well.

"He jabbered that rhyme for days," Marguerite said. "It helped it to sink in, I guess."

"It's neat," Jacob said.

I kept glancing at Joshua. He was very quiet while we talked about school. "What classes are you taking next year, Joshua?" I asked him.

"I don't know," he said. "Whatever they tell me to."

Marguerite looked at Joshua, and I could tell she also had some concerns about his demeanor. "He's starting to notice girls," Marguerite said.

"I am not," Joshua said defensively. "School's just too tough."

"Hey, Joshua," I said. "I thought you wanted to learn to fly an airplane. That takes a lot of stuff you have to learn, like some math, and science, and sociology, and debate."

Joshua swung to look at me. "I can't listen very well, Mr. Kurt," Joshua said.

I glanced at Terry, then Marguerite again. Marguerite's concern was obvious on her face.

I knew Terry and Marguerite had taken the boys to a psychologist, and they'd had several months of counseling. Had it been enough? I wondered if their mother leaving and then found stabbed to death was affecting Joshua now. I didn't think Terry and Marguerite had told the boys their father was the murderer. Apparently, their father had abused them, and then their mother took them to Carpentier Falls to get away from the abuse.

"We're going to see Dr. Goodman Tuesday morning," Marguerite said. "Maybe he can figure out why you've lost interest in school all of sudden."

Joshua wrinkled his mouth and forehead. "I'll be okay," he said.

Terry stood and said, "It's time we head to the hotel and get to bed. We've got a big day tomorrow with the race."

Christina went down the hall to tell Beau his visitors were leaving. He followed her back into the kitchen wagging his tail tiredly to say goodbye to the boys. Christina and I walked the family to their car and said goodbye. We watched them drive away, and Christina moved into my arms. "They are such a pleasant family," she said. "I'm glad it's worked out so well for the boys."

"Are you worried about Joshua's loss of interest in school?"

"No." She was so forceful it jarred me.

"You don't think it's psychological?"

"No. My bet would be that it's something physiological. Two notable culprits are eyesight or, very possibly, his hearing." Christina looked up at me. "I've seen dozens of cases where when a child's grades start falling, their parents want them tested for psychological problems like Attention Deficit Disorder, and so forth. With most of those kids, just as soon as you put a pair of glasses on them so they can read well, all the problems go away. If it's a hearing problem, then you get them hearing aids."

"Hearing aids for a fourteen-year-old?" I said. "I don't know if Joshua would wear them."

Christina paused to move dishes around in the sink. "The kids resist them and swear they won't be caught dead wearing them in public. Then they wear them around the house and see how helpful they are, and they decide they will wear them all the time. The advantages outweigh their sensitivities."

"Why didn't you mention that to Marguerite?" I asked, placing the dishes she handed me into the dishwasher.

"I'm pretty sure she already knows that, but she is very methodical and wants to start with the worst-case scenario and work from there."

"That easy, huh?" I said.

"More often than not, I'm happy to report. I'm positive that Marguerite is just the right person to run it to ground. I'm sure she'll get Joshua correctly situated on the road to a successful life."

"So am I," I conceded. "Thank you, once again, Big Guy.

We finished straightening up the kitchen, and I carried the trash bag out to the garage. I thought I heard a car in the driveway. I pushed the button to raise the garage door and watched Mutt Sparks park his Land Rover on the apron. The car had no more than stopped rolling when the passenger side door flew open, and Alisa Sharpe stepped out. She flung the door shut and ran toward me. We embraced. Alisa stepped back and said, "You really are Kurt Maxxon."

I smiled at the now familiar greeting, and gave her my standard reply, "Yes, I really am Kurt Maxxon." Today, Alisa was an attractive, healthy young woman, compared to the beaten down little girl with a Kewpie doll curl I met when I first saw her in the county jail. She was the prime suspect in the homicide of Rusty Gallegar a few years back in Kings Rapids. I'd discovered Rusty's dead body jammed under his work bench in his garage at the track. He'd been shot to death from close range. A few days later the cops arrested Alisa, since she had been Rusty's ex-live-in lover. He had kicked her out of his life a few days before he was found dead.

Her mentor at the Kings Rapids Times-Democrat newspaper, Mutt Sparks, who just happened to be one of my closest friends, proclaimed, "Alisa is incapable of killing a fly." He asked me to get involved. Eventually I flushed the real killer, and Alisa was off the hook.

Shortly after that, Alisa surprised us all by announcing, "I'm going to go to community college and get a certificate in Police Science. I want to be a cop." She gained the respect of her instructors, and they recommended her to the Kings Rapids Police Department. She went through the Police Academy, graduating at the top of her class. She became a favorite partner of several patrol cops. Then, in one tragic moment, Alisa and her partner careened into a bridge abutment which caused severe injuries to Alisa. They were chasing a lunatic spraying UZI gunfire as he was racing down a busy avenue. Alisa recovered from all the injuries, except one. She was blind in the right eye—which forced her off the police force.

Terry Grossman invited Alisa to join his detective agency in Kings Rapids, and she very quickly became Terry's most trusted investigator. To add to the good things that happen to good people, Alisa married Mutt Sparks, even though Mutt is thirty years older, and they have been living on a honeymoon ever since. Mutt retired from the Kings Rapids Times-Democrat and became a free-lance writer doing assignments for a major racing tabloid in London.

As I reminisced, Mutt climbed out of the driver's side and walked toward us. He shook my hand with his unique firm grip and emphatic herky-jerky motion. "Mutt" was the moniker of Rudolph Michael Sparks who was eight inches taller than my five foot eleven, but weighed about sixty pounds less than me. "You've put on a little weight," he said. "Not driving is catching up with you." Mutt liked to throw barbs at his friends.

"Yes, I know," I said. "I'm getting lazy, I think."

Mutt's hair today was silky white, but in his younger days, as an aspiring newspaper reporter, Mutt sported a head of black hair and a comb-like mustache. He had been teamed up with a short, rotund photographer, and they became known as the "Mutt and Jeff" team. The nickname "Mutt" had followed Rudolph Sparks ever since, and he still reminded me of Augustus Mutt of the Mutt and Jeff comic strip I loved as a kid.

Christina came out into the garage with Beau on her heel. When she saw what the commotion was about, she smiled. "You are looking very good," Christina said to the radiant Alisa. The last time Mutt and Alisa met Christina and I for dinner, about four months ago, Alisa had premiered her "glass eye" which made her handicap totally invisible.

When Beau leaned against her legs, Alisa bent down to pick him up, cradle him, and scratch his ears. Beau looked totally blissful, eyes closed, and grinning. After Alisa put him down, he trotted after her, glancing at me with a look that said, "I'm going home with her because she treats me so much better than you do."

"Terry and Marguerite just left about thirty minutes ago," I said. "They told us they thought you were coming over this evening. We kind of waited for you, but the boys were getting tired."

"I just wrapped up a major case," Alisa said. "I wanted to put it to bed before I left town."

"You know Ms. Alisa," Mutt said, with a wide smile. "I couldn't budge her until she'd proofed it for the hundredth time and checked all the dates, again and again. Then it had to be folded just right to fit into the envelope."

"So what's your point?" Alisa said, with a shrug and grin.

We wandered into the kitchen and sat around the dinette table. Christina reheated the apple strudel. I enjoyed a second helping. Beau received a covert bite from Alisa and once again made sure I noticed that Alisa treated him better than I did.

"That strudel is absolutely delicious," Alisa said. "Can I have the recipe?"

"It's an old family recipe," Christina said.

That's Christina's code for "there is no recipe written on paper." Christina usually cooked by instinct. To Alisa, Christina said, "Let me see if I can find it, and I'll copy it for you."

No time limit was mentioned, which alerted me to that possibility that there would be another batch soon, so that Christina could write down the ingredients as she went. Her apple strudel was one of my favorite desserts. Ah, contentment.

"Are you staying at the Holiday Inn tonight?" I asked Mutt, hoping he had made reservations many weeks before due to the fair crowd and race weekend.

"Yes. We're there tonight and tomorrow night, too," Mutt said. "Don Epperley will be driving over tomorrow morning for the race, then he'll stay tomorrow night and go home Monday morning. We're planning to have dinner with him tomorrow night. You and Christina are invited, obviously. We just never have time to get together in Kings Rapids anymore."

After we'd eaten our fill of apple strudel, we drifted toward the murder at the track.

"Terry played a round of golf with Brad Langley this morning up in Maplewood," Alisa said. "He told Terry you were the one who found Melvyn's body."

"Actually, I'm not involved at all," I said, nervously, hoping Brad Langley wasn't preparing to give me another tongue lashing. He and I had been friends for two-thirds of our lives. We met the day we were inducted into the Marine Corps aviation program and we learned we had grown up fifty miles apart. We became roommates and inseparable buddies for the next several years, moving up through the ranks in leap frog fashion. Brad and I were best man for each other when we each got married. Brad was the Godfather to my two children and I was Godfather to his two children. Brad retired three years before I did due to health problems caused by taking a dunk when his engines flamed out while trying to abort a carrier landing. He returned to the valley and secured a job with the state police. Not being one to sit around, Brad started climbing the ladders and very soon was the chief of the Central Investigations Division of the state police's Major Crimes Unit.

"Brad told Terry he was monitoring it very closely," Alisa said.

"Damn," I said, and Christina gave me a sidelong glance.

A few years ago, when I "helped" solve the murder of track manager Elaine Willowby, in Masonville, my moves nearly killed Christina. Brad had come down on me hard and warned me to stay out of the amateur sleuth business. When I met Alisa, while I "helped" solve Rusty Gallegar's killing in Kings Rapids, Brad was less adamant, but still advised me to stay out of the cop business. Then when I "helped" solve the murder of Irene Faye Wallace in Marysville, a town just a few miles north of Kings Rapids, and then "helped" solve the death of Carlos Guerrero in Carpentier Falls, Brad even congratulated me. After his admonitions, I still wondered what Brad would say about my activities—even accidentally getting involved. Except for the Irene Wallace death, I was the one who knew the victims. I worried about who killed my friends, and my wheels were turning. Solving the crime was just a happenstance.

"Terry didn't seem all that interested," I said. He didn't mention anything about it."

"He's up to his ears into a major fraud investigation," Alisa said. "That's about all he's thinking about right now—other than golf, of course. However, I do want to see the crime scene."

"I had the scene cleaned this morning by professionals," I said. "Not much to see I'm afraid." I really hoped to dissuade Alisa, but sensed I couldn't. "If you really want to see it, we can run over to the track now. The fair ended tonight, and so the traffic should be cleared out by now. Tomorrow morning there will be a steady stream of drivers in and out of the men's room from sun-up on."

"She's wound up," Mutt said. "She's been floating around on cloud nine ever since she broke her case wide open a couple of days ago."

Christina stood and started gathering dishes. "You all go to the track," she said. "I've got some paperwork to get caught up on." Alisa stood and began to help her. Christina shooed her away. "You guys need to get going if you're going to be home before midnight."

"I never get to bed before midnight," Alisa said with a chuckle.

"Tell me about it," Mutt said.

Mutt drove to the track. I sat in the back seat, which I liked to do whenever I got the chance, especially when in a car like Mutt's Range Rover, which had ample leg room in the rear seat. At the track I climbed out and used my key card to open the admin gate. I walked to the driver's lounge door and was surprised it was locked. I looked around to survey the drivers in the auxiliary area. Several pickup trucks and trailers along with race cars were scattered around the lot. I opened the door with my key card.

Mutt moved to buy a bottle of water from the Coke machine. We kept free bottles of water in the refrigerator, but Mutt never took advantage of freebies. Before he retired as the Senior Sports Editor at the Times-Democrat newspaper in Kings Rapids, Mutt had been in this lounge dozens of times and every time I told him to get water out of the fridge.

It was Mutt Sparks who destroyed my anonymity many years ago. Before I won my first race in Kings Rapids, nobody knew who I was. After that win, Mutt's news coverage made me a celebrity. I had his articles framed on my wall of accomplishments in my master bedroom.

Since none of the other drivers were in the lounge, I led Alisa on a tour of the driver's lounge building, showing her where I'd found Melvyn's body in the men's locker room. Alisa viewed the location very carefully, moving to take pictures from several angles with her cell phone.

"I can get blood spatter photos from Brad," Alisa said, "When Terry told him we were coming to Centralia for the race, Brad told Terry to have you show us the scene." Her eyes sparkled with merriment. I looked at her in shock.

I could still visualize the blood spatter on the lockers. I tried to reconstruct it for Alisa. The cleanup crew had removed nearly all of the evidence of a killing and investigation residue.

"How's the investigation going?" Alisa asked. She had acted like she knew everything that was going on.

"If we could just find Melvyn's car," I said.

"The car is missing?" Alisa said with concern furrowing her forehead.

"I thought you knew that."

"No, I didn't," Alisa said.

"It's probably here at the track locked in one of the garages," I said. "Nick decided it might not be worth the time and expense to get search warrants for all fifty-some garages that are locked. Karl Albertson and I are going to do our own search tomorrow after the race."

"If Nick comes by evidence like that without getting it by due process, it might not be admissible." Alisa pursed her lips. "Is someone renting the garage?"

"We don't know," I said. "We'd have to go back through a year's worth of records to see who is renting which garages, and if one of the garages isn't actually on record as being rented. That will take checking the receipts against the accounting records to see who's paid up and who has yet to pay for garages they're using this weekend."

"Lotta work," Alisa said. "And finding the car might not help find the killer. Nick's probably right on the money."

I said, "Karl Albertson, the track's general manager, and I talked about opening all the garages doing a track inspection for contraband, which is perfectly legal. If we found the car, we could call the police to check it out, since the garage wasn't rented legally. But even that might not be admissible in a court."

When Alisa and I walked back into the lounge area, Mutt was pacing around talking on his cell phone. "Oh, sure, I can be there," he said. After a few moments of chatting, he ended the call, walked to Alisa and gave her a hug. "They want me to cover the Grande Premio Do Brasil the first week in November. You should try to go with me."

"I'll try to do that," Alisa said.

As a freelance writer, Mutt had covered Indy car racing in the United States, and Formula 1 racing in Europe, Asia, Australia, South Africa and South America. He's traveled to all the Formula 1 racing venues—Monte Carlo, Monza, Valencia, Melbourne, Kuala

Lumpur, Istanbul, Montreal, and a dozen other places, including the middle east countries of Bahrain and Abu Dhabi. Alisa accompanied Mutt as often as she could, but always kept her casework for Grossman Investigations foremost. She had never let Terry down.

"You want to go, too?" he asked me.

"I don't think so," I said. "I've been there, done that."

"I didn't know you'd been to Brazil," Mutt said. "You've never mentioned that."

"I've never been to Brazil," I said. "And I have absolutely no desire to go there, either. But I've done most of the other racing cities, especially in the Middle East."

"That was during the war," Mutt said.

"That part of the world is always at war," I said matter-of-factly. "If they can't find somebody else to fight, they kill each other just for the fun of it."

"You're becoming a political analyst, Maxxon," Mutt said. "Personally, I like the gulf cities of Sakhir and Yas Marina."

"I've seen both from forty thousand feet, and wasn't really impressed with either," I said, hoping to add a humorous lilt to my voice.

"Boys, stop your bickering," Alisa said, snuggling up to Mutt. "Let's take Kurt home so we can get to the hotel."

*   *   *

Lorianne Hightower

Every time she slid into her car she wondered how long she would be driving it. She had dreamed of owning a Porsche 911 since her nineteenth birthday when she and her friends went to Chicago and she saw one in a dealer's showroom. When she bought it four months ago, it was two years old. It only had twenty-eight thousand miles on it. She loved the color—Ruby Red Metallic—at least, that was what the documents called it. Even in the dim night light and street lights around the storage buildings, it gleamed with a special sparkle.

She glanced at her watch. Damn her. Lynnette is always late. She's a damn good salesperson, though. That's the only reason I put up with her lack of punctuality. A pair of headlights rolled up to the gate, someone punched in the entry code, and a vehicle drove toward her. The Dodge pickup truck pulled up to storage room and parked to allow boxes to be loaded into the truck bed. A big-boned, chunky woman climbed down out of the truck and walked to meet Lorianne. "What's up?" the woman asked.

"Big problems," Lorianne said. "I want you to buy all the stock you have."

"Good, Lord, Lorianne, I don't have the bucks to do that. You know that."

The same answer she had gotten from Teresa and Elberta earlier in the evening. "Okay," she said. "I'm giving it to you on consignment. All I ask is that you give me a twenty-five percent cut and not mention my name to anyone who asks you."

"What's going on?" Lynette asked.

"You haven't read the newspaper, huh?"

"I usually just look at the weekend garage sales in the Thursday edition."

"Melvyn is dead," Lorianne said, and wondered if her voice sounded as shaky as she felt.

"Dead?"

"Yeah! Yesterday morning," Lorianne said.

Lynette frowned and bore into Lorianne's eyes. "How?"

"Someone shot him dead."

Lynette screwed up her face with a deep frown. "Did you shoot him?"

"No! Of course not." Her flapping mouth had gotten her in trouble again. "The cops are watching me. The wife is always the first suspect, you know."

"Yeah, sure," Lynette said.

"Anyway, here's my key to this unit," Lorianne said. "I don't want the cops onto me and this operation."

"I sure as hell don't want them to get involved, either," Lynette said, and her voice quivered slightly. Lorianne didn't like that, but there was nothing she could do about it. Teresa and Elberta had been just as equivocal about her giving them their respective inventory of stock on consignment. Lorianne didn't like doing it this way, but she'd convinced herself it was the only way to handle it on such short notice. Her operation had been very successful because she had three independent mules out peddling and delivering—three separate people who didn't know about each other and three separate storage rooms used to store the products.

Now all she could hope was the three women would honor their pledges to not name her if they got caught. Lorianne didn't really care about getting a cut of the current inventory. Over the last twelve years she had made huge profits in the business. A few bucks here didn't bother her, especially if she could get through the problem of Melvyn's death. After everything calmed down, she might think about reopening the business.

Lynette took the key and pushed it into the watch pocket of the men's jeans she always wore. She kept the key to the padlock on the storage room door on the key ring with the truck key on it. "Do you need an inventory?" she asked.

"I know what you got in there. In this envelope are the names of people to contact for new inventory when you need it. I've already alerted them that I'm not going to be the one getting the stuff anymore, at least for a while."

"So, you're not bowing out permanently," Lynette said. "How long is this going to take?"

"I have no idea," Lorianne said. "But, for now, like I said, I'm out of this operation and don't want anyone to know I was ever involved."

"Okay," Lynette said. "Are you sure the cops didn't follow you out here?"

"They didn't follow me here," Lorianne said. "I made sure of that. But I may not be able to keep them from following me from now on."

"Should I contact you?" Lynette asked.

"No. I'll contact you."

*   *   *

Kurt Maxxon

Alisa and Mutt literally dropped me off at the curb in front of my house and left to check into their motel. When I walked through the kitchen door, Beau met me. I picked him up and scratched his ears as we walked through the kitchen into the living room. Christina was asleep in her recliner with the TV on, but muted. The ten-o'clock news was just getting to tomorrow's weather, which was exactly what I wanted to see. Everything had pointed to a rain free day for tomorrow's race. Unlike the NASCAR races, which used smooth tires and couldn't race safely in rain, the SRVSCRA used treaded tires and could run in the rain, albeit at a lot slower speed. Safety is always an issue.

I sat down in my recliner next to Christina, and she roused from the noise. She sat up straight and looked groggily at me.

"I think I'll just head down the hall to bed," she said.

Beau lost interest in me when Christina mentioned bed. In one move, he jumped off my lap and into Christina's lap. "You ready for night-night?" Christina crooned. Beau looked at me, and then rolled his eyes toward Christina. He gave a small gurgle that sounded like "Yeah." I stood up and helped Christina stand. I gave her a kiss. "Goodnight, you two. I'll join you in a couple of minutes."

I clicked the closed captioning on. It was delayed so much it was almost impossible to follow, and I wasn't real interested in the news as my mind wandered around the universe. Melvyn shot dead in the locker room—after taking a shower. Lorianne Hightower had threatened Melvyn. But a man had called me and it sounded like he was just getting even with Melvyn for some kind of deal that had gone bad.

I replayed what I remembered of the conversation. "I took out that double dealing Melvyn Hightower, so I can do the same to you," the caller had said. "I just did in that lying, cheating, stealing Melvyn Hightower." The killer obviously had had a problem with Melvyn. What kind of problem? In his carpet business? The racing business? Something else?

Did the killer's problem with Melvyn involve his car? Is that why the car is missing? I would have continued that line of reasoning except I saw Nick Boynton on TV following a uniformed officer who was loading a handcuffed person into the back seat of a squad car. I read the closed captioning as it caught up with the story. It eventually said the police had arrested a suspect in the murder at the track. I followed the captioning and eventually realized that Nick had arrested Jason Tobias. It took a minute or two for that to register—Jason Tobias was Helen Tobias's soon to be ex-husband.

Did Jason Tobias have something against Melvyn Hightower? Then logic started to settle in. Were Melvyn and Helen having an affair? Was that the problem Jason Tobias had with Melvyn Hightower?

I sat watching and letting that information stream through

my brain. Helen's husband? I grabbed the remote and un-muted the TV, but the news had gone to an armed robbery of a convenience store the night before.

The kitchen light went on and I looked to see Christina and Beau getting a glass of milk out of the refrigerator. "You want a warm cup of cocoa?" Christina yelled to me.

"Sounds good," I yelled back. The news, however, had moved on to a fatal pedestrian accident in the south part of town.

When Christina arrived with two cups of warm cocoa, I said, "Nick arrested Helen Tobias's husband for Melvyn's murder."

"Why?" Christina asked.

"They didn't say on the news," I said. "I'll have to talk to Nick to find out."

"Do you think the case is closed?" Christina asked. "If it is, you can get some sleep."

"I don't know," I said. "I don't feel comfortable yet. Was that Jason Tobias on the phone last night?"

Christina stood, looking at me as she picked up Beau. "Do you know this Jason Tobias?"

"No. I've never met the man."

"So you wouldn't have recognized his voice."

"He had something over the phone mouthpiece," I said. "Probably a towel, to distort his voice."

Christina and I followed Beau down the hall to the bedroom. As I laid awaiting sleep, the voice that had called me came flooding back into my mind. The words:"lying, cheating, stealing" might connote Melvyn's involvement with his wife. But did the words "double dealing" make sense in a love triangle?

I decided that analysis was way beyond my reasoning powers. I settled into the sheet, and heard my cell phone ringing out on the kitchen counter. Christina and I swung out of bed together. When you have children and grandchildren, every phone call might be a call you need to answer. When we arrived in the kitchen, the ringing had stopped and we saw the message light on my cell phone flashing. I punched the voice mail button and entered my password. I had four messages. I punched the buttons and listened to the first three, none of interest. The fourth finally played: "Kurt, this is Steve Cosburn. Have you seen the news? The cops arrested Jason Tobias for killing Melvyn. I'm pretty sure he didn't do it. Call me as soon as you can. Thanks."

I looked at Christina. Her expression said "let's go for it." I glanced at the clock. Twelve-thirty. I switched on the speaker, and looked for Cosburn in my contacts list. I punched the send button. Steve answered on the second ring.

"God, thanks for getting back to me so fast, Colonel." Steve said.

"You sounded pretty confident that Jason Tobias didn't kill Melvyn. Why?"

"I'd rather not talk about it on the phone," Steve said. "And there's nothing we can do tonight, anyway. I'll be at the track early tomorrow morning. Can we get together then?"

"Sure," I said. "Give me a call when you get to the track. I'll be running around somewhere in the garage area or the driver's lounge."

"See you in the morning, Colonel."

We hung up and Christina, Beau and I went back down the hall to bed. The alarm clock read 1:15. Damn! Not much sleep again tonight.

I figured I could tell if Jason Tobias was the one who called me if I talked to him. That shouldn't be a problem if he was in jail. Should it?

CHAPTER EIGHT
Sunday Morning, August 26

Kurt Maxxon

"The parking lot's only about half-full," I said as we drove to park behind Pepper's Diner. We'd driven past Rodger's Café, which was only four blocks from the racetrack, and the parking lot was not only full; the side streets had cars parked along both sides of the street for two or three blocks all around. The waiting line flowed out the front door and snaked around to the back of the building. I still remembered the last time we ate Sunday breakfast at Rodger's, after having to wait in line for fifty minutes to get seated. I wasn't the type of person who waited in line for anything, especially food.

Pepper's was close enough to the racetrack that it was easy to get to, but far enough away not to be packed with crowds. I imagined Rebecca Pepper would love to have the crowd problem. Rebecca's grandfather, Sherman Pepper, started the eatery in the late 1920s a half block south of its current location. The original building that seated twenty-six people comfortably was gone, replaced by a steel and glass office building. Rebecca's father, Clifford, made plans to build a new building to seat sixty people and bought the corner lot next door. He passed away a month before the new building opened, but since Rebecca had been managing the diner for several years, the change in ownership went unnoticed. Pepper's Diner benefited from the extra notoriety when Clifford passed due to his long history of philanthropy in Centralia.

Rebecca was at the maitre d' podium when Christina and I pushed through the door. She smiled and said, "Good morning Christina, Colonel Maxxon," as she picked up two menus and led us toward a window booth. "I hope you're hungry," Rebecca said over her shoulder.

"I am," I said.

"It's going to be hot for the race," Rebecca said, "but it's going to be a beautiful day."

"Yes, it is going to be a great day," Christina said.

"It'll be an even better day if your girl wins the race," Rebecca said.

"You're preaching to the choir, young lady," I said.

Rebecca hurried away to get us coffee.

"It would be nice if Angie could win a race," Christina said.

"Good, Lord," I said. "This is just her seventh start. She's learning very well, but we shouldn't be pushing her too hard to win. I didn't win a race until my twenty-first try."

"Boys are notoriously slower learners than girls," Christina said, spreading a mischievous wide smile.

I watched Rebecca come toward our table with two steaming mugs of coffee. She set them in front of us. "You're still drinking decaf, right?" she said to Christina.

"Yes, thank you for remembering."

A young woman arrived in standard Pepper's waitress uniform—beige dress with white collar, epaulets, sleeve highlights, and trim—wearing a pink apron with Pepper's Diner embroidered on the bib. She was short, perhaps five foot three and no more than 120 pounds, soaking wet. Her hazel eyes were strangely penetrating. She held back while Rebecca was at our table. When Rebecca noticed her waiting, she said, "Your server this morning will be Maggie."

The waitress stepped up to the table and said, "Hi. My name is Maggie. Do you folks know what you want for breakfast?" Her hazel eyes went from sparkling to dull and unfocused, then back to sparkling, and sporadically went into a frenzied blinking. The effect was unsettling.

I'd been waiting all morning for a cholesterol jolt, so I ordered the Breakfast Supreme—three eggs, three bacon strips, three sausage links, a pile of hash browned potatoes, and toast.

"How do you want your eggs?" Maggie asked.

"Over easy."

"You said over easy, right?"

"Yes, over easy."

"What kind of toast?"

"Sourdough."

"Sourdough toast," Maggie said as she wrote on her pad.

"You like the same things I do," Maggie said. She stood, looking at me. "You're Kurt Maxxon, aren't you?"

For a moment I wondered if we were in some kind of a melodramatic play. "Yes. I am," I said, glancing toward Christina, who was studying the menu.

"I'm a big fan of yours," Maggie said.

"That's great," I said. "I always like to meet my fans."

Maggie kept staring at me for a long time, in an occasional unfocused way, which made me a little uncomfortable. Finally, Maggie looked at Christina. "What would you like, ma'am?

Christina said, "I'll have a bowl of oatmeal and a plate of fresh fruit."

Maggie wrote on her pad, and then said, "You want oatmeal and fruit, right?"

"That's right," Christina said.

Maggie spun around and went to put our orders in. When she returned, she stationed herself nearby and kept my coffee mug filled to the brim. When she offered to fill Christina's mug, Christina said, "I'm drinking decaf."

"Oh, I'm sorry," Maggie said and left. She delivered our breakfast plates and then seemed to remember Christina's decaf coffee. "I hope everything is alright with your breakfast, Mr. Maxxon," she said. "If you'd like anything else, anything, please let me know." She lingered, watching me.

I took a few tentative bites, uncomfortable at her watching me. "It's delicious," I said.

Maggie seemingly felt released, so she walked back toward the waitress station. As I ate, I noticed she was always looking at me. The minute I finished my plate, she came to retrieve it. "Was everything alright?" she asked.

"It was great," I said.

"Do you need more coffee?" Maggie seemed to be ignoring Christina.

"No, thank you. Give me the check so I can get moving. I've got a lot of work to get done today."

Maggie laid the check on the table, making sure it was face down. On the back she had printed in block letters: THANK YOU / MAGGIE. I looked up and saw Maggie watching me as I read the check.

She walked toward us as we stood to leave. "I hope you come back, Mr. Maxxon," she said. "Just ask for Maggie's table when you do. I really like taking care of you."

Rebecca took my check and cash. She looked around and said, "Was Maggie pestering you?"

I shrugged. "Not really. Why?"

"Maggie has some problems. I get an occasional complaint about her," Rebecca said. "I sometimes worry about having her working here."

"She seems to be a good waitress," I said.

Rebecca smiled at me. "If you say so, Colonel Maxxon. She's been kind of upset about Melvyn Hightower's death. He came in here a lot and always sat in one of Maggie's booths. She left early last Friday; said she was going to the track to watch Melvyn practice."

As I helped her into the truck, Christina said, "Maggie may not have bugged you, but, it was obvious to the casual observer that she was coming onto you like a dancehall girl."

"All waitresses do that," I said. "So they can get bigger tips."

"That was more than trolling for tips, Mr. Maxxon," Christina said curtly. "Has she been your waitress before?"

"I don't come to Pepper's that much."

"Do you come here alone—without me, I mean?" Christina seemed more agitated than I had ever seen her before.

"Well, since you and I married, I've not been to Pepper's alone. Maurey and I meet salespeople here once in awhile. I don't remember Maggie being here before, so I think she is just trolling for tips. Believe me."

"Or she's an overzealous fan," Christina said. "I'm having trouble trying to decide which."

As I pulled onto the street, it struck me like a left upper cut. "What did Rebecca say about Maggie going to the track?" I pulled over to the curb.

"Oh." Christina squinted like she did when she was

searching her brain to remember something. "Oh, yes. She said Maggie left early and went to the track to watch Melvyn practice."

"Yes," I said. "That's it." I let it sink in, thinking it through. "If Maggie was at the track, she might have seen the person who killed Melvyn. She might have—"

"Would she have been in the driver's lounge?" Christina said. Her brow knitted into a deep frown.

I said, "Even if she just went to the grandstand and sat and watched, she might have seen another person. If she was watching Melvyn, she probably would have stayed in the shadows, so to speak, so the killer might not have seen her there. We need to talk to her."

"Nick needs to talk to Maggie," Christina said slowly. "The Maxxons do ... not ... need ... to ... talk ... to ... Maggie."

I reached over and put my hand on her shoulder. Her shoulders were tensed, like her hackles had been raised. "Why are you so upset?"

"I'm sorry, Kurt," Christina said. "You know I'm not the type to react like this, but that girl strikes me the wrong way. It's something instinctive."

"If it makes you feel any better, I sense something strange there too." I drove south toward the track. Maggie kept popping into my mind. She was definitely a unique person—different in a way I couldn't put my finger on. Rebecca's words kept playing in my brain "... Maggie has some problems."

Christina was probably right. Did I really need to know what kind of problems Maggie

*　　*　　*

Maggie Decker

Maggie stood leaning against the hostess station podium, absently staring out the front door. The breakfast rush was over and there were only three tables occupied, none of them her responsibility. It had been a very busy morning with all the race fans in town and the drivers and their wives or girlfriends. Two other waitresses sat in a booth next to the station chatting. Maggie listened to their conversation.

"Wasn't that terrible, that guy murdered at the track?" the first waitress said.

"Yeah," the second waitress said. "Christ, why they let

people like that drifter run around loose is what I want to know."

"The cops arrested another guy for the murder, though," the first waitress added.

"Yeah, but, the picture of the vagrant in the paper looked scary to me."

"I worry about guys like that when I get off work."

"Yeah, you usually work the late shift."

"Did you know the dead guy?" the first waitress asked.

"Oh, sure, Melvyn Hightower came in here for breakfast a lot."

"He did?"

"Yeah, he was here last Friday morning, in fact. Maggie served him."

Both waitresses turned to look toward Maggie.

"I don't know who he is," the second waitress said.

"He owns that carpet showroom out on the east side. Always on TV advertising—what is it—Economy Carpet Mart or something."

"Oh, the hunk who says 'come see me, and let me fill your house with carpet at bargain prices.'"

"That's the one."

"He can come lay my carpet anytime."

"You mean he can come lay you on the carpet anytime."

"That, too."

Both waitresses giggled like teenagers.

Maggie looked out the door and watched Rebecca Pepper, the owner of the diner, walk back to the hostess station. She shied away at Rebecca's approach and went to the coffee station, filled a cup with coffee, and then moved to another booth near the two waitresses.

Maggie let her mind wander to Melvyn Hightower. Where had he gone? She had vague images of watching the man go into the locker room. She remembered hearing the men arguing. That had frightened her so badly; she got out from behind the pool table and ran out the door. She'd run to the fair parking lot before she stopped to look back. Then she scrambled into her car and drove home. She had to search, but she eventually found a marijuana roach from the night before and lit it.

Rebecca noticed Maggie's absent look. "Maggie? Are you

okay?"

Maggie looked up to see her boss standing next to her booth, looking down at her. "Oh, yeah, I'm fine," she said. "I was just trying to remember what I needed from the grocery store."

Rebecca Pepper walked back toward the hostess station.

"I'm going to the race this afternoon," Maggie said aloud, then looked around to see if anyone had heard her. Root for Kurt Maxxon. Yeah, he's just as cute as Melvyn.

*   *   *

Kurt Maxxon

When I pulled into the admin parking area, I saw Nick Boynton coming toward me from the garage area. I waited for Nick at my truck door while Christina went into the driver's lounge to start the coffee pot.

"Good day for racing," Nick said as he came near.

"A little hot," I said, and led him into the lounge to the chairs at the dinette set. Christina finished loading the 50-cup coffee maker and set it to perking, then went to get a folding chair. "How did you arrive at Jason Tobias?" I asked Nick.

"I got to wondering if Melvyn might have been the reason for Helen's divorce," Nick said.

That made me remember my own rationalizations the night before.

"So I went to talk to Tobias," Nick continued. "He told me he was with his boss, the regional sales manager, at a big meeting over in Farmer's City."

"And his boss didn't back up his alibi?"

"Oh, his boss backed up his alibi, alright," Nick said. "But, then we got a tip the boss wasn't anywhere near Farmer's City. He was over in Ford Junction tied up in a hot poker game at the Hoopla Casino. We have him on surveillance cameras from about ten o'clock in the morning until late afternoon. He pulled money out of the ATM at eleven-twenty-two and again at two-sixteen. So we checked with the president of the company they were supposedly meeting with and found out that the president had canceled the meeting the afternoon before because their client put the project on hold. Then we found out that Jason was seen here in Centralia about the same time as the homicide."

"That doesn't sound all that incriminating," I said.

"Yeah, well, here's the coup d'état." Nick paused, as he sometimes did for effect, and glanced around to ward off any eavesdroppers. "Last month, Lorianne Hightower wrote three checks to Jason Tobias for eight thousand five hundred bucks each, which totals a cool twenty-five thousand and five hundred dollars."

"Damn," I said. Christina gave me a guarded look.

"Right," Nick said. "So all of a sudden, I forgot about the possibility of Melvyn and Helen having an affair and started visualizing Jason as a hired hit-man to take Melvyn out. Hired by Melvyn's loving wife, Lorianne."

"Have you arrested Lorianne?" I asked.

"Not yet. We're going to let her squirm a little. She might just break down and come in to confess. Killers often do that, you know."

Nick glanced toward the coffee pot, now gurgling happily along, filling the room with the wonderful aroma of fresh brewed coffee.

"So how did Jason set up the murder?" I asked.

"The way I figure it," Nick said, "I think Tobias might have come to the track to see his wife; maybe something about the divorce. She's over in Maplewood, and he doesn't know that. He sees Melvyn going to shower after practicing. Tobias thinks: now's as good a time as any to earn my twenty-five K. So he goes out to his car to get the gun, comes back and shoots Melvyn in the locker room. Drops the gun on the floor and leaves. It's a stolen weapon anyhow. Who cares?"

"If he went out to get the gun—," I said, thinking aloud, "It's not his gun, right? The gun was stolen in a burglary several months ago, right? So, you can't tie the gun to Jason before this, right? Do his prints match?"

Nick had nodded at each of my points. "He might have come by the gun in any one of a dozen ways," he said. "Once he accepted the job, he probably went looking for a weapon on the streets that couldn't be traced to him."

The coffee pot made its thrashing final perks. Nick and I walked over and drew a cup and sat back down.

"Do you have a problem with Tobias as the shooter?" Nick asked me.

"My only problem is with the gun."

"Do you know Jason Tobias?" Nick asked.

"No. I don't," I said. "I've never met the man."

Nick emptied his cup and stood. "I've got to get downtown and work this thing out."

I led Nick toward the driver's lounge door. "Have you got a tail on Lorianne Hightower?" I asked.

"Not really," Nick said. "We know where her car is most of the time."

Nick walked toward his car parked just inside the admin gate.

* * *

Lorianne Hightower

She sat at the breakfast nook with a cup of coffee in her hand. The Sunday newspaper lay open on the table in front of her. She reread the headline again. Man arrested in Hightower death. In the first paragraph she saw the name Jason Tobias. Why? Why would the cops think Jay killed Shag?

She took a long sip of her coffee. Cold—Dammit! Dammit all to hell!

What if the cops picked up on the check I paid Jay? Dammit. Dammit.

You've screwed yourself again, girl

Dammit. When are you going to learn?

* * *

Kurt Maxxon

My phone jangled and I answered it. Steve Cosburn said, "I'm sitting in the grandstand just as you come through the chute."

"I'll be there in a minute," I said. "I'm going to the track," I told Christina, and walked toward the grandstand. I saw Steve the minute I cleared the passageway and walked to sit down beside him.

"So you're convinced Jason Tobias didn't shoot Melvyn," I said.

"Not just convinced, but pretty damn sure he couldn't have done it." Steve looked around and waved to a couple of drivers in pit row.   I pursed my lips and shrugged. Okay, tell me all about it."

"Jason wasn't even in town when Shag was shot," Steve

said.

"First," I said. "How do you know Jason Tobias and, more importantly, how well do you know Jason Tobias?"

"Melvyn Hightower, Jason Tobias and I graduated from Centralia Northwest high school; Class of 1979," Steve said. "We were the three Amigos all during senior high school. We all rode Harley Davidson motorcycles. Shag was born the first of October, I was born the first of November, and Jason was born the first day of December. We were known as the "First of the Month" gang. We chased the same girls, but we always played fair about it."

"Fair about it?"

"Yeah, well, you know. We never tried to move in on each other's girls."

"What happened after high school?"

"Shag went to Centralia College," Steve said. "Shag's folks had money. Jason and I went to Vo-Tech over in Maplewood."

"Where did Melvyn pick up the nickname Shag?" I asked, hoping not to break the flow, but really interested in knowing.

"That's what his dad called him," Steve said. "I have no idea why. All the rest of us picked it up from his dad."

"What does Jason do for a living?"

"He's a regional sales manager for one of the big electrical supply companies. He travels all around the valley—wining and dining construction company execs."

"Did he start out as a mechanic?" I asked.

"No. Jason was never the mechanic type. I had to fix his motorcycle whenever it broke down. I had to fix Shag's, too. Jason went into the electrical shop. Then when we got out of Vo-Tech, I went to work in my dad's garage here in Centralia—same place I'm still at. Jason went to work as an estimator for a small electrical contractor over in Maplewood."

"How did Jason and Helen get together?"

"Helen was a clerk working for the same electrical contractor Jason went to work for," Steve said. "Helen was taking secretarial courses at the community college over there. Jason got the sales job here in Centralia, and they moved here. You know the rest about Helen."

"How did Melvyn meet Lorianne?" I asked.

"Shag and Lorianne got together while he was going to

Centralia College. Lorianne was going to Valley Women's College. She got an AA in Business and then went to that beauty school downtown. They married about the same time she started beauty school."

"Was Lorianne from Centralia?" I asked.

"Yeah. In fact, she and Shag went to Madison Middle School out west during the seventh grade. But something happened and Lorianne's folks moved her to St. Joseph's School for the rest of high school. Jason and I, of course, went to Eisenhower Junior High up north."

"So Lorianne was not with you three amigos at Centralia Northwest High School," I said.

"No. She wasn't."

"Helen often mentioned that she lived in Maplewood," I said.

"Yeah, she and Jason lived in Maplewood for, oh, about five years," Steve said. "Carline and I went to Maplewood once in a while to meet up with them. Then they moved to Centralia. Helen's mother still lives there. Too bad about her dad."

I'd met Steve's wife Carline several times at various parties, subsidized by major parts suppliers, I'd thrown for the biggest customers of my auto parts store. Of the three wives involved in the triangle, I knew Helen Tobias the best, then Carline Cosburn. I'd only met Lorianne Hightower a few times.

"Jason still rides a Harley?" I asked. I knew Steve owned a Harley Davidson and that he rode it frequently. I also knew that Melvyn Hightower owned a Harley, but whenever he wanted to ride it, he usually had to have the battery charged before it would start.

"Yeah, he still rides," Steve said. "That's how I know Jason didn't kill Helen and Shag."

"How's that?" I asked.

"Jason called me Friday morning. He couldn't get his Harley started. He'd spent the night with a woman he's been dating. He asked me to run down and help him get it started. It turned out he'd thrown a valve, so we had to load it into the back of my pickup truck and haul it up to my shop."

"Where'd you have to go to get him?"

"Down in Fairmont Acres."

"That's seventy miles south of here," I said. "Over an hour's drive."

"Right," Steve said. "Jason called me at about eight-thirty. I got down there about ten. We left Fairmont Acres about ten-thirty and drove back to Centralia. We stopped for lunch at Lefty's Truck Stop. We got to my shop about twelve-thirty. After we unloaded Jason's motor, I took him to his apartment."

Someone yelled, "Hey, Steve," and Steve turned to see who it was. He waved to the person and turned back to me. "What's the latest on Melvyn's Chevy?" he asked.

"Probably in one of the garages over there," I said, pointing with my chin to garage row. "You've given Jason a solid alibi. Can you back it up?"

"I don't know what the Time of Death is," Steve said.

"Christina and I arrived at the track about noon," I said. "Melvyn was dead at that time."

"Well, there you go," Steve said. "Jason and I didn't get to his apartment until shortly after one o'clock in the afternoon."

"People saw you down there and along the way?" I said.

Steve nodded, "Of course."

"So why call me about this instead of the cops?" I asked.

"I thought you could handle the information better.

I suddenly remembered I'd not heard a Time of Death. I'd have to call Nick. The TOD would be an excellent way to get the conversation going.

*   *   *

I had the driver's lounge set up for the pre-race meeting with three rows of ten chairs. We had twenty nine entrants signed up for today's race. If a driver wanted to compete in the race, they were required to attend the meeting. Occasionally, we had drivers show up and register at the meeting. I stood looking at the rows of chairs and decided to add another chair to each row.

"What are you going to do about Maggie?" Christina asked from her chair at the kitchen table.

I hadn't thought too much about Maggie, but apparently, she was high on Christina's radar. "What can I do?" I said.

"We need to decide how you handle her," Christina said. "She's thoroughly infatuated with you, Mr. Kurt Maxxon. If you make the wrong moves—say the wrong things—you'll just encourage her to continue. If you push back too hard, you might upset her and she'll do something she shouldn't."

"You tell me," I said, half flippantly. "You're the psychologist in our family."

"Just be very careful around her," Christina said. "The less direct contact she has with you, the better off you are going to be."

A noise at the door drew my attention, and I watched Rafe Komminski come hobbling into the room and move to sit down. "You said you'd ask the drivers if I could sit in on the meeting," he said. "Make some more notes. Pick up on the jargon; get a feel for the drivers."

"Anything new about Jason Tobias being arrested for killing Melvyn?" I asked Rafe.

"The cops aren't saying anything," Rafe said. "Hell, they won't even confirm they have the murder weapon. You've got a better pipeline than I do."

I could have confirmed the cops had the murder weapon, but for whatever reason, Nick wasn't letting that information out.

"Angie starting in the number two position is history," Rafe said after looking at the white board at the front of the room.

"It sure is," I said, hoping not to sound like a proud father.

Christina returned from getting sugar sacks and creamer out of the truck. She and Rafe exchanged greetings.

The pre-race meeting was very efficient. We had another memorial moment for Melvyn Hightower. Since some drivers had just arrived, we reviewed the minor changes to the racetrack's rules and a couple of rule changes from the SRVSCRA. The drivers pledged to have a competitive but friendly race, and I adjourned the meeting. The drivers scattered and were puttering with their cars or resting, relaxing and psyching themselves up for the race.

Rafe came up to me and said, "That was a pretty dry meeting, compared to the qualifying meeting yesterday."

"The pre-race meeting is designed to get the drivers to focus on the latest rules and regulations of safe racing," I said. "Concentration is important to our safety. I would never record that meeting for use as a training program on good management communication practices."

*   *   *

It had become an accepted ritual that all of my out-of-town friends would come to my garage on race day to wish me good luck, and then they would go with Christina to their seats in the grandstand. This year, with Angie driving Nikki, we changed the practice to where they came to the driver's lounge. The main contingent of my friends were those from Masonville, Kings Rapids, and Carpentier Falls—all within reasonable driving distances of Centralia.

Christina and I were sitting in the lounge at the kitchen table when Don Epperley arrived.

"It's hotter than hell," Don said as he pushed through the door. "You can fry eggs on that asphalt out there."

"It is hot," I said. We shook hands and Don moved to give Christina a hug. Don was a retired Lieutenant Detective from the Kings Rapids Police Department. He took a bullet to the shoulder while shielding a couple of innocent bystanders during a shootout with a couple of felons trying to get away. The crooks went down, never to get up again. Don fought back and went through four surgeries before he could tolerate the pain in his shoulder. He was forced to retire and left the force with a gold shield he carried all the time.

Don was taller than me and outweighed me by a lot. He'd been adding to his girth annually. I worried about his weight gain, but there was little I could do about it. Don shaved his head rather than deal with the random wispy strands of hair that remained. He was an African-American man who preferred to be called "A Black man." Since Mutt Sparks introduced me to Don, we'd been close friends. Of all my friends, Don was the one who complained the most about everything—mostly things none of us had control over.

"At least there's a breeze," Don said. "That'll help keep us cool sitting in the stands."

"Think of what it's like in the cars," I said.

"I know. I know," Don said. "I've heard. You used to suffer more than we did being in the car on the track that was probably one-hundred-and-twenty-five degrees. And for us sitting in the stands it was only ninety-five."

"Now, it's Angie suffering in the car," Christina said.

"Ol' Kurt here used to sweat off about twenty pounds every race," Don said. "So Angie will sweat off about half that much I'd guess."

"Angie doesn't sweat," Christina said.

"She doesn't?" Don said.

Christina laughed. "Men sweat," she teased. "Women perspire!"

"Oh, I forgot about that," Don said.

"Bottom line," I said, "is at the end of the race Angie will be soaking wet and several pounds lighter."

"That's what I was getting at," Don said.

Christina retreated in the face of overwhelming odds.

We were just about to seal a truce when Joshua and Jacob Wallace came crashing through the door. Both headed for me, and I greeted them. Then they moved to Christina. They realized Don was present, and they both went to hug him. Don had been a surrogate grandpa to the boys since Marguerite and Terry Grossman took legal guardianship of them.

Marguerite came into the room and moved to hug Christina. She hugged Don and then moved to me. Terry strolled in next, and he hugged Christina and shook hands with Don. Terry Grossman was the man who took Don's Lieutenant Detective position when Don retired. Later, Terry and Marguerite became lovers. Then Marguerite was named acting chief of the Kings Rapids Police Department. A month after they married, Marguerite was appointed Chief of Police. So Terry decided to retire from the force and start his own Private Investigation firm to avoid any charges of nepotism.

"Are you leaving for home after the race?" Christina asked Marguerite.

"No, Terry wants to do some stuff online after the race. He doesn't want to drive home tonight. So we extended our stay at the hotel. We'll drive over to Kings Rapids tomorrow morning early. So long as I get to work about nine or ten, it'll be okay."

"That's good," Christina said.

Terry Grossman looked at me and wrinkled his smile. "How come Nick Boynton solved the murder case before you did?"

"I'm not sure he's solved it," I said.

"Oh, oh," Terry said and screwed his face into an exaggerated look of disbelief. "Kurt Maxxon doesn't like the cops' solution. Further details at ten."

I smiled at him. "I've obtained some information that makes Jason Tobias an unlikely suspect." I hoped they would leave it go from there.

"Wow, this I've got to hear about," Terry said. Marguerite had been drawn to the discussion.

"I'd really prefer not to discuss it at length," I said. "Until I can get with Nick and let him know what I found out. For now, just accept my word that I know a man who says Jason was not in town when Melvyn was killed, and he can prove it."

"That would work for me," Terry said and looked at Marguerite who nodded agreement.

I tried to change the subject. "I've been totally focused on helping Angie run the race," I said, having noticed that everyone in the room had heard our discussion and was looking at me. I was saved from further discussion of the subject when Alisa Sharpe and Mutt Sparks entered the room. The boys galloped to Alisa, and she gave them a warm greeting.

Mutt looked at Don Epperley. "You made it, huh?" he said.

"I always make it," Don retorted.

"Where are we going to eat supper?" Jacob asked Terry.

"We'll find a nice place," Terry said. "Are you hungry already? The race hasn't even started yet."

"No. I was just wondering," Jacob said.

"Can we help time Angie?" Joshua asked.

"Sure," I said. Since Jacob turned twelve this year, he can be in the pit area. The SRVSCRA rule against children in the pit areas originally set the minimum criteria as being sixteen years old. Then it had been lowered to fourteen. Five years ago the drivers had voted to lower it to twelve.

Joshua and Jacob were fidgeting. They didn't have time to get the pool table set up before they had to go to the grandstand for the race.

"What else did you guys do this summer?" I asked them.

"We went to see Auntie Jean," Joshua said.

"You did!" I said. "How is she doing?"

"She be the same ol' Auntie Jean," Jacob said. "She's living in the same place."

Marguerite started to speak, then went quiet. I glanced

toward Christina who was smiling.

"Is the elevator working?" I asked.

"Yeah, it was," Jacob yelled. "Auntie Jean, she uses it every once in a while. We had supper at Sam's."

"What'd you have?" I asked, with a goofy grin on my face.

"You know what we—" Joshua started to say.

"We had big Sloppy Joes," Jacob reported. "We love Sam's Sloppy Joes."

"I know," I said. "I really like them, too. They're really good."

I glanced at Christina. She nodded agreement.

Terry said, "I had to do some research in Carpentier Falls. So I took the boys with me, and we did the town. I met with Sergeant Hoppy. She's still praising you for your help in solving the Carlos Guerrero homicide."

Mutt said, "Hey, folks, it's time for us to get on over to our seats. The race starts in about thirty minutes."

Shocked, I looked at my watch to see it was one twenty-five. I needed to get the timing equipment ready for the SRVSCRA track officials who would manage the race from now on, and I needed to meet up with Angie to answer any last-minute questions she might have and encourage her—motivate her—to do her best. I watched as my group of friends filed out of the room. Christina came to me and gave me a kiss. Then she followed the crowd.

I walked out of the driver's lounge and stood watching, like a proud father, down garage row as several cars emerged from their garages, including the rear end of Nikki pushed out by Maurey and Tugs. Angie walked toward her car—a striking figure in her red and white racing uniform with several of our sponsors names prominent. The clearest name I saw was Kurt Maxxon Racing on the back of her uniform. Angie made me proud to be her sponsor.

Just in time, I dug my earplugs out of my shirt pocket and stuck them into my ears. Nikki roared to life along with a dozen other engines down garage row. In an unpracticed but efficient move, the cars lined up in roughly the starting order and then moved slowly toward the track. Other cars filed into the lineup from the auxiliary area, and eventually, the pack moved to parade around the track in proper starting order.

Nikki was starting the race in the number two. I realized

Tugs must have been the one who waxed and polished Nikki to a lustrous sheen.

I walked along on the driver's side as the pack moved toward the track, and looked down at Angie. She had her skid lid on, but the face shield was up. She wore a contented smile. She was in charge. "Any questions?" I asked.

Angie wobbled her head. "Nope."

"Good luck," I said. "Run safe."

I walked toward the track. You've got one damn good driver, Maxxon.

CHAPTER NINE
Sunday Race, August 26

Kurt Maxxon

The cars were parading from the garage area to the racetrack. I was strolling along beside them, and when I looked back toward the admin building, I saw a beat-up old red Dodge Caravan pull in and park next to my truck. Kimberly and Brittany Grenwahl got out and stood watching the cars. Damn, Maxxon, you spaced out about Kimberly and Brittany. I walked back toward them. When Brittany saw me coming, she yelled, "Momma, there's Mr. Maxxon." She ran toward me and leaped into my arms. "I love you, Mr. Kurt," she said. I lifted her up and carried her as I moved to welcome Kimberly.

"I'm going to watch the whole race," Brittany bubbled. "Momma said we can stay for the whole race, like me and Uncle Chuck always did."

"That's great," I said.

"I wish I could root for you," she said. "Like me and Uncle Chuck used to do."

"I'm not driving today," I said.

Her little face clouded slightly. "Howcum you don't drive anymore?"

"I get too tired driving," I said, hoping she might understand.

"Can't you just take a nap before the race?" Brittany asked.

I smothered a laugh. Kimberly couldn't control hers.

The sun was past directly overhead, a slight breeze moderating the ninety-plus temperature. I put Brittany down, and she ran ahead to the entry gate and then came back to report, "It's full of people like it always is."

I led Kimberly and Brittany to the grandstand and up to my group of friends, where I introduced them all around. I glanced around and realized several people from our rooting section had not yet arrived.

The cars had arrived at their respective pits and were undergoing final pre-race checks. I sat down and Brittany climbed up into the seat next to me. I looked across the track at Angie's pit stall. Maurey was buttoning up the hood; Tugs and the two boys were tinkering with the lap timing equipment. I couldn't see Angie. I knew, though, from past experience that she would be totally hyper at this time; it would take one or two laps to dissipate her tensions.

"Angie's doing really good, isn't she?" Brittany said.

"Yes, she is," I said, smiling at Brittany. "Angie is going to be a very good driver."

"Do you think I can be a racecar driver when I grow up?" Brittany asked.

"Why, sure!"

"I really wanted to be an astronaut," Brittany said, pursing her lips and frowning. "But, maybe I'll drive racecars."

"You can do whatever you want to do," I said. "You've got plenty of time to decide what that will be. Maybe you'll decide to become a nurse."

"No!" She said with force. "I don't want to be a nurse."

"Nursing is a good job," I said. "Nurses help people."

"Yeah, but they just help sick people. I don't want to work with sick people."

Mikie quickly came to mind, and I wondered if Brittany was dealing with some kind of a psychological situation from dealing with Mikie's condition. I decided to let Christina deal with that if it came up again. "You can drive racecars or you can be an astronaut" I said. "You can do whatever you want to do."

"I guess I'll decide that later," she said and stopped to watch a very brave mouse venture out to take on a kernel of popcorn, then dash off with it.

The engines of all twenty-nine racecars roared to life, and that was the end of the quiet in the stands for the moment. Brittany jumped down from her seat and yelled something that I figured was "Go Angie." She turned and said something to me, but I shook my head and yelled back to her, "Wait until the cars get around the first turn."

Brittany looked at me and her quizzical look turned to a slight frown. She climbed back into her seat and sat silently. Unfortunately, just as the pack of roaring engines from the front straightaway went around the first set of turns, the roaring engines from the eleven cars on the back straightaway pit stalls came around to go past us. We both sat in silence and watched the cars form up in two rows. Then the race started the cars spread out and the noise settled into a dull roar.

"Uncle Chuck always calls the turns corners," Brittany said, reinforcing the small frown that creased her forehead. "How come he calls them corners?"

"There are a lot of reasons some people call them corners," I said. "Probably the biggest reason is that the granddaddy of all races is the Indy five-hundred race at the Indianapolis International Speedway. That track is a huge square racetrack with sharp turns that have always been called corners. Another reason might be that the Daytona race was run for years on the beach, using part of a highway for one leg, so there were sharp turns involved."

"They're not corners like on a street. We live on the corner," Brittany protested.

"To some people whenever you change direction, that's a corner." I hoped I could make her understand it was a concept, not a concrete item. "It's not so much what it looks like, but what it does. In a turn on a racetrack, you change direction."

"Oh!" Brittany said and swung toward the roar of the pack flying past us on the track.

I looked toward Christina and said, "I'm going over to the pit, just to be doing something."

Christina gave me an understanding nod.

"Can I go, too?" Brittany asked.

"I'm afraid not," I said. "You have to be twelve years old to be in the pit area during a race."

A pout crossed her face, but Brittany seemed to accept it. "Okay, I'll stay here."

Christina invited Brittany to sit next to her, and I left the rooting section to make my way to the tunnel under the track to pit row. I used my keycard to open the gate and went down the steps. When I emerged on the infield side, I looked across the infield and could see that the grandstand along the back stretch was also filling nicely. It looked like we would have a good gate to split among the top ten drivers.

There are two pit rows, with twenty stalls in each. Angie's pit stall is on the front stretch facing the original grandstand, where the pits were assigned to the first eighteen cars in today's race; the second pit row on the back stretch were assigned to the next eleven cars. If you viewed the racetrack from ten thousand feet, it looked like someone took a circular track and added straight sections between two half circle ends. It was what I called an oblong. The long sides of the oblong ran east and west. Outside the east end of the racetrack was the garage area, RV parking lot, and the admin building which housed the track management offices and the driver's lounge.

As I walked toward Angie's pit stall, several drivers, mechanics, and race officials waved or yelled at me. I stopped to talk to Jimmy Davison—starting in the twelfth position. Jimmy drove the number eighty-nine Trattoria Restaurant car. A couple of years ago, I helped solve the death of Carlos Guerrero, the owner of the Trattoria Restaurant in Carpentier Falls. Jimmy was Carlos's favorite nephew and had been driving the Trattoria car for two years. He won his first race that weekend, which helped him deal with the loss of his favorite uncle.

When I arrived at Angie's pit stall, the first shock to my psyche occurred when there wasn't anything for me to do. Maurey was sitting on the concrete barrier, waiting for the cars to go past so he could listen to Nikki to determine if she was having problems. Tugs, Joshua and Jacob were monitoring the timing equipment. I could not miss the Rangers baseball caps on each boy—like Maurey's, except newer—and a fresh blue shop rag hanging from their rear jeans pocket. I looked across the track and saw that Marguerite and Terry Grossman had arrived and were being greeted by the others. The grandstand had filled up fast, as well as the bleacher seats in both directions as far as I could see. Maurey walked toward me. "How's it going?" I asked.

"Just great," Maurey said. "Wha'cha doing over here? Why

don't you go over and relax in a grandstand seat?"

Maurey is ten years older than I am, and he's advising me to relax in a comfortable seat. "I just need to feel involved," I said to Maurey's back as he walked away. I watched Tugs and the boys prepare to time Angie as she zipped past.

My mind wandered back to the conversation with Nick earlier in the morning, and then to my conversation with Steve Cosburn. My thoughts locked onto the "three Amigos" story Steve had told me. Melvyn, Jason, and Steve in senior high school—three Amigos on Harley Davidson motorcycles—simply being teenagers. Now, Nick theorized that one Amigo had gunned down another Amigo. However, with what Steve had just told me that appeared to be totally wrong. The real question was whether Jason was even in town. According to Steve Cosburn, he and Jason were somewhere between Fairmont Acres and Centralia when Melvyn was shot.

I needed to find out the time of death from Nick. If Jason wasn't even in town at the time of death, he couldn't be the shooter, especially if it took Melvyn several minutes to die after being shot. If Jason wasn't the shooter, it wasn't his voice on the phone threatening me.

Then it hit me like a sledge hammer: If Maggie was at the track as Rebecca Pepper indicated, what, if anything, did she see? Did Maggie see the killer? Could she identify the killer? Hopefully Alisa could help. I turned my mind back to the race, satisfied I'd found a way to deal with Maggie.

*   *   *

Angie started in the number two position behind Dave Kellogg's number 4 Ford Taurus in the pole position. The problem with being in the pits is that you can't see turns two and three along the back stretch due to all the communication trucks in the infield.

When the first car came out of turn four, it was Angie. I was ecstatic and at the same time fearful. My racing philosophy was: I never wanted to lead the race in heats one or two. In the SRVSCRA each race consisted of three heats of fifty laps each. There was a twenty minute break between heats one and two, then a thirty minute break between heats two and three. Only during the last break could a driver lift the hood of the car for reasons other than mechanical failure. I usually didn't worry about leading the race until the third heat, rarely making any moves to lead before laps twenty-five or so of the third heat.

My gut argued: Angie is her own driver; she has her own philosophy and modus operandi. It's a driving force making her want to be out front all the time. My fear roared back. Angie shouldn't be this cocky, this early in the race.

Dave Kellogg came out of turn four in the fifth position, and I wondered what had happened to move him back so far. As he roared past, I was truly thankful to see there were no dents or scratches. I hadn't paid any attention, but I couldn't remember seeing any dents on Nikki. I'd have to wait until the break between heats to find out how Angie got past Kellogg? Nikki has a two-way radio—I had it installed, but used it only a few times to talk to Maurey during the race if I was having problems or hearing strange noises. Angie had yet to even want to use the radio.

I told Maurey I was going over to the grandstand. He waved me away. I walked to where Tugs and the boys were watching the timers. All three of them were so engrossed with the timing that they didn't even see me watching.

When I came out of the tunnel into the grandstand, I scanned the area to see if "my" gang was where I had left them. They were gone. I looked up and spotted them higher up. I figured the men had gone up to the highest point in the grandstand with the rest of the fans. I made my way to the men's room and then got in line to get a cup of coffee at the concession stand. I joined Christina, Kimberly, Brittany, Marguerite and Alisa.

"Mr. Grossman, Mr. Sparks, and Mr. Epperley went up there," Brittany said to me, pointing up toward the top of the grandstand, as she climbed into my lap. I let the women continue their discussion and focused on the race. I noticed the noise was a little quieter higher up in the stands. From my vantage point, I could see turns one, two, four and most of the backstretch very well. Turn three was visible piecemeal through various communication trailers.

Each time we heard the engine roar nearing, we swung our heads toward turn four in hopes that Angie was still leading the pack. Several times Brittany jumped off my lap, waved a tiny fist and yelled, "Go, Angie; Go, twenty-seven." Then she would let me lift her back up onto my lap.

"When you beat all those other drivers, did they get mad at you?" Brittany asked.

"No! We we're just playing a game," I said. "The other guys win as much as I do."

"You won a lot of the races," Brittany persisted. "And they didn't get mad?"

"Don't you play games with Daniel and Mikie?"

"We play Chutes and Ladders so Mikie can play," Brittany said. "When it's just Danny and me, we play Clue or Monopoly. It's just for fun. The boys don't get mad because I win all the time."

"You win all the time?"

"Most of the time," she boasted. "It's okay 'cause they just like to play."

"Well, it's the same with the other race drivers," I said. "They just like to race. So they don't get mad when someone else wins and they lose."

"That's good," Brittany said.

As they roared past at the end of lap forty-nine of the first heat, Christofides was menacingly close to Angie's back bumper as they headed for turn one. I could tell they were racing hard—too hard! Christofides, Dejarnet, Kellogg, Depeuw, and Danielson were all older, more experienced drivers. Would they let Angie lead them for long?

Angie was on the inside, a half-car length ahead of Christofides. It would be a drag race to the finish line—a drag race I knew Angie could win with one of Maurey's engines. What would be the tradeoff? Was Nikki holding up? It was hot and humid. How about the tires?

In the SRVSCRA we were only allowed two sets of new tires per race—one on the car to start the race and one extra set. We had started the race on four new tires, which meant we had one set of new tires and the worn set of tires used for qualification runs. Those tires were in pretty good condition, and as we usually did, we would start the next two heats with new tires on the right side and two of the better worn tires on the left side.

I moved down to the lowest level across the track from the pits as Angie arrived at her pit stall and noted that she slowed down to let Dave Kellogg pull into his stall ahead of her. I figured if there had been some kind of an incident on the first lap, Dave would say something after he climbed out of his car, and I would hear it across the track. Dave climbed out of his car and pointed at Angie and I thought Oh, oh, here we go. But Dave just yelled, "You are one hell of a driver, lady."

I grinned and let the tension ease in my shoulders.

Angie climbed out of Nikki, grabbed her backpack, and dashed to the pink port-a-john that now sat next to our pit stall. She was gone for several minutes.

I wondered if she had gone and picked up the piddle pack I lined up for her.

I decided to go back to pit row and ask her. I made my way down under the track through the tunnel and arrived in Angie's pit stall just as she came out of the port-a-john.

"Did you go get the piddle pack?" I asked.

"Yeah."

"Are you wearing it?"

"I am now. Had a hell of a time with that damn catheter," she said curtly.

"How did you get around Kellogg on the first lap?"

Angie grinned widely. "He got a little too high and I just scooted past him coming off the banking," she said. "It was easy."

"So he lost it?"

"He lost it and I took it—fair and square."

I helped with tires while Maurey pampered Nikki. "Nikki's as good as she's ever been," he declared after he walked all around her, listening for any complaints. Joshua and Jacob followed Maurey's every step and they seemed to be listening to Nikki also. Maurey never needed to lift the hood to commune with Nikki. He could tell how she was feeling by the sounds she made.

After Angie and Nikki left to start the second heat, I told Maurey I was going back over to the grandstand and that I'd be back to help between the second and last heat.

Maurey said, "Hell, just stay over there. That girl can change those tires."

"I'll see," I said. I always felt guilty about making Maurey do all the heavy lifting.

*   *   *

Christina Maxxon

Christina stood and said to the others, "We probably should go to the Ladies Room now, so we can avoid the long lines during the break."

Marguerite and Alisa nodded. Kimberly took Brittany by the hand and said, "You learn quick. We used to get caught in the mobs at the baseball games when Jim and I …" Kimberly stopped, and a sad look spread across her face.

"We've all got caught," Marguerite said.

From their seats they made their way down to the midpoint landing that was a wide walkway to the center of the grandstand where the concession stands and restrooms were. As she descended, Christina noticed Maggie Decker, the waitress who had come onto Kurt at breakfast this morning, sitting where she could watch Kurt in Angie's pit stall just across the racetrack.

When she came out of the rest room, Christina saw that Maggie was still sitting watching Kurt. "We can get some snacks before the crowd arrives," Christina said and led the group to the concession stands. Brittany wanted a Coke, and all the women all ordered coffee. Then they walked back to their seats single file, with Christina leading.

As they settled back into their seats and chatted, Christina hoped the others didn't notice that she wasn't making eye contact with them. She was keeping a very close eye on Maggie.

*   *   *

Kurt Maxxon

I walked the length of the pit area again. You're going to wear out a pair of shoes doing this. As I came out of the tunnel and climbed the steps up into the grandstand, I looked up toward the concession level. I wanted a cup of coffee and was happy to see the lines at the snack bars had dwindled down to only four or five people in each. As I climbed the stairs, I caught motion to my left and turned to come face-to-face with Maggie Decker, the waitress from Pepper's. She was wearing a pair of cut off jeans, pretty tight fitting, and a very revealing polka dot halter. Her hair was flying in the breeze. She was smiling like she just got away with something.

"Hello, Kurt. How are you?" she asked.

"I, uh, I'm fine."

"I've been watching you in the pit. That girl is a good driver. I'll bet you taught her how to drive, huh?"

"No," I said. "She learned that on her own."

"She's as good as you," Maggie said.

"Uh-huh."

"Would you like to meet me after the race?" Maggie asked. "I'd like to show you how much I like you—I really do like you. I used meet Melvyn after the races. We did the same thing."

"Uh, no. I don't think so," I said, backing away.

"Why not?" Maggie asked, her smile dimming. "Don't you like me?"

"It's not whether I like you or not," I said as I watched Christina and Marguerite coming to my rescue. "I just don't do that."

Christina stepped directly in front of Maggie and kissed me. Marguerite was wearing a very stern face. Maggie shied away from the two women. Then she turned and moved quickly in the direction she had arrived. Christina, Marguerite, and I watched her walk away. She seemed to be leaving the grandstand. The two women and I moved up the stairs to the concession level.

"Thanks," I said. "That was getting uncomfortable," I said.

"What did she say to you?" Christina asked.

"Oh." I paused, deciding whether to give it verbatim or the short version, as I watched Maggie moving away. "I think you're right. She may be trying to offer me sex."

"Do you think that was why she came to the race?" Christina asked.

"She mentioned she came often to meet Melvyn after the races."

"I'm convinced she came today to watch Kurt Maxxon," Christina said.

"She asked me to meet her after the race somewhere," I said. "She said she wanted to show me how much she likes me." Christina's brow furrowed, and her jaw muscles hardened.

"You may have a problem, here, Maxxon," Marguerite said.

"I'm sure we do," Christina said. "We need to get out in front of it."

Alisa said, "It's good when younger women chase older men." She giggled.

"I'm not interested in being chased," I said, then hoped I hadn't offended Alisa. I glanced toward Brittany who wore a bewildered look. I moved to sit next to her. "You like the race?" I asked her.

"I wish you were racing," Brittany said.

"Angie is just as good as I was."

"It's not the same," Brittany said.

"The racing is still a lot of fun to watch, isn't it?" I said.

"I want to yell for you, like me and Uncle Chuck always did," she said, and her voice took on a sad tone.

I was at a loss, and I looked around for Christina, hoping she would come to my aid. I'm not very good at comforting females, no matter what their age. Christina realized my situation, and she called for Brittany to come sit next to her.

Suddenly my conversation with the weird voice last Friday evening came roaring back to mind; along with weird thoughts about a sniper hiding somewhere. I made a quick survey of all the places my imagination had conjured up where a sniper could hide to gun me down. I was somewhat relieved to see that each of the hiding places was currently surrounded by race fans, cheering on their favorite drivers. The few that were seated down low in the seats proved to be groups of women—wives of drivers and fans—who didn't come to watch the race.

I'd missed the first six laps of the second heat, so I focused on the race. The pack was running in the same order as at the start: Angie, Kellogg, Dejarnet, Christofides, and Depeuw. During lap twenty-two, Jeffry Depeuw blew his transmission coming out of turn two on the backstretch. He immediately headed for the edge of the track, but had left a swath of transmission oil across the track. Cars running behind him immediately took evasive action and most avoided the oil slick.

Angie hit the oil slick and Nikki fish-tailed severely. Angie fought to get Nikki under control. In the process she got low on the track. I knew she was worried about using up her tires this early, so she slowed down until she could safely move up to a better line. She wound up in fifth position. I read the leader board in the infield. It read: #4 – (Kellogg); #51 – (Danielson); #33 – (Greene); #89 – (Davison); #27 – (Prescotte). They ran in that order from lap twenty-three to lap forty-five.

I looked across the track and studied Maurey. He was wearing his usual "we're going to win this one" face. I focused on the two boys who were jabbering about the loss of time on the lap. Tugs said something to them, and all three watched intently the cars coming off turn number four and into their timer zone. When Angie appeared, they went to reading their equipment.

Exiting turn four in lap forty-five, Greene got too high and nearly took Davison with him into the wall. Angie used the banking to shoot herself into the third position behind Kellogg and Danielson. As they ran toward the finish line, I said to Christina, "I'm going back to the pit to help during the break."

Christina nodded. "I'll be right here."

In lap forty-seven Angie passed Danielson coming out of turn two. As I arrived at the pit stall at the end of lap 47 the running order read: #4 – Kellogg; #27 – Prescotte; #29 – Forester; #51 – Danielson; #114 – Christofides; #49 – Flanders; #125 – Dejarnet; and #33 - Greene.

Tugs and the boys were timing Angie's laps. Maurey sat in his truck reading a magazine—one of the many he subscribed to about auto repair and body work. During laps forty-eight and forty-nine, the leaders switched positions a little. At the end of lap forty-nine Kellogg continued to lead, with Angie in second, Christofides in third, followed by Forester, Dejarnet, Danielson, Davison, and Flanders. I waited for them to come out of turn four at the end of lap fifty. When they arrived, Angie was in third. The final order for the second heat was Kellogg, Christofides, Angie, Forester, Dejarnet, Danielson, Davison, and Flanders.

*   *   *

Angie came to a stop in the center of her pit stall, and climbed out of Nikki calm and controlled. She didn't dash toward the pink port-a-potty. Maurey moved to Nikki and unlatched the hood. His two sidekicks, with identical baseball caps and blue shop rags in the rear pockets, moved in lock-step with Maurey.

I measured the tires and selected the best two of the worn tires. Then I loosened the lug nuts on the right side tires. Angie slid the jack under Nikki and pumped it up. We swapped the tires and I started air hammering the lug nuts tight. We moved to the driver's side, and I loosened the lug nuts. Angie jacked Nikki up. We finished the left side tires, and I let Angie carry the jack to stow it in Maurey's pickup. She also turned off the compressor since we were done using the air wrenches. Tugs dug three bottles of water out of the cooler in back of Maurey's truck. He leaned into Nikki to put them in the holders installed on the crash frame, within reach of Angie.

Maurey had Nikki's hood up and was fiddling with her computers. He crooned, "You're running great. You've got this one won." I glanced at Angie who grinned widely.

"Two wild women on the track," Angie said. "Do those men think they stand a chance?"

I screwed my face into a goofy grin and wobbled my head. "No chance at all."

Tugs grabbed Angie and gave her a big kiss. He said, "Go get 'em, girl."

Maurey lowered the hood just as the timer called for the drivers to form up for the parade lap. He carefully latched it secure using a blue shop rag so as not to leave any fingerprints. Then he walked around Nikki in inspection mode. Joshua and Jacob copied every move Maurey made—sometimes in uncoordinated, comical actions.

Angie climbed into Nikki, pulled on her skid lid and strapped herself into the seat. "You're the best boss I've ever had," she said to me. I looked at Maurey and Angie said, "He's the best mechanic I've ever had."

Maurey gave her an "Aw, get out of here" wave of his hand.

Tugs said, "What about me?"

"You're the best of something," Angie said. "I ain't figured out what yet." She started the engine, which meant talking was no longer practical.

The running order was unchanged: #4 - Kellogg; #114 - Christofides; #27- Prescotte; #29 - Forester; #125 - Dejarnet; #51 - Danielson; #89 - Davison; and #49 - Flanders. If I was in third position just fifty laps from the final lap, I always felt pretty good. But there were so many things that could go wrong. Over the years I drove, there were several things that did go wrong—even on the last lap—even in the last one-quarter lap.

I waited until the green flag waved and the cars were roaring around the track. Then I walked back over to the grandstand. When I came up into the grandstand from the tunnel, I quickly looked around to see if Maggie was still around. I spotted

Christina and the other women. The lines were a little longer since the concession stands could start selling beer after the third heat started. I stopped by the men's restroom and then stood in line to get another cup of coffee.

I swung to look at the cars coming out of turn four. It was the end of lap ten, and they were still running in the starting order. I watched the pack go by, and then my hair stood on end as I watched Nikki fishtail in turn one and go up too close to the wall for me. Angie kept Nikki running high, waiting for an opening so she could get back in line in the sixth position.

During lap twenty-one, Sean Forester went down to a low line where he got stuck. Before he was able to move back up he had dropped back to the sixth position, moving Angie up to fifth. During lap thirty-seven Angie was able to get past Danielson coming off of turn two and moved into the fourth position. Laps thirty-eight through forty-five had Kellogg leading, Christofides in second, Dejarnet in third and then Angie.

In lap forty-five Christofides made a mistake in turn two and moved back to fourth, while Angie moved into third behind Kellogg and Dejarnet. "You're moving just right," I yelled.

Christina had her hands wrung out already, so I knew she was worried. "There's only five laps left," she said.

"Plenty of time," I said, hoping it was true. It usually worked for me. "I'm going over to the pit side, again," I said to Christina. When I came up on pit row, they were just finishing lap forty-six.

In lap forty-eight, Dave Kellogg slid high on turn three and wound up in fifth. Jimmy Davison somehow moved up to second, while Angie stayed in third. Two laps to go.

During lap forty-nine Angie whipped past Jimmy Davison coming off of turn two. She was running bumper-to-bumper with Dejarnet as they flew past us toward the white flag waving. Last lap. The crowd noise suddenly became a barometer for me. The louder cheering by all the fans high enough to see the entire track proved to be fuel for Angie, who moved into a side-by-side race with Dejarnet. Angie had the low line, a better engine, and probably better tires than Jacques. Coming down out of turn four, Angie shot ahead into first place and ran as hard as she could for the finish line. Dejarnet tried to catch her, but he didn't have enough horsepower.

"Angie won," Tugs yelled. "Yessss. She won!" He moved to shake Maurey's hand, then mine, and then both the boys who were jumping up and down and screaming at the top of their lungs "Angie Won!" When Christina arrived, Tugs embraced her and yelled, "Angie won the race!" Christina smiled and covered her ears. Joshua and Jacob walked around high-fiving anyone who would reciprocate.

We started moving with the crowd toward the Winner's Circle at the center of pit row. The SRVSCRA didn't allow burnouts or any overt demonstration of victory other than yelling and jumping.

Several Press and TV reporters gathered around the Winner's Circle and waited for Angie to climb out of the car. Suddenly I worried she might not know how to handle the media attention. Angie was cool and composed—more than I ever was.

The media people each got a sound bite from Angie and left to interview other drivers. The rest of us swarmed in to congratulate Angie. When Christina embraced her, Angie's face relaxed noticeably. I looked at the milling crowd and yelled, "Everyone is invited to a victory party this evening."

Jacques Dejarnet walked up to shake my hand.

"Where's it at?" someone yelled.

"At my place," Jacques yelled back.

"Good idea," I said. "It's big enough and the food is great." Dejarnet's Restaurant was a popular family operation, serving French cuisine on the east side of Centralia.

"We close at six on Sundays," Jacques said. "I'll call and get some volunteers to stay over for the party." Jacques fished his cell phone out of his pocket and punched a speed dial number. I heard him telling someone to get ready for a party—probably about one hundred people—no, not mine—yes, we'll need a couple of cooks and a half dozen wait staff—yes, keep the bartender—and get some more beer into the coolers.

A fierce "Yippeeeeeeeeeeee!" grabbed my attention, and I turned to see Angie leaping off the hood of Nikki into Tugs' arms. I watched Christina move to Angie's side and stay there, daring anyone to try the normally rough-house congratulations practiced among the drivers and overzealous fans. The SRVSCRA discouraged beer outside the grandstand and bleacher areas during the race, but after the race was over, there were no sanctions if a driver or fan popped a beer in the pit area. While the other drivers never did it to me, since they all knew I didn't drink beer, or anything else, there were several drivers who had been doused with beer after a win. I surmised that Christina had positioned herself to make sure no one resurrected the beer dousing part with the first female to win a race in the SRVSCRA.

Joshua and Jacob both moved toward Angie and she paid them special attention, leaning down to kiss both boys on their cheeks. Suddenly, I saw Brittany standing at the edge of the crowd—looking very lost. I looked around for Kimberly and saw her on the other side of the milling crowd, frantically searching among the legs. I walked toward Brittany and when she saw me coming toward her, she ran to me and I scooped her up. She wasn't crying, but she was close. "I thought Momma was right behind me," she sobbed. "I don't know where she went."

"I see her over there." I pointed with my chin and walked around the crowd toward where Kimberly was searching. I felt Brittany's body relax. As I neared Kimberly, I said, "Kimberly, Brittany is with me."

Kimberly stopped and looked toward my voice. Her frown eased and she ran toward us. "Where did you go?" she said.

"I thought you were following me, Momma," Brittany said.

I handed Brittany to Kimberly, not realizing Brittany had grown too heavy for Kimberly to lift. I recovered enough to help Brittany sink gently to the ground. Kimberly knelt down to embrace her daughter. Both their faces brightened.

It's going to be one special victory party.

* * *

Maggie Decker

Maggie watched Kurt Maxxon and Christina walk down and disappear into the tunnel under the track. She saw them emerge on the other side and followed their movement to Angie's pit stall. Maggie got up and quickly followed through the tunnel, even though the ushers had opened the gates to let people in the grandstand walk across the track. Maggie made her way to the Winner's Circle, hanging at the edge of the crowd. She watched

Kurt Maxxon hug Angie for a long time. *I hope he doesn't like her more than he likes me.*

She thought about going home and having a toke. As she walked away from the crowd, she heard Kurt Maxxon yell there was going to be a victory party. Then she heard another driver yell it was going to be at his place. *Who is that driver?*

Maggie stopped and turned to a man standing nearby. "Who is that driver who just said the party was going to be at his place?" she asked the man.

The man looked at her for a long moment. "That's Jacques Dejarnet. His parents own Dejarnet's Restaurant on the east side of town."

Maggie frowned. She had been east of Centralia to Melvyn's Economy Carpets several times. "I'm new to town," she confessed. "How do I get there?"

The man wrinkled his face, and then said, "Go out east First Avenue. It's just before you get to the city limits."

"I was out there once at Economy Carpets," she said. "Is that the same area?"

"It's maybe a half-mile farther, on the north side of the street," the man said. "There's a big sign out front."

Maggie hurried off to the parking lot, got into her car. *I'll find the place. Maybe Kurt will show me how much he likes me if I go.*

CHAPTER TEN
Sunday Evening, August 26

Kurt Maxxon

Christina, Kimberly, Brittany and I arrived at Dejarnet's Restaurant, and I pulled under the awning to let everyone out. "Looks like we're the first ones here," I said. "The parking lot is nearly empty."

"All the drivers have to shower and clean up," Christina said as she stepped down out of the truck and helped Brittany and Kimberly out of the back seat. "I wonder how many will show up?"

"Probably quite a few," I said. "I told Jacques to plan on fifty to seventy-five. Of course I'll pay any extras. Any driver's first win is an occasion, but Angie is the first woman to win a race in the SRVSCRA. That makes this one historic."

I parked in the far corner of the lot and walked to the front door as several other cars arrived. When I pushed through the front door, I saw the women and Brittany waiting for me while several of the wait staff scurried around setting up tables and laying out place settings. I mentally congratulated Jacques for being able to recruit the number of people I saw working on such short notice. I led the party to a table in the far corner away from the bar. A waitress materialized; Christina and I ordered decaf coffee, while Kimberly ordered a chocolate milk for Brittany and a diet Pepsi for herself.

"This place makes me feel like a princess, Momma," Brittany said. We smiled at her.

"It is a nice place," Kimberly said. "I've never been here before."

"They serve very good food," Christina said.

I nodded agreement. "It's mainly French cuisine. They have great steaks and seafood, too."

"Do the French eat a lot of seafood?" Kimberly asked.

"No more than Americans," I said. "If you live on the seacoast, in the U.S. or France, then you eat a lot of seafood. If you live inland, it's beef, pork or lamb."

Kimberly said, "I guess that makes sense."

I didn't expect Angie and Tugs to arrive until later. Because of the crush of people, I told Tugs to take Angie to the nearby Holiday Inn Express and get a room for the night. That way Angie could shower in peace and get ready for her victory party. It would also keep them from having to make the hour and a half drive back to Carpentier Falls after the party.

The first driver to come in was Jimmy Davison and his wife, Vinita. Jimmy had finished third in the number eighty-nine Trattoria Restaurant car. Jacques Dejarnet banged through the swinging kitchen doors carrying a tray of dinnerware. He set the tray on a table and came to our table where he sat down on one of the chairs.

"We have beef roasts we can finish and barbequed chickens that'll be ready by the time the people will want to eat," he said. "We're making our popular pork casserole. Anything else you'd like to have?"

"That sounds great," I said. "That ought to be enough, as long as you've got some potatoes to go along."

"We've got plenty of potatoes," Jacques assured me.

There were seven drivers standing in the bar area when the bartender came from the back room, tying on his apron as he walked. He waved to the crowd and went about setting up the bar for the action about to commence. Eventually he said, "What'll you have?" and drew glasses of beer for all the drivers in line, starting with Jimmy Davison.

The fifth place finisher, Dave Kellogg, arrived and got in line for a beer. Eugenios Christofides, the fourth place finisher, slammed through the front door and stood looking around the room. He made his way to bar line and went to talk to the drivers sitting at Jimmy Davison's table.

I looked toward that table and decided this might be the last time tonight all of them would be together, so I nodded for

Christina to follow me. We walked toward the table and all the men leaped to their feet and elbowed each other to give Christina a hug. As if prompted, Jacques Dejarnet, the second place finisher, came from the kitchen and walked to the table. I shook hands with each driver and congratulated them on an exciting race. Angie was the only top five finisher not here yet.

Jacques grinned and said, "Damn, I thought maybe I could outrace that driver of yours, but she had the inside track and one hellava engine to boot."

"You're not going to outrace a Maurey Kennedy engine," Davison said. "I'm hoping to convince Kurt to include me on a race team." He winked at Christina. "Would you put in a good word for me, Christina?"

"I sure will," Christina said.

I shook Jacques hand. "You are a class act, my friend, throwing a party for a competitor."

"I have a wonderful friend and mentor in Kurt Maxxon," Jacques said. "You make it easy."

As Christina and I retreated to our table, the waitress delivered our drinks. I heard a thumping noise and looked around to see Rafe Komminski wobbling toward our table on his matching canes followed by his wife Katarina and Eugenios Christofides. Eugenios and Rafe were good friends—Rafe an immigrant from Czechoslovakia and Eugenios from Greece. Eugenios pulled two chairs out from the table and said to Rafe, "Sit here, old man."

"Old man, my ass," Rafe shot back as he sat down in the proffered chair. Katarina smiled and sat down in her chair.

The waitress waited through the exchange. "Would you gentlemen like something to drink?" she asked.

"Gentleman," Rafe shot at her, pointing with his chin toward Eugenios. "This guy is no gentleman. Believe me when I say that."

"Another Ouzo," Eugenios said, ignoring Rafe.

"Double Jack Daniels on the rocks," Rafe said.

Christina shot Rafe a withering look, forcing him to follow her eyes to Brittany sitting next to her.

"You're the only man here older than me or Kurt," Eugenios quipped as he sat down.

"That's true," Rafe said. "Excuse my French." He looked

around the room. "The cameraman is coming. Do you mind?"

"I don't mind," I said. "Everyone will appreciate our party making the news."

"This is a memorable event," Rafe said. "Angie is the first female to win a race in the SRVSCRA. I'm going to shout it out on the front page of tomorrow's edition."

If any of the males within earshot had quibbles, they didn't show it. Maybe they hoped Rafe would mention them all as supporters of women's rights.

"That's wonderful," Christina said. "Angie is a special girl who has a great future in racing."

"Think she can move up into NASCAR?" Rafe asked. "Where is she, anyway?"

"She'll be along—" I started to say.

"Yes," Christina said. "She definitely has what it takes to race in NASCAR."

"Can I quote you?" Rafe asked.

"You can quote me," Christina said. She nodded to me. "Him, too."

I nodded agreement.

Rafe had already scribbled something on his notepad, and I knew from past experience, it would be as accurate as if he had taped it.

More people were arriving all the time and, at one point, I worried that there might be more than the fifty to seventy-five I'd estimated. Jacques wandered to our table. "What if five hundred people show up?" I asked him.

"No problem," Jacques said. "We can handle it."

I introduced Kimberly and Brittany to Jacques. I watched Kimberly's eyes as they brightened. Jacques was a flamboyant Frenchman who, for whatever reason, had never married. His parents had put him through parochial schools; elementary grades at St. Joseph's Catholic School and then high school at Sacred Heart Catholic School in east Centralia. Jacques had matriculated at St. Gregory Catholic College in Jamesboro, where he attended one semester and dropped out. He came home and went to work in the family restaurant.

Angie and Tugs came through the door, and several people stood and started applauding. Angie, suddenly shy and red-faced, dipped her head and walked straight toward our table. Christina got up to give Angie a hug and whispered something in her ear. Then Christina led Angie to her seat at our table. Tugs walked around the table, whipped out a chair and sat down next to Eugenios. They started chatting, and soon they both got up and headed toward the bar. I stood and held the chair out while Angie sat down next to Kimberly. I would have to work on training Tugs on the intricacies of gentlemanly manners, like holding the chair while your lady sat down. Other drivers and their wives or girl friends came to congratulate Angie. I was sure I saw a little envy in the eyes of a few of the women. Then it hit me with full force. Angie Prescotte was the first female to win a race in the SRVSCRA. I felt like a new father. I was old enough, obviously, to be Angie's father. Now she was the first woman to win a SRVSCRA race. I wished I could have talked Maurey into going home to get Hazel and coming to the party. Maurey was slowing down as he should because he was over seventy years old. It would have been nice, however, to have him here enjoying his success as Angie's mechanic. I was thinking about phoning Maurey when Terry and Marguerite Grossman and the boys arrived.

They led Joshua and Jacob Wallace to our table. Both boys were taking in all the activity. Most of the drivers were wearing shirts announcing their car numbers and sponsors. Many were wearing ball caps also. During the race, the boys had donned their Texas Rangers baseball caps that Maurey had rounded up for them to wear a couple of years ago for the Carpentier Falls race. The boys left those caps in the car, so Terry offered to go get the caps for the boys.

I introduced Brittany to the boys. Jacob sat down next to Brittany, and they set up a brisk conversation. Eventually I wondered if the conversation would ever end. Joshua was watching the crowd. He recognized various drivers. Dave Kellogg came to the table and shook Joshua's hand and welcomed him to the party. Joshua was enjoying the attention.

"Dave gave you and Jacob a rousing recommendation at the driver's meeting," I said.

At the sound of his name, Jacob swung to look at me. Joshua grinned. "That's good," Joshua said.

"What's good?" Jacob asked Joshua.

"Mr. Kellogg gave us a good recommendation as lap timers," Joshua said.

"Oh, yeah!" Jacob said. He jumped up to shake Dave's hand. "Thanks, Mr. Kellogg."

"Yeah, thank you," Joshua seconded. "We appreciate that."

I realized that Rafe had called Manchester to take photos of the party when camera flashes started filling the room. I watched him move from group to group, rearrange them a little and then take a picture. After a while, the flashes just blended into the background.

Marguerite was chatting with Christina. I looked around the room. Dejarnet's staff had removed the five dozen four-person tables and set up a banquet room arrangement with eleven huge round tables that each would seat ten diners. Making the rounds of the tables would give me a good chance to connect with the drivers in a casual way. Some of the best ideas were developed in the relaxed atmosphere or a meal and camaraderie.

Suddenly I looked up and watched Don Epperley walking toward our table with a highball glass in hand. I was a little ashamed. I had been so busy visiting I wasn't greeting new arrivals like I should be.

"You drinking and driving?" I asked.

"I am not!" Don declared. "I had a taxi bring me, and I'll call a taxi to get back to the hotel." He gave me a smug look. "Unless I can catch a ride with some friends of mine. I'm staying at the same hotel as Mutt and Alisa."

I liked to give Don a hard time once in awhile. He was a no-nonsense man, who was considered to be a by-the-book cop, and a damn good one.

After Don's retirement, the Kings Rapids Historical Society enlisted his help putting together a history of black people in the valley. Don enjoyed that so much, he got involved with the history of the entire Swift River Valley.

"Why did you wait until this morning to drive over?" Christina asked Don when she realized he had arrived.

"I didn't," Don said. "I drove over Friday afternoon. I've been staying on the north side."

"You didn't call us?" I quipped. "What were you

thinking?"

"They just discovered another major station on the Underground Railroad," Don said with a smug look on his face. "Just north of here, in Harrisonville, about twenty miles."

I knew Don had become very active in the research into the Underground Railroad. My first direct experience with the Underground Railroad was a few years ago, the year I helped solve Elaine Willowby's death in Masonville.

"That would be on the same route that ran through Grief Mason's place, in Masonville," I said.

The founder of Masonville, Grief Mason, let his place, known then as Mason's Acres, become a major stopover on the Underground Railroad that linked the southern states north to the Canadian border.

"The very same route," Don said, beaming. "The next stop after Mason's Acres."

Grief Mason was born in Virginia to a black father and a white mother who died giving birth. Grief was, however, as fair skinned as his mother and could pass as a white person. Grief's life changed for the worse when his father moved to Philadelphia and married a black woman. His stepmother hated Grief. She abused him physically and emotionally every way she could. At one point she broke Grief's leg, and he crawled away and hid out in the caves along the Schuylkill River. He met a dozen other homeless waifs, and they helped each other survive.

Grief eventually became a teamster and adept at handling an eight-mule team capable of hauling heavy loads. Everything else I know about him until he arrived in the valley, with a pile of money, was hearsay. The most common legendary theory was that Grief worked as a teamster for the U.S. Mint in Dahlonega, Georgia, a facility established to process the gold found in the mountains of northern Georgia in 1838. The most acceptable theory held that he acquired his money by pulling off a huge heist of gold coins while driving them to Atlanta for shipment.

Through a roundabout way, Grief arrived at Greene's Ferry and became a regular on the Society pages of the local newspapers in Greene's Ferry and Kings Rapids. He had accounts at several banks in both towns. He dressed impressively. He courted several of the local ladies, who competed for his attentions.

Grief bought 120 acres on the north side of the Mink River about fifty miles east of Kings Rapids. He developed the land as a cotton farm and built a mansion on the property. In the process he met and fell in love with Phoebe Lindquist, the Kings Rapids lumber store owner's daughter. Grief offered Phoebe permanent residence in the new mansion and she accepted. They were married and produced a dozen children—six boys and six girls.

As the debate over slavery went from a murmur to a shouting match, most of the residents in the valley were anti-slavery. Many of Grief's neighbors were aghast when they found out Grief had bought six slaves and added more slaves each year. The neighbors didn't know Grief freed the slaves and offered them a home, a share of the farm's produce, and an annual allowance. Visitors did note there were an exceptionally large number of individual huts, a little bigger and a lot more elaborate than the typical slave shack. But the anti-slave neighbors could only see the things they felt were wrong; the pro-slave neighbors saw a man treating his slaves better than he should. The neutral neighbors simply came and went without thinking about it.

Don's research also extended to the beginnings of the civil rights movement during the 1930s. Don's articles in the historical society's newsletter and the local newspaper also chronicled the activities of several Negro bootleggers who operated in the valley during Prohibition from 1918 to 1932. Those characters were the most interesting to me, since two of them figured prominently in the evolution and development of the SRVSCRA.

The photographer arrived at our table and rearranged the women so their faces were all visible in the pictures. He fired away, making sure he included Rafe in as many shots as possible.

*   *   *

Maggie Decker

She'd gone home and made a futile search for a joint of marijuana. After several minutes, she decided she would have to go buy some new joints. Since she had to go out, she also decided to go see what was happening at the party, then stop at the store on the way home. She drove to the restaurant and finally found a parking place in the farthest corner of the lot, next to Kurt Maxxon's big white truck with www.KurtMaxxonRacing.com in red letters along the bottom of the two doors on each side. Before entering the restaurant, she carefully peeked in through the door windows. No one was guarding the door. She went in and made a quick survey of the dining room. People were standing in groups talking, as well as moving between tables, the wait staff ferrying drinks from the bar to the tables. In the far corner, she caught a glimpse of Kurt Maxxon sitting at a large table with several people seated around it.

Maggie carefully maneuvered to where she could see most of Kurt's table, but Kurt couldn't see her with a clear view. That woman who was constantly beside him was right there—next to him and talking to a tall elegantly dressed African-American woman, who looked familiar. She was with that woman at the track today.

"Do you want something from the bar?" Maggie jerked to look up at a waitress.

"Uh, yeah, bring me a Whiskey Sour." She watched the waitress walk away, and then swung her attention back to Kurt Maxxon, who now was talking to an African-American man, older, shaved head, heavy-set. They were laughing.

Then another couple came through the door, walked past her and to Kurt's table—a tall man with a comb mustache. Maggie didn't pay any attention to the woman, even when Kurt stood and embraced her. He shook hands with the man. Then the man and woman went to talk to that female racecar driver. What was the girl doing driving a race car? Maggie could see Kurt's side profile pretty well with only minor disruptions by passing people. If Kurt looked in her direction, she could duck a little to get out of his line of sight. Kurt was enjoying himself. She thought about going over and trying to talk to Kurt, but decided this was not the place to do it. She'd just sit and watch Kurt for a while, then stop for some stuff on the way home. Maybe Kurt will see me and come over to talk to me.

The waitress had delivered the Whiskey Sour, and Maggie paid her out of the roll of tip money in her pocket. She threw a dollar tip on the table, but she didn't touch the drink and sat for several minutes. Eventually she lost interest in Kurt and the party. She stood and made her way quickly out the door and to her car.

It took awhile before Melvyn paid any attention to me. Kurt Maxxon will like me. When I show him how much I like him. And I'll do that just as soon as he lets me.

*　　*　　*

Kurt Maxxon

A Karaoke machine sitting on a chair in the corner started playing. A few couples took to the small dance floor in the corner. I wasn't paying too much attention until I realized that Brittany was watching her mother on the dance floor with Jacques Dejarnet. "Way to go, Kimberly," I said under my breath.

My thoughts were interrupted when Alisa and Mutt arrived. I stood to greet them and then let them congratulate Angie. I sat back down. Mutt wandered off and returned in a few minutes with a cocktail glass in each hand. He handed one of them to Alisa and walked around to sit down between Don Epperley and me.

"You staying in town tonight?" Don asked.

"We're out at the Airport Holiday Inn," Mutt said.

"Who's driving?" Don asked.

"Alisa."

"What's she drinking?" Don asked

"It's non-alcoholic," Mutt said.

"Good," Don said. "Mr. Maxxon, here, is concerned about drinking and driving."

"He should be," Mutt said smartly. "He travels all around the valley talking to teenagers about safe driving." Mutt and Don had been friends for many years—long before I'd met either of them. I was always hard pressed to tell why they bickered with each other at the drop of a hat.

Alisa had sat down between Angie and Marguerite. She looked at me and said, "That girl who approached you in the grandstand today is sitting over there all by herself."

Christina gasped. "What? She's here? Where?"

Alisa tuned toward the entrance. "Yeah, she's sitting over there behind the wall of the Women's Restroom."

Christina leaped to her feet and almost ran across the room. Several people were startled by her movement, and they followed her progress. When she rounded the wall, she stopped and looked around. Then she came walking back to our table. "She's not there now."

"It looked like she was either just getting there or getting ready to leave when we came in," Alisa said.

"Did she see you?" I asked Alisa.

"I don't think so," Alisa said. "If she did look at me, I doubt she looked at me long enough to remember me."

A plan was developing in my brain. I would have to work it out. "Didn't you work as a waitress at one time?" I asked Alisa.

"Among other things," Alisa said. "Waitressing is a first job for a lot of girls out of high school."

"Would you be comfortable going undercover as a waitress?" I asked Alisa.

"Sure, why not?" Alisa smiled. "Whatcha got in mind, Colonel?"

Christina looked at me. "Have you got a plan, Maxxon?"

"It's in the preliminary stages right now," I said.

"Best not take too long," Marguerite said. "Else we might have to take care of it ourselves."

Since they put me on the hook, I decided to think aloud. "I thought about talking to Rebecca Pepper about getting Alisa in as an undercover waitress. Hopefully, she might be able to get next to Maggie and ask the questions I want answers to."

"That's not what we were thinking about," Christina said. Then she stood up. "I just had a thought," she said and walked away. A few minutes later I watched Christina lead the Manchester, Rafe's photographer, toward our table. He sat down next to Christina and held the camera so they both could view the pictures. Eventually Christina said, "There she is!"

Marguerite and Alisa walked to stand behind Christina and view the camera. All agreed that Maggie Decker had been to our party.

"Kurt's plan might be a good way to find out what she's up to," Marguerite interjected. "And hopefully we can find out her involvement with Melvyn at the track."

Alisa was nodding vigorously. "I like it," she said.

I breathed a sigh of relief. I had been a little concerned about what Marguerite meant when she said, "Else we might have to take care of it ourselves."

The women went back into conversation. I heard my name mentioned often. I heard Maggie's name mentioned occasionally. I wondered what the women were plotting. Since one of them was a cop, I decided they weren't plotting anything illegal or unlawful. I'd never noticed it before, but Marguerite did a lot of hand talking. Alisa moved her head to stress words. Christina usually spoke with a smile on her face.

Fortunately Kimberly returned to the table and was a distraction. She sat down across the table from me, and said, "Whew, I haven't danced this much in years. In fact, it's been longer than four kids ago."

"Enjoying yourself?" I asked, then grinned widely.

"I sure am," Kimberly said. "This is great. You have done so much for me in just a couple of days; you've changed my life completely. Thank you so much."

Over the next several minutes I let everything I knew about Melvyn's killing flow through my mind. Then my mind wondered about Maggie's involvement in the case.

Joshua had gone off circulating among the drivers and holding his own on the conversation front. I was impressed with the way he moved from group to group chatting, laughing, and gesturing. I started hoping intensely that Joshua's disinterest in school was some correctible physical problem—eyesight, or perhaps hearing.

I was surprised when Jacques came out of the kitchen and walked toward our table. He held his hand out to Kimberly, and they rushed back to the dance floor. Brittany watched them go. She swung her huge brown eyes at me and said, "Momma sure likes that man," she said.

"It looks like it," I said.

Brittany was ignoring Jacob and totally focused on watching her mother dance with Jacques. Christina, Marguerite, and Alisa were still huddled and I heard Christina say, "I'll bet she was just sitting there watching Kurt."

Angie and Tugs were making the rounds of tables and groups. When I told Angie I didn't drink alcohol, she replied, "Neither do I. I've never touched the stuff." Tugs was taking care of Angie's share of beer. At one point I wondered if he was a little tipsy, but he seemed to right himself and carry on. Terry and Mutt were also making the rounds of the standing groups. I knew Terry would nurse one highball all night and probably not need Marguerite to drive them to the hotel. Mutt would have two or three, and rely on Alisa to get him and Don Epperley safely to the hotel. Don would have four or five without showing any ill effects. "The man can hold his liquor," Christina had declared after she met Don the first time at a party.

As I surveyed the room, the only person I felt sorry for was Jacob. He was sitting at our table plainly in a dreamy daze. "What you thinking about?" I asked him across the table.

"My science project," he said. "It's pretty complicated. I want to show how they use gravity to slingshot satellites off Jupiter and Saturn and Uranus and Neptune to get them into outer space."

"Wow," I said. "That does sound complicated."

"I'm thinking about how to do that." He put his elbow on his knee and held his chin in his left hand—in true Rodin style for The Thinker.

"If you need any help," I said, "I'll do what I can. I probably wouldn't be much help, though, on such a complicated subject as that. I'm glad you're putting your heart into the things you're learning. You're doing great, Jacob. I'm really proud of you."

Jacob's chest swelled a little.

After the wait staff served the main entrée, the conversation level lowered as many hungry people dug into the entrees. Jacques gave up dancing with Kimberly long enough to supervise the serving of the main entrée. Kimberly sat down at our table and nibbled at her dinner plate. Brittany finished her plate and was taking bites from her mother's.

"Do you like that man, Momma?" Brittany asked.

"He is a very nice man," Kimberly said. "I like him a lot."

"Okay, Momma," Brittany said. "I like him, too."

Kimberly leaned back and looked at Brittany. "That's great, Brit."

I was so enthralled in the Brittany-Kimberly conversation I didn't see Karl Albertson come up behind me. He put his hand on my shoulder, and I turned to look. "I figured you'd lost interest in looking in all the garages after the race," Karl said with a smile.

"I forgot about it. I sure did," I confessed. "You want to do it now?"

"Hell no." Karl held up his hands with both palms toward me. "It's way past my bedtime," he said and turned and walked away.

I returned to the conversations around the table as the

waitress arrived to check our drink and dessert choices. All the adults refused dessert and ordered refills of their drinks while the boys and Brittany ordered ice cream sundaes.

I would have gladly had an ice cream sundae—chocolate, strawberry, and butterscotch.

*   *   *

Lorianne Hightower

She drove north on Hoover Street and pulled into a convenience store in case she was being tailed. The only problem with the Porsche was it wasn't big enough to carry more than four banker's boxes in one trip. Two boxes in the back seat, a third box on the front seat, and a fourth in the tiny trunk—or hood—on a rear engine car like the Targa. If she moved them by car, she would have had to make five trips to get the sixteen boxes of documents to the storage shed.

I need another plan! She thought about it, and an idea started to form—one that would speed up moving the boxes from the Salon to the storage shed. Fortunately the storage room had been rented late last year after she decided to take on another mule: by New Age Beauty Products.

If the cops went looking, they would have to dig pretty deep to find her name on the lease—the same with the other three storage units used by New Age Beauty Products. Over the years Lorianne had kept all the records. Now she wondered why? If the cops got their hands on the papers in any one of those dozen boxes, they would start to ask questions. And those questions could mushroom. If they managed to track any one of her three mules it might be all over—especially if they spilled the beans.

After a rather circuitous route, Lorianne arrived at the storage complex. Using her practiced routine she drove past turned around sharply and parked a half block away. After several minutes, she entered the complex and drove to her storage unit. She unloaded the three boxes into the room and left to drive home, following a different route, with several stops to make sure she wasn't being tailed, each trip a total of thirteen miles to cover what was about five miles as the crow flies.

Back home, she sat waiting for the garage door to open. What if … what if the cops put one of those tracking things on her car and could tell where she was all the time? "Dammit, they're probably watching me all the time and I don't know it," she said to the rearview mirror. What if they get a search warrant and look into the boxes in the storage shed? "Dammit, dammit. I've got to get rid of those papers."

The new plan became clearer in her mind.

"That might work," she said aloud as the garage door ground closed. "Yeah, that'll work." She felt like a giant weight had been lifted off her shoulders. In the next few days, she would take care of all those papers for good. She was going to lose some sleep, but that was okay. It was going to be much safer to have those papers gone. She sat in the car staring at the work-bench across the front of the garage cover with Shag's tools and junk. Thoughts of Melvyn filtered into her mind. "Dammit, Shag, you made me do it," she whispered. "You never let me have enough money. All you wanted to do with money was save it. Save, save, save. You saved more money than we could ever
need. Dammit. Damn you."

CHAPTER ELEVEN
Monday Morning, August 27

Kurt Maxxon

There were two dozen cars in Jalopy's parking lot. I parked and made a quick survey, then looked toward Christina. "Kimberly's car isn't here yet," I said.

"Getting four children ready for the day has to be a circus," Christina said, smiling. I had fleeting remembrances of raising Vanessa and Little Kurt, and it appeared Christina was having her own memories of raising Tabetha and Mason. We walked to the front door, went in, and as we passed the vacant hostess stand, we each grabbed two booster seats. I led Christina to a large round table in the far corner where I could watch the parking lot. The few occupants of the booths and tables seemed to be a normal Monday morning crowd, some recovering from an overly active weekend, others facing a long hard workweek.

Behrooz Sherafat, affectionately known as Bay, came out of the kitchen. When he saw us, he waved and went to get mugs of coffee, which he brought to our table with one for himself. He looked at the booster seats on four of the chairs and went to get another chair from a nearby table which he swung around and sat down straddling it. "You two are a little early this morning. Someone bringing children?"

"We're meeting a special family we just adopted," Christina said.

"You adopted a whole family!" Bay said.

Christina smiled. "It's a wonderful family. The mother is going to work for us at Maurey's place. Kurt and I are going to take the children to our neighbor's daycare for today."

"That's wonderful," Bay said. "You two do so many good things." He sipped his coffee which I recognized from its aroma as Strong Turkish coffee made white by half cream.

I'd known Bay since he bought Jalopy's in 1994. Behrooz was of Iranian heritage; his ancestry was well documented back to an old line Persian family. Bay spoke Farsi as fluently as he spoke English. However, I decided the few words I'd heard him utter in Farsi, were—well, cursing.

Bay's father had been a Physics professor until recruited by the Shah's government to be the science liaison officer to the United Nations delegation. The family moved to New York City. Bay was accepted as a senior in a local high school after scoring 100% on the entry test. Bay graduated with a B.A. in Business Mathematics from American University in 1983. He married Gelsey Mehran, who he met in his junior year at AU and they have two children, Christopher Michael and Sarah Lealah.

I saw Kimberly's rusted out old red Dodge Grand Caravan drive into the parking lot and park. I watched as Kimberly got out and moved to the passenger side. Brittany, Daniel and Mikie tumbled out as Kimberly reached to undo the safety seat of Madison Jane. Kimberly carried the baby and led the three others to the front door. Christina followed my stare and got up to go hold the front door open for Kimberly and the children. Bay sat with me, watching the gang come toward us.

"That is a lovely family," Bay said and excused himself. He walked toward the kitchen.

Brittany ran to me and climbed into the chair next to me, reaching for a hug. I snuggled her, and she giggled. That was what I had been waiting for, and the reason I didn't get up and go to the door. Christina, Kimberly, and the waitress arrived and helped the other children into their seats. I helped Brittany get into her booster seat. Eventually we were all seated and the waitress took our order. The kids all wanted waffles. Christina and Kimberly ordered fruit plates and oatmeal. I ordered one of Jalopy's famous breakfast platters that carried three days worth of cholesterol— ignoring Christina's disapproving look.

As they chatted, I heard Christina say, "Our neighbor lady has agreed to watch the children today and maybe tomorrow. But, she isn't set up to get Brittany and Daniel to and from school when school starts in a few weeks."

Kimberly nodded.

"I'll call a couple of other friends," Christina said, "to find an acceptable daycare center that can get Brittany and Daniel to and from school each day."

"Did you tell her about Mikie?" Kimberly asked.

"Yes, I did," Christina said. "Olivia isn't set up to handle Mikie every day. But I told her that Brittany can help when Mikie has a problem. So she agreed to watch them today."

"That's great. Brittany is a big help," Kimberly said, and looked away. "I can't believe you're helping me so much."

"We want you and your family happy," Christina said. "And you should not have to worry about them."

"Are you going to take care of us, Mr. Maxxon?" Brittany asked.

I noticed Kimberly jerk to look at Brittany, then look away again. "Brittany, your mother will take care of you. I'll help with the things she needs as I'm able," I said and watched Kimberly for a few moments. Something seemed to be bothering her, and I wondered what it was.

*   *   *

Kimberly Grenwahl

As she watched her children enjoying their waffles, her thoughts returned to the night before. Jacques Dejarnet. That name had kept her from going to sleep last night, and this morning it was the first thing on her mind. She replayed their meeting the night before, the party, their dancing—close in each other's arms. Jacques Dejarnet, the Driver of car number one 125 Monte Carlo.

Brittany seemed to like Jacques—nothing like her infatuation for Kurt Maxxon. And Jacques had responded favorably to Brittany. But what about the other three kids?

She and Jacques had danced most of the night. Fortunately, they were the only ones dancing on the postage-stamp sized dance floor to the music of the karaoke box. She had felt his heat, and she would have surrendered to that heat if not for Brittany being with her.

What was the song on the jukebox that really turned Jacques on? Kimberly struggled with her memory. Oh yeah, it was "Please, help me; I'm falling …" by Patsy Cline. It had made her body tingle also.

Jacques Dejarnet! Is this the start of something special? Lord, what a find. She'd only been a part of the Maxxon family for a couple of days, but already her life was changing—definitely for the good.

*   *   *

Kurt Maxxon

The waitress bussed the dishes almost as fast as we emptied them. Three of the four Belgian waffles seemed to evaporate on their plates after the proper amounts of butter and syrup had been added. Madison Jane was still sleepy and picked at hers. Daniel and Mikie accepted pieces of fruit from Kimberly's plate; Daniel liked strawberries, while Mikie liked grapes. Brittany only liked cantaloupe. I'd raised two children and knew they were as different as day and night—beyond being male and female. Now I was learning the traits of four new children and loving every minute of it.

From her actions, I sensed that Christina was enjoying it as much as I was.

"Okay, gang," I said. "Time to get going for the day." Four little faces swung to stare at me. I could feel the tension of the unknown building in each of them. The plan we had developed was for me to take Kimberly to Maurey's place and get her comfortable in her new job. Christina would take the four children to Olivia's daycare and stay with them while they adjusted to the other kids. Then she would go home to let Beau out, before leaving for her dentist appointment. I was to pick the kids up at Olivia's and bring them to Maurey's shop so they could ride home with their mother when her day ended.

Christina had picked up on the anxiety clouding the faces of the children. "You will really like Olivia's Daycare," Christina said, looking from child to child. "I'll stay with you this morning, and I'll put on a little play on how to care for pets. Would you like that?"

All four little faces brightened, and tiny smiles grew on each mouth. "Yeah, we've never seen a play about pets," Brittany offered.

I carried Madison Jane out to Christina's car. The little girl was anxious to leave her mother and go with Christina, but

Kimberly soothed her and finally got her to agree to go with Mrs. Christina.

Kimberly and I stood watching as Christina drove away with the children. I glanced at Kimberly and could see the tension easing on her face.

"They are a handful," she said.

"You deserve a lot of credit for keeping the family going the way you do," I said.

"Thank you."

"I'll meet you at Maurey's."

At the repair shop that Maurey managed for me, I introduced Kimberly to the five mechanics we employed at the shop. There was a glass-enclosed office space in the corner of the building that Maurey used for the phone and a file cabinet. He hadn't spent much time in it, so I wondered if the ancient air conditioner hanging out one of the windows even worked. If it didn't, I'd get a new one installed this afternoon. Probably not a bad idea to get a new one installed anyway.

*   *   *

Maggie Decker

Maggie sat in the booth used by waitresses when traffic was slow. She'd cleaned her assigned tables, set up the silverware and plates needed for the lunch crowd that would descend on the place in another hour. The morning newspaper's Sports Page was opened in front of her. There was a large photograph of a smiling Angie Prescotte next to the number twenty-seven car that had won the race yesterday—Kurt Maxxon's car.

She let her mind wander back to the night before, at the restaurant. I shoulda gone over and talked to Kurt. He likes me, I know he does. Why did I leave so soon? That other woman was always next to him. Kurt kept talking to people, even that bratty little girl who hung next to him most of the night.

Maggie needed to figure out how to talk to Kurt alone. She wanted to show him how much she liked him. That's what grownup people do. She vaguely remembered being involved with another race driver—showing him how much she liked him. But that driver had gone somewhere. How could she find out where Kurt Maxxon lived?

Another waitress walked by and glanced at the newspaper.

"That girl driver won the race yesterday?" the waitress asked.

"Yeah, she did," Maggie said. The other waitresses rarely socialized with her.

"That's neat," the other waitress said. "She drives for Kurt Maxxon. God, he was a great driver himself. My dad was a true-blue fan right until the day he died."

"What does Kurt Maxxon do?" Maggie asked. "Do you know where he works?"

"He owns a store over on Monroe Street. Maxxon Auto Parts, I think is the name of it. It's easy to spot; it's a big store, nearly fills the whole block."

"Oh, yeah," Maggie said. "That's cool."

*   *   *

Kurt Maxxon

Maurey Kennedy had seemed a little defensive when I asked if the air conditioner in the office worked.

"I don't know, I've never used it," Maurey said.

"You've been in this building for five years and you've never turned the air conditioner on?"

"Don't like air conditioning," Maurey countered.

I helped Kimberly clean off one of the desks and find a chair that would get her by until I could get a new one delivered. I tried the air conditioner and found the fan worked, but it didn't cool the air. "It may just need to be charged," Kimberly said.

"It's an old model that uses Freon," I said. "Which isn't available any more. I'll call a friend of mine and have him install a new one." I speed dialed Centralia Appliance Center, who sponsored Sean Forester's number twenty-nine Pontiac, and asked him to deliver a new air conditioner. He promised to have a technician run by and install it later in the afternoon.

Maurey and Kimberly sat down at her clean desk, and Maurey explained what he did when he needed parts and how he ordered them, then waited for them to be delivered. Maurey gave Kimberly a handwritten sheet listing the suppliers he typically used with addresses and phone numbers.

"Are these people online?" Kimberly asked.

Maurey looked at me.

"They probably are," I said. Fortunately, I had brought a laptop computer with me for Kimberly to use until I could get a desktop installed. "But we probably don't have an ISP here in the office. I'll call the telephone company and get a DSL installed."

Maurey shook his head. The Internet was even more Greek to him than to me. He stood up and walked toward the office door. He stopped and turned around. "What's the latest on Melvyn Hightower's death?" he asked.

"Nothing new that I've heard," I said.

"Matilda called Hazel last night," Maurey said.

"Melvyn's Aunt Matilda?" I said.

"Yeah, the leader of your major fan club," Maurey said and wandered back into the shop area.

A few years after I started winning regularly in the SRVSCRA, I heard that a group of "older women" had formed a Kurt Maxxon Fan Club in one of the local independent living facilities. Of course that stirred my interest, so I went to meet the women. The woman who spearheaded the formation of the group was Matilda Stauffer. She told me she rooted for me in the SRVSCRA and for Melvyn Hightower who, at the time, was racing in a local sports car league. "But," she'd said with a twinkle in her eye, "even if Mel raced in the same league as you, Kurt, I'd still root for you."

Over the years I'd visited Aunt Matilda every few months and, as she aged, she eventually moved into a Green House—an assisted living elder group home up on North 41st Avenue, between McKinley and Monroe Streets.

Centralia was laid out with the Swift River as the major physical feature affecting its plat. The river angled from northeast to southwest. In 1920 the city fathers radically changed the city plan, and therefore, its future growth. There had been six bridges built over the river, usually perpendicular to the river. Traffic patterns were so complicated that when the wood planking of one of the bridges burned to ashes in 1898, it caused quite a bit of frustration for the residents. When another bridge was closed in 1916 because of the heavy loads imposed by the heavy new trucks, the citizens of Centralia raised an outcry. The city fathers responded by completely changing the city's plat. The new grid provided that the east/west Avenues would start with 1st Avenue, at the time thought to be the future northern most avenue, and increased to the south with bridges over the river at every mile. The first bridge built was on 11th Avenue. Then bridges were built at 21st Avenue, 31st Avenue, and 41st Avenue.

A marker next to the bridge at the 71st Avenue Bridge marked the approximate location of the original Greene's Ferry settlement one hundred and fifty years ago. The ferry crossing on the west bank generally landed just north of 81st Avenue, near the present day fair grounds and racetrack. Greene's Ferry generally grew northeast along the east bank of the river. However, over the years several folks built homes on the west bank and commuted by boat or raft. The ferry crossing was abandoned in 1835 after the residents built a bridge across the river where the present day 41st Avenue Bridge was located.

In 1847 all but a dozen structures in the Greene's Ferry settlement burned to the foundations when a wild fire blew up from the southwest. The settlement was rebuilt northeast about a half mile and renamed Greenesville.

In the 1920 re-plat of the city, the north/south byways were labeled Streets and every mile carried a Presidential name, with bridges built across the river every two miles. The streets with bridges were Hoover, McKinley, Monroe, Jackson, and Davis, an admission that the city had southern leanings during the War Between the States. The east-west byways were designated as Avenues and numbered.

Between the 1920s re-platting and today, the city limits had expanded significantly in all directions, especially to the southeast.

*　　*　　*

After I had ordered a new desktop computer delivered, a new chair delivered, and a DSL from the telephone company, I bid Kimberly goodbye and told her I was going to visit Aunt Matilda. Kimberly gave me a blank smile. I decided to tell her who Aunt Matilda was later.

When I knocked on the door of the Green House, an older gentleman peered around the cracked door. I told him I wished to visit Matilda Stauffer. He eyed me then swung the door wide. "You're Kurt Maxxon, huh?" he said as he led me to a sitting area with two sofas and three easy chairs.

"Yes, I am," I said. "Are you a race fan?"

"Sure am," he said. "I root for Drew Westlake. I worked with Drew's dad."

"You were a cop?"

"Yeah, I was," he said, dipping his head in pride. "You know Davy?"

"Yes, I do," I said. "He's an old friend of mine. And Drew is an exceptionally good driver."

"I'll go get Matilda," the gentleman said and walked toward the hallway.

Matilda Stauffer was an elegant, statuesque lady, taller than most women, with an aquiline face. Her silvery blue hair always coiffed, and her eyes were sparkling brown. Her lips were always curved in a smile, her cheeks prominent, and her eyebrows natural. Even if I didn't know her so well, her appearance came across as an intelligent, experienced woman. She had been a librarian for fifty-five years, and I suspected she had read more books than I've ever seen.

"Ah, Colonel Maxxon," Aunt Matilda cooed as she wobbled toward me in her aluminum walker to accept my hug. Early on we had adopted embracing as the standard method of greeting because Aunt Matilda was not a person who shook hands.

I followed her to the open seating in one corner. She eased herself down into one of the easy chairs, while I sat at the end of one of the sofas. 'It's just terrible about Mel," she said after she was comfortable. "I read in the newspaper that you were the one who found him. I'm so glad you came to talk to me. What can you tell me about his murder?"

"Not much, really," I said, wishing more had been resolved. "But I know Melvyn came to see you often. Did he mention anything about problems? Business problems? Social problems? Any problems at all? With anyone?"

"Mel's only problem was with his wife, Lorianne."

"With Lorianne?"

"Mel was a stickler about money. He pinched pennies and Lorianne spent money like a drunken sailor."

I let this information soak in. "I didn't think Melvyn and Lorianne had financial problems," I said.

"I don't think they were in any financial trouble. You know, they weren't hurting," Aunt Matilda said. "But, Mel always worried about Lorianne's spending habits. She was spending money on things she didn't need. The latest thing was that car of hers—it cost over a hundred and fifty thousand dollars, Mel said."

I didn't know what kind of car Lorianne drove. My interaction with Melvyn and Lorianne Hightower had never been on a personal level—it had always been as president of the SRVSCRA and a competitor on the track. "I don't know Lorianne that well," I said.

Aunt Matilda scooted back in her chair. "Lorianne loves the trappings of wealth. She likes to act wealthy. She likes to think wealthy. She likes to talk as if she's wealthy. Now, she and Melvyn were successful business people, but they were not millionaires as Lorianne liked to think and act."

I nodded. My own business was successful, but I didn't consider myself terribly wealthy. I would have to find out what kind of car Lorianne was driving.

"Mel complained to me regularly about Lorianne's spending habits," she said.

"Okay," I said. "Were there any other problems?"

"Not that I know of," Aunt Matilda said. "I think Melvyn hoped he could straighten Lorianne out and get her using money more responsibly. I think he was too optimistic."

Aunt Matilda and I watched two men go into the kitchen area and get cans of soda from the refrigerator. "I haven't seen Lorianne for two, three years, now," she said. "Not since I moved up north here. Mel came to see me once a month, sometimes more often. But Lorianne didn't. Before I moved way up here, Mel and Lorianne would take me out for a dinner every once in awhile."

"Did Melvyn ever mention divorce?" I asked.

"No. Mel was raised to stay in the marriage, no matter what." I decided their marriage was no longer a matter of discussion at this point. There was no evidence that either had decided to end the marriage.

"The daughter of a friend of mine goes to Lorianne's salon every other week," Aunt Matilda said. "She can probably tell you more about Lorianne than I can. She lives in Albertstown somewhere. Let me get you her name and phone number. I can never remember her last name. She's been married four times."

Aunt Matilda got up and trudged off toward her room, guiding her aluminum walker deftly. She returned with a note sheet in her hand. The gentleman who had admitted me came strolling into the room. "Hank, come over here and meet Kurt Maxxon."

"I know Colonel Maxxon," Hank said. "I told him I root for Drew Westlake."

"That's okay," Aunt Matilda said. "Who has won more races?"

I felt rather small in the room.

Fortunately, Hank smiled and said, "Colonel Maxxon is one of the greatest drivers in the SRVSCRA. But I still root for Drew Westlake. He's Davey Westlake's boy."

"That's good," Aunt Matilda said.

The man smiled and walked away.

"I'm not happy that you quit driving, you understand," Aunt Matilda said. "I do like the young lady you picked to drive your car. She's a good driver. I'm starting an Angie Prescotte Fan Club. We'll run it alongside yours."

"That's great. She's a winner," I said, sure that Aunt Matilda had followed Sunday's race on the radio.

Aunt Matilda remained standing and handed me the sheet with her friend's daughter's name and phone number. I realized she was getting tired, so I let her walk me to the front door and I gave her a firm hug. I walked to my truck with mixed emotions. Her input about Lorianne had jolted my thinking. What were the implications?

Then I remembered my conversation with Steve Cosburn yesterday morning. With the race, Maggie showing up, Angie winning, and her victory party, I'd spaced out the significance of it. Jason Tobias could not be Melvyn's killer—not because of his history as one of the three Amigos, but simply because he wasn't in town at the time Melvyn was shot. Even if Lorianne Hightower had paid Jason twenty-five thousand dollars to shoot Melvyn, Jason could not have done it. I should have passed that information on to Nick sooner. I hoped Nick would cut me some slack for forgetting it.

I pulled my cell phone out and dialed Nick's number. It went to voice mail, and I had just said, "Nick, this is Kurt Maxxon," when Nick came on the line and said, "What's up, Maxxon?"

"A couple of things," I said. "One pretty important, the other not so much."

"Okay. Give it to me."

"First, the not so important thing," I said and told Nick about my interview with Aunt Matilda and the information she gave me regarding Lorianne.

"What was the important item?" Nick asked.

"Jason Tobias couldn't have killed Melvyn," I said, expecting an explosive reaction.

"Yeah, so," Nick said in a calm voice. "How'd you come to that conclusion?"

"He was with Steve Cosburn," I said. "He called Steve to come get him and his motorcycle Friday morning—" I paused to see what Nick's reaction was going to be.

"Was Cosburn the guy with Tobias when they stopped at Lefty's?"

"Yeah," I said. "You know about that?"

"Lefty called me. Told me about them stopping for lunch at his place. Told me they had just come from Fairmont Acres. We checked with the Quick Stop store in Fairmont Acres. They have a receipt for Tobias using his credit card to buy gas about ten-twenty-three in the morning."

"Where's Jason now?" I asked.

"About to be let out on his own recognizance," Nick said. "He's still a person of interest to us until we clear up the twenty-five K Lorianne Hightower paid him last month."

"What do they say that was for?"

"Their stories are that it was a business loan made by Jason two years ago," Nick said. It's just now being paid back. We can't track it because there was never any paperwork done for it. They say it was just a loan between two old friends."

"I probably believe that," I said.

"They were old friends?" Nick said. "How?"

"It's a long story," I said. "For now, I'd accept what they say as true and forget about Jason Tobias as the killer. I'll fill you in later."

"Okay," Nick said. "If I hear you right, you don't like Jason Tobias or Lorianne Hightower as Melvyn's killer."

"That's a pretty good summary of my thoughts," I said. I thought about telling Nick about Maggie Decker, but then decided to hold off for a while. Christina wouldn't be happy with me, but I needed to get a little more information first. From my perspective, Maggie didn't appear to play a major role in Melvyn Hightower's death. However, she might have seen the killer. She might be able to tell us if someone else was around.

Then I remembered something I wanted to know. "Do you have the time of death?" I asked.

"Not with me," Nick said. "I'm on my way to the county jail. I can get it when I get back to my office and dig out the autopsy report."

"Okay."

"You got something in mind, Maxxon?" Nick asked.

"Just curious."

"I'll call you," Nick said.

*   *   *

I drove to my store. There was an awful lot of stuff running around in my head, and I needed to write it down while I could still remember most of it. I wanted to run by Pepper's Diner after the lunch hour was over and Maggie had left for the day.

At my desk, I dug out a yellow writing pad and a new pen. The first thing I wrote down:

Where is the #35 Chevy Impala?

Then I wrote:

3 amigos = Melvyn Hightower + Jason Tobias + Steve Cosburn

Then I doodled geometric designs and wrote:

Harley Davidsons

Lorianne Hightower knew Melvyn in middle school / but she was not with the 3 Amigos at NE Sr high

Then I remembered the man on the phone Friday night. The man claimed Melvyn had cheated him. How did the man word it? I'd made a note about that on the scraps next to the phone. Hopefully I could find that note.

Then my memory kicked in, and near the bottom of the page I wrote:

??MAGGIE DECKER??

I flipped to a new sheet, and at the top of it I wrote:

Is Lorianne Hightower connected?

The desk clock on my desk dinged. It was one o'clock; time for me to go talk to Rebecca Pepper at Pepper's Diner. I carried the writing pad with me as I went down the steps to my truck. From now on I would rely on that writing pad to keep me tracking correctly. I'd jot notes as they flashed through my mind— if I could remember them long enough.

Hopefully, I'd collect enough of them to figure this mess out.

CHAPTER TWELVE
Monday Afternoon, August 27

Kurt Maxxon

The parking lot at Pepper's Diner was nearly empty which meant the lunch rush was over. As I pushed through the front door, I stopped to let my eyes adjust to the dim light inside, then scanned the room quickly. I didn't see Maggie, which eased my mind. Rebecca Pepper was at the cashier's station. She grabbed a menu, came around the counter, and led me to a window table. "I need to talk to you when it's convenient," I said.

"Let me take care of a couple of things," Rebecca said, "and then I'll come back to talk. In the meantime, I'll get you an iced tea and Tina will be your waitress."

Tina arrived with the iced tea and I ordered a Tuna Melt plate with french fries and cole slaw. As I watched the traffic flowing by on the street, I let my mind wander frequently coming back to questions I wanted to find answers to. Tina delivered my sandwich, and I nibbled at it and the French fries with about the same gusto as Christina does on her perpetual diet. I was about half way through the sandwich when Rebecca sat down with a steaming cup of coffee that smelled awfully good.

"What do you want to talk about?" Rebecca asked.

"I'm—Christina and I are worried about Maggie," I said.

"Maggie?" A deep frown wrinkled Rebecca's forehead.

I nodded. "Maggie showed up at the track yesterday during the race. And she was really coming on to me."

Rebecca's frown deepened. "There's not much I can do about her activities away from the diner," she said.

"Oh, I know that," I said. "We don't want to cause any

problems if nothing is amiss, but Christina is concerned about her mental condition. You mentioned Maggie left work early Friday morning to go to the track, and I'm wondering if she saw anything out of the ordinary."

"Maggie's always been a big race fan," Rebecca said. "She followed Melvyn Hightower, you know, rooted for him. She went to the races a lot."

"How involved was she with Melvyn Hightower?" I asked and watched another waitress move to sit down in a nearby booth. I wished we could move further away; Rebecca realized what was happening and lowered her voice.

"I have no idea, actually," Rebecca said, worry lines forming between her eyes. "Melvyn Hightower came in earlier Friday morning for breakfast, and Maggie was his waitress. Then Maggie asked to leave early so she could go to the track—I guess she did say something about watching Melvyn practice."

"I have a friend who is a private investigator," I told Rebecca. "I'd like to get her next to Maggie for a couple of days, you know, let her meet Maggie and get to know Maggie. After that we'll have a better idea if Maggie knows anything about Melvyn's death."

"You think Maggie is involved with Melvyn's murder?" Rebecca's face took on a look of panic.

"Maybe not involved, per se. However, I'd like to find out if she saw anyone or anything that might help solve who did it," I said.

"If your friend can waitress, it works out nicely," Rebecca said. "One of the girls didn't show up this morning. She just called to tell me she quit." Rebecca looked around the room. "I was lucky it turned out to be a slow day. Has your friend ever worked as a waitress?"

"As a matter of fact she has."

"Can she start tomorrow morning?"

"I'm pretty sure she can," I said. "She's waiting for me to call her."

"Call her and tell her to be here tomorrow morning at five-thirty—no later than five forty-five."

"You got it. Thank you for your help," I said.

"I'd say you've solved a problem for me," Rebecca said.

"At least in the short term."

When I walked outside I saw Maggie sitting on a park bench across the street, her eyes focused on my pickup truck. She didn't act like she saw me, and I hoped I could get into the truck and drive away without her coming to talk to me.

* * *

Lorianne Hightower

She drove to Mid-Town Service Center and left her car to have it serviced. She went into the waiting area and then slipped out a side door. She stood, surveying the area. Satisfied no one was watching her, she crossed the street, walked two blocks south and then went into the pharmacy on the opposite corner. She bought a bottle of water, paid for it at the cashier next to the side door, and went out the side door. Her timing was nearly perfect, as the city bus pulled around the corner and stopped at the curb. This was a time-stop for the bus and she had watched the time very carefully. She got on the bus and was just seated when the driver pulled away and merged into traffic.

Lorianne rode the bus for several minutes then got off and walked back the way it had just come for a block and sat down on the bus stop bench and watched traffic going by. A Centralia Police car went by, and she looked away before realizing the cop car didn't seem interested in her. After several minutes, she walked further up the street, crossed over and walked two blocks west to the Montpellier Hotel. She sighed slightly as the cool air engulfed her before she went to the pay phone section off the lobby and dialed a nearby Enterprise Rental Car office. "This is Mickey Watson," she said. "I'm at the Montpellier Hotel. Can you come get me? I reserved a pickup truck."

A few minutes later a white Ford F250 pickup pulled into the covered parking at the front door to the hotel. A young man with sun-bleached blond hair and handsome face and powder blue eyes came in and looked around. He walked toward Lorianne and asked, "Are you Mickey Watson?"

"I am," Lorianne said. She had scanned the man's entire physique as he approached. He had all the qualities that made a woman swoon. If she didn't have pressing business, Lorianne would have been more interested in getting to know the guy.

The man led her to the pickup and opened the passenger

door for her. He watched as she climbed up into the truck. "So your apartment was damaged by fire? Was that the one over on 29th Street?" the man said as he climbed into the driver's seat.

"Yes, it was a kitchen fire next door. You know, in the wall above our stoves," she said. "There wasn't a lot of fire damage, but water and smoke ruined a lot of my stuff. My ex is coming over to help me, and I need the truck to haul off the furniture and trash."

"This truck will haul a lot of stuff," he said. "Sorry we didn't have a smaller half-ton available."

"I just need it for today and tomorrow," Lorianne said. "Any truck will do."

At the rental office, Lorianne filled out the paperwork, all the time worrying that the driver's license she bought from the street guy and made hastily on equipment in a briefcase looked like a fake. If the blonde haired man noticed, he didn't mention it. "Since you're paying in cash, you'll have to accept all of our insurance options."

Lorianne signed the papers and drove to an Office Depot on the west side of town. She went in and bought a professional-sized document shredder. A clerk helped her load it into the truck.

One thing Lorianne liked about driving a pickup truck was that there were three large rearview mirrors. She was constantly scanning behind her, and she pulled into several convenience stores to make sure no cars followed her or parked to watch her. She eventually arrived at the Self-Store complex on the north side of town. She backed the truck up to where the bed was inside the room. Using 2 x 4 boards, she eased the heavy shredder out of the truck bed onto the floor. Against the back wall, there were eight banker's boxes full of papers. Lorianne climbed into the truck bed and reached to take out the overhead light in the room's ceiling fixture and installed an adapter that allowed the light bulb along with two electrical outlets. She plugged in an extension cord, let it dangle down, and climbed out of the truck bed.

She moved the pickup out of the room and parked it on the apron. Uncrating the shredder took more time than she planned for. She glanced at her watch and decided she wouldn't have time to do any shredding today. She had to be back at the salon for her three-forty-five appointment with Mrs. Harris, who wanted a rinse and trim. Tomorrow afternoon she would do some shredding and then return the pickup truck and rent a van to use to keep the cops off guard. She would haul the garbage bags full of shredded paper in the van to the common dumpsters at the edge of the local low income housing project.

She closed the storage room door and drove back to her salon. She could park the pickup at the far end of the strip mall where her salon was. No one would know who it belonged to.

I definitely have got to get rid of those papers! As soon as possible.

*   *   *

Kurt Maxxon

After my chat with Rebecca Pepper, I drove the few blocks to my store and climbed the stairs to my office. I carried my writing pad, threw it on the desk, and made four cups of coffee. When I sat down, I studied the notes I'd made. At the bottom of the page I had written:

Maggie Decker.

As I thought about it, I made additional notes under Maggie's name:

Was she at the track?

Rebecca Pepper had indicated she left work early to go to watch Melvyn practice. Did she really go to the track to watch Melvyn practice?

Where was she? In the grandstand? In the driver's lounge?

My mind drifted to Melvyn Hightower, and then Lorianne came to mind. I flipped back to the sheet with her name on it and scribbled:

Big Argument = About What? Other women? = Helen Tobias?

My cell phone jangled. I thought about ignoring it, but reluctantly dug it out of my pocket. The Caller ID said Restricted.

I punched the SEND button and listened.

"Mr. Maxxon, this is the Emergency Room at Hopewell Memorial Hospital. Christina Maxxon has been in an automobile accident and has been transported to our hospital and is about to go into emergency surgery."

"How badly is she hurt?"

"You need to come to the hospital, sir," the voice said. "As soon as you can get here!" I started the engine and pulled the gear shift into position. I had the presence of mind to punch Maurey's speed dial number and told him what had happened and that neither Christina nor I would be bringing the children from the daycare. Let Kimberly leave early and go get them. "Good, God," I remembered Maurey saying.

As I pushed through the emergency room doors, I took my glasses off to let my eyes adjust to the brightly lit fluorescent lights. I saw Jay Penworthy, the head of surgery at Hopewell Memorial Hospital, walking toward me. He reached for my hand. "They're still working on her," he said.

"How—how bad is she?"

"I can't make an assessment of that, Kurt." Jay put on his professional face. "I really didn't see her when she got here. Phil Schroeder is the surgeon. You know Phil. Don't you?"

I nodded that I did.

"He's as good as we've got," Jay said.

"I know. Does anyone know what happened?"

"I doubt we know too much. The fire department paramedics transmitted a couple of pictures of her as they found her in the car before they started peeling the roof off to get to her. I suspect the patrol people are still writing their report."

"Were—were her injuries life threatening?"

"I can't say, Kurt," Jay said. "Like I said, I don't want to make an assessment based on what little I know."

"I understand," I said, even though I didn't.

"Go on into the waiting room," Jay said, pointing toward the room in the corner. "I had the nurse brew a fresh pot of coffee for you. Christina will go the ERICU, probably for several hours after the surgery. If she's recovering satisfactorily, they may let you sneak in to see her in an hour or so. That'll be up to Phil."

I walked to the waiting room, poured a cup of coffee and sat down at the dinette table in the corner. I'd shoved my cell phone into my shirt pocket after calling Maurey. I made it to the hospital in seven and one-half minutes. I had not driven the speed limit during any portion of the trip. Where was Beau? We'd left Beau home alone with his doggy door locked. He's been home alone several times and nothing bad came of it. How long is this going to take?

A young woman drifted into the room and sat down in a

chair. She held her hands between her knees and worked a huge wad of tissue. Her eyes were red-rimmed and tears streaked down her cheeks. Her forehead was a mass of worry lines. She sniffled and blew her nose into the tissue. She stared fixedly at the door we both knew led to the surgical theaters. Husband, boyfriend, child? Who was she waiting for?

The woman looked around the room and saw me. I wondered how I could comfort her. Christina was the one good at that. Damn, Christina is in surgery, too. "He was just running—" The woman gulped and swiped at tears in her eyes. "He was just running across the room—" She burst out sobbing. Fortunately, a young man charged through the ER doors and rushed to embrace the woman. Then the tears flowed freely as she told the boy's father how the little boy had tripped and fallen against the coffee table. There was a bad cut, a lot of blood, and terror as she drove to the hospital.

I remembered the time when Little Kurt fell down the stairs of a school bus and was rushed to the hospital. I had been out with my squadron mates partying late into the night. When our neighbor found me asleep in my pickup truck in the driveway, she immediately took me to the hospital where I found Vicki ready to collapse from worry about me and relief that Little Kurt was going to be okay. That was the day I quit drinking alcohol.

I sat sipping coffee, happy that the young couple had each other for support. When the doctor came in to talk to them, I tried not to pay attention, but it was impossible not to overhear. "There's no fracture of the skull, just a rather bad cut, which we've stapled up. There's a concussion, so we're going to keep him overnight. I'm sure he'll be alright tomorrow morning."

How is Christina doing? Lord, please do what you can for her.

I gazed at the muted TV—a game show… my eyes blurred the picture. Lord, I need Christina. I don't want to lose her.

In the minutes, hours, days and months after Vicki, my wife of thirty-three years, passed away from ovarian cancer there was a constant aura of support hovering around me in the presence of Christina Zouhn. She took me by the elbow and guided me from the room where Vicki had taken her last breath, down the hall to a table in the cafeteria. She got me a cup of coffee. She said comforting words. When our minister arrived, she took him to Vicki's room. When the people from the funeral home arrived, Christina took charge of the operation. She led me out of the hospital and took me to her house. She cooked supper for me. Then she drove me to my house and made the place livable enough for me to get through the night.

Christina was a veteran of losing a loved one. Her husband, Bill, had passed away two years before. Vicki had been at Christina's side during that entire trauma. Vicki had comforted Christina. Vicki had helped Christina deal with the aftermath of the loss.

The next morning Christina arrived to fix breakfast. Then she helped me start dealing with the many tasks I had to do to take Vicki's name off deeds, car titles, pension plans, retirement funds, credit cards, stocks, bonds, and bank accounts. She made phone calls for me, since I hate to talk on the phone when I'm upset. She carefully noted exactly what I had to do with each entity—Death Certificate and a …. Every entity wanted different documents. Every document had to be signed in a certain way. Some had to be notarized. Some had to have a green Medallion stamp. Without Christina's help, I would never have gotten through it so smoothly and quickly.

Vicki had passed away in November. I hadn't been racing for several months at the end of the 2002 season. Over the winter I thought long and hard about quitting. It wouldn't be any fun anymore—not without Vicki. When the Masonville race came around the last weekend of May 2003, I was thinking more and more about getting back on the track. Normally, during the off season, I made a deal with Riverside Flats International Speedway, the Centralia racetrack, which was really my home track, to run practice laps every week. But in the wake of losing Vicki, I hadn't been on the track for eight months.

Christina and Maurey Kennedy had hovered nearby—not pushing, but always letting me know they were there—ready to go racing again. Maurey had all three of my engines ready to go. He had two cars ready to go. So in the middle of April, I went to Centralia track and tried to practice. I crashed into the wall during the third lap. Nothing too bad—just scraped the hell out of the right side of the car. Christina soothed my wounded pride. Maurey downplayed the damage and moved me into our second car while he pounded out the first one.

Between the ministrations of Christina and the encouragement of Maurey I regained some level of confidence. By the time the Masonville race came around, I ran it with a little trepidation, but finished the race in seventeenth place. That was a major victory for me. Christina and Maurey threw a mini victory party at Kin Folks place in Naomi. I felt like a winner.

Over the next four years Christina had been by my side a lot. She didn't travel to every race, but she made it to more than half of them. She was the reason I had adopted Beau. She was the reason I did a lot of things. We were so close, yet living apart.

When we married a couple of years ago, many friends, neighbors and relatives on both sides said, "God, it took you two long enough!" Since our marriage, we have been inseparable. Christina did her volunteer work with the animal shelter north of town. I did my thing with the auto parts store, Maurey's garage, and racing. Every night we came together at home, Christina in her recliner with me next to her in mine.

My eyes were filling with tears, threatening to spill down my cheeks.

What would life be like without Christina?

Don't go there Maxxon!

For God's sake, don't think about that.

I almost missed Phil Schroeder's approach. He shook my hand. His face was very somber. He walked to the coffee pot and filled a cup then came to sit across from me at the table. "She's resting well," he said, studying his coffee. "She was banged up pretty badly. We fixed the clavicle and the shoulder. The humerus needed a couple of pins because of a compound fracture. She'll need some follow up surgery to get them fixed right. There were two broken ribs, and one of them punctured her left lung. But we got it re-inflated, and it appears to have sealed up very nicely. We'll have to watch it closely, though. The left hip should heal without any trouble. But, again, we'll have to watch it, too. There appears to be some nerve damage to the thoracic vertebrae, probably where the ribs were broken, that we need to watch and it will need some follow-up therapy."

"Is she in any danger?" I asked.

Phil sipped the coffee. "This stuff is actually fresh," he said, holding his cup up. "Is this because Kurt Maxxon is a guest of our waiting room?" He smiled. "I'm reasonably sure Christina will survive this. It's just going to take some time," Phil said. "She'll need therapy."

I heaved a grateful sigh of relief. Thank you, Big Guy. I remembered the crashes I'd had on the track and the many and varied therapies after. "I imagine it will be extensive," I said.

"We'll send her directly from this hospital to a rehab facility. I'd recommend Our Lady of Grace over on Fitzgerald Boulevard. It's the best in town."

"Then that's where she goes," I said.

"We'll have to see if they have an opening," Jay Penworthy said from the coffee pot. Neither Phil nor I had seen him come into the room. "They only maintain forty-five beds, and they very often have a waiting list."

"Hell, Jay, if you can't get Christina Maxxon into Grace, you'll lose my vote for administrator of the year," Phil said, and let a wide grin spread over his face.

"If they don't have a bed available when we discharge Christina," Jay said, "we'll have a backup plan. That's all I'm saying. We can transfer her to Madonna for a week or so, if we have to, then move her to Grace. But, it would be best to move her straight to Grace."

"How long will she be there?" I asked.

Phil raised his hands, palms up. "I'd say a week, maybe ten days. That's because I know Christina—her tenacity. It will depend on how damaged the nerves are. It's in an area where many people become paralyzed, but the electrical activity we see tends to indicate it won't be that bad. We're watching it."

I nodded acceptance. "Just so she's getting the best treatment available," I said.

"We'll make sure of that, Colonel," Jay said.

"The impact must have been horrific," I said.

"Yes, it was," Phil said. He rolled his lips into a stupid grin and shrugged. "That driver's compartment looked like something you could do to Nikki by hitting the inside wall. I saw a photo of it before they peeled the roof off."

"Too bad she didn't have a crash cage like I have in

Nikki," I said.

"That probably would've helped a whole lot," Jay said. Being an ex-race driver, he had some experience with crash cages.

Phil Schroeder emptied his cup and looked at the pot. Then he wagged his head. "I don't need any more caffeine today."

"I do," I said as I stood and went to the coffee pot.

Phil glanced at the clock on the wall. "With any luck, I may get home in time for a hot supper for a change."

"That would be a change," Jay said.

"How soon before I can see her?" I asked.

"Give it another hour, and then we'll let you sneak in for a peek. Just a minute or so. Christina will be out of it all night. We're dripping her with a sedative to help her body deal with the trauma. After you've seen her you might as well go on home and get some sleep. Do you need something to help you sleep?"

"I never take any of that stuff," I said.

"Just for the sake of it all," Jay said, "I'll have my nurse bring you a sample package of a sleep aid. If you can't get to sleep, try it."

We shook hands all around.

Phil walked toward the door. "I'll tell the nurses to let you in to see her in about an hour. We had to put her down pretty deep and now, like I said, we're dripping a strong sedative."

Jay and I watched Phil walk out of the room. "We'll take good care of Christina, Colonel," Jay said.

Jay gave up racing two years ago and retired his car—the number 16A Ford Thunderbird. Jay's father, Henry B. Penworthy, M.D. had founded a racing family that was as near to legendary in the SRVSCRA as you can get. Henry raced his old number 16 Ford Fairlane to relieve the stress of being a doctor. When twin sons were born, Jay and Ray, old doc Penworthy raised them the racing world. Both sons followed in their father's footsteps and became medical doctors as well as racecar drivers. Jay had gone on to become a well respected surgeon. Jay and I chatted over coffee until the PA system summoned him to his office. He'd only been gone a few minutes when a nurse came through the surgery door. "Colonel Maxxon," she said. "I'll show you where Christina is; you can stay about five minutes. We're checking her vitals every few minutes."

I followed the woman down a hall that I knew went past the six surgical theaters in the hospital, through a set of double doors into the ERICU. The room was divided by moving curtains and, since visitors were kept to a minimum, most of the recovery rooms were virtually wide open with the resident in full view of the central nursing station. Christina was in the first room. She had tubes hooked to arms, her nose and one that penetrated her left rib cage. I could see a bruise forming on her left temple area. I hoped she wasn't in pain. Then, for the umpteenth time, I remembered the many times I'd been in the same position, and I didn't remember ever having any pain.

Her breathing was slow and regular. She looked so peaceful—so beautifully peaceful. I was glad there were no lacerations or contusions to her beautiful face. I looked straight up. Thank you, Big Guy. I reached for her hand, and leaned down close to her ear, remembering just before Vicki passed, the nurse had said, "She can still hear you." I swallowed hard, because I wanted my voice to be strong, clear and full of optimism. I said, "My love, my wonderful love, come back to me. Please come back to me. Soon."

I left the ICU unit to go home and take care of Beau. A nurse came up to me and handed me a flat box of sleep aid pills. I thanked her and walked toward the door. I was so deep in thought I nearly walked into Nick Boynton. He'd been waiting for me in the main lobby.

"How's she doing?" he asked.

"Pretty well," I said.

"You need anything?" He asked.

"Not really," I said. "Just would like to know how the accident happened—all the details."

"You going home?"

"Yes."

"I'll have one of our people run a copy of the accident report by your house as soon as it's officially on file. It might answer some of your questions. That work for you?"

"That'll work for me."

"Oh, by the way," Nick said. "The time of death you asked me about. Melvyn died at eleven twenty-two."

"That means Jason Tobias absolutely won't work," I said.

Nick eyed me for a long moment, then shrugged and said, "Tell me about it." He turned and started to walk away then turned back to me. "We still haven't ruled out a hired gun."

"Okay, but the guy who called me didn't sound like a hired gun. That tirade was strictly personal. He was angry with Melvyn for some reason."

*   *   *

Beau was very happy to see me. He dashed down the hall to get his favorite chewy toy and then dashed back, dropped it at my feet and ran toward his locked doggie door. "It's been a long day," I said, feeling guilty for not calling the lady next door to unlock his door. "Are your teeth floating?"

Beau barked urgently and rushed through the door as soon as I unlocked it, and disappeared. I checked his food bowl as I refilled his water bowl. He hadn't eaten much, if any of the food. I went to the bathroom and washed up. I noticed my face looked a lot older than I remembered from my morning shave. I returned to the kitchen and looked in the refrigerator. Beau banged back into the kitchen and stood up against my leg. "You want me to call for a pizza delivery?"

I heard a growl that sounded like a definite "Yeah!"

I turned on the TV news, muted it, and sat down in my recliner. I was reaching for the phone when they showed the crash scene and what was probably the fire department digging Christina out of one of the cars. I couldn't tell for sure, the cameraman was a half block away. I watched the entire sound bite with interest, trying to analyze every movement by the fire personnel, and straining to see the person they were working on.

I would stay up to watch it again at ten o'clock—after I'd watched it as often as possible on the local all-news channel. I called the pizza shop a few blocks away and, in forty-five minutes, Beau and I were munching on our favorite five-meat double cheese pizza. As I started on my fourth slice, I noticed Beau was looking for Christina. What're you doing to yourself, Maxxon? Was I celebrating the fact that Christina was out of pocket and couldn't protect my diet? You need to eat. Beau jumped up on Christina's chair and looked at me.

"Mom's in the hospital," I told him. "She's hurt pretty bad and won't be coming home for a while. You and I are going to have to get by without her." My voice quivered. Beau tilted his head and sat staring at me. He jumped in my lap and laid his head on my shoulder, looking out through the window. It was as close to a hug as he'd ever given me.

When I muted the TV set, it suddenly struck me how alone I was. The house phone rang. It was Hazel Kennedy.

"What's the latest on Christina?" she asked.

I told her all that I'd been told by the surgeon, that Christina was going to be sedated for a while, and they were going to transfer her directly to a rehab hospital.

"Maurey is very upset about it all," Hazel said. "He wants to go to the hospital. I called for you at the hospital, but they said you'd left."

"No sense sitting at the hospital tonight," I said.

"Will you let us know how she is tomorrow morning?"

"I will do that."

CHAPTER THIRTEEN
Monday Night, August 27

Kurt Maxxon

I decided to call my daughter, Vanessa, first since I knew she was the least emotionally attached to Christina. She would give me a chance to practice keeping my composure. When I dialed the number, a recording told me I had reached a disconnected number. Then I remembered an email in the last few weeks with a new phone number. I booted up my computer and looked for the email. When Vanessa answered, I said, "You're back in North Carolina again."

"You should know what it's like to be a career Marine," Vanessa said, and I could tell from her voice she was smiling. She was born while I was in the Marine Corps stationed at Cherry Point Marine Air Station in North Carolina. Although we moved several times, when it came time for her to choose a life-mate, we were back at Cherry Point. Vanessa graduated high school and then started college. Eventually she married Brian Harrington, a Captain in the USMC cargo services and moved to Southern California when Brian's squadron of C-130 Hercules cargo planes was transferred to Okinawa for thirteen months. When they came back stateside, they were to be stationed at El Toro Marine Air Station in Tustin, California. Vanessa decided to move to Southern California to live while Brian was overseas.

While living in Santa Ana, Vanessa had our grand-daughter, Ashley Jane. Vicki and I flew out to see our first grandchild and spent two weeks getting to know her. Our grandson, Tyler Kurt, was born three years later while Brian was stationed at Jacksonville, Florida.

I told Vanessa about Christina's accident.

"Good Lord," Vanessa said before I finished. "Is she okay?"

"She's banged up pretty bad, but the doctors are saying she'll live."

"When you need me," Vanessa said, "I can fly over anytime. I've got several weeks of leave time built up. You want me to call Little Kurt?"

"I'd appreciate that," I said. "I don't know if I have Little Kurt's latest phone number." All I remembered was that he had called and left a voice mail message that he was going on embassy duty in Oslo, Norway. He'd been in the Marine Corps sixteen years now.

Where in the world has the time gone?

Next I called Christina's son, Mason Lamont Zouhn. He was a math instructor at the Western Wyoming Community College, which was in either Rock Springs or Green River, Wyoming—I'd been through both towns while driving on I-80, but they both seemed like a blur to my mind. When I told him about the accident, he asked, "Is she going to live?"

"Yes, we think so," I said.

"She's a tough old broad," he said. I frowned, although I knew Mason usually said what he was thinking. "Mercy and I will run over on the weekend for a few days. The fall quarter doesn't start for another month. It'll give Mom a chance to meet Mercedes."

Mason and Mercedes had married in Las Vegas during the New Years break over a year ago. Christina had tried to plan a trip to meet Mercedes, but so far it hadn't been worked out. Mercedes was a top executive with a large coal mining company in southwestern Wyoming and northeastern Utah and traveled all the time.

"Is Tabby coming, too?" Mason asked.

"I'll be calling her in a minute, so I don't know."

"It'd be nice if both Mom and Tabby could meet Mercy," Mason said.

I hung up from Mason and walked to the kitchen. I looked under the sink and in the pantry. If there had been a bottle of Scotch—any booze at all—I might have broken down and had a drink. But that would probably lead to a second one, and then to a third one, and so on. You don't need that right now, Maxxon.

I dialed Christina's daughter. Tabetha Faye Downing was a social worker in Pueblo, Colorado. "I'll drive over since I want plenty of room for Isabella and the boys," she said. "I'll wait a couple of days and then drive down so I can help Mom when she gets out of the hospital."

"Your mom is going straight to a rehab facility from the hospital," I said.

"That's okay," Tabetha said, undeterred. "I'll plan on driving on Friday and stay over in Wichita on my way. I can help Mom adjust to the rehab place. I still have seven weeks left on my maternity leave."

"Okay. You and the kids can stay here," I said. "Beau will love having the boys to play with."

Tabetha gave birth to Isabella eleven weeks ago. Christina was still aglow that Tabby and Greg now had a daughter after two sons, Brandon James and Anthony Wayne. Christina and I had made a trip to Pueblo to see our new granddaughter.

Christina said, "I'm going to fly out and help Tabby with the new baby."

"I'll go with you. In fact, I'll fly you there and back," I said.

I can still picture Christina's look, her head cocked to the left. "That's right, you are a pilot," she said.

"I am," I said. "I can rent a plane at the Centralia Airport. We can leave whenever we want to. We don't have to worry about taking our shoes off to get through security. We don't have to worry about what's in our suitcases as snoopy TSA people rummage through them. We just pack, drive to the airplane, climb in and leave. No hassle."

"Don't you have to do a flight plan, or something like that?"

"Yes. But you can do a flight plan in ten minutes, even after you take off. I'll chart the course and have everything ready to give them before we leave—except the exact headings."

"You can't do that before we go to the airport?"

"I won't know what the winds aloft are until a few minutes before we depart. I know how to do this—trust me."

"What kind of airplane can you get?" Christina asked.

"Randy has a Beechcraft King Air that I like. I've flown it several times over the years."

"Is it a jet?" Christina had asked.

"No. It's a twin turboprop, but it's fast enough for our trip. It's very comfortable."

"Let's do it," Christina had said. And so, I took Christina up for her first flight with me as the pilot. At first, she was a little tense as she listened to my radio transmissions with ground control and then the tower. She listened as I talked to the regional control centers while we winged our way to Colorado. She hung on every word as I called the Pueblo tower for instructions on entering their airspace and their landing pattern at Pueblo Memorial Airport.

After we landed and I taxied to the ramp at the local fixed-base operator, Christina said, "I'm impressed, Colonel Maxxon. Do you have any idea how many times you've landed an airplane?"

"I've never counted," I said. I'd never thought about it before, and certainly hadn't done the calculations. "I'll give you an estimate when we get home."

Every takeoff was an adventure—an adventure to somewhere. Every takeoff led to a landing. It was the landings that made a pilot successful.

"Every landing is a controlled crash" the instructor who taught the first courses in my aviation training program had said. "If you walk away from that crash, able to take off again, you just made a successful landing."

Made sense forty years ago and still made sense today.

*　　*　　*

We spent nine days in Pueblo. Helping Tabetha with Isabella sent Christina into seventh-heaven, where she remained for the nine days. Edwin Jamison had asked Christina to help me get familiar with the internet, especially e-mail, so he could communicate with me while I was gone. In two intense sessions, Christina gave me enough to make me reasonably proficient with electronic communications. I'm not as terrified of e-mails now.

On the flight back from Pueblo, I chose to fly around a low-pressure trough to avoid the turbulence we probably would have experienced, which lengthened our trip by over an hour. But, once again, we arrived and made a successful landing which we walked away from. About mid-way back, Christina said, "I want to learn to fly. Can you teach me?"

"No!"

"Why not?"

"I don't have an Instructor's Tag." I wanted to avoid confessing that I didn't have the patience, but more importantly, she was my wife. "Just talk to Randy," I said. He'll take care of you. You'll have to go get a medical exam—a Pilot's Medical Certificate."

Christina told all her friends and associates about the trip, mostly about the beautiful little girl named Isabella, but also how, "My husband flew us out and back. That is the way to fly."

The important point about it all was that Christina had shed her initial fear of flying in small airplanes and her natural fear of flying with me as the pilot. Those were major milestones in our relationship.

After we got back home, Christina brought the calculator to the kitchen table one night and said, "Let's estimate how many landings you've survived."

"I've obviously survived them all," I said and accepted the challenge. "If you take twenty-six years of flying in the Marine Corps, flying on average three days a week," I punched numbers on the calculator, "twenty-six years times fifty-two weeks per year times three flights per week, that gives you four thousand and fifty-six flights," I said. "Since I retired from the Corps, I've flown about thirty days a year, so fifteen years times thirty equals four hundred and fifty flights, and you wind up with a grand total of about forty-five hundred flights—takeoffs and landings."

"That's why you do them so well," Christina said.

"No. I do them well, because I don't like the results of not doing them well."

*   *   *

The doorbell jerked me awake. I opened the door to see Alisa Sharpe standing on the porch.

"You really are Kurt Maxxon," she said.

"Yes, I really am Kurt Maxxon," I answered, feeling terribly guilty about forgetting she was coming. With all that happened today, I'd spaced out about our plan.

I led Alisa into the living room and watched as Beau trotted in from the bedroom, where he had gone to bed. Beau loved Alisa because she spoiled him worse than any other human being he knew. She picked him up and began scratching his ears.

Alisa looked around. Then it struck me. "Christina is in the hospital," I said.

Alisa's eyebrows rose. "Why?"

"She was in a car accident this afternoon, and she had to have surgery."

"That's terrible," Alisa said, a frown creasing her forehead. "Is she going to be okay? You could have canceled this gig."

"I just forgot about it, what with the events of the day. The doctors think she's going to be okay. She's still in ICU."

"You still want me to go to work at Pepper's tomorrow morning?" Alisa asked.

"Yes. We need to find out how Maggie Decker was involved with Melvyn Hightower," I said. "We also need to know if Maggie actually was at the racetrack Friday morning; if she was, did she see anyone or anything suspicious. I'd be particularly interested in knowing the descriptions or names, and if possible, of any other people at the track."

"I need to go check into the hotel," Alisa said and stood. "I need to get some sleep. You told me I had to be at work at five-thirty, so I'll have to get up at four o'clock to be ready for work at five-thirty." Beau wasn't happy about Alisa abandoning his ears. He curled up in Christina's chair, resting his head on his front paws, rolling his eyes and wagging his tail. "Beau," Alisa cooed. "I'll see you tomorrow. You be a good boy until then."

*   *   *

Lorianne Hightower

She felt exhausted. After the sun went down, she had loaded the remaining boxes of records from her salon basement into the pickup truck and made her way to the storage room. She had planned to spend an hour or so shredding—she was anxious to get started. But lugging the boxes up the stairs of her salon and unloading them into the shed had exhausted her. She plugged the shredder into the overhead outlet and opened a box. How long it this going to take?

Standing in front of the pile of boxes, Lorianne did a quick mental calculation. If each of the sixteen boxes holds four thousand pages, that meant there were … what, sixty-four thousand pages to be shredded.

Good Lord, if the cops are watching me, how do I cover this? I've probably only got a week or so before they start really leaning on me.

She held her watch up and tilted it in the dim light so she could read it. One o'clock. One part of her brain said, "Go home and get some sleep. Do the shredding tomorrow night." Another part of her brain said, "You've got to get rid of this stuff. The cops are watching you. Do some of it now."

She dragged one of the boxes next to the shredder and sliced it open. She glanced at the roll up door and worried about it being full open, so she lowered it to where there was a one-foot opening. She turned the shredder on and was startled by how noisy it was. The little shredder she had in their house wasn't too loud, but this big hog was a roar. She reached for a handful of pages. The instructions recommended you shred twenty sheets at a time. How the hell do you know how thick twenty pages are?

If there were sixty-four thousand sheets—good lord, this was going to take—she stopped to do math, then gave up. Oh, hell, it was going to take hundreds of hours. Through experimentation, she finally had a pretty good idea of how thick twenty pages were, and got into a rhythm. The roar of the shredder gave her a headache. She shut it off to take a rest. "Go home! Get some sleep," one voice in her head said. "Keep going—" Suddenly she realized someone was banging on the rollup door. Oh Christ—no, no, no.

She stood still for several moments, then moved to raise the door. Standing outside was a security guard, his car idling just behind her pickup truck. He was a tall, bulky African American, with bushy eyebrows and a heavy mustache; he eyed the shredder and the stack of boxes. "Ma'am," he said. "I hate to bother you, but I heard you in there. It's awfully late."

Lori had chosen this storage facility, like the others, because it was outside the residential areas so there wouldn't be nosey neighbors who might see her and her mules transacting business. Being away from neighbors also meant no complaints about late night noise. She hadn't thought about security people, even though each storage company advertised they had it.

"I just lost track of time," she said. "I'm going to do this shredding during the day, but I got out here and wanted to try it. Is the noise bothering anyone?"

"No ma'am," the guard said. "I was just checking the buildings and heard you."

Lori looked at her watch. Two ten. "I'm bushed anyway. I need to get home and get some sleep."

"That's good, Ma'am," the guard said. "This ain't the best neighborhood for a woman to be out in alone at this hour."

That was something Lori hadn't thought about. "Yes, well, thank you for checking on me. I'll be leaving now."

As she sat waiting for the electric gate to grind open, Lori saw the security guard park in front of the office and turn on the overhead light in his SUV. He was writing something, probably a report. He hadn't asked her name. It would take a lot of digging to find out the name of the tall woman who rented unit number 429. At least she hoped it would. But, dammit, what if he wrote down the license number off the pickup truck. And the cops went to Enterprise. How long would it take an expert to determine that the driver's license she used was a forgery of her real driver's license with a phony name on it?

And he could tie her to this storage room if they came looking before she could shred all the evidence. Dammit. Dammit.

*　　*　　*

Kurt Maxxon

I'd stayed up to watch the ten o'clock news to see the collision site again. Since I'd seen it on the six o'clock news on CBS, I punched in the ABC affiliate for this second viewing and was rewarded with a different view, a little closer in. I recognized one of the EMTs working the scene and decided I would talk to her to see what she remembered about the accident and the car. Christina's car was a one-year-old Lincoln MKX. It seemed sturdy enough. But, in accidents, the forces sometimes were more than the body and frame could deal with. I needed to run by and look at the remains of Christina's car. Our insurance agent would probably be calling me about it.

The doorbell rang again. I worried about who could be calling at this time of night, and was relieved to see it was a uniformed Centralia Police officer. He shook my hand and said. "I've rooted for you for a long time, Kurt. But I switched to Davy's boy last year."

"Drew is an excellent driver," I said.

The cop handed me a large white envelope. I remembered Nick had promised to have a copy of the Accident Report run by my house. I thanked the cop and went back to my recliner. Beau jumped up beside me and snuggled in. I tore the envelope open and scanned the report. Vehicle #1 was a Volvo tractor with a fifty foot box; Vehicle #2 was a red Chevrolet Impala; Vehicle #3 was a white Lincoln MKX. The driver of vehicle #1 had failed to see a stop sign and had T-boned vehicle #2 going west and then vehicle #2 struck vehicle #3 nearly head on. Even at speeds as low as thirty-five to forty miles per hour, accidents like the one described could be deadly. Two lines caught my eye. The first one read the driver of the Volvo Truck was cited for Negligent Driving; the second read driver of red impala was not wearing a seat belt. My mind went on high-alert.

In all the confusion, and then the worry about Christina, I hadn't even thought about the other people involved in the accident. On the news broadcast I'd just watched, I saw a man pacing around the scene and the reporter identified him as the driver of the truck. So the truck driver had survived, apparently unharmed. But what about the driver of the Red Impala?

I phoned the hospital. No one there knew anything about the other driver. "They probably were transported to Municipal Hospital."

I called Municipal Hospital.

"What is the patient's name?"

"I don't know their name. My wife was in the same accident, but she was taken to Hopewell Memorial."

"Sir, we see twelve, fifteen accident victims a day. If you don't know the victim's name, we can't begin to help you."

"I'm sorry," I said and hung up.

Then I remembered the names and addresses were on the Accident Report. Dumb-dumb.

I called Municipal Hospital back. Fortunately, I got a different voice that sounded older than the young female voice of ten minutes before. "This is Kurt Maxxon," I said—

"The race driver?"

"Yes, ma'am."

"How can I help you, Colonel Maxxon?"

Ah, a race fan. "I wanted to check on the condition of, uh," I squinted at the writing on the report, "Pamela Williamson."

I heard keys clicking on a keyboard. "Are you related to Mrs. Williamson, Kurt?" the voice asked me.

"No," I said. "It's just that my wife, Christina, was in the same accident and I was curious."

"Where is Christina?"

"She's at Hopewell Memorial," I said.

"Is she okay?"

"Yes, she's doing fine. They did surgery this afternoon, and they're confident she'll be okay. I noticed on the Accident Report that Mrs. Williamson was not wearing a seat belt."

"A seat belt might have saved her," the voice said. "Other than that, I can't give you any more information. I'm sorry."

"Thank you, anyway," I said and hung up.

But ... she had revealed all I needed to know. I sat quietly, sadness overtaking me. Life is so short. "Dear Lord, please help the Williamson family."

Beau jumped down and walked down the hall. I knew I should follow him and force myself to go to bed. At least two of the three people in the accident had survived it. The most important one to me is Christina. And she's still alive.

I looked toward the ceiling. Thank you, Big Guy.

I turned on a local twenty-four hour news/weather channel and muted it. Maybe they would cover the wreck again. I leaned the recliner back, hoping to fall asleep. When I noticed the lamp light was bothering me, I turned it off and sat with the room lit by the pale, flickering blue glow of the television screen. Occasionally, I read the news banner scrolling across the bottom of the screen. Pretty boring stuff—but not boring enough to make me fall asleep.

I looked at Christina's empty recliner and let the many wonderful memories we'd had since we started sharing one house flit through my mind. In the three short years, there were some funny ones too—the funniest memory being from the period while we were merging our two homes together. We had decided to live in my house and keep Christina's house as a rental unit. Then my washer gave up the ghost. We decided to buy a new front loader washing machine and matching dryer. Front loader washing machines intrigued my engineering curiosity. Several months later I went into the laundry area and saw the washing machine running. As I looked at it, the machine seemed to be doing things it had never done before. I leaned down and looked into it. It was pumping water and spinning wildly, but contained no clothes. I walked to the living room where Christina was sitting in her recliner, and said, "Why are you washing an empty load of laundry?"

I still remember her blank look, then her body heaving a chuckle. "My dear," she said between chuckles, "the washing machine … is in the self cleaning mode."

I never got sucked into that trap again.

I went back to focusing on the glowing, flickering TV screen. The news did cover the collision site with yet another view, however, further away and more generic than the other two stations. I let my mind wander again. But nothing came.

I watched the news as it cycled through the local, national, and the international news. I wondered what was on the other channels, but I sat transfixed—the deer in the headlights. I was hoping sleep would overcome me, like it had dozens of times before while watching the boob tube.

And yet, I sat wide awake. Maybe I should try one of the sleeping pills the doctor gave me.

Memories of Christina flooded my mind. Memories from when we were merely close friends, then from when we were very close friends, then from our marriage, and all the wonderful benefits that had brought.

What would I do without Christina?

I didn't even want to consider that question. I went to the kitchen and took one of the sleeping pills.

I was wide awake and just sitting reminiscing about life with Christina, so I decided to go sit at the kitchen dinette and rummage through my notes. I'd left the writing pad on the table when I came home earlier.

I scanned over the notes, not letting anything sink in until I got to the name:

MAGGIE DECKER

Was she at the track? = Rebecca Pepper had said she left

work early to go to the track = Where was she? = In the grandstand? = In the driver's lounge?

"Did Maggie have sex with Melvyn?" It's only supposition right now!

I studied that notation for a long time, and then underlined it.

Who or what did she see? If Maggie was in the grandstand watching Melvyn run practice laps, was she paying attention to other people? Were any other people even around?

If she was there mainly for sex, she probably would go to the driver's lounge? Had she and Melvyn had sex and that was why he was showering?

Then it struck me: Was Maggie offering me sex Sunday? At breakfast? At the track?

I wondered if this whole mess would involve simple psychology.

I was reaching for a red pencil I keep in the napkin basket on the table when I saw the annotation: find the note sheets i wrote after talking to the man on the phone Friday night.

Before I got up, I circled several items on my writing pad with the red pencil, and next to each circle I wrote: does not make sense.

I went to my desk in the third bedroom and looked for the note sheets I'd made Friday night. They were on top of the pile.

I read through the notes.

"Maxxon," I remembered the voice saying. His voice was distorted.

I wrote down voice distorted = towel??

Traffic noise in the background.

He knew I had found Melvyn's body = "I know who you are" I wrote.

"Name, rank and serial number," = man used that term.

"I know you, but you don't know me."

I'd drawn a blank on what he'd said exactly, but I understood he was warning me to leave the case alone. I also understood he said he had done Melvyn Hightower, so doing me wouldn't bother him. The bravado of a killer who has just killed and kind of enjoyed it.

I sat a long time pondering the adjectives he used for

Melvyn—which I'd written down on my tablet.

Double dealing was one. Lying, cheating, stealing were the others, I thought. That was a term I'd heard used often by others.

I asked how Melvyn had cheated him.

The Road & Track magazine I'd written the phone number on was just under the notes. I glanced at it.

I remembered telling Nick about his use of the terms name, rank, and serial number. The way he used it made me think he might have been in the military when they still used serial numbers as an ID number rather than Social Security numbers.

Beau came in and jumped up on my lap. That brought me back to reality. I cradled Beau in my left arm and carried the notes to the kitchen, picked up the writing tablet and walked to my recliner. The TV set was filling the room with flickering blue toned light. I put Beau in Christina's chair, then sat down and levered the chair back to nearly flat. I propped the writing tablet on my legs and studied the notes … until … they … blurred ….

CHAPTER FOURTEEN
Tuesday Morning, August 28

Kurt Maxxon

Beau bounced up onto my lap and jolted me awake at 3:45 AM. I realized I'd fallen asleep in my recliner again. "Hey, Beau," I said. "I didn't let you out before beddy bye, huh?" I struggled to my feet and led Beau to his doggy door.

As I was stripping down to my skivvies, Beau came trotting into the bedroom and jumped up on the bed. He curled and lay down next to Christina's pillow. I didn't have the heart to shoo him off the bed so I snuggled into my side. For the next hour I tossed and turned, maybe falling asleep for a few minutes at a time. Eventually, I came wide awake and knew I wasn't going to get any more sleep. I got out of bed and went to the kitchen to set the coffee pot to perking.

A quick shower helped wake me up a little more. Beau was still asleep. After I dressed, I went to Beau's bed and physically lifted him out of his nest. "Come on, Beau. Dad's got to go see how Mom's doing."

Beau growled and apparently realized the futility of fighting me. He followed me to his doggy door and went out. I filled his bowl with fresh water, and added some food to his dish. I dug out my big old thermos bottle and, when the coffee finished perking, I filled it. Beau came back in, sauntered into the living room, jumped up on Christina's chair, made a couple of circles, and then settled in. I locked Beau's doggy-door and went out through the garage to get in my truck. I felt slightly guilty about not phoning to check on Christina's condition the night before.

I glanced at my watch: five-ten. Alisa was probably on her

way to Pepper's Diner. I climbed into my truck and drove to the hospital.

*   *   *

Alisa Sharpe: Very Early Morning

Alisa Sharpe dug her mini-recorder from her purse, a special police-issue woman's style, that allowed her to carry several things, including handcuffs, a weapon, and extra ammunition. She'd parked her car two blocks away, since not too many waitresses drive BMW 330ci cars. She glanced at her wristwatch. She had more than twenty minutes before she had to report for work. To make sure the mini-recorder was operating; she pressed the start/record button, and watched the small lights blinking. Satisfied it was working, she spoke into the small microphone:

"Alisa Sharpe reporting, regarding the homicide of Melvyn Hightower at Centralia Race Track. It is Tuesday, August twenty-eight, at five-thirty A.M. I am just about to arrive for work at Pepper's Diner. I parked my car two blocks away and am walking to the diner."

She clicked the mini-recorder off and stuffed it into one of the large pockets of the beige uniform she bought last night, along with a small writing pad and two pens. She checked her eyes in the rearview mirror; she was always conscious of her glass eye. Satisfied, she got out of the car and walked toward the diner. The lights on Pepper's Diner sign came on as she approached.

"Don't blow this assignment," her brain said quietly as she tried to remember the tasks from the last time she worked as a waitress over eight years ago.

*   *   *

Maggie Decker

Maggie sat on the edge of the bed, trying to get her eyes to track together. She glanced at the alarm clock. "Damn," she muttered, as she tried to stand, but her head ached and pain shot down her spine. "Dammit, I'm going to be late for work, again."

She sat back down and looked around the room. Her uniform dress was lying on the back of the easy chair. She tried to stand up again, and this time suffered through the pain and kept standing. On the floor at the foot of the bed she saw a pair of feet, toes pointing straight up. She moved tentatively to the foot of the bed on her way to the bathroom.

Berry Atwater was asleep on the floor, flat on his back, naked as a jaybird. Maggie padded to the bathroom. She needed to hurry. Rebecca Pepper was constantly harping about getting to work on time. She doesn't open until six. The other girls can get the coffee going and the place ready. Rebecca is just picking on me—trying to make life hard for me. None of the other girls like me anyhow.

Maggie splashed water on her face, then combed her hair so it wasn't flying all over the place. She dressed without underwear and ran out to her car. The first time she turned the key, the car merely clicked and Maggie gasped. "Not again. Dammit." But, with the second twist of the key, the engine cranked and eventually caught.

As she drove to work, Maggie wondered what Rebecca Pepper was going to do about Janet quitting. It had been on short notice. Janet just didn't show up yesterday and then called to say, "I'm quitting today." Yesterday had been bearable. This morning could be hell to pay. It was always hard work when someone didn't show up for work. She'll make me do all the dirt work, just watch.

When Maggie got to work at six fifteen, she noticed a new girl in a gleaming new uniform talking to Rebecca. Rebecca waved Maggie over to her.

"Maggie, this is Lisa Goldman," Rebecca said. "She's Janet's replacement. I'd like you to show her where to get a fresh apron and teach her the ropes. Would you do that, please?"

"Yep," Maggie said. "You from around here?" Maggie asked as she led Alisa to the uniform closet at the back of the building.

"No, I just moved here from Masonville," Alisa said.

"I ain't never been down there," Maggie said. "I come from north of here."

"Okay," Alisa said. "Show me around."

"You been a waitress before?" Maggie asked.

"Oh, sure," Alisa said. "Although I haven't done it for a couple of years."

"Whatcha been doing?" Maggie asked as she watched Alisa put on a crisply pressed apron.

"I tried to be a file clerk in an insurance office. That was awful work."

"Why?"

"No windows, but mainly, no tips," Alisa said and laughed.

"Oh, yeah," Maggie said. "I'd miss them too."

Maggie led the way back to the main dining room. There were only a half dozen people sitting at the counter. The other waitresses were standing around the waitress station. Maggie introduced Lisa Goldman all around. The waitresses exchanged greetings and a few asked questions about her background and family.

People began arriving for breakfast and the demands of serving the people meant that Alisa and Maggie did not have a chance to talk for nearly two hours. Eventually the breakfast crunch waned and after cleaning their respective tables and booths, Alisa and Maggie had a chance to take a break. They each got coffee and sat down in a booth to chat.

*　　*　　*

Kurt Maxxon

I checked with the receptionist in the Emergency Room, who told me Christina had been moved to the ICU on the second floor of the main hospital. I nearly ran upstairs. The nurse at the ICU desk told me Christina had rested comfortably all night. I went over and looked down at Christina, who seemed peaceful as she slept. I studied the three bags of medicine hooked by tubes to the IV into the back of her right hand. All three bags looked to contain the same colorless and transparent liquid. Each, however, had a different label giving names I couldn't even pronounce, let alone know what they were doing inside her body.

I thanked the nurse and went down to the cafeteria for breakfast. They were setting up a buffet breakfast line that opened in ten minutes at 6:00 AM. I got a cup of coffee and sat reading the newspaper I'd bought on the way down, and waited for the buffet. If you get bacon on a buffet within two hours of it being cooked, it probably isn't too tough yet. The bacon this morning was exceptionally good. I went for a second helping.

*　　*　　*

Alisa Sharpe

Whenever the opportunity presented itself, Alisa went into the restroom and pulled her mini-recorder out and added information she had gleaned. She tried to be discreet, but one time Maggie walked into the restroom just as she was putting the mini-recorder back in her pocket.

"What'cha doing?" Maggie asked. "Whatcha got there?"

"A grocery list," Alisa said. "I had to move here pretty fast, so I need to go get some things on the way home. And I use a mini-recorder to make my shopping list."

"I should do that," Maggie said as she went into an empty stall and banged the lid up against the tank.

"Yeah, these little recorders are handy as hell, and easy to use," Alisa said.

"Nah, not that," Maggie said from behind the stall door. "Make a grocery list. My mother always made a shopping list."

"You don't make shopping lists?" Alisa asked.

"Nah. I always wind up with no food in the place."

"I have to make shopping lists so I can stay within my budget," Alisa said.

"I need to do that, too," Maggie said.

"What?"

"Do a budget."

"You don't have a budget?" Alisa said.

"Nah, hell, I just buy stuff when I have the money," Maggie said.

Alisa exited the restroom and watched Rebecca Pepper seat a couple in one of her booths. She went to the wait station and grabbed two glasses of water and two menus and walked to greet the new diners. The early breakfast wave had gone pretty well. Alisa had only screwed up a few things, which everyone seemed to accept with no adverse comments. And I've already made $18 in tips.

At one point mid-morning, there were only three couples, in booths serviced by other waitresses, finishing up their breakfasts. Alisa joined Maggie in the booth next to the wait station. Two other waitresses were sitting in the booth across the aisle talking.

Alisa said, "So, how long have you been working here at Pepper's?"

Maggie studied a spot somewhere behind Alisa. "I think— 'bout a year. I don't really remember." Maggie took her cell phone out of her pocket and turned it on. "What's your phone number?" She asked.

Alisa hesitated for a minute, but then gave Maggie the cell number of the phone she was using. It was one of the agency's and not traceable. Maggie punched the number into her speed dial system.

Alisa responded by adding Maggie's cell phone number to her phone. "Do you like working here at Pepper's?" Alisa asked.

"It's okay. The tips are good. 'Specially the mornings when there are races at the track."

Alisa looked around and then at Maggie. "I heard there was a murder a while back at that track. Did you know that person?"

Maggie frowned severely and looked like she was trying to decide what to say. "I think I knew the guy," Maggie said, looking around to make sure no one was listening to her.

"Melvyn Hightower?" Alisa said.

"Yeah, I think that was his name," Maggie said. "He and I. Well, he showed me how much he liked me a few times."

"Showed you how much he liked you?"

"Yeah, you know, he put himself in me."

Alisa's alarm systems went on high alert. "He what?"

"You know," Maggie said, watching the other waitresses across the aisle. "His pee-pee thingy got hard and he put it in where the pee comes out of me."

Alisa eased back in the seat. "That's how he showed you how well he liked you?"

"Yep," Maggie said. "That's how boys show girls they like them."

"Okay," Alisa said. "So he did that a couple of times? Or did he do that more?"

"More," Maggie said, and smiled. "Whenever I saw him at the track."

"You went to the track to let him show—" Alisa went silent as she saw Rebecca Pepper walking toward them.

"Maggie," Rebecca said as she approached them, "would you stay for the lunch hour? Sissy's got to go to the dentist at eleven-thirty."

"Yes, ma'am," Maggie said.

"Good," Rebecca said. "Lisa, you can stay too, if you want to."

"I hope I'm doing okay," Alisa said.

"You're doing fine," Rebecca said. "You were a big help today." She went back to the cashier's station.

"I like you," Maggie said, as she watched Rebecca walk away. "I like working with you. You're nice."

During the additional two hours they worked together, Alisa asked more questions, but didn't get a lot more answers. Alisa was more impressed by Maggie fading in and out and the mood swings. At one point Alisa wondered if Maggie was in denial about what happened at the track last Friday morning. When their shift ended, Maggie was anxious to leave. "See ya," Maggie said as she hurried to her car.

"I'll see you tomorrow morning," Alisa said. She hung back long enough to let Maggie get into her car and drive away before she walked to her car, glad she'd parked so she couldn't be seen from the diner.

*　　*　　*

Kimberly Grenwahl

"No. Please God, no," Kimberly said aloud, and looked around to see where the kids were. They were watching TV in the living room. Kimberly sat down on the edge of the bed. She buried her face in her hands. Oh, God. What have I got myself into?

Kimberly lowered her cell phone and stared at it. The message had been garbled, but very direct. "I had to cough up an extra two hundred and fifty bucks to get a runner on short notice after you backed out with less than a day's notice. I expect you to pay me back. You've got a month to pay me, or I come after you."

*　　*　　*

Kurt Maxxon

Life felt surreal after yesterday's blur. Christina filled my thoughts and dominated my mind. I left the hospital in a daze from my lack of sleep. I drove to Maurey's place to help Kimberly with her children. I parked next to Kimberly's beat up old Dodge Grand Caravan and went in. Everybody looked at me with questioning expressions. "She's sleeping. She had a good night. There's no change," I said.

Every face I looked at relaxed just a little bit. Kimberly sat down at her desk. I noticed that all four of her children were sitting quietly on folding chairs near her. Then I remembered. Christina had mentioned she wanted to find a permanent day care center and had some thoughts along that line.

I walked to stand next to Kimberly. The mechanics went back to working on their respective vehicles. Maurey answered the ringing phone on his desk. "Did Christina tell you if she found a daycare center for the kids? Specifically, did she tell you where it is?"

"No, she didn't," Kimberly said.

"She didn't tell me either," I confessed. I stood trying to remember if Christina had said anything to me. Nothing came to mind. "Knowing Christina as well as I do," I said, "I'll bet she made a note on her desk pad. I'll run home and take a look." I noticed Brittany perk up and walk toward me.

"Can I go with you, Mr. Maxxon?" Brittany asked.

I looked at Kimberly, who smiled and nodded approval. I worried about taking Mikie. I looked toward Daniel. Kimberly smiled again and nodded.

"Danny, you and Brit can go with Mr. Maxxon," Kimberly said.

Mikie didn't seem too interested and Madison was definitely not interested as she moved to climb up onto her mother's lap. "You and Mikie can stay here," Kimberly soothed. "But you have to sit over there and be good, while Mommy works."

I helped Brittany and Daniel up into the front seat of my truck. I stretched the seat belt across their laps and buckled them in. Even though both sat up straight, neither could see where they were going. Neither one seemed to care.

As I drove to my house I called Edwin Jamison at my store and asked him to have three child seats sent over to Maurey's place. At my house I led the children inside and sat them at the dinette table in the kitchen. After we calmed Beau down, I got each a glass of milk and dug out some chocolate chip cookies and put a plate of them within reach. I looked at the coffee pot and remembered I had a thermos of cold coffee under my seat in the truck. Oh, well!

I walked into the third bedroom which Christina and I use as an office. When Christina moved to my house, the first thing she wanted moved was her desk and office chair. I sat down in

Christina's chair and searched the desk pad. It took a few minutes, but eventually I saw what I was looking for. Children's Development Center with a phone number written below. I punched the speakerphone on and dialed the number. Four rings and a voice said, "Children's Development, this is Nancy; how can I help you?"

I said, "My name is Kurt Maxxon—"

"Oh, hi Kurt," Nancy said in a somber voice. "How is Christina doing?"

"She's stable and resting well," I said. "Thank you very much. Did Christina talk to you about taking care of the Grenwahl children?"

"Yes, she did. She called me Saturday afternoon and explained the situation. She said she would like to get them in as soon as possible. We've had two cancellations last month. I talked to the staff yesterday, and we all agreed to take them in. Do you want to bring them in this morning?"

Once again, I raised my eyes heavenward. Thank you Big Guy! "Oh, that's great," I said. "I'll be bringing them over in an hour or so. Can you give me your address?"

"We're at 2101 North Newton Street," Nancy said.

"I'll see you in a few minutes," I promised as I wrote down the address. Brittany and Daniel had heard my conversation and were standing in the door to the office. Their chocolate smeared mouths and fingers told me they had devoured the cookies. Hopefully, they had drunk the milk. I smiled and said, "Okay, you two, let me get you cleaned up."

Beau showed up to continue playing and seemed miffed that I led them to the bathroom for a washcloth and towel.

I led the two children back to the living room. Brittany seemed to be hanging back. On the bookshelf in one corner I had several model cars of well-known NASCAR drivers I have rooted for over the years. The most notable display was the Number 28 Texaco Havoline Thunderbird driven by Davey Allison during his first win. It was sealed in a clear plastic cube, and it drew Brittany's attention immediately.

"Is that a special car, Mr. Maxxon?" Brittany asked.

"Yes, it is. That car was driven by a great young driver named Davey Allison," I said. Vicki and I met Davey after he won the spring race at the Talladega Superspeedway in May 1987, the year he went on to be named Rookie of the Year in the old NASCAR Winston Cup series.

That Talladega race turned into one of infamy for NASCAR. In lap twenty-two Bobby Allison, Davey's dad, blew a tire and went airborne, flying into the fence in front of the grandstand at the start/finish line. Bobby landed back on the track and caused a massive crash. Neither Bobby, nor any of the drivers were hurt, but several of the spectators were injured by flying debris. That wreck led NASCAR to first reduce the size of carburetor ports and eventually require restrictor plates in the carburetors, to reduce the speeds on the huge super speedway tracks.

"Did he win a lot of races?" Brittany asked.

"Not enough," I said. "He was killed when he was just 27 years old." I paused to remember the incident. Vicki and I were both enchanted by the twenty-six year old Davey. He had a million watt smile, was an illustration of the word charisma—he was the JFK of NASCAR racing. A friend of mine sent me the replica of Davey's number 28 Texaco-Havoline Ford Thunderbird.

At the time of the crash at Talladega, Davey was running ahead of his dad, so he was spared being involved. The race was red-flagged—stopped dead still—for over two hours. The race eventually got back underway and Davey passed Dale Earnhardt to take the lead. A few laps later, the race was called due to darkness, ten laps short. But, Davey Allison had won his first Winston Cup race.

"What happened to him?" Brittany persisted.

"Davey was killed in July of 1993 when his helicopter crashed into the infield of the Talladega Superspeedway while he was returning from a race in Vermont," I said.

Brittany frowned hard. "That was bad, huh?"

I recalled how hard Vicki and I took Davey's death. It felt like we had lost one of our own children. "I chose to race Fords—Thunderbirds and then Mustangs—mainly because of Davey Allison," I said.

"Uncle Chuck really likes his Mustang," Brittany said. "He's just like you, Mr. Maxxon."

I keep a couple of model cars so visiting children can play

with them. Daniel was a prime candidate for that today. As he zipped and zoomed around on his knees, I led Brittany back into the kitchen.

"Something's wrong with Mommy, again" Brittany said bluntly. "She's not happy anymore. And she's crying again at night after we go to bed."

"Why is that?" I asked.

"I don't know," Brittany said. "I just know that something is upsetting her."

This girl was going to be a leader of mankind some day. "I'll see if your mother will talk about it." I smiled at her and gave her an exaggerated wink. She smiled back and I think she relaxed a little.

I loaded the kids back into the truck. "Let's go get Mikie and Madison, and I'll take you all over to your new day care center."

"Madison won't like that," Brittany said.

"Oh, yeah," I said. "Is she afraid of new places, or things?"

"Yes, she is." Brittany sat staring ahead even though she couldn't see where we were going.

"I don't want to go either," Daniel said.

"We've got to," Brittany lectured him. "Mommy has to work to make money to take care of us, especially Mikie. We can't stay at the garage."

"Why not?" Daniel argued. "We can stay out of the way. We don't bother anyone else."

"We have to go the day care center," Brittany said with authority. "It won't be too long until you and I will be going back to school. Then we won't have to stay all day there."

"Oh, yeah," Daniel said. "I like school."

"So do I," Brittany agreed. "So all we have to do is get by until we go to school."

We arrived back at Maurey's garage. Maurey and I installed two small-child seats and one booster seat for Daniel in the back seat of my truck. Then Kimberly and I loaded the two youngest children into the back seat of my truck, strapping them in to the new child seats. Daniel was happy to graduate up to a booster seat from the old seats his mother had in her car. Brittany seemed content to ride in the front seat between Kimberly and me, strapped in with a seat belt which made it impossible for her to see out the windows.

We arrived at the Children's Development Center and I parked in the spaces for unloading children. I carried Madison and led Kimberly and the children into the lobby where we were met by an athletic thirty-something red headed woman who appeared, wearing a pink jogging suit. She nodded at Kimberly, smiled at me, and said, "Hi Kurt. Welcome to Children's Development Center." She led us through an electric gate to where two dozen children were playing and interacting at various tables.

Madison shied back and Brittany took her by the hand and led her to a table with several board games set up and some being played by other children. They selected a game and went to playing. Daniel and Mikie ran off to get involved with the other kids in some of the action areas. No one seemed to mind the new kids. They seamlessly blended in and the games went ahead.

Nancy watched with interest. She looked at Kimberly and said, "Christina told me one of your children has Epilepsy. Which one is it?"

"It's Mikie, the youngest boy," Kimberly said. "The one wearing the blue shirt."

Nancy swung to search the boys playing in one corner. "Okay," she said. "Let me get Rene to talk with you. Rene is our Registered Nurse, and she'll be keeping tabs on Mikie."

"That's great," Kimberly said.

Nancy went out of the room through a double door. As she left, a twenty-something woman in a dark blue jogging suit came out of the back room. "Hi, Kurt," she said to me. "That Angie is really a great driver. She's going to win them all."

"We hope so," I said with a surprised smile. "What's your name? I like to keep track of Angie's fans."

"Henrietta Atchison," she said with a fetching grin. "I go to all the races here."

"I'll get you a Pit Pass," I said as I dug out one of my Kurt Maxxon Racing cards from my shirt pocket, scribbled PIT PASS on the back, signed it, and handed it to her.

Henrietta's face beamed as she studied the front of the card and then the back. "Thank you," she said. "Thank you so much."

Nancy returned with a serious looking young woman, dressed in blue scrubs. She had a round face with dark brown eyes, black eyebrows, and a pointed nose. Her black hair was long, parted in the middle of her head and hung over her shoulders. A brass name tag above her left breast read: Rene Tocqueville. Rene let a smile spread on her face as she moved toward us. "What treatment is your son getting for his epilepsy?"

Kimberly looked at me. I stepped forward. "Mikie is going to get a new diagnosis this coming Thursday," I said. "We have a doctor's appointment Thursday afternoon. If the doctor wants other testing or evaluation, we'll be getting that."

Rene said, "Okay, please let me know what the doctors tell you."

"We'll do that," Kimberly said.

Rene asked a few more questions about symptoms, lengths of seizures, etc., which Kimberly fielded with ease. Eventually, Rene reiterated wanting to know what the doctors say.

"Well, I guess that takes care of everything," Nancy said. "Do you have any questions?"

Kimberly looked at me, then at Nancy. "How do I pay for all this?"

Nancy looked at me. "We've set it up to bill Maxxon Auto Parts. That's what we'll be doing. Whatever arrangements you've made with the Maxxons is between you and them."

Kimberly swung to look at me.

"Didn't I mention one of your benefits was childcare?" I asked.

We made a quick survey of the four children. Kimberly probably would have liked to go to each of her children and wish them well. I think she knew her children would have to deal with separation anxiety. She turned and walked toward the front door. I followed her. Neither of us looked back.

*　　*　　*

We left Children's Development Center and I knew Kimberly had mixed emotions about leaving her children. I drove back toward Maurey's garage.

"You know how perceptive Brittany is," I said, to start the upcoming conversation.

Kimberly swiveled in her new chair to look directly at me.

"Yes."

"Brittany tells me there is something wrong. You cried last night after you went to bed. She's worried about you."

"That girl," Kimberly said. She sat silently, staring through the windshield. I could see she was rummaging through several different lines of thought.

"Is there something wrong?" I pushed.

Kimberly continued to stare out the windshield. Then the pressure of it took over. She buried her face in her hands and started to sob. "I really screwed up," she squeaked between sobs.

I pulled into a convenience store on the corner and parked toward the back. "You want a cup of coffee?" I asked.

Kimberly ignored me for a few beats, and then nodded. "I need one."

I went in and got two large cups of coffee. When I returned to the truck, Kimberly had obviously regained control. I handed her a cup and settled in to the driver's seat. She shook her head slowly and wiped tears from her cheeks with her left palm.

"Let's hear it," I said. "Tell me about it."

"I ... uh, I screwed up royally," Kimberly said, her voice breaking. She stopped to suck air into her lungs. "God, did I screw up."

"Can't be that bad," I said.

"Oh yeah, it can."

"What did you do?"

"I needed money to buy groceries," Kimberly said slowly. "A friend of mine told me to call a phone number and do as they told me." She paused.

I hoped not to think through how she was going to talk to me.

"I got involved with delivering drugs to dealers," Kimberly's voice seemed to be gaining strength. I made a delivery to Farmer's City the week before last, and it was easy enough. So I agreed to make another delivery last Sunday evening."

I sat studying her face. She was sincere enough to convince me she was leveling with me.

"When you offered me a job Saturday, I decided it wasn't worth the risk. So I ... I—" Tears started to streak down her cheeks. She put her face into her hands and sobbed visibly.

I reached over and patted her on her shoulder. She shuddered at my touch, but then relaxed a little.

"So, I called and cancelled my delivery."

"Good," I said.

"Yeah, but then I got a message from my contact saying he had to find another runner on short notice. It cost him two hundred and fifty dollars extra. He wants me to pay him that two fifty plus interest. That it'll probably total over five hundred before it's all over."

"Okay," I said. "He knows you, but you don't know him."

"He mentioned my kids." Kimberly's sobs returned, and she buried her face again. From under her hands I heard her say, "When he called me yesterday, he said something that made me think he would hurt my kids. That scared me. He said I had a month to pay up."

"Okay," I said. Anybody who would threaten a woman's kids had to be dealt with and dealt with in a straight forward, no nonsense manner. "Do you have any idea how to find these people?"

We sat in the parking lot, sipping coffee. After I pressed for more information, she said, "I think the big boss uses Dudley's Bar and Pool Hall on the south side of Centralia to conduct business."

I decided Dudley's would be my next stop. I dropped Kimberly off at Maurey's garage and drove to Dudley's Bar and Pool Hall. I'd met the owner, Dudley Simpson, seven years ago at the annual Marine Corps birthday celebration in November shortly after he retired from the Marine Corps as a Sergeant Major. Dudley and I became instant friends. Dudley was an African-American male, six foot three inches tall and now going about two hundred and eighty pounds. He shaved his head bald and wore a mustache and beard of black hair, now flecked with gray. His fierce gray eyes never smiled, even when his lips did. He didn't openly espouse political ideals, but there was no candidate who was too conservative for him.

When I strolled in, I looked around to see if there were any shady-looking characters hanging out. No one seemed to fit that description, so I walked to the back of the room and climbed onto a bar stool that let me see the entire room. Three pool tables were being used, but the participants looked to be local players of no particular interest. Dudley was behind the bar, and it took him a minute before he realized who I was. Dudley walked toward me. "Hey, Colonel," he said. "Whatcha doing, bud?"

"I'm looking for a man—"

"You think he killed that guy at the track?" Dudley said.

"No. He has nothing to do with that killing," I said.

Dudley frowned. "Damn," he said. "Sounds interesting."

I told him all I knew about the circumstances, from what Kimberly had told me.

"There's one guy," Dudley said. "He's in here a lot. Meets a lot of other people here. I've always kind of felt—I don't know—you know, I just never really cared for the guy. But, hell, I gave up trying to keep the place just for honest people. You know what I mean."

"What's his name?" I asked.

"I don't know. I mean, nobody wears name tags here." Dudley studied the players at the pool tables. Then he yelled "Hey, Mitch,"

The room went silent. One of the pool shooters straightened up and faced Dudley. "Yeah," he said.

Dudley waved him toward us. Mitch moved cautiously to the bar, watching the game he was part of—and eyeing me. "Yeah," Mitch said.

"What's the name of that guy who comes in pretty often to meet other people—you know, sits over there at the round table in the corner, talks to people, kinda dark haired, short, usually in a suit and tie?"

Mitch looked at me and then to Dudley. "Hell, I don't know what his name is; I've never heard it. The person who might know is Kelly Gates."

I hoped I could remember all these names.

"Let me check with Kelly Gates the next time she comes in," Dudley offered. It was the best I could do. "Better yet, if the guy comes in, I'll see if I can get his license number. Hell, maybe I can get the license numbers of the people he's meeting with, too. That work for you, Colonel?"

I saw recognition spread across Mitch's face. "You're Kurt Maxxon, huh?"

"I am."

Dudley looked at Mitch. "I thought you knew Kurt Maxxon."

"I recognize him now," Mitch said as he walked back to the pool table.

Life worked a whole lot better—faster and easier—when people knew you were a good guy.

CHAPTER FIFTEEN
Tuesday Afternoon, August 28

Kurt Maxxon

My trip to the hospital was rewarded by an angelic Christina laying peacefully, her mid-length blonde hair flaring out on her pillow. I gripped her hand and squeezed as hard as I thought proper without hurting her, leaned down, and said, "I love you Christina; never forget that." I moved to her guest chair and sat watching her while the nurses made frequent trips to monitor her vital signs and machines. I dozed a little in the chair. I woke up painfully with a crick in my neck and stiff joints. One nurse came in, looked at me, and said, "Dr. Schroeder ordered her to be kept on propofol until the night shift. She's in a light coma."

Not being a patient person, I thanked the nurse, and went down the stairs to the cafeteria for a sandwich and a cup of coffee. After the snack, I walked the halls of Hopewell Memorial's first floor and then climbed the steps to the second floor. At the end of the hall past Christina's room on the second floor I had discovered a small waiting room with a motel sized writing desk in the corner. Four reasonably comfortable chairs with a magazine table between each pair lined the other two walls. No coffee pot, but I could get by.

I walked the short distance back to Christina's room and sat fidgeting for about ten minutes before I went down the stairs and to my truck. The air was warm and muggy and dark clouds lined the southwestern horizon. I hadn't paid attention to the weather forecast. The rain was likely since the wind was blowing the clouds toward me. Storms never bothered me, but lightning and thunder bothered Christina and especially Beau. I dug my writing pad out of my brief case and walked back into the coolness of the hospital, and climbed the stairs to my new "mini-office."

I'd made notes on the first three pages of the tablet. Unlike the other murders I'd been involved with, everything about this one seemed to be totally disconnected; no threads from one item led anywhere else. The only commonality of the notes was the frequency of a couple of names—Maggie Decker and Lorianne Hightower. I'd written down, as close as I could remember, what Maggie had said to me Sunday morning while serving us breakfast. I'd also written down what I remembered her saying to me when she intercepted me in the grandstand during the race.

I scanned the notes from my talk with Melvyn's Aunt Matilda—things I remembered her saying about Lorianne Hightower. I fished around in my shirt pocket, but I was wearing a different shirt from when I met Aunt Matilda yesterday. Where did you put the note with the name and phone number of her friend's daughter? A thought, or more like a suspicion, crossed my mind; I walked back out to my truck. Sure enough, the note sheet Aunt Matilda gave me was lying on the dash of my truck. I went back to my cubby-hole on the second floor.

I copied the name and phone number onto my tablet page. Gayle Peterson. After I wrote her phone number, I dug my cell phone out and dialed the number. A female voice said, "This is Gayle. How may I help you?"

I introduced myself as a friend of Matilda Stauffer.

"I haven't been up to see Matilda in several months," she said. "Is she okay?"

"Yes, she's fine. I just saw her yesterday morning."

"That's good," Gayle said.

I asked Gayle if I could talk to her and explained, in a roundabout way, that I was interested in talking to her about Lorianne Hightower.

"The hairdresser?"

"Yes."

"I suppose," Gayle said. "I don't know her all that well."

"Aunt Matilda told me you go to Lorianne's salon often."

"Yes, I do. Every other Thursday."

"I'm just interested in getting some backup information." I decided to be a little deceptive. "I'm the president of a racing league that her husband competed in—"

"That's where I've heard your name before," Gayle said.

"I'm concerned about keeping Melvyn's car in the SRVSCRA. I'm hoping Lorianne will sell it to a local driver," I said. "I have an appointment to meet Lorianne tomorrow for lunch."

"Where are you now?" Gayle asked.

"I'm at Hopewell Memorial Hospital—"

"You're only half a block away from me. I work at the Ryder Insurance Agency just up the street."

"Have you had lunch yet?"

"I was just getting ready to get lunch. Let me walk over to the hospital. They have the best salad bar in town. And it's cheap, too."

"I'll meet you in the cafeteria," I said, and punched the off button, then wished I'd asked how I would know her. I went down to the cafeteria. It shouldn't be too hard. Everyone except myself and another man wore hospital scrubs.

*   *   *

The cafeteria never seemed crowded and I decided the hospital staff rotated lunch breaks to achieve that. Several tables were empty, and I grabbed a cup of coffee and sat down at one. I'd only waited a few minutes when a woman walked into the room, looked around and walked toward me.

"Colonel Maxxon," she said.

I stood and shook her hand. I noticed she had a newspaper clipping clutched in her hand with her purse. "I dug out a picture of you. So I'd know you."

I smiled. "Smart woman. I was wondering why I didn't ask how I'd know you."

She was my age, medium height, and a little chunky in the middle. Her hair was auburn, cut business-woman short, and I realized her bi-weekly visits to Lorianne probably involved a rinse, along with a trim. She smiled with her lips and dark brown eyes that twinkled with a little mischief. Her penciled on eyebrows were also auburn. No other makeup marred her appearance. She was wearing a business suit with matching skirt and jacket, an ivory colored blouse buttoned to the neck and a plain blue scarf that imitated a tie.

I held a chair for her, but she said, "I need to get a salad, I only like to take about an hour for lunch."

Realizing my faux pas, I said, "I'll get one, too. This is my treat."

We made our pass through the salad bar and went to the cashier who weighed each plate. While Gayle went back to the table, I paid the tab then followed her. Gayle ate while she talked.

"You're interested in Lorianne Hightower? Good or bad?"

I looked at her and she must have read my confusion.

"Are you looking for praiseworthy stuff, or smut?"

"Oh, I'm not interested in smut," I said emphatically. "I'm just curious about what you think of Lorianne and her salon."

"Her salon is about the same as the dozens of others in town." Gayle paused to think about what she was going to say. "I like Lorianne. She does good work. I've never had to wait for her to start on me."

"Has she ever mentioned any marital problems? Financial problem? Anything like that?"

"I read about him being killed over at the track." Gayle chewed her food. "The only thing Lorianne ever talked about was how big of a tight-wad Melvyn was."

"Was she angry about it, wanting to get revenge?"

"Oh, I don't think she was after revenge," Gayle said. "She just complained about Melvyn a lot. You know, he controlled the purse strings, wouldn't give her money, and took her off the checking account. Every once in awhile she'd talk about things around the shop, like needing the plumbing repaired, but Melvyn wouldn't let her have the money. I asked her one time about the ratty old sneakers she wore at the shop, and her response was 'Melvyn won't let me have the money to buy a new pair.'"

"Did you get the impression that Melvyn was being deliberately mean to her?" I asked.

"Oh, not really," Gayle said. "Lorianne has a big ego that she lets get in her way at times. I think Melvyn was probably just trying to rein her in. She bought that car last year, and I think that may have been a major turning point in her relationship with Melvyn."

"What kind of car?" I asked.

"I don't know the brand," Gayle replied. "But, rumor has it, that it cost over one hundred thousand dollars."

I decided to cut to the chase. "Do you have any reason to believe that Lorianne might have killed Melvyn or had someone do it for her?"

"I'll respectfully take the fifth amendment on that one," Gayle said matter-of-factly, then let a smile spread across her face. "Why do you ask?"

"Because if Lorianne proves to be involved, she'll not be able to sell Melvyn's car for a long time. I was hoping to keep the car racing in the league, even this year."

"In that case, if you want my gut feeling, I'd say Lorianne is not involved." Gayle pursed her lips and nodded conviction.

"Thanks," I said. "You've been very helpful."

Gayle smiled. I asked her what she did at the insurance agency.

"I handle several large corporate accounts," she said.

We talked about other people we both knew. I walked Gayle to the front door and then went up the stairs to my cubby-hole office on the second floor. I jotted notes in my tablet about what Gayle told me about Lorianne. As I compared those to the notes I made from Aunt Matilda, I realized that Aunt Matilda was biased, being related to Melvyn. Gayle Peterson, on the other hand, was not a relative, and didn't have any connection other than being the daughter of a friend of Aunt Matilda. And she couldn't say whether Lorianne had something to do with Melvyn's death. I scribbled INTERESTING below the note.

I walked back to Christina's room and looked in on her. She was sleeping peacefully. I left and went out to my truck. The dark clouds had moved closer and the wind had picked up.

I drove home. Beau greeted me at the door, and I unlocked his doggy door. He dashed through, but was back inside in only a few minutes later. I looked out the living room bay window and saw the birch trees out front whipping around in a strong wind. Huge rain drops crashed against the window as I stood watching. Beau jumped into Christina's recliner and sat watching me. Christina kept an old blanket in the coat closet that she let Beau crawl under whenever it was storming outside. I went to the coat closet and got the blanket. When I tried to put it over Beau, he jumped up on the arm and growled lowly. A bright flash of lightning lit the room. A few seconds later a building rattling boom told me the storm was very close. Beau gave up his bravado. He dove under the blanket and let me tuck it around him.

My cell phone jangled and the caller ID gave a number I didn't recognize. I answered. It was Alisa.

Alisa said, "Man, I've got a real load to dump on you."

"Let me call you right back on my landline," I said. "That way I can talk to you on a good speaker phone."

"I'm on the motel phone. My cell phone is charging." She gave the phone number.

I turned the speaker phone on and punched in the numbers, then listened as the beeps paced quickly to a ringing on the other end. After we went through the small talk, Alisa said, "Man, this Maggie girl is something else."

"What have you got?" I asked.

"I'm still working on my report," Alisa said. "But I wanted to give you the highlights so you can be thinking about them, too. This story is going to knock your socks off."

With my interest piqued to maximum, I grabbed my writing pad and a pair of pencils. "Tell me what you've got."

"Okay," she said. "I think we'll find that Maggie was involved with Melvyn, sexually and all. Also, Maggie is probably a lot more disturbed than anyone really realizes." I heard papers shuffling.

"Maggie told me that Melvyn showed her how much he liked her; which involved sexual intercourse. She said something like." I heard papers shuffling again. "She said, 'He put himself in me.' I've got to do some research, and I wish we could talk to Christina about this, but it sounds like Maggie may be sexually immature—I mean totally infantile about it." Alisa paused, and I figured she was studying her hand-written notes. "I often have to do some imaginative interpretation of my hand writing," Alisa said.

"I do too," I said.

"Okay," Alisa continued. "Maggie definitely was at the track Friday morning. She said she went there to meet up with Melvyn for, basically, sex. Her story is very interesting, but the most interesting part of the story is that Maggie had a pistol—a pistol she says she found in one of the booths a few days before."

"A pistol?"

"Yes. Maggie told me she had a pistol in her fanny pack."

Alisa went into another pause. "I asked her where the pistol was now. She said she didn't know. The next interesting part of the story is that Maggie claims that a second man showed up, and she hid behind the pool tables. She heard Melvyn and the man get into an argument in the locker room, then they moved into the shower room. Maggie says she got scared by the arguing and ran out to go home. I tried to connect the pistol to before and after the man arriving and arguing with Melvyn, but Maggie has blanked it out."

I tried to analyze what Alisa had just told me. I'd jotted notes on my tablet, but there were so many disconnected jottings, I wasn't sure I could ever make sense of them.

"Here's what I've surmised," Alisa said. "Maggie had a gun. She went to the racetrack to meet up with Melvyn Hightower, intent on having sex with him; although she might not have a mature idea of what that involved."

I made notes while I listened to Alisa. "We need to run Maggie's pistol to ground," I said. "Did she even take it to the track? Is it the murder weapon?"

"Right," Alisa said."

I jotted: Maggie went to track to meet up with Melvyn. Maggie had a pistol in readable lettering on my tablet; even though somewhere just above was a scribble saying about the same thing.

"Was it a revolver or a semi-auto?" I asked.

"She probably doesn't know the difference," Alisa said. "Why?"

"The question is, obviously, was that the murder weapon?" I said. "The weapon that killed Melvyn was a revolver. I saw it. That dude pointed it at me."

"Oh, yeah, that's right," Alisa said.

"For some reason," I said, "I doubt the guy who pointed it at me was the same guy who argued with Melvyn. Can Maggie describe the man?" I asked.

"Not too well—let me find it." Alisa paused while she leafed through papers. "Yeah, here it is—medium height, fat, black hair, she doesn't remember the color of his eyes. Hair looked dyed, she said. When I asked her how old he was, she said, and I quote, 'about the same as Kurt Maxxon.'"

I ignored the comparison and said. "That's not the dude with the gun when I got there. What was the part where she said the man argued with Melvyn in the locker room and followed Melvyn into the shower room?"

Alisa riffled through her notes. "Let's see. Here it is. What it sounds like is she was waiting for Melvyn—oh, yeah, she said she was sitting on the pool table when she heard this second man coming through the door. She ducked behind the pool table. The man went into the locker room. They started shouting at each other. Shouting is the word she used. She says Melvyn was naked and he walked toward the shower room. The two men continued arguing. Maggie says that scared her and she got up from behind the pool table and ran out to go home."

In my mind, I tried to picture the pool tables when Christina and I arrived at the track. After encountering the drifter with the gun, however, I wouldn't trust my memory too far. "The pool tables were in their normal playing positions I'm pretty sure, from the association who used the track last weekend. Maggie could easily hide behind them. The police probably moved the tables, and then I pushed them aside for our meeting."

After a long pause, I said, "Maggie said she ran out to go home?"

"Shouting appears to upset her," Alisa said. "Which I think is consistent with mental retardation. From talking to Maggie, I'd be surprised if she is much more advanced than a twelve- or thirteen-year-old mentally. I think she has the body of a thirty-something, but her mind is not too well developed in a lot of areas—especially sexually."

"How does she do as a waitress?" I asked.

"Well that was kind of a tip-off for me. Being a waitress is not an easy job. I'd never belittle the job. But, a person like Maggie can operate as a waitress. I noticed that she writes down every order, even asking several times what the customer wants. I also noticed that Maggie can't remember who ordered what when she delivers the food. That tends to indicate either a lack of interest, or a lack of mental capacity to keep things in order."

I remembered Maggie taking our breakfast order last Sunday morning. She had asked us to repeat things and wrote a lot on her pad. "I miss Christina," I said.

"She has great insight into people," Alisa said. "As I remember from what little psychology they taught us in police science school, human beings learn to read and write during their first three to eight years. It's probably taken Maggie thirty years to get to where she is." Alisa paused. "I wish I knew more about it. But things like reasoning and judgment develop later, and that's where Maggie is lacking."

"Did she hear any shots?" I asked.

"I don't know yet," Alisa said. "I need to do some follow up. I'll be working at Pepper's again tomorrow morning."

"Good," I said.

"I'm making notes on questions I want to ask Maggie tomorrow."

I said, "Well, she probably isn't going anywhere, so there's no rush to get Nick involved. See if you can get her to place that gun at the track. Was it hers or did the drifter bring it with him?"

"That's what I was thinking," Alisa told me. "Let me have tomorrow to get more."

*   *   *

Lorianne Hightower

"I need to keep some personal stuff out of the weather," Lorianne said to the man behind the counter, "While the workmen are running around inside my apartment."

She wondered where the young blond haired, blue-eyed Adonis was. He had been much easier to talk to. The current counterman was older, sterner looking. She hoped he didn't look too closely at her driver's license.

The man finished the paperwork for returning the rented pickup truck and threw the paperwork into the proper basket. "We have a Chrysler Town and Country or a Ford E-250 van," he said, pointing with his chin toward the vehicles lined up in the parking lot out front.

"Which is the biggest?" Lorianne asked.

"The Ford," he said.

"I'll take the Ford."

Lorianne left the car rental lot and drove east several blocks; then pulled quickly into the parking lot of a strip mall. She parked and watched to see if any cars followed her. None did. After a few minutes she drove out of the parking lot and drove back the direction she had come. No cars turned around to follow her, and none of the cars behind her seemed to be tailing her.

It had started raining while she was driving to the rental office, and now the rain came down heavier. It beat on the roof of the van and the wind whipped it around. The rain was a mixed blessing for Lorianne. Both of her afternoon appointments would probably call and cancel. They were elderly ladies who had to catch cabs to get there, and rain nearly always deterred them. If they did show up, the other girls were covering for Lorianne.

She took a new route to the storage shed and, when she arrived, she spotted the security guard's car parked in front of the office. She steered the van straight past the storage facility. She drove two blocks and then turned around and parked at the side of the road. In a few minutes the security car left the storage facility and drove toward her. She slid down and looked toward the passenger seat as he drove past, not sure he could recognize her. He had never seen the van before.

The rain had lightened, but still drummed on the roof of the van. Lorianne drove to her storage unit and parked the van in front of the door to partially block the view into it. When she first got out, she noticed it was parked too close to the door and the rain was glancing off it into the room. She dashed back to the driver's side and moved the van out a couple of feet. That worked. She tried the shredder and did about twenty handfuls of paper before she shut it off and walked to look around outside the storage room. No one was in the area. The office was a football field away and facing away from the row of storage units. Plus the rain, wind, and thunder were making more noise than the shredder. She went back to work and continued shredding. She hadn't planned on the shredder getting hot and shutting itself off after about thirty handfuls of paper. And it took a long time to cool off.

That's alright! I need to break from that damn noise. Next time I come up here, I need to grab a pair of Shag's earplugs from the garage. I need to bring a water bottle, too.

* * *

Kurt Maxxon

Beau had wiggled under the blanket in Christina's chair after about three crashing, loud thunder rolls. As the rain let up, occasionally, he would look out at me, but not come out. I sat looking at the notes I'd made while talking to Alisa.

I hoped I could manage to get to the hospital without

getting drenched. Beau watched me as I put my tablet into a large plastic sleeve, locked his doggy door and went out through the garage to climb into my truck. I drove to the Hospital.

Seeing Christina so still and quiet discouraged me a little. So I went down to the cafeteria for a sandwich and coffee. I was about to take my tablet out of the plastic cover when Phil Schroeder wandered in, filled a cup with coffee and waked to my table. He turned the chair to straddle it. "How you doing, Kurt?"

"I have to admit, I'm a little discouraged."

"I understand," Phil said. "I decided to keep her under a little longer. That should help reduce the stress factors on the body."

"When will she be transferred to Our Lady?" I asked.

"Oh, I'm still shooting for Friday afternoon; Saturday morning at the latest."

"Can she be transferred, what with all the casts and bandages and all?"

"Oh sure," Phil said. "Don't be too worried about her now. She's out of the woods. I just stopped the propofol drip. You'll be surprised how quickly she wakes up. We'll have her up and walking," Phil glanced at the clock on the wall "... oh probably tomorrow morning; by noon for sure. The reason I continued the coma was because she apparently banged her head against the door frame harder than we originally thought. The EEG last night showed that area might be swelling more than it looked at first. We'll look at it again later. The good news is that her legs, hips and pelvis weren't damaged. There are some contusions on her left hip, but nothing serious. That means we can get her up and moving soon."

"The last time I broke my arm at Masonville three years ago," I said, "they wanted me to start therapy the next day."

"We like to get people like her into rehab quickly," Phil said. "So the therapists can start working the muscles, tendons, cartilage and the bones. The therapists will work with her even with the casts and bandages. It is a rehab hospital."

"Is her lung okay?"

"Yes. Once we got the piece of rib out, it sealed itself nicely. There's no sign of leakage."

"Will her arm and shoulder be impaired in any way from

the compound fracture?"

"We don't think so, and that's why I want to get her to the rehab people as quickly as possible. We pinned the femur together in almost perfect alignment. We might have to do some follow-up surgery on tendons and cartilage, but it'll be minor."

"I have a friend who lived in absolute agony after a broken arm and shoulder," I said, thinking of Don Epperley.

"How'd he break the arm?"

"He got shot. He was a cop."

"Oh, well, yeah. Gunshot wounds are a different animal all together," Phil said. "If a bullet strikes a bone and breaks that bone, it usually takes part of the bone with it as it moves on. Putting all the bone, muscle, tendons, etc. back together after a gunshot wound can be challenging. Christina's arm and shoulder were much different."

"I feel better after talking to you," I said.

"The nurse told me you looked kinda pale. That's why I decided I needed a cup of coffee. I've got to go," Phil said as he stood, swung the chair around and pushed it under the table.

I watched him walk rapidly out and head for the elevators across the lobby.

My cell phone jangled. It was Alisa.

"I got to wondering," she said, "about the murder weapon. I need some information you should know because you saw the gun the drifter had."

"Okay," I said. "Nick told me it was a fake S&W thirty-eight caliber."

"Nickel or blued?"

"It looked to be stainless steel," I said, trying to see the weapon through the mental warp of denial.

"I'm going to try to figure a way to get Maggie to describe the gun. Maybe even pull a picture of one off the Internet."

"It had about a five inch barrel. I think Nick said it was a seven shot. I didn't count the number of cylinders while the guy was pointing it at me. Nor could I see that the shells were empty." I smiled.

"Good," Alisa said. "Let me see if I can find a picture of an S&W seven short with a five inch barrel. I'll figure out a way to see if Maggie can identify it as the gun she had. If it isn't the same gun, then we might have two guns involved."

"I saw the murder weapon," I said. "Pointed right at me."

"Right," Alisa said. "But if Maggie convinces me the gun she took to the track was actually a nine-millimeter Sig Sauer semi-auto, she's less culpable. Hell, she might have thrown the gun away somewhere running away and not remember where. If it's not the murder weapon, do we really care?"

"Let me ask you something," I said and paused to formulate how to go about asking. "Maggie had a gun. What if it was the murder weapon? What if Maggie shot Melvyn—accidentally or otherwise—and then fabricated this guy who shows up and argues with Melvyn?"

"I seriously doubt she's capable of doing that, Kurt. I really do." Alisa went silent for a long moment. "No, that's too big of a stretch. She couldn't do it."

"You're working tomorrow at Pepper's?"

"Yes, I am," Alisa said. "I think Rebecca Pepper would like me to stay forever."

"That's good," I said. "I wonder when we should tell Nick about Maggie."

"Let's keep Maggie between you and me for now," Alisa said.

"Works for me," I said. "You okay with all this time here in Centralia?"

"I'm having a ball. Give me tomorrow to see what else I can come up with," Alisa said.

"No problem," I said. "There's probably no good reason to implicate Maggie until we find a good reason to."

"You sound like Yogi Berra," Alisa said.

"What?"

"Do you remember what you just said to me?"

I thought for a long time. "No, as a matter of fact, I don't."

"Good." She hung up.

CHAPTER SIXTEEN
Wednesday Morning, August 29

Kurt Maxxon

I woke up about five-thirty with Christina on my mind. The doctor had said she should come out of her coma sometime this morning—at least by noon. I was anxious to talk to her, hear her voice. It seemed like an eternity since we had chatted.

I made a pot of coffee, showered, shaved, dressed, and then sat at the dinette table in the kitchen sipping coffee and watching the early news, weather and traffic on the TV in the living room. I'd unlocked Beau's doggy door, and he went out. While he was out, I filled his food and water bowls. When Beau strolled back through the kitchen, he glanced at me then jumped up on the blanket in Christina's recliner and curled up. "Not ready for the day, Beau?" I yelled. He raised his head on the arm of the Christina's chair and glared at me. After a few seconds, he decided to ignore me.

After the first pass of news and weather, I let my mind wander. Several of the facts of the case flooded my mind, and I got up to retrieve my writing tablet to review my notes. Then I decided to go to the hospital in case Christina woke up. After all, people in hospitals rarely awaken or do anything in accordance with our solar clocks. I clicked the TV off, locked Beau's doggy door, grabbed my writing tablet, and went out to climb into my truck.

During the drive to Hopewell Memorial, I wondered again what had happened to Melvyn's car. Where is the number thirty-five car? I was sure Nick and the CPD was watching the racetrack for it. I hadn't been to the track since Sunday. Cecil Bjornlund was the grounds keeper who worked at the track and the fairgrounds every Monday through Wednesday. I promised myself I'd run by the track and see if Cecil had seen anything in the last two days.

At the hospital I looked in on Christina and was heartened to see that she was moving ever so slightly—pre-awakening movements. I stood by her side for several minutes, and then sat down in the easy chair where I could see her face. To my chagrin the movements ceased and she went back to a peaceful sleep. My growling stomach argued against putting breakfast off any longer, so I went down to the cafeteria. I gulped my food down and went back to Christina's room. I sat for an anxious hour with Christina still sleeping soundly. "Wake up! My love, I want to hear your voice again," I whispered.

I stood and paced out into the hall. After a half dozen circuits, I looked in on Christina and went down to my truck to get my writing tablet. When I returned, Christina was moving a little, so I sat on the edge of the chair, ready to jump up the minute her eyes opened. Once again, however, she went into another quiet period. I settled back in the chair and opened my tablet and scanned through the notes I'd made. I was now up to seven pages. The lack of connectivity struck me as odd. The dots were not connecting—not even forming any type of pattern.

I'd made an appointment to meet Lorianne for lunch and I swung the full sheets up to a new, blank page. I jotted notes about the information I wanted to get from her. My main quest: what she planned to do with the number thirty-five car. If we ever find it?

Lorianne Hightower hadn't been charged with anything yet, so she retained ownership. However, the car could not be dealt with until she was cleared.

After several minutes of dead-end thinking, all I had written on the blank page was:

What was the argument Steve overheard about?

Melvyn's Car? Where is Melvyn's car?

I went back to the front of the tablet.

As I read the notes through again, I moved further away from any hypothesis that Maggie could have shot Melvyn. With the infatuation Maggie had for Melvyn, it just wasn't logical that she would shoot him. It would be interesting to find out about the gun Maggie told Alisa she had in her fanny pack. Was it the murder weapon? Did Maggie drop the gun in the driver's lounge? How did the killer get the gun? Did he find it lying on the floor—like the drifter claimed he found it?

Maggie Decker was a major enigma in the case. From what she told Alisa, she had gone to the track to have sex with Melvyn.

But does Maggie even know what sex really is?

Who was the man that argued with Melvyn?

Was it Jason Tobias? According to Steve Cosburn's time schedule, Jason wasn't even in town.

Were others involved? Who? After several minutes of concentrating on it, no one else came to mind. So, I flipped to a new page and made a new list of suspects: (1) Lorianne Hightower, (2) Maggie Decker, (3) the man who argued with Melvyn. As an afterthought, I wrote (4) Angelo ??, since I couldn't remember the drifter's last name. But Angelo had been shown not to have fired the weapon.

I sat studying the new list, frequently flipping pages to review other notes.

Then I remembered the man on the phone. The voice. The voice telling me to leave the case alone. I flipped to the page where I'd scribbled: The Voice.

I flipped back to my new list and wrote:

(5) The voice = definitely the voice= How does he connect??

I drew a line from (5) The Voice to (3) The man who argued with Melvyn.

Who was he? Maggie is the only connection to the two!

I replayed my encounter with Maggie Sunday at the track. I remembered Alisa's comment about Maggie perhaps not really understanding the meaning of sex. Also, Alisa's theory that Maggie probably wouldn't know what she had done if she had actually been the one who shot Melvyn:

What is Maggie's developmental age?

"Developmental Age" was a term I'd heard Christina use with reference to children who are challenged.

I glanced at my watch and realized Alisa was probably dealing with Maggie at Pepper's again today. I hoped she could wrap up her investigation this morning, so she could get back to Kings Rapids and a normal life. Terry Grossman and Alisa had already declared they didn't expect me to pay for their services—no matter how much I protested.

Christina stirred and said something I couldn't understand. I leaped to my feet and jumped to her side. An alarm went off on one of the machines connected to her, and a nurse came streaming into the room. I moved out of the way, hoping I hadn't set the damn thing off. The nurse moved to Christina and began the vitals routine. Christina woke up and looked at me. She smiled, and I hoped I didn't start crying. But before the nurse got out of the way, Christina was back to sleep again. The machines were beeping rhythmically. I was the only thing in the room out of sync—at least it felt that way to me.

I worried about leaving Christina as my lunch date with Lorianne Hightower approached. As the time passed, however, I realized that Christina would not be wide awake until later in the afternoon. After a lengthy debate, I left and drove to Celeste's Bistro.

*　　*　　*

The overnight storms were gone and only a heavy overcast lingered. The mid-day air was heavy with humidity and felt like it might start raining any minute. My collar was soaked by the time I made it from the air-conditioned truck to the air-conditioned Celeste's Bistro.

I'd met Lorianne Hightower a few times, but wasn't sure I would recognize her. Women change their hair style and color and look totally different to me. I searched the crowded room and, when no one stood up to wave at me, I let the hostess seat me at one of only three empty tables. I didn't care to be surrounded so intimately by people I didn't know. As I settled in, however, the couple sitting next to me nodded and the man said, "Hello, Colonel Maxxon." Ah, good. I wasn't totally surrounded.

The bistro was a small room and the noise of conversation drowned out the four televisions, each with a different noon newscast. A waitress appeared and wiped the table with a wet cloth. "What ya want to drink?" she asked.

Iced tea," I said. "I'm meeting Lorianne Hightower."

The waitress looked around the room and declared, "She ain't here yet."

Lorianne came through the door as the waitress delivered my iced tea. The scuttlebutt had it that Lorianne has played tennis at least four days a week since she was nine years old. She was the same height as me and muscularly built in an attractive female way. Her reddish auburn hair was highlighted and framed a squarish masculine face that probably favored her father. She designed her makeup to highlight her feminine features, resulting in a very attractive woman. She stretched her hand and gripped mine firmly in a businesslike manner, then quickly moved to hug me.

The waitress waited while I held the chair out for Lorianne, and she sat down gracefully. Then the waitress said, "Hello, Mrs. Hightower. Would you like a drink?"

Lorianne surveyed my glass of iced tea and said, "I'll have the same as him." The waitress thanked her and walked away. "Normally I'd have a vodka martini for lunch," she said. "But, today I have a customer who swears she can smell vodka on my breath. She's a Bible-toting Southern Baptist, so I avoid drinking at lunch when she's scheduled for an afternoon appointment." Her smile showed a lot of gleaming teeth.

"I'm glad you came to meet me," I said.

"I'm sorry I only have a few minutes," Lorianne said. "But that's my life with the salon and all."

I sipped on my iced tea casually. "I just have a few questions,"

"Okay," she said, "although I can't imagine what else you could ask. I mean, after I spent five hours with the local police. Are you working with Detective Boynton on the case?"

I wrinkled my nose and shrugged. "Nick would love to have me do his work for him," I said. "But, right now I've got too much on my plate. My wife—"

"I heard about Christina's accident," Lorianne interjected. "How is she doing?"

"She's doing okay," I said. "The doctors expect to move her to Our Lady of Grace Rehab Center Friday afternoon or Saturday morning."

Lorianne looked around the café. "I know the police still consider me a suspect. I don't think the cops think I pulled the trigger, but they haven't given up on the idea that I might have hired it done. But I can tell you in all honesty, neither Jason nor I killed Melvyn."

I remembered Nick telling me about Lorianne writing

checks to Jason for twenty-five thousand dollars, and thought about asking her about that. Then I decided against it. Nick had confided that information to me, and I shouldn't scatter it around. As close as I felt comfortable going was to ask, "Is there any reason why people would think you paid someone to have Melvyn taken out?"

"Is that the first of a few questions?" Lorianne said, and smiled broadly.

"No. It just popped into my mind from what you just said."

"Well," Lorianne started, then paused to think through what she was about to say. "I told Detective Boynton that I made some rather crude remarks about what I wanted to do to Melvyn. I know Steve Cosburn told the cops that I threatened to kill Melvyn. And I probably said something like that. I don't remember."

"I've been told they were incriminating?"

"Taken out of context, I suppose," Lorianne spoke slowly, reminiscing. "I regret ever saying them. But we were having a knockdown drag-out fight."

"About what?"

"Money, of course."

"Not other women?"

"Other women?" Lorianne said and smiled. "I don't thing Shag and I have ever worried about other people."

"The argument was about money—like the family budget or something like that?"

Lorianne studied me for a long moment. "Shag was literally a tightwad. He was worse than ol' Scrooge. He always has been. When I bought my car, he suddenly went crazy. He set up a new checking account in his name only. He did the same thing with our savings account. He took my name off of everything he could. The investment accounts are all in joint tenancy. He claimed I had blown all the money I inherited from my folks and was starting to blow his money. I make pretty good money at the salon. But Shag made more with his carpet business."

"Okay," I said. "Let's get to the questions I really wanted to talk to you about. Did Melvyn ever talk about selling the number thirty-five car?"

"Shag has been going to sell that car for—I don't know—

probably three years now," Lorianne said. "He'd line up a buyer, and then at the last minute, he'd back out of the deal. He'd decided he wanted to drive it just one more season."

"Do you think that upset someone bad enough they would kill Melvyn?" I asked.

"Shag pissed off a lot of people for a lot of different reasons," Lorianne said. "He got several phone calls over the last few weeks. I heard him arguing with one, but he hung up and calmed down. Shag was like most of you drivers have to be, I assume. You flare off, but then cool off real quickly."

"Any idea how much he was asking for the car?" I asked.

"I think he mentioned fifty-five thousand once," Lorianne said. "Something like that."

"Had he lost interest in racing?" I asked.

"Oh, not really," Lorianne said. "Shag had hemorrhoids. They got so bad at times, he could hardly walk. He really suffered after some races, and that was usually when he started talking about selling the car."

"Hemorrhoids can make your life miserable," I said. "Do you know the names of any of the people he talked to about selling the car?"

"I was never involved," Lorianne said matter-of-factly. "If Shag ever mentioned a name, I probably wouldn't have remembered it anyhow, unless it was someone I knew."

"What do you plan to do with the car?"

"I'm going to sell it," Lorianne said. "For a fair price."

"I'm glad you're being reasonable about it," I said. "Did Nick put a Mechanic's Lien against the car's Bill of Sale? Assuming he ever finds it."

"I don't think there's an official lien of any kind," Lorianne said. "But you can bet I'm not about to do anything with the damn car until Detective Boynton tells me I can."

"I will help you find a new sponsor if you decide to keep it," I said.

"I appreciate that, Kurt, but I don't think I want the memory and especially the hassle involved with owning a car and hiring drivers. I know Steve would keep the car running, but it is just too much for me." Her smile showed more gleaming teeth.

"I suppose it could be," I said. "I'm interested in keeping a good car racing in the SRVSCRA and bringing more businesses into it," I said with a smile.

*　　*　　*

I drove back to the hospital and went to Christina's room. She was more awake than she had been for several days, and staying awake longer each time. The pain meds kept her from becoming alert and chipper, and she was losing the jaundice caused by the adrenaline flow during the accident. Her normal golden glow aura was returning. I leaned down to kiss her, and she smiled.

"Wher' ... 'ave ... y ... been?" Christina said.

"I went to talk to Lorianne Hightower."

"How ... is ... sh ...doing?"

"Pretty well," I said. "I can't make up my mind whether she hired someone to take Melvyn out. She does seem contrite. And she seemed to regret making comments about wanting to kill Melvyn. But I don't know. The jury is still out on that one, I guess."

"Judge ... nt ... lest ... ye ... b ... judged."

"I agree, my love," I said. "Lorianne knows she's still under suspicion. I wanted to talk to her about what she plans to do with the number thirty-five car. She told me she is going to sell it."

"That's ... good," Christina said.

A nurse came into the room and took Christina's vitals. "You want the TV on?" the nurse asked Christina.

Christina shook her head.

The nurse looked at me.

I shook my head. If Christina didn't want the TV on, I sure didn't want it on.

As the nurse went out the door, Phil Schroeder came into the room. He shook my hand as he walked past me toward Christina. "How are you feeling, young lady?" he said to Christina.

Phillip Schroeder graduated Albertstown High School the first year Christina was the school administrator for the district. What is this "young lady" business?

"We got you lined up for Our Lady of Grace Rehab," Phil said. "Friday afternoon. Saturday morning at the latest. So you try to get a lot better between now and then."

"I ... will," Christina promised.

"Alright," Phil said as he listened to her lungs and heart.

"Did they have an opening?" I asked.

Phil simply gave me a sidelong glance. "Why, naturally, they had an opening."

I decided to let it go. "Is she going the way she is?"

"I'd expect she will. What are you talking about?"

"You're going to leave all the tubes, casts, bandages, and supports?" I asked.

"The only thing that will change is that we'll disconnect the IV drips and switch her to new ones in the ambulance. When she gets to Our Lady, they'll hook up their IV drip equipment. The major difference will be their drip won't have a sedative in it. Ours does so she'll be comfortable during the transport." Phil gave me a look that said: Don't ask any more stupid questions, Colonel Maxxon

*   *   *

Alisa Sharpe

Alisa hung back. She did not want Maggie walking with her to her car. Maggie probably didn't know the difference between a BMW and a Chevy, but there was no sense testing her. Maggie walked toward Alisa. "You going home?" Maggie asked.

I'm going to get a Coke to go," Alisa said. "I'm waiting for a phone call and wanted to take it inside."

"It's not raining," Maggie said. "I'm going to go. I really like you," Maggie said. "You talk so smart."

"Thank you. I like you, too," Alisa said, although she wondered where this was going.

Maggie went out the back door and walked to her car parked in the rear of the lot. Alisa watched as she drove onto the street. Alisa looked to find Rebecca and went to talk to her. "Did that girl you interviewed this morning accept the job?" she asked.

Rebecca Pepper wagged her head. "No. She didn't."

"I can work tomorrow," Alisa said. "I may want to follow up on some stuff with Maggie."

"That would sure help me," Rebecca said.

Alisa walked to her car and dropped down into it. She took out the mini-cassette recorder and listened to her recorded notes. She made several notes on her tablet, then drove to the hotel. "After a long, hot shower, I'll call Kurt and report in," she said aloud.

*　　*　　*

Kurt Maxxon

In one of her lucid moments, I told Christina I had to leave and take Kimberly and Mikie to a doctor's appointment.

"That's ... good," she said. "I'm ... okay."

I left Hopewell Memorial and drove to Maurey's garage for Kimberly, then to the daycare for Mikie, and then drove to Dr. Watson's office. While Kimberly filled out the forms about Mikie's latest health, I filled out the forms that would cover Kimberly and her family under the insurance plan I had for Kurt Maxxon Enterprises, LLC employees.

While Mikie was being examined, I sat reading magazines, even getting interested in an article in the latest Popular Science about the newest astronomical discoveries. Mikie came dashing out first and ran to me. He was smiling and seemed happier than when we arrived. "How you doing, partner?" I asked him.

"I'm good," he said. "The doctor gave Mom a 'scription. I have to take a pill every morning."

"Great," I said and watched Kimberly come through the door. She was smiling a little brighter also.

"The doctor is confident we can control it," Kimberly said. "And it might be kind of a temporary condition."

"That's really good," I said as I led them out of the clinic and back to my truck. I opened the rear door, and Mikie scrambled up into the truck. I helped Kimberly climb in the front after she fastened the belts on Mikie's child seat. "You need to get a prescription filled?"

"Yes, but the doctor gave me four sample packages, which is four weeks of pills," Kimberly said. "So we don't need to get it filled today."

"I'll go to the pharmacy we use and sign you up for our plan," I said. "When you need it, let me know. I'll go get it filled the first time so we can see what it will cost."

"I hope it doesn't cost too much," Kimberly said, a worried look on her forehead. "Until I get back on my feet."

"The maximum it will cost you is twenty bucks," I said. "We have a prescription plan as part of our insurance."

"Really?" Kimberly swung to look at me, her eyes large.

I nodded.

Kimberly looked into the back seat at Mikie who sat alert, watching out the side window. "It would just be wonderful if this thing was temporary," she said.

"That would be an answer to our prayers," I said.

At Maurey's garage, I followed Kimberly and Mikie in. Maurey walked directly toward me, and all the other mechanics followed him. "How's Christina?" he asked.

"She's staying awake longer," I said. "Phil Schroeder said they might have her up and walking this afternoon." The crowd gave a group sigh and returned to their workstations. Kimberly kissed Mikie goodbye and said, "I've got several parts I need to track down. I need to get busy." She walked toward her office.

I delivered Mikie back to the daycare center. My cell phone jangled. It was Alisa Sharpe, and I pushed the speaker phone button.

"The gun Maggie took to the track could very well be the murder weapon," Alisa said. "I ran a copy of the S&W Model 686 off the Internet last night. I got Maggie talking about guns and told her I was thinking of buying one, and I showed the picture. She said, 'that looks like the gun I found in the booth over there.'"

"Did Maggie take the gun to the track?" I asked.

"I've pretty well confirmed that Maggie had that pistol in her fanny pack when she got to the track."

"I'd be interested in knowing what happened to the gun," I said. "If it is the murder weapon, how did the shooter get hold of it?"

"I'll be working at Pepper's again tomorrow morning," Alisa said. "I'm going to try to develop new questions I want answers to. Talking to Maggie is like trying to find a doorway into a labyrinth. We need to move fast; however, I suspect we'll eventually need Nick to look into exactly who Maggie Decker is."

"Can you stay in Centralia that long?"

"This case is getting more and more interesting," Alisa said.

"Where are you now?"

"I'm in my hotel room."

I heard a knock on the door to Alisa's room, and Alisa told me to "hold on for a minute." In the background I heard her open the door and say, "Come on in here. Damn, am I happy to see you." Then I heard Mutt's voice. Alisa came back on line. "Mutt just showed up."

"That's good," I said. "Were you expecting him?"

"No. He surprised me."

"That's even better," I said.

Alisa said, "It's Kurt. Say hello, Mutt."

Mutt asked, "How's Christina?"

"She's starting to wake up—and stay awake. I'm on my way back to the hospital now."

"I figured we'd run by to see her, later," Mutt said. "That's why I ran over. Do you think she'll know who we are?"

"I think she will," I said. "Why don't you plan on doing that this evening?"

I dropped Mikie off at the Daycare and drove to the hospital. Christina was sleeping when I arrived, but she woke up shortly after. I walked to stand next to her. She smiled at me. "Where ... ha ... yo ... been?"

"I took Kimberly and Mikie to the doctor."

"Good."

A nurse came in and took her blood pressure and checked the machines connected by tubes. She stood at the foot of the bed looking at Christina. "You need anything, Mrs. Maxxon?"

Christina shook her head. "No."

My cell phone jangled, and I went out into the hallway. Cell phones are no-nos in hospitals. The caller ID told me it was Nick Boynton. I walked down to my mini-office at the end of the hall. I called Nick back.

"You had lunch with Lorianne Hightower," Nick said unceremoniously.

"Yes, I did," I said. "Are your people tailing her?"

"Not really," Nick said. "One of my guys was there having lunch, too. He saw you, and he knows who she is. Did she say anything about the GPS we put on her car?"

"No. She didn't mention it. I wanted to find out what she is going to do with Melvyn's car," I said.

"Did Lorianne tell you anything worth talking about?" Nick asked.

"Not really. I found out the argument Steve Cosburn heard was over money, not women. But I do want to talk to you about another woman." After I said it, I wished I'd taken a different tack.

"Another woman?"

"Yes. Can you meet me about five o'clock?"

"Where?"

"Let's meet in my office," I said. "It's on the second floor over my auto parts store. There's a stairway at the middle of the building. I'm going to ask Alisa Sharpe to talk to you also. We'll tell you the whole story when we meet."

"Okay," Nick said. "I can be there."

I called Alisa and invited her and Mutt to the meeting.

"That was fast," Alisa said.

"Nick called me, so I asked him to meet with us. He's anxious for anything new. We can grab a bite to eat after the meeting and then come here to the hospital to see Christina."

"Is Christina awake?"

"She's staying awake longer each time. She should be reasonably alert by then."

*   *   *

I trudged up the steps to my office. My auto parts store was a two story building. The second floor, which only covered the front half of the lower floor, was all offices and file storage. I had six office people: a secretary, a bookkeeper, two clerks, and two buyers. Each of them had office space. The back third of the second story was my office. It was the most spacious of all, but at some time in the future, I planned to hire another clerk and buyer, and I would carve the new offices out of my space. The desk, credenza, and file cabinet in my office were there when I bought the place in 1993. I had a new phone system installed with a modern intercom feature. Since then, nothing else had changed. The carpet probably needed to be replaced. I remembered several offers from Melvyn Hightower to replace my carpet. Now I wished I'd taken him up on it.

At the front of the office space there was a stairwell for the office people to use regularly. The stairway at the side led to my office only, and allowed me to invite people I might not want the employees to see. Nick Boynton and Alisa Sharpe fit into that category. All but one of the buyers, who was a workaholic, would be leaving at 4:30 PM.

I didn't spend that much time in my office, even when I was racing. I held a staff meeting every Wednesday at ten o'clock, which lasted about an hour. Some weeks that was the only time I was in my office. During today's staff meeting, I'd called in to see if there were any pressing problems they needed me to resolve. The only thing they wanted was an update on Christina.

I started the big coffee pot in the private rest room adjacent to my office, arranged the chairs around the round conference table in my office and laid pencils and tablets on the table. My supply of writing tablets was down to three—time to reorder a couple dozen of them.

Alisa and Mutt arrived five minutes to five, and Nick came huffing up the stairs at five after five. We made small talk for several minutes and then got down to business. I filled Nick in on what Alisa and I had been doing with Maggie Decker. Then Alisa read from her notes. Maggie had found a pistol in a booth, and she had the pistol in her fanny pack when she went to the track. She was waiting for Melvyn to shower so they could have sex, when another man arrived. The man argued with Melvyn.

Nick made notes in his notebook. He listened intently. When Alisa wrapped up, Nick said, "You say this Maggie can't describe the man who showed up to argue with Melvyn?"

"No. It was a pretty generic description," Alisa said, flipping pages in her notebook. "Fat, black hair, age about the same as Kurt Maxxon."

"That old," Nick said as he pulled up a clean page in his notebook. "Description fits about twenty-five percent of the men in Centralia."

"Right!" I said.

Nick pulled his cell phone from his jacket pocket and punched a speed dial number. After someone answered on the other end and some small talk, Nick said, "I need an IAFIS run on a woman named Maggie Decker compared to that weapon we have in the Hightower homicide." Nick listened and then said, "Hold on." He covered the phone and asked, "Is Maggie her real name or nickname? Is Decker a maiden name or married name?"

"Nothing is ever easy," I said.

Alisa, ever the consummate investigator, said, "Margaret, aka, Maggie, nee Bronson, Decker. DOB March 20, 1969."

Nick relayed the information. He said, "Thanks, let me know." He folded his phone closed and stood up, stretching his lower back muscles. "I'm getting old," he said, then looked at Mutt, then me. "Ah, hell, most of us in this room know what it's like to get old. But I've got a slipped disk."

"You need an elevator," Mutt said.

"There's no place to put one," I said and smiled.

"Disc problems are nothing to mess with," Mutt said. "I've had two surgeries for ruptured disks."

Nick left. While Alisa and Mutt waited, I tidied up the office—emptying the coffee pot and moving the waste basket next to the office door where the janitor would empty it.

Alisa, Mutt and I went down the side stairs. We'd decided to go to the hospital and eat in the cafeteria after we checked in on Christina.

CHAPTER SEVENTEEN
Wednesday Evening, August 29

Kurt Maxxon

Alisa, Mutt and I spent almost forty-five minutes with Christina. Amazingly, she was fairly alert through most of it. I was thrilled to have her talking to me, and me talking to her, and didn't want it to end. Eventually, Christina started fading out, and we realized it was time to leave her for a while.

"Let's go down and get something to eat," I suggested.

In the cafeteria, the three of us chatted during supper. Alisa and I didn't want to bore Mutt with the Melvyn Hightower homicide investigation, so we tried to keep the conversation about the weather, about Beau and about racing. Mutt talked about his upcoming trip to England to cover the Formula 1 race there.

Alisa was the one who saw Nick Boynton come into the cafeteria and look around. She pointed her thumb toward Nick and said, "Detective Boynton has arrived."

I looked to see Nick scanning the tables. When he saw us, he went to get a cup of coffee and then walked toward us. He was in shirt sleeves, and his gun and badge holsters weren't visible. He greeted each of us.

"Christina looks good," Nick said. "I went up looking for you. She was asleep. I decided you'd probably be where the food is. She's doing okay?"

"Yes, she is," I said.

"We didn't get any matches," Nick growled. "Mainly because Maggie Decker has never been fingerprinted. She's not in the IAFIS."

"Never printed?" I said.

"It happens," Nick said. "More often than you might think, especially young females who just become invisible in our society—no college or military—just become wives and mothers."

"Alisa is going to be working with Maggie again tomorrow morning," I said, nodding toward Alisa. "She can grab a glass or a coffee cup with Maggie's prints on it, and you can run the check."

"That won't work," Nick said. "It'd never be admissible in court."

"How do we get a set of Maggie's prints?" I asked.

"I'm looking for better suggestions than yours, Maxxon." Nick glared with an authoritative stare.

"Maggie is on pot, heavy," Alisa said.

"Oh, yeah?" Nick said, pursing his lips as he studied Alisa. He pulled his cell phone from its holster on his belt. "I'll check with the DE guys," Nick said. "Maybe they know about her. If they have her on their scopes, they might be able to bust her when she makes a buy. With her in custody for a few hours, we can print her."

"How long will that take?" I asked.

"Could happen tonight. Might take a week." Nick was in his basic reporting mode. He stood and walked out into the hallway to talk on his phone. When he came back, he didn't sit down. "They know about her, and may be able to set her up in a sting."

"So, you'll be working at Pepper's tomorrow," Nick said.

"Yes. Tomorrow morning," Alisa said. "Probably not much longer, however."

"If I come up with something I'd like you to get out of her, would you do that?" Nick said.

"Sure," Alisa said. "My cell phone number is on my card." She handed Nick a business card.

"I doubt you're in much danger, operating undercover like this," Nick said. "But if you feel threatened, let me know."

"I'm just fine," Alisa said.

Nick's cell phone rang, and he walked back out into the hall. After a few minutes, he waved goodbye to the three of us from the hallway and walked toward the front door.

I walked Alisa and Mutt to their Land Rover in the parking lot and bid them good evening. I went back to Christina's room and sat, hoping she would become lucid again. But after an hour, she was sleeping deeply. I leaned down to kiss her and said, "I'm going home to take care of Beau."

At the sound of Beau's name, Christina stirred slightly and her eyes fluttered open. "How's t' ... Li'tle ... Guy ... ?"

"He's fine. He misses you," I said, but she was asleep before I finished the sentence.

I left to go home.

*   *   *

After Beau had gone out to do his business, lapped water and nibbled at his food bowl, he jumped up and curled up in Christina's chair. I sat down at the dinette table in the kitchen with my writing tablet and studied my notes. Once again, the fact that Maggie Decker and Lorianne Hightower dominated the notes was blatantly clear. But my gut feeling was even more convinced that Maggie probably would not have killed Melvyn, and I secretly hoped Maggie would not be connected with the murder weapon. I tore two sheets from the tablet and added them to the stack I stuck at the back of the tablet. At the top of a new page, I wrote:

Man arrived & argued with Melvyn (per Maggie)

I underlined that line of writing and tried to remember all the things I'd heard about the man who argued with Melvyn. Then I tried to replay the voice that had called me last Friday night. I flipped through the previous pages of notes, scanning them again. I let my mind go blank and decided to write down my thoughts as they came to mind. I wrote it on a new empty sheet:

Cheating

Stealing

Double dealing

Lying

Those were the words I remembered the voice using. I wrote them down in the sequence I thought I'd heard them: That lying, cheating, stealing Melvyn Hightower!

Then I wrote: Was the voice on the phone the same man who argued with Melvyn? I had assumed it was. But was that a good assumption?

Was the voice on the phone really the one who killed Melvyn? He said he did it!

Did the argument Maggie described lead to the shooting? Was there something else involved?

I jotted: This is like riding a Merry-Go-Round!

Then my mind wandered to Melvyn's car. Where is Melvyn's car? Why can't we find Melvyn's car? Reality set in, however. What good will it do to find Melvyn's car? Fingerprints? DNA? From hair. Anything else?

I glanced at my watch and decided to turn on the all-news channel. After the TV came to life, the weather man did his thing, and then they went to sports.

As I scanned over my notes, I suddenly realized: Colonel Maxxon, you are looking at one huge disconnected mess.

*   *   *

Lorianne Hightower

She arrived at the storage shed and went right to work, shredding handfuls of paper for several minutes before she stopped to allow the shredder to cool off. The earplugs she'd pushed into her ears helped prevent the headaches from developing. But with the earplugs in, she worried about someone sneaking up on her. The sun was low on the western horizon and, while there was a layer of low clouds, they were light in color, not the kind of cloud that produced rain. It would be dark in less than an hour, and she worried about the security guard arriving again. That guard had spooked her enough that she had decided not to stay in the area after dark even if it meant the shredding might take longer.

After the shredder cooled down, she returned to shoving handfuls of papers into it. Suddenly, she realized there was a man standing in the doorway. Her breath caught. Her muscles tensed. She recovered and switched off the shredder and mustered as calm a voice as she could. "Yes, can I help you?"

The man smiled. "You're making an awful lot of noise," he said.

"I'm sorry," Lorianne said. "Is it bothering you?"

"Nooo," The man said. "I was just wondering what you were doing. I've got a unit three doors down. I heard the noise and just wondered what was causing it."

"Oh, I've got to shred all these documents," Lorianne said. "I'm a small bookkeeper, and I have to get rid of client's documents each year. It's a pain in the ass and takes a lot of time, but I only need to keep records for a certain number of years."

"You store the client's documents here in this shed?"

"No, no. I keep them in my office, but to shred them in my office, I'd have the neighbors calling the cops to complain about the noise."

"Oh, I see," the man said. "It is noisy."

"I'm about done for today," Lorianne said. "I want to get home before dark."

"This is not a good area to be in after dark," the man said. "Even hardened criminals get hurt here after dark."

"Oh, yeah," Lorianne said.

"Didn't you see on TV about the drug bunch that used this storage unit to stage their shipments? The ringleader was found dead in one of the units toward the back a few months ago."

"I don't watch that much news," Lorianne said.

"I've got to get unloaded and get out of here myself," the man said. "Best of luck to you, ma'am." He walked away.

"I've got to keep going," Lorianne said. "But I'll be out of here before dark." The man's comments augmented the security guards warning. I've got to get rid of these papers. But even if it takes months, I'm not going to put myself at risk.

Another person had seen her at the shed—could place her here shredding documents.

"Dammit," Lorianne said aloud. She went back to shredding and, once again, didn't notice the person standing in the door until she stopped and turned the shredder off to cool. When she looked up, she saw the short, chunky woman with platinum blonde hair holding a pistol pointed straight at her.

"Maxine!" Lorianne said. "What are you doing?"

"I think you know," Maxine said. She looked at the boxes of paper, then at the shredder, and then at Lorianne. "I can't believe you were stupid enough to keep the evidence all this time."

"What are you talking about?" Lorianne said, hoping her voice sounded stronger than it sounded to her.

"The cops knew about the counterfeit cosmetics being brought into the valley over the last dozen years. They just have bigger fish to fry. It's hurt Jarvis Beauty Supply quite a bit all along. Eventually, I started doing some research after I decided that the only way someone could do so much without getting caught was to be an insider—someone in the business. I made of list of operators I suspected could be doing it. You were way down near the bottom

of the list, so it took me a while to track you down. But I've been
following you ever since I figured out it was you."

Lorianne frowned. "You've been following me?"

Maxine shrugged and looked away. "You were looking for
suspicious cop cars," Maxine said. "I just boogied along behind you
in my old Jeep."

"Okay. What do you want?"

"We can do this the easy way, or we can do it the hard
way," Maxine said.

"What's the easy way?" Lorianne asked.

"You transferred your inventories to your three mules,"
Maxine said, "so you could go into hiding, thinking the cops were
watching you. You didn't want them to discover your nefarious
enterprise."

Lorianne stood transfixed.

Maxine walked toward the boxes. Lorianne turned,
wondering how to disarm her.

"Do Teresa, Elberta and Lynette have the moxie to keep
the enterprise going?" Maxine asked.

Lorianne remained silent.

"I seriously doubt it," Maxine answered her own question.

"So, to keep it going, you'd have to get back into the
command position—to do the reordering and marshal the
distribution—as quickly as possible."

Lorianne stood staring at Maxine. "I suppose," she said.
She was not surprised at Maxine's perceptiveness and tenacity. You
let yourself get caught, dummy.

"I doubt any of those three women can keep the supply
flowing—unless they have your help."

Lorianne nodded.

"So the easy way that you and I handle this matter is that
you simply close down this operation. You don't help your mules
keep it going, and you just decide not to start it up again, if or when
the cops stop watching you."

"What's the hard way?" Lorianne asked.

Maxine pulled her cell phone from its holster and held it
up. "I call the cops right now."

"I understand," Lorianne said. "Not much need to shred
all those papers."

"I'll take a couple of the later boxes over there, as a security deposit," Maxine said, pointing to the stack of boxes with the gun. "I've gathered samples of the fake cosmetics that I have gotten tested. I've got you surrounded girl—lock stock and barrel." She waved the gun in the air over her head.

Lorianne shrugged and nodded again.

"Hell, if I were you," Maxine said, "I'd just haul the rest of those boxes to the landfill."

"You need a paper shredder?" Lorianne asked.

"You can donate it to the Kiwanis auction," Maxine said. She walked to the stack of boxes, stuck the pistol into her waistband, lifted one, and then carried it to the door opening. She repeated the process with a second box which she stacked on top of the first. Lorianne felt her legs getting weak.

Maxine walked out the door and a few minutes later drove up and backed her camouflage painted Jeep with canvas top and sides next to the rollup door. She loaded the two boxes into the back seat and walked back to the driver's door. With one leg into the Jeep, Maxine paused to pull the pistol out of her waistband and shove it under her seat, and turned to face Lorianne. "It's been a pleasure doing business with you, Lorianne. Good luck to you. I'm sorry about Melvyn—if, of course, you didn't have anything to do with it." She hiked her leg up onto the driver's seat, started the engine, waved goodbye, and drove away.

Lorianne let various emotions flit through her mind. Eventually she walked out and lowered the roll up door. She put the padlocks on each side of the door, and walked toward the van.

I'm glad it's all over.

As she drove away, she realized she had left the shredder plugged into the ceiling fixture and the overhead light burning.

Waste not, want not. But if you're going to waste, do it big.

*   *   *

Kurt Maxxon

I was still trying to find connections in my notes. But nothing jumped out at me. I was ready to give up and just relax when my cell phone jangled. I answered it on speaker.

"Dudley, here," Dudley Simpson said.

"Hello, Dudley, how're you doing?"

"I'm good," Dudley said. "I've got some license plate

numbers for you."

"Great," I said. "Go ahead."

"You got a pencil?"

"I'm ready."

"Walt Murdock drives a red Corvette with license number JK 9834," Dudley said. "I got that one nailed. Then there's two people he met today, same people he's met at other times. One drives a blue Continental Mark IV, license number JL 2946. The other drives a black Hummer with license number JK 4905."

"That's great, Dudley," I said. "I really thank you for doing this for me."

"You gonna get Brad Langley to ID those plates?"

"No. I'll get Nick Boynton to ID them."

"You involved with Boynton?" Dudley asked.

"He's the lead detective on the homicide case," I said.

"Be careful of Nick Boynton," Dudley said.

"Why?"

"Just be careful," Dudley repeated and hung up.

Undaunted, I dialed Nick Boynton's number. He answered and I said, "I need a favor."

"Yeah? What da ya need?"

"The names and information for a couple of license numbers."

"Give me something hard," Nick quipped. "Go ahead."

I read the numbers to Nick.

"What's this about? Does it have anything to do with the homicide?"

"Nothing to do with the homicide," I said. "It's a personal thing for a friend of mine."

"I assume it's nothing illegal, immoral, or unethical," Nick said, and I could visualize his worried frown.

"It's one of them," I said. "But not terribly bad."

"I'll get back to you in a little while," Nick said and hung up.

"Thanks," I said to a dial tone.

*   *   *

Maggie Decker

She'd worked both the breakfast and lunch crowds at Pepper's Diner and, when she left work, she drove to the Cinema Seven at the Westside Shopping Mall. She watched the movie twice, since her mother had always told her that was a way to get the most for your money. The movie was about a man and a woman who struggled against many adversaries to have children and raise the children. Where do children come from? Maggie had never been able to answer that question.

Maggie left the cinema and drove home. She rummaged around the apartment for a joint of marijuana, but she couldn't find any. When she looked in the refrigerator, all she saw was a moldy package of cheese and two cans of beer. She decided to go to the grocery store for bread and lunch meat, and to buy a few joints of marijuana.

As she walked toward the grocery store from her car, a man stepped toward her. "You looking for joints?" he asked.

Maggie stopped and looked at the man. "You got joints?" she asked.

"I sure do. Really good stuff, too. Better than you can get from those dudes inside."

"I'll take a couple of them," Maggie said.

"You got cash to pay?"

Maggie dug money out of her fanny pack. "Yep, see," she said, holding the money up.

"You sure do," the man said. He took the money from her, and handed her an envelope.

Maggie spread the envelope and saw two neatly rolled marijuana joints. She smiled at the man. "Thank you," she said.

The man nodded, and then said, "You're under arrest for possession of a banned substance." He moved to gather her hands into handcuffs.

"What?" Maggie said. "What're you doing?"

"You are being arrested for possession of a banned substance," the man said. He produced a badge as a female moved next to her, also flashing a badge. "You have the right to remain silent," the man said. "Anything you say can and will be used against you in a court of law."

Maggie didn't know what to do, and said in an agitated tone, "I don't really need the stuff. You can have it back." The cops walked her to a plain white car and put her in the backseat. "Where are we going?" she asked.

"To the police station," the cop said.

At the police station, she was forced to empty her pockets and give up her fanny pack. She was put in a holding cell with several other people, but she shied away from all of them. Then a lady cop came up to her and asked if she wanted to call someone? Who can I call? No one came to mind. She sat for a long time worrying about what was going to happen next. Then she remembered her new friend. "Can I have my cell phone, please?" she asked.

"No," the lady cop said.

"I need to call a friend whose number is in my cell phone," Maggie said.

"I'll see if I can get your cell phone," the woman said. "Long enough to get the number."

After a time, the woman brought Maggie's cell phone to her and supervised as she went into her contact list and found her new friend, Alisa Sharpe. She punched the number on the black wall phone. The phone buzzed and buzzed. She was about to hang up when she heard Alisa say, "Hello."

*   *   *

Alisa Sharpe

She was snuggled against Mutt. It took several seconds before she realized the noise bothering her was her cell phone ringing. She threw the cover off and reached for the phone. "Hello."

The voice on the other end was barely audible, but she eventually realized it was Maggie Decker. "Who is this?" Alisa said.

The voice strengthened a little, "Maggie. Uh Maggie Decker."

"What's up?" Alisa asked.

"I'm in jail," Maggie said.

Mutt stirred and rolled over on his side facing Alisa. "What?" he said.

Alisa waved him silent. She was straining to hear Maggie.

"You're in jail?" Alisa said. "What are you in jail for?" Alisa was coming awake and realized that Nick had already got the drug guys to bust Maggie. "You're in jail for buying a joint?" she repeated.

Alisa watched Mutt get up and go to the bathroom.

She listened as Maggie whined about not knowing what

was happening; could "Lisa" come to the jail, and help her talk to the cops?

"Yes, I can come and help you get out of jail," Alisa told Maggie. "I'll be there in a half hour."

Mutt gave Alisa a withering look. "You don't need to be bringing stray animals home."

"I have to go," Alisa said, as she was dressing. "I've got a lot invested in this case already." She thought about calling Kurt, but decided against it. He was probably sleeping—it was ten-thirty—but she needed to keep Maggie confident in her. This was a great way to do that.

*　　*　　*

Kurt Maxxon

I'd studied my notes off and on, then gazed into space for several minutes, then went back to studying my notes. But nothing was making sense. My cell phone jangled, and I answered it.

Nick said, "I got your license information."

"Great," I said. "I'm ready."

"JK 9834 is a red Corvette registered to Walter P. Murdock, an operator in everything illegal and immoral. JL 2946 is a white Lincoln Continental Mark IV registered to Monroe V. Sullivan, a known minor hood. JK 4905 is a black Hummer, registered to Owen C. Kelso, a local attorney with suspected mob ties."

"Damn," I said.

"I hope you haven't landed yourself into something you can't handle, Maxxon."

"So do I."

"You want to talk something over?" Nick asked.

"Not yet. I think I can handle it," I said and hoped it was true.

"We're partners," Nick said. "If you need help, you just gotta let me know."

"I appreciate that," I said. "But for now, I'll try it alone."

"You've got my phone number," Nick said as he hung up.

CHAPTER EIGHTEEN
Thursday, August 30

Kurt Maxxon

I arrived at Christina's room as the sun was clearing the eastern horizon. When I walked to stand near her, Christina stirred slightly, but didn't come awake. I stood stroking her silky blond hair, waiting. After a long time, Christina's eyes fluttered open. She blinked a few times and went back asleep. I waited. I was about to give up and sit down when Christina moved her head, opened her eyes, frowned slightly, then focused on me. She said, "G'd ... mor'ning ... love."

Those were the most beautiful words I had heard in several days. As the minutes passed, Christina became more and more alert. A nurse came in and did a vitals check.

"Can I get you anything, Mrs. Maxxon?" the nurse asked.

"Coffee," Christina said.

I jumped to my feet. "I'll get it for her," I said and took off at double time down the hall and down the stairs, to the cafeteria. I was thrilled to see that the coffee carafes looked fresh. I poured two cups, put lids on, and went to pay the cashier. I made it back to the room in less time than I estimated it would have taken for the nurse to order it delivered from the kitchen—and it was fresh.

Christina sipped on her cup. "Ta'stes ... good," she said.

At least she was talking to me. I raised my eyes to the ceiling. Thank you, Big Guy.

"Wh'at hap'n'd?" Christina asked.

"The Accident Report says that a truck driver was talking on his cell phone, and he failed to see a stop sign. He T-boned a car going westbound and sent that car careening into your car nearly head on."

"Ummm." Christina was back asleep.

* * *

Alisa Sharpe

Both Alisa and Maggie were tired. "I got to bed about one-thirty," Alisa said to Maggie as they sat in the booth drinking coffee during a break. The breakfast rush was over and only seven people were scattered around the room.

Maggie smiled. "I didn't go to bed, just sat on the sofa and dozed. When I got home, Berry was in my bed."

"Who is Berry?"

"Berry Atwater. He's a guy that used to live in the alley," Maggie said. "I told him he could sleep in my place."

"Does Berry show you he likes you?"

"Nah. I think he only likes boys."

"So the cops just busted you for buying a couple of marijuana joints last night?" Alisa brought the discussion back to the subject.

"Yep," Maggie said. "I go to that grocery store to buy the stuff all the time."

"They sell marijuana in that store?"

"Not in the store," Maggie said. "Any of the guys that work there have it for sale. They always go outside to deal."

"Did you go into the store?" Alisa asked.

"Nah. I hadn't got to the store yet." Maggie gazed off into the distance. "This guy comes up to me and asks do I want to buy some stuff."

Alisa knew why it had happened, and it appeared Maggie was remembering that it was Alisa who had come to get her out of jail.

"Have you talked to anyone else about what you saw last Friday at the track?" Alisa said in a confidential voice.

"Nah," Maggie said. "I didn't see anyone. Not even Kurt Maxxon. I like him."

"You like Kurt Maxxon?"

"Yep, he's cute. Just like that other driver. I'd like Kurt Maxxon to show me how much he likes me."

Alisa eyed Maggie. "You'd like to have sex with Kurt Maxxon?"

"Whatever you call it," Maggie said. "I like men showing me how much they like me. It makes me feel good."

"Melvyn showed you how much he liked you," Alisa said.

"A lot of times," Maggie said. "That's why I went to the track." Maggie sipped on her coffee.

"To have sex with Melvyn?" Alisa asked.

Maggie didn't seem to hear the question.

"Yesterday you told me you waited out in the lounge for Melvyn to shower. You said you were sitting on the pool table."

"Uh, yeah, that's right." Maggie sipped her coffee again.

"You had a gun in your fanny pack," Alisa continued. "But you don't know what happened to it."

"Yeah. It's gone."

"The reason I'm asking," Alisa said, "Is because I got to thinking if you still had the gun, I might buy it from you. I really need one, I think."

"I don't have it," Maggie said, frowning. "I don't know what happened to it."

"Maybe we can find it," Alisa said. "Did you have it in our fanny pack when you got to the track?"

"When I jumped down off the pool table," Maggie said. "It banged against my leg. That hurt."

"When did you jump off the pool table?"

"When the other guy showed up."

"Did you have it when you got out from behind the pool table to leave?"

"Uh, I don't remember."

"Did you have it when you got home?"

"I, uh … I don't think so."

"What happened when the other man arrived?" Alisa asked. "How did that come down?"

"Uh, well, he opened the door, and, and he looked into the men's room," Maggie said. "And then he yelled, 'Mel, are you in there?'"

"Did he see you?"

"No, the door wasn't open. When the door started to open, that's when I jumped down off the pool table."

"And the gun banged your leg?"

"Yep. It hurt."

"So what happened next?" Alisa hoped she wasn't stretching the interrogation too far.

"Uh, Melvyn yelled, 'Yeah. What do you want?'" Maggie frowned in deep thought. "The new guy came through the door and went into the men's room. I heard them talking. Then they started yelling at each other. That scared me so I ran away."

"You left?" Alisa said.

"As fast as I could."

"Was your fanny pack closed?"

"I've never been able to zip it closed. I found it in the trash at work."

"And the gun was gone when you got home?"

"Yeah. I don't know where I lost it. You want to buy it?"

"I'd buy it if you can find it," Alisa said, almost sure she knew the gun they were talking about was in the CPD evidence locker as evidence in the Hightower homicide.

*　　*　　*

Nick Boynton

Nick sat at the desk he shared with another senior detective. The desk and the two-drawer file cabinet next to it were heaped with file folders and paperwork. One pile of folders on the floor showed the results of spilling a cup of coffee on it while it resided on the desk. To let it dry it had been slammed to the floor.

"Detective Boynton," a voice said behind him, and Nick spun around to see one of the lab technicians walking toward him with a large manila envelope. "Lab results on the Hightower homicide, sir," she said.

The lab tech was one of the new ones hired right out of college. These latest techs were smart, fast, and thorough. Nick also noticed they all were attractive females. When I started in this business the only women were the clerks and secretaries on the first floor. The name tag on the lab tech's white coat lapel read: ADRIAN.

"Good," Nick said, as he took the envelope and opened it. He scanned the top sheet then shuffled to read the second sheet. "So, three of the latents appear to be partials of Maggie Decker?"

"Yes," the lab tech said, as she pulled a straight wooden chair from another desk and sat down crossing her shapely legs. "All three are partials," she said. "But if we integrate all three prints into one composite, we can see that they fit together very well, and that they are from Ms. Decker's left thumb. The frosting on the cake is that this composite print matches several prints we lifted from the lounge door and from the edge of the one pool table."

Nick studied the graphics on the following sheets. He could see what the lab had done. He knew what they were saying was true. But, could he convince the ADA that this provided sufficient probable cause? "Maybe a little iffy," Nick said.

"We're reasonably sure we can make it stick," the lab tech said. "It is very convincing."

"Convincing as hell to me and you," Nick said. "But is it even reasonable to a jury of twelve people, probably CEE students, who are always rooting for the underdog in the case?"

"Juries are fickle," Adrian agreed.

"Fickle is not the right word," Nick said. "But I'm not going to tell you what the right word is—"

"I've heard it before."

"I'll talk to the DA's office and see what they think." Nick promised.

*　　*　　*

Kurt Maxxon

My cell phone vibrated, and I went out into the hall to answer it. It was Dudley Simpson.

"Walt Murdock just arrived," Dudley said.

"How many Marines can you get there in an hour?"

"How many do you want?"

"Enough to be convincing," I said.

"You got it, Colonel," Dudley said and hung up.

I went back into Christina's room and said, "I've got some very important business to take care of. I'll be back in a couple of hours."

"What kind of business?" Christina frowned slightly. "You're not into something you shouldn't be?"

"Well, I probably am," I said, and smiled broadly. "But, at this point, it has to be full speed ahead."

"Take care of yourself."

"I plan to." I left and went down the stairs two at a time.

While I drove to Dudley's, I rehearsed what I was going to say to Murdock. I planned to start out mild and meek, but get tough only if I had to. When I walked into the dimness of Dudley's, I looked toward the table in the corner. Two men sat talking. Which was Walt Murdock? Who was the other guy?

Dudley came toward me and stood blocking my view of the table. "The guy in the red polo shirt is Murdock. The suit is Owen Kelso."

I nodded understanding and walked toward the table where I sat down opposite Walt Murdock. Murdock tried to ignore me, but he had gone silent.

"Me and my friend here were having a friendly conversation," Murdock said. "We didn't invite anyone else to join us."

"What can we do for you, Colonel Maxxon?" Kelso asked, checking the knot of his tie to make sure it was presentable.

At least the guy is a race fan.

"I want Mr. Murdock, here, to back off shaking down a friend of mine."

"What is your friend's name?" Kelso asked.

"Kay Hinds," I said.

"I don't know who Kay Hinds is," Murdock growled.

"She backed out of making a drug run for you last Sunday, and you're trying to shake her down for two hundred and fifty bucks." I watched Murdock's eyes as they moved side to side. I glanced at Kelso's face. He was calm and collected—typical lawyer.

Murdock said, "I don't know if you know who you're dealing with, Colonel Max … whatever. But I'm backed by an organization that doesn't scare real easy."

Dudley and fifteen ex-Marines came from the pool room and walked to stand around the table.

I watched the procession, noting the reactions of Murdock and Kelso.

"I'm backed by a much bigger organization that doesn't scare at all," I said, never taking my eyes off Murdock. "They've hurt people professionally, and they can hurt you, personally."

Murdock surveyed the group of Marines.

"Exactly what would you like Mr. Murdock to do, Colonel Maxxon?" Kelso asked, all the time staring at Murdock.

"Like I said, just leave the Hinds family alone." I kept staring at Murdock.

"I'm sure Mr. Murdock would prefer leaving the Hinds family alone rather than take his chances with the United States Marine Corps," Kelso said, never taking his gaze off of Murdock's face. "Isn't that true, Mr. Murdock?"

Murdock hesitated for a long time.

"Mr. Murdock?" Kelso said.

Finally, Murdock nodded. "Okay."

"You need anything else, Colonel?" Kelso asked.

"That's all I need. I thank you all for your cooperation," I said to all the people around the table.

*   *   *

Lorianne Hightower

As she loaded the last of the boxes into the van, Lorianne wished she had kept the pickup truck. It would have been much easier to haul the boxes. After she pushed the last box up onto the pile in the middle of the van, she wiped her brow with her hand and leaned against the side of the van. Unloading would be much easier. She could merely let the boxes fall out. As she pulled the rollup door down, she looked at the shredder. What do I do with it? Maybe like Maxine suggested, I should donate it to a charity. But not her damn Kiwanis Club.

Lorianne sipped on her bottle of water. The sun was midway toward sunset. The temperature was in the nineties, and the humidity felt like it was about the same. All last night she had wrestled with the question of whether to shred the papers or just take them to the landfill. The tipping point was the thought of spending months coming to this shed to shred the papers. Then I'd just have to haul the bags of shredded paper to the landfill.

Maxine Jarvis knew about her operations, bringing counterfeit cosmetics in from Brazil. It was good stuff, not dangerous. It was just un-taxed. No one was ever injured. Will Maxine Jarvis let me off the hook—completely? Thankfully, Maxine was just interested in eliminating the competition—not in retribution.

What can I do if Maxine reneges? What can I do if Lynette, Teresa or Elberta try to keep the business going?

Lorianne locked the storage shed door and drove to the landfill. She pulled onto the scales at the entrance. The sign on the wall read: $55.00 PER TON.

How much does this damn stuff weigh? Would it have weighed less if I brought it here as shredded paper? She thought about that for a long moment and concluded it probably would weigh the same, but the volume would be greater.

As she drove to the active area of the landfill, Lorianne saw a huge bulldozer pushing the piles of trash out into flat layers. Several trash trucks had dumped their loads and were pulling out. Lorianne backed into one of the empty slots, as close to the working bulldozer as she could. She threw boxes out of the van. As the last box went out, Lorianne sat down on the floor of the van. There, all those damn papers are gone. Thank God for small favors.

She pulled the van out of the way, parked at the edge of the driveway, and watched the bulldozer push the boxes into the chasm next to the active area. A huge earthmover rumbled over the chasm and dumped a load of dirt. A second earthmover followed the first. Lorianne relaxed. There go those damn papers!

On the drive home, Lorianne began thinking about the $500,000 insurance policy on Melvyn. There's no way I can speed that up. And you probably don't even want to try as long as the cops think you might have had Shag done in. Dammit all to hell.

"I should never have paid Jason back all at once," she said aloud. But the twenty-five thousand he loaned me from his bonus check helped me buy the Porsche at a good price, since I had cash.

"Right," she said. "But you're going to need some cash flow before this mess is all over."

Be patient. Good things come to those who wait.

*　　　*　　　*

Kurt Maxxon

When I returned to Christina's room I was thrilled that she seemed much more alert. I could tell she had been worried about what I was up to.

"You going t' tell me 'bout it?" she asked.

"Not right now," I said and sat down in her easy chair.

"I'm thinking better," Christina said. "Don't remember much about the ac'id'nt, but I'm thinking better."

"That's good," I said. "Because I need your input on Maggie Decker."

"Who is Maggie Decker?"

"She's the waitress who served us breakfast at Pepper's Diner last Sunday. Then she confronted me during the race in the grandstand."

I could tell Christina was searching her memory. Without any luck.

"Sorry, but I don't have a clue."

I gave Christina a quick overview of what I knew about Maggie from Alisa's undercover work. Christina listened intently and nodded occasionally. When I finished, I sat silent for a long time. Then I asked "Is it possible that Maggie could have become an adult—a working adult—and not know what sex is? Is that what Freud talked about when you talked about infantile sexuality development?"

Eventually, Christina said, "Freud talked about infantile sexuality, but not like you're thinking. Freud's infantile sexuality is part of the normal human development, during an infant's early years—birth to three, four years old. If this woman, what's her name?"

"Maggie. Maggie Decker." I watched Christina's face.

"If Maggie experienced abnormal sexual activities—like sexual abuse—in early periods of development, those could cause abnormal behavior later in life." Christina paused. "I suppose it's possible for a woman to become an adult and not fully understand the emotional or psychological aspects of sex. She might very well realize the physiological pleasure of sex, which is hormonal and instinctive. But she may not understand why she enjoys it."

I sat looking blankly at Christina.

She smiled. "It's complicated, huh?" I said.

"Very complicated," Christina said. "How well do you know this woman?"

"Not very well at all."

"Why are you involved with her?"

"It's—it's the Melvyn Hightower homicide."

"At the track?'

"Yes."

"I remember a little about that. I remember you and I arriving at the track."

"I'm concerned that Maggie—the woman I'm talking about—might have been involved sexually with Melvyn." I paused for breath. "But she doesn't appear to know what sex is. It also appears her idea of a man showing her he likes her involves having sex with him."

"Was she abused as a child?"

"I don't know."

"The first thing I would check on would be sexual abuse, at a very early age, and then continued until she was eight, nine or ten years old by someone she trusted."

"Damn." I've never been able to fathom men who sexually abuse very young children.

"We know it happens," Christina said. "No matter what we think of it. It happens."

I thought about it and then asked, "Is it possible that a girl can grow up to become a waitress, not know what sex really is, and not know she had shot a man to death?"

"You think she shot Melvyn?"

"It's a possibility," I said. "Right now I'm just fishing. Do you think she could have shot Melvyn?"

"I doubt it," Christina said. "But you need to talk to a psychiatrist, like Dr. Steinberger."

"Maybe I'll make an appointment with him, and chat with him." I grinned at Christina. "Maybe I should have him give me a session, then ask him about Maggie."

"You don't need a session now," Christina said. "If you let this thing eat at you, however, you might wind up needing one." She smiled.

My phone vibrated. I dug it out and looked at the number. It was a local number that I didn't recognize, so I closed the phone and put it back into my shirt pocket.

"Who was that?" Christina asked.

"I don't know," I said. "I'll go down to the cafeteria in a little while and call them back."

"I'm tired," Christina said. "You go ahead, and I'll take a nap."

* * *

On the way to the cafeteria I realized it was after one o'clock. I hadn't thought much about lunch, but now I did. I walked down the stairs and took advantage of the quiet spot at the basement stairwell to dig my cell phone out and dial the caller back.

When the female voice said, "Jalopy's Diner," I knew who had called. "Is Bay there?" I asked. I heard the female yell "BAY" and heard the phone clunk against the wall.

"This is Bay," the man said.

"This is Kurt Maxxon," I said.

"Hey, Kurt. Hey, I tried to call you because I've got a fellow asking if I'd like to sponsor his racecar. I figured I should talk to you about that first."

"Who is it?"

"I don't know," Bay said. "He called me this morning. I told him I'd talk to you, and he said he needed to get hold of you, too."

I frowned. "Did he tell you about his car?"

"No. He said he's staying just down the street in a motel and can come by any time."

I said, "How about now. Do you have any of your lunch special for today left?"

"Sure," Bay said. "You coming over now?"

"Yes. See if you can get the other guy there. It'll take me about ten minutes to get there."

I drove to Jalopy's in record time, six minutes. I parked and went in to a room with three other men sitting at one of the booths. Bay was sitting on a stool at the end of the lunch counter. He waved and pointed me to a booth away from the front door. I slid into the booth and watched a waitress walk toward me with a glass of water and a cup of coffee. I looked, but Bay had disappeared.

"Bay went to get your plate," the waitress said.

"What's the special today?"

"Dolmeh yeh Felfel," the waitress said. "Bay is preparing you a new plate of it."

Dolmeh-yeh Felfel was one of my favorite dishes at Jalopy's, and Bay knew that. It was the Iranian version of stuffed green peppers with a lot of herbs and spices and made with ground lamb. The waitress walked back to her station, and Bay came out of the kitchen with a large platter of food. He walked to my booth and set the plate down, then went back to get himself a cup of coffee.

"How is Christina doing?" he asked as he sat down across

from me.

I already had my mouth full of the wonderful stuffed pepper. "She's doing fine," I said between chews. "This Dolmeh-yeh Felfel is absolutely delicious."

"I know you like it," Bay said. "The stuff we made for the lunch special didn't turn out that good. So I made you a special batch. I still had green peppers and the fixin's. The fellow who called will be here in a few minutes."

I had just finished my plate and was chatting with Bay when a young man pushed through the front door, stood looking around, dismissed the three men in the booth and focused on Bay and I.

The man was thirty-something with reddish auburn hair and a face full of freckles. He was short, five-seven, perhaps, and quite thin. His ears were big for his head and stuck out prominently. His incisor teeth were also oversized and prominent. His eyes were hidden by dark sunglasses. He was wearing blue jeans and a yellow muscle shirt. I hoped I didn't make a Freudian slip and call this fellow "Rusty." Rusty Gallegar, the victim I found dead at the Kings Rapids racetrack a few years back, also had reddish auburn hair and freckles, which caused his nickname to be Rusty.

He walked toward us. "Are you Bay?" he asked as he approached.

Bay nodded and stood up. "And you are?"

"Oh, uh, yeah," the young man fumbled his words. "My name is Jeremy Uggens." He looked toward me.

"That's Kurt Maxxon," Bay said.

"Uh, man, are you really Kurt Maxxon?" Jeremy said to me.

"That I am," I said with a goofy grin.

"Uh, oh, yeah, I need to talk to you, too," Jeremy said.

"Why don't you sit down and tell us what all you need," I said.

"Uh, yeah." Jeremy sat down opposite me and slid into the booth. Bay sat next to him.

I noticed Jeremy kept looking at me.

"You said you needed a sponsor for your car," Bay opened the conversation.

"Uh, oh, yeah. I just bought a new racecar," Jeremy said. "The guy I bought it from said he had heard you mention you might sponsor a racecar." Jeremy looked sideways toward Bay.

"I guess I did say something about that," Bay said. "Probably a few months ago when I catered the Centralia Auto Dealers Convention."

"Uh, yeah, well I need a sponsor," Jeremy said. "I also need to talk to Mr. Maxxon about transferring my car into the Stock Car Racing Association."

"Transferring from where?" I asked.

Jeremy looked at me blankly for a long time. "Uh, yeah, well, I don't know where it came from. All I know is I bought the car ..."

"Who'd you buy the car from?" I asked Jeremy.

Uh, yeah. His name was Gilbert Baker."

The name didn't ring a bell. I looked at Bay, who shrugged.

"Where is the car now?" I asked.

"Uh, oh, at the racetrack over at the fairgrounds," Jeremy said.

"Where?" I asked.

"Uh, oh, in garage number thirty-two," Jeremy answered.

"What kind of car is it?" Bay asked.

"Uh, it's a Chevy Impala," Jeremy said. "I think that's what Gilbert told me."

"What color is it?" I was getting a little concerned about what was coming.

"Uh, oh, it's black and yellow," Jeremy said.

"Number thirty-five?" I asked.

"Uh, yeah," Jeremy said and brightened. "Did Gilbert already talk to you about transferring it to me?"

"I'm familiar with that car," I said as I gave Bay a wary look. Bay nodded understanding. "I've got to get some paperwork out of my truck," I said. "I'll be right back. Bay will tell you about his diner here." I stood and casually walked out of the diner, but had my cell phone out and dialing Nick's number before I had cleared the door. When Nick answered, I gave him the highlights and that Bay and I would try to keep Jeremy here at the diner until he could get here.

"The car is in garage number thirty-two," Nick repeated.

"Yes."

"I'll get some people over there right now." He hung up.

I got my writing tablet from the front seat and went back into the diner. "I left my briefcase at home," I lied, as I approached the table. "I'll make some notes on this," I said, holding the tablet up for inspection. Jeremy didn't seem bothered about anything. He's calm. That's good.

Bay had talked Jeremy into ordering one of his diner sandwiches.

As we talked, and I jotted notes, Christina came to mind. My mind said, you need to be with her. I said, I need to be here with this case.

My mind won the battle.

*   *   *

I got back to Christina's room just as they were delivering her supper tray. She looked at me as I walked toward her, and I felt guilty.

"I just woke up," she said. "Have you been waiting all this time?"

"No, that's okay," I said.

"You're so patient," Christina said.

"Well, actually, I didn't sit here all this time," I confessed. "I went off and found Melvyn's car."

"That sounds interesting," Christina said. "Where did you go?"

"To Jalopy's Diner."

Christina had picked at the plain food on her plate and was chewing what looked to be a baked chicken breast. "Don't start talking about Bay's wonderful food," she said. "Not while I'm dining on hospital fare."

"Okay, I won't." I told her about Jeremy calling Bay about sponsoring his new racecar. How Bay and I determined it was really Melvyn's car. Apparently Jeremy had paid One hundred and fifty thousand dollars to a Gilbert Baker for the car—three times what it was probably worth—and no one knew who this Gilbert Baker was. The only clue we had was that Bay had commented to a group of Centralia car dealers that he might like to sponsor a racecar. So Gilbert Baker might be one of the Centralia car dealers who were at the convention Bay catered several months before. Nick had impounded the car. Jeremy was terribly frightened by the proceedings. Nick had Jeremy go to the station and look through mug shots of known con-men. There didn't appear to be a picture gallery of Centralia's car dealers. Christina listened as if transfixed—in the end however, I knew she was just trying to avoid eating her supper.

CHAPTER NINETEEN
Friday Morning, August 31

**Kurt Maxxon**

As I approached Christina's room I heard her talking to a familiar voice. When I entered the room, a stocky body blocked my view of Christina, and I recognized the black hair braided into two pigtails on each side of her head. The sheriff's uniform she was wearing proved me right. I walked to where Christina could see me. Janice caught my movement out of the corner of her eye and turned to look at me. She said, "Good morning," at the same time Christina said almost the same thing, but Christina's deeper voice finished with "my love."

Janice Hoopaneewanda, better known as "Hoppy," was a member of the Weeblookaan tribe, one of the original Indian tribes in the valley.

"It's good to see you Sergeant Hoppy," I said.

"She's no longer a sergeant," Christina said. "Look at her epaulet. She's a lieutenant."

"Well, for goodness sake," I said sheepishly. After twenty-six years in the United States Marine Corps, you'd think I would have paid more attention to the rank of the person I was addressing. I'd been retired for over a dozen years now, however, and maybe my "Officerese" had gotten a little rusty. I hugged her and said, "Congratulations."

Hoppy—at any rank—was a prime mover in the Pierre County Sheriff's Department's Major Crimes Investigations Unit. I helped her resolve the death of Carlos Guerrero in Carpentier Falls a couple of years ago. She and Christina went back further than that, however, since Janice graduated from high school in

Albertstown while Christina was the Administrator of the Albertstown Consolidated School District.

"Janice heard I'd had an accident, and she drove over to see how I was doing," Christina said.

When I looked at Hoppy, she said, "You remember Damon Hertz, don't you? He was over here Monday afternoon interviewing a suspect in the hospital, and he heard a nurse talking about Christina Maxxon having just been brought in. He checked with ER and told me about it when he got back to the office. I called over, and they eventually told me she was here, but completely out of it. So I decided to wait until this morning to come over. I'm on my way to the capitol building for a hearing. So I decided to leave early and drop in to see her."

"I'm so glad you did," Christina said.

"So am I," I said. "I called relatives and close friends, but I totally spaced out on calling you, even though you are a close friend. I'm sorry."

"No need to apologize," she said as she leaned down to kiss Christina on the forehead, carefully avoiding the tubes, supports, and casts. "I've got to run. You're looking great, Mrs. Maxxon."

"I've told you a dozen times, call me Christina."

"Okay, Mrs. Maxxon, I'll call you Christina if I remember." She grinned and walked quickly out the door.

A nurse arrived to help Christina get out of bed, into her slippers and, with a robe draped over her shoulders, she pushed the "drip tree" as they walked down the hall and back. I glanced at my watch and told Christina I had to go take Kimberly's kids to daycare and would be back later in the morning. She nodded understanding.

As I arrived at the first floor I saw Nick come through the front doors, and I went to intercept him at the elevator.

"You were a great help, yesterday," Nick said. "Tracking down Hightower's car and all. We went over it with everything we could think of and came up with zilch."

"Had Jeremy been in the car?" I asked.

"Oh, yeah," Nick said with a grin. "The kid apparently sat in the car playing like he's roaring around the track at a hundred miles per hour. He left a lot of fresh prints on the door handle, the steering wheel, and the gear shifter. We're checking to make sure they're all his. Otherwise, the car had been wiped down pretty well. They used a Ninydrin spray on the Bill of Sale and phony rent receipt the guy gave Jeremy. They'll be checking those documents later this morning to see if any prints developed, other than Jeremy's."

"Is that the process I read about where they use a steam iron?"

"That's it," Nick said. "We have the most modern techniques around."

"I thought it was pretty cool," I said.

* * *

I left Nick in the hospital parking lot and drove to Maurey's garage to pick up the Grenwahl children and take them to the Children's Development Center. Then I drove to my store and carried my brief case up to my office. After I set the coffee pot to perking, I dug out my writing tablet and sat at the conference table to make notes about the events of the evening before. I sat staring at the rest of the notes, focusing on several for a long time. My intercom buzzed, and I picked it up.

"There's a young man named Jeremy Uggens down here asking for you," Edwin Jamison, my store manager said.

I'd given Jeremy one of my KurtMaxxonRacing.com cards the evening before. "I'll come down," I said, and walked toward the front stairwell. The office people greeted me as I walked through their work area. When I emerged from the stairwell, I saw Jeremy browsing in the high performance section of the store. I went to meet him.

"Uh, hi Mr. Maxxon," Jeremy said. "Uh, well, I was wondering if you've, uh, if you've found out any more about the car?"

"No, I haven't," I said. "It's only been a little over twelve hours since Nick impounded the car. I'm afraid it's going to take some time."

I wondered how this was going to play out with Lorianne Hightower, the rightful owner of the car, if she wasn't connected in any way with Melvyn's death. I wasn't sure how Nick had talked to Jeremy about the car. Did Jeremy have any legal claim to the car? I doubted it based upon what little business law I'd studied. But all that was best left to the legal eagles and the court system.

"I want to start buying some of this stuff to make my car better," Jeremy said, sweeping his hand toward the racks of engine enhancing equipment.

"Let's go up to my office," I said, after noticing Edwin Jamison and several customers watching us.

Jeremy followed me up the stairway and through the office area to my office. He sat down in the chair I offered him at the round conference table.

"Before you buy any of this stuff," I said, "I'd suggest you talk to Maurey Kennedy first."

"Uh, who's he?" Jeremy asked.

"Maurey is my mechanic," I said. "He can tell you what works and what doesn't. More to the point, what's worth buying and what's not."

"Uh, okay, would this guy be my mechanic, too?" Jeremy asked.

"I suppose he might," I said, "but, actually, the number thirty-five car already has a mechanic. His name is Steve Cosburn. Steve has worked on the thirty-five car for over five years now. He knows that Chevy inside and out."

"Uh, oh, where's he at? He and I will have to work together. I'm not going to let anyone else tell me how to drive my car."

"All great race drivers consult with their mechanics and friends on how to drive." I hoped I hadn't been too curt.

"If he wants to be my mechanic," Jeremy said, "I'll let him give me advice."

"I'll get you set up with Steve just as soon as we figure out who owns the car and it all plays out." I hoped to be helpful, but practical.

"Uh, do you think I have a chance in hell of getting the car?" Jeremy blurted.

"Well, I think you're as much a victim as Melvyn Hightower is," I said slowly, trying to formulate how to handle the mess. "We need to track down this Gilbert Baker and get your money back from him. I can check to see what Lorianne Hightower is thinking. She might agree to sell it to you, at a much more reasonable price."

"Uh, I hope so," Jeremy said. "God, I hope it doesn't take too long. I really like that car."

"I hope it doesn't take too long, too. The cops are being cautious, though. As long as they aren't totally sure, the wife remains on their scope—and as long as the wife is on the scope, she can't do anything with the car."

"Uh, well, I wish they could get it solved," Jeremy whined.

"I'm sure they're working as fast and as hard as they can," I assured him.

"I don't think I'm ever going to get that car," Jeremy yelled even louder, letting his subconscious mind take over his presence.

All the people in the office outside stopped working and looked in our direction. One picked up the phone and was dialing a short number. I hoped it wasn't 9-1-1.

Jeremy calmed down and said, "Uh, I'm sorry."

"I know you've probably already answered the questions I'm going to ask you, but I'd appreciate if you'd talk to me. I want to help you. Will you answer my questions?"

"Uh, yeah, I guess." Jeremy fidgeted on the chair and settled in at an angle. "Uh, I don't have anything to hide."

"You said you bought the car from a broker named Gilbert Baker. How did you get hooked up with this Baker?" I asked.

"Uh, a car lot down on the highway had a dragster for sale," Jeremy said. "I emailed them about it. We emailed back and forth a couple of times on Tuesday, I think. I decided I wanted a stockcar not a dragster, so I sent them an email telling them that. A couple of days later Gilbert Baker calls me on my cell phone and tells me he's seen my emails to the car dealer online and he can get me a stockcar."

"Where did you get the money?"

"Uh, I won the lottery a couple of months ago," Jeremy said, and I noticed he was smug about that. "I got four-hundred and seventy-five thousand dollars in a lump sum."

"Good chunk of change," I said, hoping to connect with Jeremy and his generation's lingo. Then I realized that was about what I would have said when I was his age. The coffee pot finished gurgling. "You want a cup of coffee?"

"Uh, nah. I'm a Coke person."

I called the office receptionist to bring a Coke from the lunch room fridge. "How did this car deal go down?" I asked.

"Uh, I met with, uh, Gilbert Baker Thursday night at the Riverside Park, right there next to the racetrack. He told me he had just about finalized the deal with the owner, but would need a couple more days to finish everything. He took me over to the garage and opened the door and showed me the car. I didn't do anything but walk around the car in the garage. But Gilbert showed me all the tools and test equipment on the bench and told me that was included in the hundred and fifty thousand dollar deal."

"So this Gilbert Baker had a key to the number thirty-five garage?"

"Uh, yeah, he sure did."

My mind raced through the possibilities of how Baker could have gotten the key to the garage. Melvyn was selling his car? Gilbert Baker had keys to garage number thirty-five? How? Did Gilbert Baker have access to the key box in Karl Albertson's office? "Okay," I said. "What happened next?"

"Uh, he wanted a deposit—half so he could show the owner I was serious about buying the car."

"So you gave him seventy-five thousand dollars?"

"Uh, yeah. Well, the next morning I did," Jeremy said. "I had to go to the bank to get it. He wanted cash. The banker didn't want to give it to me, but he had to."

"That should have tipped you off to a scam," I said, and then decided to back off a little so as not to put Jeremy on the defensive. "Where did you meet to give him the deposit?"

"In the park there next to the track."

"After you gave him the deposit, what happened next?"

"Uh, Gilbert called me Saturday afternoon and told me he had finalized the deal and he had the car for me. He wanted me to meet him in the park after dark to give him the balance of seventy-five thousand dollars, and he would give me the keys and title and all."

"Didn't all this meeting after dark, in the park, make you suspicious?" I asked.

"Uh, well, yeah. But, Gilbert told me the driver was a well-known local celebrity, and he didn't want the sale of his car to be known for a while. The guy was having trouble with his wife or something—I don't know."

"So you met with Gilbert Baker Saturday night?"

"Uh, yeah, about eleven o'clock. He had moved the car to garage number thirty-two, and he gave me the keys to the car and the padlocks on the garage door."

"Gilbert Baker put the padlocks on garage number thirty-two?"

"Uh, yeah. They were there when we completed the deal Saturday night."

"This Gilbert Baker might have shot Melvyn because of the car," I said. "I have good reason to believe that he and Melvyn argued about it. Melvyn may have led Gilbert to believe he would sell the car and then backed out at the last minute."

"Uh, well, Christ, I mean, uh—I just—I just wanted to own a racecar. And, uh, drive it in races," he squeaked.

"Have you raced cars before?" I asked.

"Uh—on dirt tracks. Up in Justice County, in Dalton." The stricken look on Jeremy's face eased. Poor kid. "I really like that car, Mr. Maxxon," Jeremy whined.

"Hopefully they can catch this Gilbert Baker before he blows all of your money, Jeremy," I said. "Then, if Lori Hightower isn't involved in any way, she might swing a deal with you."

"Uh, yeah. I'd like that," Jeremy said, and gulped a couple of times.

"I'll talk to Lorianne Hightower," I promised. "See if she'll sell the car to you."

"Uh, I still have some money left," Jeremy offered. "I can probably still pay her for it."

"We'll see," I said. "I don't know what the cops are doing. I'll try to find out about that, too." I wondered what Nick was doing with the Bill of Sale. Was he looking at the signature, which couldn't be Melvyn's—tracking down who really signed it?

"Do you really want to help me, Mr. Maxxon?" Jeremy said just above a whine.

"I'm going to help you as much as I can," I said. "Let me talk to Lorianne about it. And I'll also talk to Nick Boynton. Then I'll get back to you."

Jeremy seemed to accept the situation. He stood and looked toward the office door. "You can go down those stairs," I said. "They lead to the parking lot." He nodded and left.

I moved the writing tablet in front of me, glad Jeremy hadn't shown any interest in it as it lay on the conference table during our conversation. I scanned the notes again. However, Jeremy seemed to dominate my thoughts.

I dug out the phone book and dialed Lorianne Hightower at her shop. When she answered, I asked if she would be free for about fifteen minutes sometime right after lunch. She told me to hold on while she checked her appointment book, then told me she had an opening at one forty-five.

"I'll be there at one forty-five," I said.

"What's this about?"

"I want to talk to you about the car," I said. "I assume you heard about the young fellow who bought Melvyn's car from some con-man?"

"Yes, I did. This is getting to be an unfortunate mess."

"I represent that young fellow now, as well as the SRVSCRA."

"Is he a good driver?" Lorianne asked.

"If you want my honest opinion, I seriously doubt he's even a mediocre driver. But, I'm convinced he'll keep the car in the SRVSCRA. There are several drivers who just can't afford to keep their cars going since they or their wives have lost their jobs, or other reasons. I'm hoping to get one of those drivers to drive it for whoever owns it."

"Do you need a rinse or a perm?" Lorianne asked me and laughed heartily into the phone.

"I could probably use a haircut," I said, "As long as you cut the right one."

"That's a great answer, Colonel. I'll see you right after lunch."

*   *   *

At eleven thirty, I packed my briefcase and drove to the hospital. The sun was hot and the air was humid. The cab of my truck reached the comfort zone about the same time I pulled into the hospital's parking lot. When I arrived at Christina's room, she had just returned from another stroll up and down the hall. "I'm ready for a nap," she declared. "These jaunts up and down the hall wear me out."

I waited while the nurse helped Christina into bed and then, satisfied the equipment was working properly, walked briskly out into the hall. I said, "I'm going down and get coffee. You want anything?" When she didn't respond, I looked at her, and realized she had already dozed off. I kissed her lightly on the forehead and headed downstairs.

In the cafeteria, I had just finished filling two cups of coffee when my cell phone vibrated. It was Phil Schroeder.

"They're going to transport Christina to Our Lady Rehab about three o'clock," Phil said.

"That's good," I said. "I have an errand to run right after lunch, but I'll be back in time to go with her."

"Whatever," Phil said. "They won't let you ride in the ambulance."

"That's okay. I'll drive," I said. "I'm in the cafeteria. I'll buy you lunch."

"I'm not at the hospital," he said. "I'll take a rain-check."

I called Kimberly. "You'll have to go get the kids from daycare," I said. "They're going to move Christina to Our Lady at three o'clock, and I want to go with her."

"Yes you do," Kimberly said. "That's great news. I've got everything up to date. So I'll take a couple of hours off. I'll tell Maurey."

"That'll work," I said. "We'll get back to normal tomorrow morning."

Next, I dialed Nick's cell phone which I heard click through to his desk phone.

"Make it fast, Maxxon," Nick said. "I just got an offer for a cold beer from an old Army buddy who's in town for the night only."

"Just wondering if you'd had any luck figuring out who signed that Phony Bill of Sale," I said. "In other words, who this Gilbert Baker is." I cradled the phone between my shoulder and face while I took the lid off one of my cups of coffee and took a sip.

"Not a clue, yet," Nick said. "Trying to work with the handwriting proved to be a very small needle in a huge haystack. Whoever Gilbert Baker is, I'm sure he's our killer."

"Did you pick up on the fact that this Gilbert had access

to garage number thirty-five Thursday night?" I waited for Nick to reply.

"What are you talking about?" Nick said slowly.

"Jeremy told me," I paused for effect, "that Gilbert Baker opened garage number thirty-five and showed him the number thirty-five car Thursday night."

"What? Hang on a minute," Nick said, and I heard the muffling sound of his hand over the mouthpiece. I also could hear him yelling at someone. Then I heard Nick talking to someone near him. "This is Kurt Maxxon on the line. He's got some information you must have overlooked when you interrogated Jeremy Uggens. Pick up the phone and talk to Kurt."

I heard a click and a voice said, "Hello."

Nick said, "I've got Greg Potter, the cop who interrogated Jeremy, on the line Kurt. Now what is this you just told me?"

"I was talking to Jeremy this morning," I started. "He told me that Gilbert Baker opened garage number thirty-five to show him Melvyn's car Thursday night. That leads me to believe this Gilbert Baker must have some connection to the track and/or racing."

"Did Jeremy tell you about that?" Nick asked gruffly, his mouth turned away from the speaker. I started to respond, confused as to Nick's question.

"No, he didn't," Potter said. "But I didn't ask him anything about that. I mean, I wasn't interviewing him as a suspect but more as a victim. I asked him how he met up with Gilbert Baker, and he told me Baker called him saying he knew where he could get a racecar. Then I pursued how they did the deal. Jeremy told me he met with Baker and gave him half the money and then waited for Baker to call him. Baker called him Saturday night and told him he had the car for Jeremy in garage thirty-two. Jeremy went to the track, and they finalized the deal. Jeremy gave Baker the balance of the hundred and fifty grand. I didn't go after a lot of details."

"I understand," Nick said. "Does Baker have a connection to the track, Kurt?"

I paused long enough to run the name Baker through all the people I knew connected with the track. The groundskeeper, the maintenance guys, the ticket sellers, and the ushers. "It might be that Melvyn gave Baker a key to his garage so Baker could show Jeremy the car," I said.

"How would that work?" Nick asked. "This Baker person just popped onto our radar. Where'd he come from? Where'd he go?"

"It could be an alias," I replied. "If he's involved with racing, he probably didn't want Jeremy knowing his real name. He might be gaming the taxman."

"Lorianne Hightower told me at lunch the other day that Melvyn had been going to sell the car off and on for several years now. It could be that Baker called Melvyn and said, 'I've got a buyer for your car, I would like to show it to him.' Melvyn says, 'Okay, run by the carpet shop and I'll give you a key to my garage.' Baker gets the key. Shows Jeremy the car. Then when he goes back to Melvyn, Melvyn says 'I don't want to sell right now.' They argue. Baker shoots Melvyn."

"Any other scenarios running around in your brain, Maxxon?" Nick asked.

"The only other idea would be that Baker knew about the key box in Karl Albertson's office. Baker might have a keycard to the auxiliary office for some reason, although I can't imagine why."

"Who has keycards to that office?" Nick asked.

"We'll have to talk to Karl," I said. "I think the officers of the various racing associations that use the track probably have them. Track officials and state people probably have them."

"Can you track that down for me, Maxxon?" Nick said. "Albertson might talk to you easier than me."

"You're late for that cold beer, huh?" I said.

"The cold beer just flew out the window," Nick growled. "I want to go over the tapes of Jeremy's interview with Potter. We now have a whole new situation package. If this Baker fellow is inside, he might not stop with Hightower." Nick paused, then said, "Hang on a minute, Maxxon, something just struck me. Let me look here."

I heard him shuffling through papers.

"What ya looking for?" Potter asked.

"Here it is," Nick said. "Yeah. There was a vague partial print on one of the padlocks from garage thirty-five that didn't match Melvyn's. There's a note here that it might match one from the gun barrel."

"Might match?" I asked.

"Cop lingo for it looks like it matches, but we may not be able to prove it in court," Nick said.

"I hope we can catch Gilbert Baker before he spends all of Jeremy's money," I said.

"Right now he's probably in Acapulco basking on the beach," Nick said. "Can you believe that boy gave this guy one hundred and fifty big ones with nothing more than a wing and a promise?"

"Jeremy is naïve and gullible, that's for sure. But, he had a dream. Haven't you ever had a dream, Nick?"

"My last good night's sleep was in 1976—the night before I hired on as a cop in Farmer's City," Nick said. "So that probably was the last night I had any dreams worth recording."

"I didn't mean to make you reminisce about your life," I said, hoping to add some levity.

"Right now the question I still have is did Melvyn's wife pay the guy to take Melvyn out?"

"That doesn't seem apropos at this juncture, does it?"

"That is always apropos, Mr. Maxxon." Nick snorted. "I take it you don't like her as a suspect."

"No, I don't," I said. "She doesn't work for me, what with the car deal and all."

"You may be right," Nick conceded. "Let's say, hypothetically, that Mrs. Hightower isn't involved in any way with Melvyn's death. How much do you think she'll ask for the car?"

"I'm guessing probably somewhere between fifty and seventy five thousand," I said. "Melvyn paid about forty thousand for it five years ago."

"And the kid paid one hundred and fifty thousand for it."

"Naïve. Gullible—".

"How about Stupid?" Nick said.

"The boy was chasing his dream."

"Have it your way, Maxxon," Nick said. "I gotta go."

*   *   *

I carried the remaining cup of coffee to Christina's room, and she was still sleeping. I glanced at my watch and wondered why I hadn't thought about lunch while I was down at the cafeteria.

You offered to buy Phil's lunch! Even as I decided to go down to the cafeteria for lunch, a debate developed in my head between one faction who thought I should go down to the hospital cafeteria, while another faction said go to Jalopy's. By the time I had reached the first floor, Jalopy's had won the argument. I went out and climbed into my truck.

Bay welcomed me and led me to a booth. I ordered iced tea and the daily special, which was an eggplant dish with a lot of spices and beef. Bay brought my plate and put it down in front of me, then went to get himself a cup of coffee. He came back and sat down across from me.

"So, can I afford to sponsor a car in the SRVSCRA?" Bay asked as he sipped coffee.

I smiled at him. "I'm sure you can," I said.

Bay inherited a sizable sum of money when his father died, which he shared with his family. After taxes, he wound up with enough money to escape the crowded east coast, move to Centralia, and land a job working for a major national insurance company as an actuary. Through hard work and saving his money, Bay bought Jalopy's Diner, and since has grown it into a thriving business.

"How much will it cost me?" Bay asked.

"Probably only a few thousand dollars per season." I watched Bay's eyes, but they didn't change perceptively. "Here's the facts," I said. "The first thing you need to know is that some businesses sponsor cars in all the SRVSCRA races around the valley, while others only sponsor cars in their local market." I watched Bay relax and lean forward with interest. I sipped on my coffee.

"Sponsors typically agree to cover the driver's costs for entry fees, tires, and gas. A few help with maintenance costs and repair costs." I counted on my fingers and said, "The basic costs are Entry Fees at $250 per race. Nine races a year and that comes to twenty two hundred and fifty bucks. Tires are the biggest cost. Most drivers run tires that cost about five hundred dollars per set, two sets per race, that's nine thousand dollars a year. Gas is the least expensive item, runs about fifty bucks per race, or four hundred and fifty dollars a year. So, if you sponsor a car for all nine races, you're looking at about twelve thousand dollars per season."

Bay wrinkled his lips and shrugged. "That doesn't sound too bad," he said. "Do you pay that all at once? At the beginning of the season?"

"Some do, but most sponsors make it in two payments. Half just before the Masonville race the fourth Sunday in May; the balance just before the race in Maplewood the fourth Sunday in July."

"Aren't there two races here in Centralia each year?" Bay said, more as a statement than a question.

"Yes, there are," I said. "The last race of the season is the Centralia Shootout. It's by invitation only; the top fifteen points getters are invited to participate. It is a big draw, and the money paid to the drivers is all the gate money that the SRVSCRA gets." I grinned. "During the season, each race costs the sponsor about thirteen hundred and fifty bucks. If your car makes it to the Shootout, most sponsors throw in some extra money for a new paint job to make their name stand out better. I always spent about two thousand bucks to get Nikki ready for the Shootout. Then there's the entry fee, tires, and gas."

Bay glanced at his watch and said, "I've got to phone in my vegetable order for tomorrow. I really appreciate your input."

"If you get the chance to sponsor the number thirty-five car, it's a good one. All it needs is a good driver to be a regular winner."

I watched Bay walk toward the kitchen door as I finished my iced tea. I went out to my truck and climbed into it.

Will Jeremy get to buy the car? Who is Gilbert Baker?

*　　*　　*

I decided to run back by the hospital to Christina on my way to meet with Lorianne. I hadn't had a chance to tell her about my appointment with Lorianne, and I didn't want Christina to start feeling neglected. I didn't need to worry. Christina was still sound asleep. I kissed her and gave the nurse a message for her. I left and drove to Lorianne's salon.

When I pushed through the door, I noted two women sitting under hair dryers reading magazines wearing brave smiles while enduring the torturous heat. Another operator clipped away on a woman's hair at the last chair in a line of four.

"Hello, Colonel Maxxon," Lorianne said as she stood from

her perch near the door. She beckoned me to follow and walked toward an archway opening to a back room. I walked into a small office barely big enough for the desk, chair, file cabinet, and waste basket. Lorianne found a folding chair behind the file cabinet and opened it for me. I folded my frame into the tiny space between her desk and the wall, with my shoulder wedged painfully under the metal handle of one of the filing drawers.

"Okay," she said. "What do you want to know?"

"Basically, I'm just interested in finding out if you'll sell the car to Jeremy Uggens and, more importantly, what I figured you might not want to discuss on the telephone: how much you want for the car?"

"I'm glad you didn't ask me on the phone," Lorianne said. "I figure the cops have my phone tapped, so I don't talk a lot of business on it anymore."

I nodded understanding.

"The answers to your questions are: yes, I'll sell the car to the young man. I want fifty-five thousand dollars for it. That's a firm price."

"That's reasonable enough," I said. "Have the cops placed any liens or encumbrances against the car yet?"

"Nothing yet," Lorianne said. "They have the car under their locks."

"I have no idea how long they can impound the car," I said, "since it's involved with a homicide. But I would think there are limitations, since it doesn't seem to be a key piece of evidence."

"It really doesn't matter to me," Lorianne said. "I won't need the money, obviously, so let them have it as long as they want."

"I'll do all I can to get it released as quickly as possible," I said. I recalled Aunt Matilda's comment about Lorianne wanting to appear wealthy. "Does the name Gilbert Baker ring a bell with you? Someone Melvyn might have talked to or about?"

"No. I've never heard that name before." She paused to search her memory, "Absolutely nothing comes to mind."

I didn't want to disclose anything else about Baker's access to the garages. "Is there a chance Melvyn promised he'd sell the car to Baker and then backed out at the last minute?"

"That's always a possibility," Lorianne said slowly.

"Melvyn was flighty at times. That might explain the murder. If the buyer got mad about it."

"Did Melvyn have any problems with drugs or alcohol?" I asked.

"No. Shag drank a beer once a month or so; never touched whiskey; never was into drugs."

"I thank you for your time, Lorianne," I said and stood to leave.

"Let me ask you flat out, Mr. Maxxon," Lorianne said and paused. "Do you think I had anything to do with Melvyn's death?"

"No. I don't," I answered quickly. "I think the car is the key to this whole mess."

"Thank you." Lorianne led me back to the front door, and I left without another word.

*   *   *

I pulled into the parking lot at Hopewell Memorial at two twenty-five. The thermometer on the bank down the street read ninety-five degrees. Phil Schroeder had said they planned to move Christina "about three o'clock" which, I assumed, could mean any time Friday afternoon. I turned off the engine. Something I needed to do started nagging at me, but I couldn't remember what it was. I sat in my truck concentrating on what it was, and finally decided it would come to me if I changed my focus. My truck quickly became an oven, so I climbed out and went inside.

CHAPTER TWENTY
Friday Afternoon, August 31

Kurt Maxxon

As I walked into Christina's room, I noticed she wore the new gown I'd bought her. The nurse must have tipped her off about the impending move. I sat down in her easy chair. "You going somewhere?" I asked.

"I'm going to rehab this afternoon. You didn't tell me," she accused.

Before I could respond, Phil Schroeder rushed into the room.

"Are you ready to bust out of this place?" he asked Christina as he grabbed her chart book from its shelf and walked to the foot of the bed. He laid the book open on the bed, studied it for a few minutes, took his stethoscope from his shoulders, put the tongs into his ears, and walked to Christina. He listened to several different places on her back and then moved to her chest.

"I sure am," Christina said, watching the surgeon as he worked.

I turned to look at him and said, "Can't we just leave like normal people?"

Phil grinned. "Neither one of you is just normal people."

"I think she's doing great," I said.

"She is," Phil said. "I'm impressed with her attitude."

Christina dipped her head and tried to ignore us.

"Christina will be back to normal in no time," Phil said to me, then turned his attention to Christina. "The transport ambulance is here. They're clearing the paperwork now. They'll be up for you in a few minutes." He picked up Christina's chart from the bed and signed in three different places, then closed the book and tossed it back on the bed.

Three white-clad attendants came into the room, pushing a gurney. Phil introduced us all around. The lone male was the driver and the two women were paramedics. Each of them greeted me, but the one dark haired woman greeted me as "Colonel Maxxon."

"Are you a race fan?" I asked her.

"You betcha," she said. "But I root for Sean Forester. He's my cousin."

"That's okay," I said. "I'm glad you enjoy racing." I read her name tag: Shannon McNealy.

Phil and the nurse supervised the loading of Christina onto the ambulance's gurney, and the transfer of the IV drip bag to the tree on the gurney. Phil inspected the IV site and gave a thumbs up.

*   *   *

I followed the ambulance from Hopewell to Our Lady and, while they backed up to the unloading door, I parked and went inside. The sun would set in three hours. It was still hot outside, and I'd worked up a sweat in the short walk from my truck. I stood off to the side of the admissions area and watched the paramedics unload Christina and wheel her into the entrance area. Christina was in a peaceful sleep. The jaundice and contusions caused by the adrenalin rush of the accident had faded, and she was beginning to get her old radiance back—that golden glow Christina has had since I first met her nearly two decades ago. "Looks like she made the trip in good shape," I said to the two paramedics guiding the gurney.

"Oh, she's fine," Shannon said. "She was awake the first few blocks, but then she went down and slept the rest of the way. The sedative will wear off pretty fast."

I waited as the paramedics went through the paperwork transfer process to Our Lady of Grace personnel. Two nurses wearing pastel blue uniforms appeared and walked along with us as the ambulance attendants wheeled Christina to the elevator, up to the third floor, and then down the hall to her room—number 312. They paused to align the gurney with the door, and then pushed it through. Once in her room, the blue clad nurses took charge of Christina, supervising the movement of her off the gurney and onto her bed. Then one of them picked up the red-bound chart on the gurney and went to studying it. The other one started taking a round of vitals as soon as Christina was comfortable in her new bed—temperature, blood pressure, pulse and she listened to Christina's lungs with her stethoscope—which she recorded into the red-bound book.

The paramedics gathered all their gear and threw it on the gurney. "Good luck, Colonel," Shannon said as they prepared to leave.

"Thank you," I said. "I don't race anymore."

"I know," she said. "That girl driving your car is a good one. She drove one hell of a race last Sunday."

"That she did," I said.

"Take good care of Christina," Shannon said as they wheeled the gurney out of the room and toward the elevator.

With Christina situated and officially enrolled in the facility, the nurses left. I sat in the easy chair in Christina's room, watching a muted Weather Channel on the TV. I noted that the easy chair was a lot more comfortable than Hopewell's as I glanced toward Christina frequently. I came fully alert the instant she opened her eyes and moved her head on the pillow, and then I jumped to my feet to move to her side. Christina followed the movement, let her eyes rest on my face for several moments, and then smiled. A new nurse came in and did a quick survey of Christina.

"Are you hungry?" the nurse asked.

"Yes, I am," Christina said.

"I'll get something sent up for you," the nurse said. "Dr. Spenser will be in to see you in a little while," the nurse said. "She's the physical therapist who will be in charge of your recovery here at Our Lady."

Christina struggled into a more comfortable position with her multitude of casts, restraints, bandages and all else. "Can my dog come see me here?" Christina asked the nurse.

"Yes, but it has to be on a leash."

"Will you bring Beau to see me tomorrow morning?" Christina asked me.

"Sure," I said. "He's been wondering when you're going to come home."

"That's good," Christina said. "I know he misses me as much as I miss him."

*　　*　　*

They sent Christina a tray with a plate of cottage cheese, chunks of pears and pineapple, a slice of raisin toast, and a cup of green tea. She cleaned the plates and emptied the cup and said, "I feel like another nap."

I'd never seen Christina clean her plate before. I sat in her guest chair and waited for her to go to sleep. The room was a little too warm for me, but probably just about right for Christina. When she was out of it, I decided to go down and check out the cafeteria. I always enjoyed trying a new eatery, even in a hospital. They didn't have a salad bar, which I would miss, but they did have a pretty decent hot beef sandwich with a lot of mashed potatoes and covered with reasonably good brown gravy. They were sold out of meat loaf, which told me it must be a good recipe, and probably a favorite of both staff and visitors. I would check it out another time.

When I returned to the room, Christina was awake and sitting up. Since she appeared to be lucid, I asked, "Do you remember anything about the accident?"

"Not much," she said. "I remember seeing a church marquee on 27th," Christina said. "I slowed down to read it as I drove by. It said something about, 'Slow down. Be still and rest— I don't remember it all."

"What church was it?"

"That Evangelical Bible church on twenty-seventh about three or four blocks west of Randolph. You know which one I'm talking about, don't you?"

"Not really."

"Oh. I thought you did." Her eyes clouded like she was trying to remember something. "Have you seen the accident report?" she asked.

"Yes, I have. A semi truck driving south on Randolph ran the stop sign at 27th. The driver was apparently talking on his cell phone. He realized what he'd done and jammed on his brakes, which caused him to jack-knife and lose control. He T-boned a westbound car. That car careened into your car. You just got there at the wrong time."

"Maybe I got there late," Christina argued. "Maybe slowing down to read that marquee saved me from being the car he hit dead on." Christina lapsed into silence. "Did the people in the other car get hurt?"

I'd weighed the pros and cons of skirting the issue, but Christina would never countenance me lying to her. "The driver of the car that hit you died later in the hospital," I said and watched Christina's face cloud. "The truck driver wasn't injured, but he's been charged with unsafe operation of a vehicle which will probably be raised to vehicular homicide."

"So I would have died—" she said, then went silent. Big tears started to roll down her cheeks.

Damn, I made her cry. Dammit Maxxon. "I'm sorry, Christina," I said.

Christina drifted off to sleep even before I finished the sentence, which ended the discussion for now. I decided I would drive by and see if I could spot the church—and read the marquee.

I thought about going home, but decided to wait to meet Dr. Spenser. When she arrived, I was surprised. "You look like you're just graduating high school," I said after she introduced herself.

She smiled and said, "I hear that all the time. I graduated high school twelve years ago." Thankfully, she didn't seem to be insulted.

I said, "I didn't mean to insinuate…"

"No. It's okay. You wouldn't believe the number of people I meet who wish they looked younger."

Christina woke up at the sound of voices. She looked at Dr. Spenser and said, "Linda?"

"That's right, Mrs. Zouhn, uh, Mrs. Maxxon."

"Linda graduated from Albertstown High School," Christina said to me. "She was our Valedictorian that year."

Linda Spenser beamed.

"I knew you went into physical therapy," Christina said. "I'm so happy you're the one who's going to fix me up."

"I'm going to examine you. I have the x-rays before and after surgery, so I really don't need to look inside the cast." Dr. Spenser looked at me. "Would you excuse us for about an hour?"

"I hope I can stay awake," Christina said.

"I'll keep you awake," Dr. Spenser said and chuckled.

"I'll go downstairs and wait," I said, and stood and left. I decided I needed to get some fresh air, having been cooped up most of the day. I went outside and walked around the hospital campus. The humidity had gone down dramatically and the temperature was a little cooler. A high pressure ridge must have arrived. It was so nice outside; I walked for forty-five minutes, and then went by my truck to get my yellow writing pad. When I came back through the door next to the cafeteria, the aroma of fresh coffee caused me to detour to get a cup. In the cafeteria I saw Nick Boynton sitting at a table, talking on his cell phone.

"I went up to find Christina's room," Nick explained as I sat down across from him. "The door was shut, so I came down here to wait."

"Do you need something?" I asked.

"Yeah. Answers. Who the hell is Gilbert Baker? How the hell did he get into Melvyn's garage Thursday night? Other than that, I live just six blocks from here," Nick said, pointing an index finger toward the north.

The PA system overrode most of what he said, but I heard, "I don't have anything new," and ended with, "I've concluded that nothing about this case makes any sense."

"Tell me about it," I said. I saw Nick's eyes widen, and he raised his hand to wave. I turned to look behind me and saw Brad Langley coming toward me.

"You don't care who you're seen with, do you Detective Boynton?" Brad said, and spread a wide grin. Next to him was his wife Carolyn, who moved to hug me.

"As always, just ignore him," Carolyn said. I nodded. Brad shook my hand and then Nick's.

When I saw Brad and Carolyn standing side by side, I was always reminded of their wedding day. Brad was five foot nine inches tall and currently weighed about two forty five. Carolyn was five ten and slender. When they married, I was Brad's best man, and I remembered Carolyn coming down the aisle barefoot so that she wouldn't appear taller than Brad. Brad had never cared about it, but Carolyn was very sensitive about it.

Carolyn said, "We went to Hopewell, and they told us Christina had been moved here. So we came here. How's she doing?"

"She's doing very well," I said. "The therapist is examining her now. That's why the door is shut."

I looked from Brad to Nick and said, "When I see you two guys together, I get worried that no one is watching the store."

"The store is safe, buddy," Brad said.

I glanced at my watch. "The doctor should be about done with her," I said. "We can go up and wait in the hall."

My phone vibrated, and I dug it out. "I just finished transcribing all my notes," Alisa Sharpe said.

I glanced toward Nick and Brad Langley chatting across the table, and said, "Just a minute." I picked up my writing tablet and moved to an empty table several feet away.

"Okay," I said. "I can talk now."

"I've put together my final report on Maggie Decker for you," Alisa continued.

"Good," I said. "Are you and Mutt going to have a nice dinner out tonight?"

"Yeah," Alisa said. "We're going to Dejarnet's Restaurant. We were impressed with it last weekend. Then we'll run by and say goodbye to Christina."

"That's good," I said. "I wouldn't worry about seeing Christina. I doubt she'll be awake too late. She's had a busy day. Anything new about Maggie?"

"Nothing earth shattering. I want to get with you tomorrow morning, so Mutt and I can get back home. Terry is asking me how much longer."

"How about I come to your hotel and meet you and Mutt for breakfast about seven o'clock tomorrow morning?"

"They have a great breakfast buffet," Alisa said, then added, "but, I'll bet you already knew that, huh?"

"Yes, I did."

"Okay," Alisa said. "I still marvel at Maggie's concept of sex. She talks about sex like a little girl talks about someone giving her a lollipop."

"It will be interesting to figure out her part in all this," I said.

"If you need anything tonight, just give me a call. Otherwise, I'll see you tomorrow morning at breakfast," Alisa said and hung up.

I glanced toward Brad and Nick's table and saw Nick answering his cell phone. I walked back to their table.

Carolyn sat disinterested. "Do you think they're done with Christina now?" she asked.

"Probably," I said.

Carolyn stood and said, "I'm going up to see Christina."

Brad was listening to Nick on the phone. His frown told me something was of concern.

Nick folded his phone and put it into the holster. "They just finished up a call at Maggie Decker's apartment. Someone cut her up pretty bad. She's at General going into surgery."

"Who was the stud?" Brad asked.

"Don't have a positive yet," Nick answered. "Neighbor told them he lived there most of the time."

"It might have been him they were after, and she got in the way," Brad said.

"The DE guys are looking into it." Nick let the subject hang.

"Maxxon hasn't solved the Hightower homicide yet?" Brad said and smiled.

"Not yet," Nick said.

"I'm piecing it together," I said.

"You've had a week," Brad said. "It usually doesn't take you this long."

From the tone and lilt of his voice, I sensed I was in friendly territory.

"I'm convinced that a man known as Gilbert Baker is the killer," I said. "But, and it's a big but, who the hell is Gilbert Baker?"

"Yeah, I saw some reports about that," Brad said. "Sounds like you two have a real puzzle to unravel."

"I'll let you know if Maggie makes it tomorrow morning," Nick offered.

"She's that bad?"

"Yeah. Life threatening injuries," Nick said.

Brad and I left Nick as he walked toward the front doors. We went to the elevator and went to Christina's room.

Carolyn and Christina were chatting when we walked in.

Christina looked wrung out, but she was very upbeat. "I'm thrilled I know my doctor," Christina said.

"That's why this place is so highly rated," I said.

Carolyn and then Brad stayed a few minutes and left. I leaned down to kiss Christina on the forehead, and she reached up to give me a one-arm hug. Life is good. And now it's getting better. Even a one-armed hug is better than none at all.

I noticed Christina was fading fast. She was quiet for a long time and then surprised me. "God was watching out for me," she said aloud. "Thank you, Lord."

"Whoa. What brought that on?"

Christina looked at me. "I'll talk to you tomorrow, my love."

I kissed her goodnight and walked to my truck. My mind took off soaring around the universe the minute I exited the hospital door. Who is Gilbert Baker? How did he get access to Melvyn's garage Thursday night before the murder Friday morning? Gilbert Baker has to be the killer. Is there any doubt? What am I forgetting to do?

After I climbed into my truck, I sat for a few minutes reflecting on my day so far. Then Christina came back into my mind. What's happening with Christina? I let my eyes move upward studying the puffy clouds in the azure blue sky. Thanks from me, too, Big Guy.

Then I remembered what I wanted to do. I glanced at my watch. 5:15! Probably too late! I dialed Karl Albertson's cell phone number. It immediately went to voice mail. I dialed his office phone number, hoping his secretary might be working late. She was.

"Karl is over in Ford Junction at his grandson's birthday party," she told me. Of all the executives I knew, Karl Albertson was the master at "not being available." When he didn't want to be bothered, Karl could erect so many barriers to getting to him that anyone who tried, no matter how urgent, just gave up. "I can put a message on his computer screen. That's the first thing he'll see tomorrow morning when he comes into the office."

"Tomorrow's Saturday," I said.

"Doesn't matter. He'll be in here at nine-thirty."

Christina's story about the church marquee came to mind.

I decided to find it.

*   *   *

I left Our Lady of Grace Rehab Hospital and drove north. Since they were one way streets, I turned west on 26th Avenue until I was six blocks west of Randolph Boulevard then turned north a block and turned east on 27th Avenue. Three blocks west of Randolph I spotted the marquee for the Servants of Christ Evangelical Bible Church. I drove around the block so I could park on the side street to read it. The sun highlighted the marquee with bright light.

It appeared unchanged from what Christina remembered and read "Be still and rest in the Lord; wait for Him/ Yes people, slow down and stay alive". The pastor's name was J. Walker Christianson.

While I sat staring at the marquee, a battered red Ford Ranger pickup truck drove up and parked on Matthews Street across from me.

A tall, heavy set African-American man got out and walked toward the marquee, carrying a large wooden case. He wore faded jeans, a white T-shirt with a red cross at the right breast, and ratty sneakers with untied shoe laces. He set the case down on the ground and inserted a key into a key slot at the bottom of the marquee. He lifted the glass front of the marquee that was hinged at the top.

I got out of my truck and walked toward him. "Are you J. Walker Christianson?" I asked him.

"I am," he said in a deep baritone voice I associated with evangelical preachers. He turned to get a full look of me. "And you are … Colonel Kurt Maxxon, I do believe."

"Yes, I am," I said. "Are you a racing fan?"

"My thirteen-year-old son is an avid Kurt Maxxon fan. His bedspread is red and white with the Number 27 car on it. His pillows are the same. He's got a Kurt Maxxon jacket and ball cap."

"I wondered who was buying all that stuff," I said, grinning widely.

"Now you know, Colonel Maxxon," he said. "What can I do for you, today?"

A gray cloud dimmed the light on the marquee. "My wife was nearly killed in a wreck at 27th and Randolph a few days ago,"

I said. "She told me she slowed down to read your marquee and that may be why she was the second car hit, and not the first. The driver of the first car died from her injuries."

"I'm sorry to hear your wife was in that accident," J. Walker said, turning to study his sign. "I'm glad it slowed her down. In fact, that may be witness enough to leave this message up for awhile. When the congregation asks why, I'll tell them about ... I'm sorry, what is her name?"

"Her name is Christina," I said. I watched J. Walker's eyes as he memorized the name.

"How is Christina doing? Which hospital is she in?" he asked.

"She's at Our Lady of Grace Rehab, now," I said. "And she's doing pretty well."

"That's wonderful," he said. "Would either of you mind if my son and I visit her?"

"No, she'd like that. And I would, too."

He closed the large case. "We'll go see her tomorrow," he promised.

"What's your son's name?" I asked.

"J. Walker Christianson, the Second," he said. "You autographed his jacket and cap a year ago at the race. He's really growing up. I think the next thing he'll want is a Kurt Maxxon edition of a Ford Taurus."

"We'll be switching to the Ford Fusion next year," I said. "I'll call Ford and see what I can do." In the last few years the NASCAR teams who ran the Ford Taurus had switched to the Ford Fusion. I'd been kicking around the idea of switching Nikki to a Fusion. Talking to J. Walker, I finalized my decision. The sun came out from behind the gray cloud and brightened the marquee.

J. Walker face took on a brilliant smile. "It looks like God likes your move. You really are as great as everyone says."

I left J. Walker and walked across the street back to my truck. I sat staring at the sign for a long time after J. Walker had driven away. He's going to leave the marquee unchanged. That's good. I wish he'd never change it.

* * *

I drove home to take care of Beau. Beau wanted pizza delivered again. He and I spent the evening with the TV on, but muted. Beau dozed on Christina's chair, always alert to when I got up from my recliner. I brought my writing tablet to the chair and sat staring at a blank page after I wrote in big letters across the top of the page:

WHO IS GILBERT BAKER??

After several minutes of thought, the only thing that came to mind was:

Gilbert Baker knew Bay was thinking about sponsoring a racecar ... How?

CHAPTER TWENTY-ONE
Saturday Morning, September 1

Kurt Maxxon

I saw the CLOSED sign in the window when I turned to walk toward Theodore's Sports Bar off the lobby of the Holiday Inn. That's when I remembered it was Saturday and breakfast started at seven on the weekends. I went around and entered the lobby of the hotel, then looked around for a chair to wait. I'd no more than sat down when Alisa and Mutt get off the elevator. I stood and went to meet them.

"How long have you been waiting?" Alisa asked.

"He was probably here at five-thirty," Mutt said.

"About five minutes," I said. "Weekdays it opens at six thirty. I forgot it was Saturday."

As we moved slowly toward the restaurant opening, one of the wait staff arrived to undo the rope chain blocking the entrance walked away. The three of us went in and looked around. A waitress waved at us from across the room. "Sit wherever you want," she yelled.

We sat down at a large round table, and the waitress came toward us with an armful of menus.

"I think we all want the buffet," I said, looking at Alisa then Mutt who murmured agreement. The waitress kept the menus in her arm and said, "You want something to drink?"

We all ordered coffee. The waitress left for coffee, and the three of us walked to the buffet line.

"So you're going home today," I said. "I'll bet you're glad to have this assignment behind you."

Alisa smiled. "It has been interesting, that's for sure."

"I wish we could talk to Christina about Maggie," I said. "But Christina doesn't seem to remember Maggie. That's just as well as far as I'm concerned."

Alisa dug into her briefcase and pulled out a green report cover. "I hope I did what you wanted me to do."

"Oh you did everything I wanted and more," I said. "I really appreciate what you found out about Maggie and her involvement with Melvyn. But, I'm convinced Maggie didn't have anything to do with Melvyn's murder other than the murder weapon was the gun she took to the racetrack with her."

"They got some of Maggie's partials off the gun," Alisa said. "All of them tending to indicate she gripped the gun by the barrel—to carry it, not to shoot it."

"Eat your breakfast so we can get the hell out of town," Mutt said.

"Chill out, love." Alisa winked at me. "He always gets antsy when we're leaving for home."

"He's an antsy guy," I said and smiled at Mutt.

Mutt glared at me. "See if I write anything about the number twenty-seven car ever again."

"You're not covering the SRVSCRA any more, remember?" I said.

"Boys, boys, try to get along for another fifteen minutes," Alisa said.

Actually it was another forty minutes before I bid Alisa and Mutt goodbye. Mutt drove away in his Land Rover while Alisa and I watched. "He is always in a hurry to get home," she said. Alisa moved to her BMW and dropped down into it. "Tell Christina we'll run over to see her in a few days, once she's back to near normal."

I pushed Alisa's car door shut and said, "I will. Have a safe trip." I watched as Alisa roared out of the parking lot onto the highway.

*   *   *

Beau acted like a show dog on his leash as we crossed the lobby and went to the elevator. He strutted down the hall and then heeled when I told him to and followed me into Christina's room. Christina was sitting with her bed half raised when she saw Beau come through the door. I thought she was going to try to get out of bed on her own. I quickly moved to pick Beau up and put him on her lap. Beau went wild, trying to fight his way out of my grip and around the cast and tubes to give her a kiss. He finally made it to her chin and kissed her. Christina kissed him back.

I sat in the guest chair and watched Christina scratch Beau's ears which calmed him down even more. Eventually, he stretched out on her lap to soak up the attention. Christina looked at me and said, "Good morning, my love."

Ah, heaven again.

"We need to talk," Christina said, and I knew it was important.

"Okay. What would you like to talk about?"

"We need to start going to church," she said and paused to see my reaction.

"I suppose," I said. I'd always felt a little guilty about racing on Sundays rather than going to church. As a child I had been raised by a devout Lutheran mother and a moderately regular Lutheran father. Family members told me that my dad didn't go to church very often until he married my mother. As a child growing up, I remembered my dad skipping church occasionally, but never too many Sundays in a row. Up until the time I left for Atlanta and Georgia Tech, I probably hadn't missed more than a couple of dozen Sunday services.

Once in college and loaded with studies, homework, NROTC, and earning a few bucks any way I could, church became more of an option than a rule. My late wife, Vicki, was a fairly devout North Carolinian Baptist. She shamed me into attending church kind of regularly from the time we married until our daughter, Vanessa, came along and reached the age where Sunday school made sense, with Little Kurt coming along behind her. I attended church more regularly as the father of Vanessa and Little Kurt. But we never became members of a church.

"Did you and Bill belong to a church?" I asked.

"No. We took the kids to the nearest church which was a Christian Church." Christina gazed off into the space above me. "When the kids were gone, we stopped going to church."

Vicki and I went through a similar transition. When we found our nest empty, I started shirking off more and more frequently. Vicki frowned on it, but she never got too vocal. When

I started racing on Sundays, Vicki at first ignored me and went to church alone each Sunday morning, while I went to the track to get ready for the competition. Eventually, as I started winning more often, Vicki started traveling around the circuit to every race, and often did not go to church before the race, since the races always start at noon.

Christina sat scratching Beau's ears. "Would you go to church with me?"

"Sure," I said, and nodded to encourage her.

"I feel like my life has been changed. I mean in a positive way. I really feel like God—I've seen Jesus Christ in the last few days—Jesus came to me, took me in his aura, and said, 'Hello, Christina. I'd like you to follow me. Trust me. Believe in me.'"

I let my face remain noncommittal. "I believe you, Christina. I've been pretty lax about acknowledging him. I constantly thank Him, though I'm not a bow your head and pray type of guy."

"I've always believed I was a Christian," Christina said, waving her good right hand in the air to put quotes around the word. "I didn't thank God like you do, I just did my duty. Don't get me wrong, I'm blessed to have you in my life, and Vicki was a blessing, too." She paused and tears trickled down her cheeks.

"Please don't cry," I said. "You know I can't handle that."

"I know that, my wonderful love. These are tears of pure love and joy. God loves you and me."

I smiled and helped her wipe away the tears with a tissue. "I know he does," I said. "Do you want to visit some churches?"

"I'd like that," Christina said. "Maybe we could go to that church where the marquee is. God used that marquee to save my life."

"That would be okay," I said.

Beau and I stayed until Christina appeared to be dozing off more often. We got home about eleven o'clock, and I was contemplating making a pot of coffee when my cell phone jangled. I answered it on speaker. It was Karl Albertson returning my call from last evening.

"Are you in your office?" I asked him. Karl's insurance office was in a new strip mall in northeast Centralia, in an area I'd never been to. I was ready to drive to it to talk to him about the problem, rather than talk about it on the phone.

"Yes, I am. What's up?"

"I need to meet with you ASAP," I said. "About an important issue regarding the track."

"Sounds serious," Karl said. "How about we meet for lunch at Pepper's?"

"I'll meet you at Jalopy's," I said. "If you don't mind."

"It'll take me about an hour."

"I'll meet you there," I said.

*   *   *

I pushed through the door at Jalopy's and saw Bay standing next to a booth with Karl Albertson sitting in it. I walked to the booth and sat down.

"What's good to eat for lunch?" Karl asked, holding the menu up to read it.

"All of it," I said.

Bay grinned. "Kurt is my advertising manager," he said.

"I'll have whatever Kurt is having," Karl said.

I ordered "Persian Stew." Karl looked at me as Bay walked toward the kitchen.

"It's really vegetable stew made with mutton rather than beef."

"Okay," Karl said and leaned back against the booth. "What's the problem with the track?"

I gave him a short version for the basis of my concern— that Gilbert Baker apparently had access to Melvyn's garage Thursday night. "I'm wondering who all has keycards to the auxiliary office. We know the key box in your office is typically available to anyone who gets into the auxiliary office, since you never lock your office."

Karl studied me for several beats. "You don't sound accusatory," he said.

"I'm not. I'm just interested in finding out how all this came down. I never place blame. You know that. It's not worth the time."

"I know," Karl said. "I'm glad it's you asking. Truth is we've probably been too lax with the keycards. We never call for them to be returned when people no longer need them. But, I guess we've never thought there was anything of value left in the office. I mean, the entire office is just information. Yes, there are a couple of computers and a copy machine. There are about eighty-five outstanding cards out there, according to Helen."

"For what, maybe thirty people who actually need to use the office?"

"If that many," Karl said with a shrug. "Helen can tell you who needs them."

"Helen has a list of all of the outstanding keycards?" I asked.

"As a matter of fact, she mentioned this a few months ago, and said we ought to have the keycards changed. We talked about it and decided to have the electronics changed over the winter and get new keycards to those who need them next spring at the start of the season. Guys like you, who need access year round, would get new keycards just as soon as we made the change."

"I need a copy of Helen's list," I said.

"I'll call Helen," Karl said, "to find out where she keeps it. I'll ask her to work with you on it."

"Is the keycard system on one of the office computers?" I asked.

"Yes. It's in Helen's desktop computer," Karl said. "My desktop computer is just for my own entertainment. Everything of importance is on Helen's computer."

Karl's cell phone rang, and he looked at the Caller ID. He punched the button and said, "We were just talking about you." He looked at me. "Kurt Maxxon and I. We were talking about that list of outstanding keycards into the auxiliary office. Remember, you told me you'd made a list. Kurt thinks someone on that list may be the one who killed Melvyn." Karl listened. "Here, let me put Kurt on. You and he can talk about it." Karl handed me his cell phone.

"Hello Kurt," Helen said. "I was just telling Karl that the list is in my center drawer; it's in a yellow file folder."

"I'll find it. Karl said there are around eighty-five names on it."

"There were," Helen said. "I've weeded it down to sixty-seven. I called several people on the list and I got their cards back. A couple of them said they had lost their cards. I haven't called any others. I was working on it a little at a time. If you have any questions, you've got my phone number."

"How many people actively need access to the office today?"

"Well, there are the track officials who each keep a file there. That's thirteen people. Then there is the bookkeeper. She comes in once a week to do the ticket sales and all. There are the racing association officers, like you, who keep files there. That's another five people."

"Five? I thought there were seven racing associations that used the track each summer."

"Two of the racing associations are small, loosely organized, and don't use that office," Helen said. "There are only five big ones, and the SRVSCRA is the biggest."

"I'll run by later today to get the list," I said. "Probably after Christina goes down for the night."

"How's she doing?"

"They moved her to Our Lady of Grace Rehab yesterday. They've already put her through several sessions of therapy."

"That's the best rehab hospital in the country," Helen said. "Let me talk to Karl again, please. You take care, Kurt."

I handed Karl his phone.

Karl and Helen talked for a few minutes, and Karl hung up.

A waitress arrived with our food check. Karl put his phone in its holster and grabbed the check. He threw a pile of bills on the table and scooted out of the booth. "I've got a ton of phone calls to return," he said. "And then there's my email."

I thanked Karl for his help and the meal and sat back in the booth. Since it was Saturday, Jalopy's was not as busy as the weekday lunches. I waited for Bay to reappear, and when he came to my booth, I told him I needed a couple of questions answered.

"Sure, give me a couple of minutes, I'll be back." He headed for the kitchen and, in a few minutes, reemerged and came to sit down. "What's up?"

"I'm interested in the comment by Jeremy that Gilbert Baker told him you were interested in sponsoring a racecar." I spread my hands in questioning gesture. "How did that come about?"

"I don't know for sure," Bay said. "I talked to a few people about it, nothing serious. I probably made a comment about that last June when I catered the State Used Car Dealers Association's conference at the Marriott Downtown."

I must have had a questioning expression on my face. Bay continued, "I was talking with three or four car dealers who are car owners in the various racing associations. They all sponsor their own cars, but I remember one of them saying something about Jalopy's Diner should sponsor a car."

"You catered that conference?"

"I catered a special lunch on Saturday for all the dealers in Greene County hosted by the Greene County Insurance Agents. There were nearly a hundred dealers there." Bay smiled, then stood and walked toward his trophy wall. The trophy wall was about thirty feet long and separated the kitchen and rest rooms from the main dining room, and held a collage of photographs, some framed, others not.

I'd glanced at the trophy wall many times over the years I'd been dining here. There were photographs of Bay with every state governor over the last twenty years, every mayor of Centralia for the same period, several famous movie stars, and hundreds of local celebrities. He had been justifiably proud of that trophy wall all the years I had known him.

Bay walked to one photograph and brought it back to the booth. He handed me the picture. It was a framed picture showing about fifteen men grouped around Bay sitting in the center. "This was taken that day."

I sat looking at the picture. I recognized four of the men, all who owned cars in other racing associations. "Can I borrow this picture?" I asked. "I want Jeremy Uggens to look at it, see if Gilbert Baker is in it."

Bay gave me a quizzical look, and then I saw understanding spread across his face. "Sure," he said. "Take it with you."

My thoughts returned to Christina and I wanted to go see her. I thanked Bay and walked to my truck, carrying the photo of Bay and several car dealers, intent on going back to the hospital. After I climbed into the truck, I sat looking at the photo, but not really focusing on anyone in particular. Is one of you the man Jeremy Uggens knows as Gilbert Baker? I tried to remember what Maggie had told Alisa about the guy. All the men in the picture seemed to match Maggie's description: *My age and fat.*

*   *   *

Kimberly Grenwahl

Kimberly led Brittany into Christina's room and looked around. Christina was dozing, but woke up at the slight noise of someone in the room. "Oh, Kimberly," Christina said, smiling. "Hello Brittany."

"Hello, Mrs. Maxxon," Brittany said. "I hope you are feeling better."

"I'm feeling much better," Christina said. "Kurt brought Beau to see me this morning, and that made me happy, but now that you've come to see me, I'm really happy."

"You can bring dogs in here?" Brittany asked.

"Yes. Pets are great therapy for people like me."

"I'll bet that was good therapy," Kimberly said.

"Beau is cute," Brittany said. "I love him just like I love Mr. Kurt."

A nurse came in and scanned the equipment hooked to Christina.

"We want to have Mikie's birthday party here tomorrow afternoon," Brittany said with an air of excitement. "So you can come."

"That is so nice of you," Christina said. "I'm glad you thought of me."

"Could you have Kurt see about using the Activities Room tomorrow afternoon?" Kimberly asked.

"Why sure," Christina said. "I'll have Kurt get the ice cream and cake. How many will be coming?"

"Marge next door will probably bring her two kids," Kimberly said. "And our gang. That's it."

"Mikie only likes chocolate cake," Brittany said. "With chocolate icing."

"That's what Kurt likes, too," Christina said. "He'll enjoy being at the party."

"I like Angel Food cake," Brittany said. "But I'll eat chocolate cake since it is what both Mikie and Daniel like."

"Chocolate ice cream, too?" Christina said.

"Naturally," Kimberly said. "Chocolate everything."

"Can Beau come to the party?" Brittany asked.

"Sure! I'll have Kurt bring him."

"Too cool," Brittany said.

"Come on young lady," Kimberly said. "We've got to get home and get some things done."

"Do you need anything, Mrs. Maxxon? Kimberly asked.

"No. I have just about everything I'll ever need. And, if I don't already have it, you can bet that Kurt will get it for me."

"You are married to one hellava man, Mrs. Maxxon."

"I am truly blessed," Christina said. "How is the romance with Jacques Dejarnet going?"

Kimberly colored slightly. "It's going okay. I was hoping he'd ask me on a date tonight, but he's probably busy with the restaurant and all."

"That's wonderful," Christina said.

*   *   *

Christina Maxxon

Christina was forcing herself to go longer between calls for pain medication, prepared to deal with a certain level of pain in order to be able to stay focused and alert.

She raised the bed back and eased into it. What did that marquee say? Something about "be still" and "wait for Him." What did it say? What did it say?

Christina reached for the drawer in the nightstand. It was empty. She pulled on the call light string. In less than a minute a nurse appeared.

"What do you need, Mrs. Maxxon?"

"Can I get a Bible to read? One with a Concordance in the back?" Christina said. "There's not one in my drawer. Doesn't the Gideon Society leave them everywhere?"

"Not in this Catholic hospital," the nurse said with a prominent grin. "There should be a Bible in the drawer, however. I'll get you one. Would you like me to call a Priest to talk with you?"

"Not right now. I just have something on my mind, and I want to think it through. My Latin has gotten rusty. You don't use the Catholic Bible with all the Latin in it, any longer, do you?"

"Not that much," the nurse said. "The older Catholic people still use it. But the younger generation uses the New Standard Version or the Revised Standard Version."

The nurse left and returned in a few minutes with a black-bound Bible. Christian took the book and looked at the spine. "This is the King James Version," Christina said.

"We keep several versions for different guests," the nurse said. "That was the first one I could find."

The nurse stood near the door watching as Christina opened the Bible to the Concordance at the back. She studied it for a long time, unsuccessfully.

"Do you need some help?" the nurse asked.

"I have parts of a verse in my mind, but I can't remember it all." Christina leafed through the Concordance pages again.

"Let me get Sister Ludmila in here," the nurse said. "She knows the Bible forward and backward. She's just down the hall."

Christina waited until Sister Ludmila came in and sat down in the easy chair next to her bed. "How may I help you, Mrs. Maxxon?" the petite girl in a white habit said.

"I … I had an accident. I mean, you know about that. Just before the accident I remember seeing a church marquee that said something about 'be still' and 'wait for Him.' I slowed down to read it, and that saved my life. I'd like to remember the entire verse."

Sister Ludmila smiled and said, "That sounds like something from Psalms or Proverbs. Let me get my computer and we can look into it." She stood and rushed out the door. When she returned, she was holding her laptop computer open on her forearm. She sat back down and punched keys as Christina marveled at her typing skills.

"Ludmila is a pretty name," Christina said. "Is that Slavic?"

"It's Russian," Ludmila said. "My mother always says it means Love of the people. This might be what you saw."

"Is there a web site for Bible studies?" Christina asked.

"There are several of them, from kind of amateurish stuff to real professional stuff. I have a list of them at my desk. I'll give you a copy of it."

"I'd appreciate that," Christina said. "I want to start studying the Bible."

"There are also web sites for daily Bible reading," Ludmila said. "That's on the same list I'm going to give you."

"Wonderful," Christina said.

Ludmila paused to read the screen. "Here we are," she

said. "This might be it. Psalms 37, verse seven. Be still before the Lord, and wait patiently for him; fret not yourself over him who prospers in his way, over the man who carries out evil devices."

Christina had opened the Bible she held to the Psalm. "That's a little different than what I have here."

"You have the King James Version," Ludmila said. "This is the Revised Standard Version. There are several different versions of the Bible out there today."

"Yes, I know," Christina said. "I'm going to start reading the Bible every day. Which version should I get for that?"

"I would recommend you look at the different Study Bibles that are available," Ludmila said. "Besides the old line, the King James Version, the New Standard Version, and so forth, there are the newer versions; for example, the New Living Translations, or the Daily Experience Version. The newer Bibles have a little more practical meaning to some people."

"It's been a long time since I really thought about faith," Christina confessed. "My folks were never strong religious people. My mother was Methodist and my father was a Lutheran. I was baptized in the Methodist church, I'm pretty sure."

"That you were baptized is the important thing," Ludmila said. "Do you have a record?"

"I was an infant," Christina said, a slight frown creasing her forehead. "I think the only record of it is my mother's notation in my Baby Book. And if my memory serves me correctly, the date given made me fourteen months old."

"There are several good churches in the Centralia area," Ludmila said.

"Kurt and I live in Albertstown," Christina said. "We go to the Emmanuel Lutheran Church every once in a while."

"I would encourage you to go each Sunday," Ludmila said. "Even join the church and become part of its everyday activity."

"I know now that God is watching out for me," Christina said, waving the Bible with her good right hand. "Just as soon as I get out of here, we are going to join the church and start going every Sunday."

"All you really need to do, Mrs. Maxxon, is welcome the Lord, Jesus Christ, into your life and your heart. He will take care of the rest."

Christina looked Ludmila directly in the eye. "I already have."

CHAPTER TWENTY-TWO
Saturday Mid-day, September 1

Kurt Maxxon

I walked through the auxiliary office into the bullpen area and moved to Helen's desk. I sat down in her steno chair and slid open her top drawer. There was a worn yellow file folder under a letter opener and a staple remover. I took the file folder out, closed the drawer, and swiveled the chair around to use the light coming in through the side window. I opened the folder and laid it on my lap, then looked at the papers in it. There were two sheets, each with two columns of neatly typed names. The first sheet was full top to bottom, the second sheet had names about two-thirds of the way down. Several names had a thick red line drawn through them, and I assumed those were the names who Helen had contacted. Four of them had a red "L" next to it, and I assumed that meant they had lost their keycard. I'd have to check with Helen to verify if my translation of her code was correct.

I scanned the names, recognizing most of them, but there was no Gilbert Baker. I went back through the names individually, visualizing those I remembered best. Each person on the list had been a track official or officer of a racing association.

Is Gilbert Baker an alias or a purely bogus name?

The thought that Melvyn could have given a key to his garage to Baker so he could show the car came to my mind. Would I do something like that? I might! If I trusted the person I gave the key to. If Melvyn gave Baker a key to his garage, he must have known Baker and trusted him.

I racked my brain again, trying to remember if I'd ever heard the name Gilbert Baker?

I closed the file folder and walked back through the auxiliary office and out the door. As I climbed into my truck, the thought that I hadn't looked at where garage number thirty-two was located came to mind. So I drove down garage row. Garage thirty-two was directly across the tarmac from garage thirty-five. Baker could have simply released the parking brake on Melvyn's car and guided it down the slight slope into garage thirty-two. Did Melvyn leave his car on the garage apron to cool off after practicing, and then Baker saw it after he shot Melvyn and moved the car to garage thirty-two?

I turned around in the gap between garage buildings and left through the main gate. Occasionally, I glanced at the yellow file folder lying on the passenger seat.

I dialed Jeremy's cell phone, and he answered on the second ring. "Where are you?" I asked.

"Uh, at the track."

"At the track?" I said. "What are you doing at the track?" I stopped at the main gate.

"Uh, yeah, just sitting in the stands," Jeremy said, "uh, thinking about how I could be racing around the track in a race when I get my car."

This might be serious, I thought. The kid might be psychologically off kilter since his car has been taken away from him.

"I want to show you something," I said. "I'm over near the admin building. Let me drive over to the grandstand."

"Uh, yeah. Okay. I'm just sitting here near the end."

I backed up so I could turn around and said, "I'll be there in two minutes."

I parked just outside the track portal, picked up the photograph Bay had lent me and walked to where Jeremy was sitting. He was the picture of dejection as he watched me approach. I moved to sit down next to him and handed him Bay's photograph. "Is Gilbert Baker one of these men?"

Jeremy studied the photograph for a long time. Then he swung his head from side to side. "Uh, none of those guys is Gilbert Baker," he said and handed the photograph back to me.

"Damn," I said. I don't know why I'd been so sure Jeremy would see Baker in that picture.

"What's the deal about the photograph?" Jeremy asked.

I didn't hear him since my mind had already soared off into the universe. I dug my cell phone out and dialed Jalopy's Diner. When a female voice answered, I asked for Bay. "He's gone for today," she told me. "Do you have his cell number?"

"No. Can you give it to me?"

She rattled off the number, and I wrote it on my writing tablet.

"Uh, what are you after?" Jeremy asked.

I held up my hand like a cop stopping traffic and dialed Bay's cell phone number. He answered after several rings. "I need some more information," I said.

"Okay, what do you need?"

"Who took this photograph of you and the used car dealers?"

"Oh … there was a photographer from the newspaper," Bay said.

"Which newspaper?"

"The Valley Voice," Bay said.

"Did he take other photographs?"

"Oh, yeah. He took a hundred pictures—at least," Bay said.

"That's great," I said. "Thanks for your help."

"What did I do?" Bay asked.

"A lot," I said. "I'll get back to you later."

I glanced at my watch, but dialed Rafe's cell number anyhow.

"What the hell you want, Maxxon?" Rafe said when he answered.

"A photographer from the Valley Voice took a bunch of pictures at the State Used Car Dealers Association conference in June," I said.

"Yeah, that was Manchester, the guy you met last weekend."

"What happened to all the pictures he took?"

"They should be down in the Morgue."

"Can I look at them?" I asked.

"I suppose," Rafe said. "Have you noticed today is Saturday? Is this important?"

"I hope to figure out who murdered Melvyn Hightower."

"Damn, Maxxon, why didn't you say so to start with? Hell yes, you can look at them. I'll get Manchester in, and we'll help you any way we can."

"I want to get Jeremy Uggens and Behrooz Sherafat to look at all the photos Manchester took at that conference to see if Gilbert Baker is in one of them."

"When?"

"As soon as possible," I said.

"In an hour?"

"That will work."

"Meet me at the front door to the newspaper in an hour," Rafe said. "Bring whoever you want."

I called Bay back and asked him if he could join us. "Yes, I will," he said.

Jeremy and I waited for several minutes before we left to go to the newspaper, which was way east on the edge of the city limits. When we arrived, there were only a half dozen cars in the parking lot. I parked my truck so I could see cars arriving. Jeremy sat quietly, but his demeanor radiated, "I'm on a mission," and he accepted his role as a major component. I watched Manchester arrive and park in his reserved space and go into the building using a key.

When Rafe arrived, I got out of my truck telling Jeremy to follow me. We intercepted Rafe about midway to the front door. "Hello Rafe," I said in greeting.

"I wouldn't do this for anyone else, Colonel Maxxon," Rafe said with a gruff voice as he hobbled along with his twin canes clattering on the concrete. He used a key to unlock the door and led us to the security guard's station where the receptionist normally held domain. We signed in as guests, and then Rafe led us to Manchester's office toward the back of the main floor of the building.

Manchester greeted us and then led us to the elevator, down to the basement level, where he led us to a huge room. There were rows of microfiche readers and hundreds of odd-sized file cabinets. Rafe led Jeremy and me to a large round table in the corner, and we watched as Manchester went to a reader and then moved into the labyrinth of file cabinets. He returned with a large box which he set down on the table. He pulled a large group photo from the box and a sheet of paper. "This is our master photo," Manchester said as he laid the two pieces on the table within easy reach.

My cell phone vibrated, and I looked at the caller ID. I didn't recognize the number, but I answered anyhow. It was Bay at the Security Guard's station. I told Rafe, who used a phone on a nearby table to clear Bay, and asked the guard to bring him down to the Morgue.

Manchester had already started showing photograph proof sheets to Jeremy. By the time Bay arrived, Jeremy had looked at three dozen proof sheets. The proof sheets were small and hard to see. Manchester walked to a nearby desk and returned with three magnifying glasses. Bay began looking at proof sheets. We were in a routine production mode of viewing the proof sheets: Jeremy first and then Bay.

Suddenly Jeremy jumped up and yelled, "That's him!" He pointed to a man in one of the photographs. We all focused our attention on the man in the photograph. I recognized the face, but I couldn't remember his name. Manchester took several seconds, but eventually declared, "That man's name is Boyd Gardner."

"Boyd Gardner," I said. "I know him."

Rafe picked up a sheaf of papers and leafed through them. He said, "Boyd Gardner owns Quality Used Cars down on south Hoover Street."

"Are you sure that's the man who said he was Gilbert Baker?" I asked Jeremy.

"Absolutely positive," Jeremy said emphatically. "That's him."

I pulled my cell phone from my shirt pocket and dialed Nick's number.

When Nick answered he was at home, and instantly went on duty. "Where are you?" he asked.

I told him. He said, "I'll be there in fifteen minutes."

It only took him twelve.

Nick was instantly convinced that my group was trustworthy. He called the duty officer and told him he wanted three squads of patrolmen to meet him near Boyd Gardner's car lot. "Will you go along and make an identification?" Nick asked

Jeremy. "We won't put you in danger or anything—he'll never see you. We just want to make sure we're getting Gilbert Baker."

"Uh, sure!" Jeremy happily agreed. He followed Nick toward the elevator. Bay, Rafe, Manchester, and I followed Nick and Jeremy to the front door. There, we all went our separate ways. I drove to the hospital and went to Christina's room.

*   *   *

Kimberly Grenwahl

Kimberly and Brittany returned home from visiting Christina. Brittany ran to the neighbor's house to fetch her siblings and led them home. In very short order the three younger children were lying on the floor watching cartoons on TV and Brittany lounged on the end of the sofa reading a library book.

"What do you guys want for supper?" Kimberly asked from the kitchen as she finished putting away dishes.

"Chef Boyardee skeddies," Mikie yelled.

"You had Chef Boyardee spaghetti last night," Kimberly said. "You need something a little more nutritious tonight."

"I don't care, then," Mikie said.

"How about mac and cheese?" Daniel offered.

"Yeah, and put some wieners in it," Mikie said.

"I was thinking more like some vegetables," Kimberly said. "Like green beans."

"Not green beans," Mikie said. "Brit's the only one in this house that likes green beans."

"Don't you like green beans, Daniel?" Kimberly asked.

Daniel looked toward Mikie, and said, "I guess I do."

"Green beans are good for you," Brittany said. "That's what I'd like to have Momma."

"Ah, geez," Mikie said. "Brit always gets what she wants."

"You got what you wanted last night," Brittany pointed out. "I ate Chef Boyardee spaghetti with you last night. So, you can just eat green beans with me tonight."

"I'll fix some french fries," Kimberly said, "and boil some wieners to go along with the green beans."

The phone rang. Kimberly answered it. "Oh! Oh, yes!" She looked away from the children. "Hi, Jacques. How are you?"

Kimberly peeked around and saw Brittany staring intently at her. "My weekend?" She brushed her hair back over her right ear. "Oh, this afternoon I'm going to go to Kurt's store and Edwin Jamison is going to show me how the parts are catalogued and stored in the bins and racks so I can just go get parts Maurey needs. I'll probably be there most of the afternoon."

The three younger children were now paying attention to the conversation,

"Tonight?" Kimberly said as she turned to look away from the children. "Oh, yes, I'd love to. Uh huh. I'll have to find someone to watch the kids. My neighbor is going out also."

Kimberly noted Brittany's face eased as a tiny smile crept onto her lips.

"She will?" Kimberly said. "Yes. Yes. That would be wonderful. Yes. Yes. Okay. I'll see you tonight." She hung up the phone and turned to look at four little faces staring at her. "That was Jacques Dejarnet," Kimberly said. "He wants me to go out with him tonight. His sister has volunteered to babysit you guys."

"Will you be home tomorrow morning?" Brittany said, a small frown creasing her otherwise smooth forehead. "We have Mikie's birthday party tomorrow afternoon, right?"

"Oh, sure. We'll have Mikie's party," Kimberly said, "You guys will be okay." She couldn't explain what was happening inside her stomach and chest.

"Do you know his sister?" Daniel asked.

"Not too well," Kimberly admitted. "But, she is a very responsible lady; she helps Jacques manage the restaurant."

"Is that where we went for Angie's Victory Party?" Brittany asked.

"Yes."

"It'll be okay, Momma," Brittany said. "I'll help her take care of the kids."

Kimberly's eyes filled with tears and she looked away again. Then she smiled at her oldest child. "You are so grown up, Brittany. You are such a big help."

"I'll help her, too, Momma," Daniel said.

"Me, too," Madison said timidly. "Me, too, Momma."

"Come here, you guys," Kimberly said, kneeling down and opening her arms wide. All four children crammed into her arms. "You're all growing so fast and Momma's proud of you. This will be fun for all of us, okay?"

CHAPTER TWENTY-THREE
Saturday Afternoon, September 1

Kurt Maxxon

I had no more than settled into the Christina's easy chair when a man and boy appeared in the doorway. I stood and moved to shake their hands. "Christina, this is J. Walker Christianson and his son, J. Walker Christianson the second."

Christina looked at me blankly. "J. Walker Senior is the pastor at the church with the marquee you slowed down to read."

Christina's face instantly brightened. "Oh my goodness," she said. "I am so pleased to meet you Pastor Christianson." She held out her hand and J Walker Senior walked over to shake it. "I'm even more pleased to meet you," J. Walker Senior said.

I looked at J. Walker the second and could tell instantly he was J. Walker Senior's son. He was two inches taller than his father, with big bones like his father so he would carry his heft with the same ease as his father. Both men had intense brown eyes set under black eyebrows that made a straight line across their foreheads. Both wore perpetual smiles. "I hear you're quite a race fan," I said. I noticed J. Walker the second was in some kind of swoon.

"You autographed my jacket, see," he turned around to show me the back of the jacket where I'd scribbled my signature.

"I sure did," I said.

"Ninety-four degrees in the shade and he wants to wear that jacket over here," J. Walker Senior said.

"I hear you might want a Kurt Maxxon Ford Fusion," I said to add a little levity.

"In two years and seven months," J. Walker the second

said.

"That'll give me some time to talk to the Ford dealer," I said.

Christina struggled to a more upright position and picked up a Bible lying on her tray table. "The message on the marquee saved my life," she said, "In more ways than one."

J. Walker smiled. "Kurt told me about your slowing down to read it."

I remembered the slip of paper in my pocket on which I had carefully copied the message for her. I pulled it out and handed it to her. She looked at it.

"Is this the message on the marquee?" she asked.

J. Walker Senior walked over and took the paper from Christina. "Yes, that's what the message says," he confirmed.

"What version of the Bible is it from?" Christina asked.

J. Walker Senior stopped for a moment and looked at Christina. "The basis for it is from the New Living Bible, but I took some liberties with it to make it fit on the marquee."

"Psalms thirty seven, verse seven in my Bible there reads, "Be still before the Lord, and wait patiently for him... You left out the word patiently."

"Not one single person in my flock mentioned that, Mrs. Maxxon. You are very perceptive. Note the first part of the verse, 'Be still and rest in the Lord.' which isn't in the King James Version you are reading there." J. Walker Senior gave a hearty laugh. "I like that part of the verse as a reminder to slow down. The Psalm is really talking about ignoring people who achieve success by devious means."

I told the group I wanted to go get something from my truck and hurried out the door. I went to my truck and dug around in the glove box, eventually finding a plastic permanent PIT PASS. I carried it back to the room and presented it to J. Walker the second. The boy was ecstatic with it. "I'll come to every race your car runs in."

"That pass will get you into the pit area in all the races at River Flats Speedway," I said. "It covers all the racing associations."

"Wow," J. Walker the second said.

"You can go see Ruth's brother race in that truck league,"

J. Walker Senior said.

"Cool." J. Walker the second was grinning so wide I thought his face might crack.

"We're going to start going to church every Sunday as soon as I can get around," Christina said. She looked at me. I nodded acceptance.

"You're welcome to visit our church," J. Walker Senior said.

"We'll do that," Christina said.

"Yes, we'll do that," I agreed. "He'll have to change the marquee before we get there."

"I don't know why," J. Walker Senior said. "If the message saved one life, it may save another and for that I'll stand the cost of another marquee for new messages." He laughed again. This man was well suited to be a pastor. His upbeat personality was infectious and made everyone feel good.

A white-clad person came into the room. "Mrs. Maxxon?" he said.

Christina held her good right hand up and said, "That's me."

"Oh. Okay. I wasn't sure," he said with a broad grin. "I'm here to take you down for another therapy session. We want to work on the muscles under that cast."

I walked with J. Walker Christianson and his son out into the parking lot and watched as they drove away in the beat up old pickup truck. I was walking back into the cafeteria when my phone vibrated and I answered it. Steve Cosburn asked me where I was and I told him.

"I'm headed toward your store to get some parts and got to wondering if you'd like to meet Jason Tobias," Steve said. "If you would, maybe you'll meet us there."

"I'm about ten minutes away," I said.

"I'm glad you're finally going to get to meet Jason. We'll see you there." I was inside the store talking to Edwin Jamison when Steve walked in leading a tall, lanky man with a smooth shaved head. He was wearing camo-cargo style shorts, and a black muscle shirt. His dark tan arms bore witness to many hours in the sun. The two men walked directly toward me.

"Kurt, this is Jason Tobias."

Jason shook my hand with a firm grip. "I'm pleased to meet you," he said. "Of all the people that were around the track, Helen talked about you more than any of the others. She thought you were the best driver of them all."

"I'm glad it was always good," I said.

"I had to come get some parts for work I've got in shop," Steve said, "and Jason was hanging around, so I decided to bring him along to see if we could meet up with you."

"If he ever gets my motorcycle running," Jason said to me, "I'll stop hanging out there."

"I've told you a dozen times," Steve said tersely, "I had to order the valves from Harley Davidson, and they are being shipped."

Jason grinned. "He's a good mechanic because he always has a good excuse for everything."

Steve wandered off to order parts from the counter person. Jason said, "Let me look around to see what you got. I like to browse around auto parts stores."

"If you need any help, just ask one of the people," I said and went upstairs to see if anything needed attention. Since it was Saturday, the only person working was a buyer who works six days a week just because he does not know what to do with his time if he isn't working. I waved to him as I walked through the area to my office.

I glanced at my watch. It had been a couple of hours since Nick and Jeremy had left the newspaper building. I was hoping Nick would call me to tell me they had Boyd Gardner in custody. When my phone rang I answered it immediately on speaker.

"He's gone," Nick growled.

"Boyd Gardner?"

"His trailer is empty. His car is gone. He's probably in Acapulco like I said."

"Damn," I said. "I doubt Jeremy will see any of his money again."

"I gotta go." Nick hung up.

I lost interest in anything other than going back to Christina's room. She should be done with her therapy session by now. Just spend a quiet evening with her.

*　　*　　*

I walked down my private stairway and clicked the remote to unlock my truck. I climbed up into the truck and put the key in the ignition. I was reaching to close my door when the passenger side door flew open and a man climbed in. In an instant I recognized the man as Boyd Gardner. My door was still open. Boyd shut his door and sat looking at me, a semi-automatic weapon in his left hand pointed straight at my chest. I thought about jumping out of the truck and running. Could I outrun a bullet?

*   *   *

Brittany Grenwahl

When they came to a wide aisle, Brittany let her mother and Edwin Jamison go ahead as she focused on the bright sunshine streaming in through the back door. She heard Jamison's voice droning on about part numbers, bar codes, rack and shelf locations, and other things. Occasionally she heard her mother's soft voice ask a question. The adults turned into another row of shelves in the labyrinth building. Brittany stood transfixed by the sunshine at the back.

If I'd stayed home to watch the other kids, we could be playing outside in the sun, doing what we wanted to. She had come with her mother because she thought it would be interesting to learn about auto parts—and it was Mr. Maxxon's business. She had hoped Mr. Maxxon would be here so she could talk to him more about racing. Mr. Jamison explained the code on the shelves and bins, and her mother seemed to understand how parts were cataloged. Brittany thought her mother was learning quickly.

Brittany glanced around the dimly lit building, but the only real attraction was the sunshine flooding the area around the back door. She walked slowly toward the door, occasionally hearing Mr. Jamison murmuring about numbers, codes, and sub-codes. When she reached the door she tried the knob. It twisted, the door opened, and she walked out onto a landing with a stairway down to the parking lot.

Suddenly a noise grabbed her attention. She looked toward it. There was Mr. Maxxon's big pickup truck. She saw Mr. Maxxon sitting in the driver's seat as he reached to close his door. He started the engine.

Can I get his attention? Brittany started down the steps.

"Mr. Maxxon! Mr. Maxxon!"

She stopped when she saw Mr. Gardner coming running up and bang on the door of the pickup, and then climb into the passenger side. *He has a gun! Mr. Gardner has a gun!*

Through the rear window of the truck she saw Mr. Gardner wave the gun toward Mr. Maxxon. She slipped back to the top of the landing and inside the building, leaving the door open. She peeked around the door sill. Why does Mr. Gardner have a gun? Why doesn't he like Mr. Maxxon?

She watched as Mr. Maxxon's pickup truck backed up and drove toward the street. She turned to find her mother. She heard Mr. Jamison's voice. Brittany ran to find her mother. "Momma! Momma!" she yelled as she ran looking between rows of shelves.

"We're here, Brit," she heard her mother yell.

When she spotted them she turned up the row. "Momma, Mr. Gardner just kidnapped Mr. Maxxon. Something's wrong, Momma. You gotta call the police."

"What are you talking about?" her mother asked. "Who is Mr. Gardner?"

"He's ... he's the guy who led the races to start. Uncle Chuck liked his Mustang. He ... he was ... I don't know Momma. Please, Mr. Maxxon needs help. Mr. Gardner was pointing a gun at him. I don't want Mr. Maxxon to get hurt."

Edwin Jamison ran toward the front of the store. "A gun?" he yelled as he banged through the office door.

"Please, Momma, call the police. Mr. Maxxon needs our help. Mr. Maxxon is in trouble," Brittany shouted.

Kimberly dug her cell phone out of her fanny pack and speed dialed the number Kurt had put in her phone for Detective Nick Boynton. When he answered, Kimberly said, "Hi Detective Boynton, this is Kimberly Grenwahl, Kurt Maxxon's new clerk. I'm worried about Kurt. My daughter Brittany says she just saw somebody she calls Mr. Gardner get into Kurt's pickup and point a gun at him. She says ... Oh, ah, we're at Kurt's store. Yes, in the parking lot here. Yes, yes, we can stay here."

Jamison ran back from the front of the store. "Kurt turned left and is going north on Monroe Street."

"Nick," Kimberly shouted into the phone, "Are you still there? Edwin Jamison says Kurt is driving north on Monroe Street right now."

"That's good. I'll get my resources up looking for them."

Brittany, her mother and Edwin Jamison lost interest in the auto parts and they went to the front of the store where they paced around waiting.

"I didn't know Kurt was here," Brittany heard her mother say.

"Yeah, he was up in his office," Mr. Jamison said. "He came over to meet with Steve Cosburn and Jason Tobias. I never know when he comes and goes. There's a private entrance to his office from the parking lot."

After a few minutes a blue and white squad car roared into the lot and slid to a stop in front of the store. A uniformed police lady jumped out of the passenger side and dashed through the front door. Jamison intercepted her and led her toward Kimberly and Brittany said, "Kurt's truck left here and drove north, oh, probably five minutes ago."

"We've got that," the lady officer said. "Who saw the gun?"

"My daughter, Brittany," Kimberly said putting her hand on Brittany's shoulder.

The lady police officer knelt down in front of Brittany, and she read the name tag over the lady's left breast pocket: *OFR: K. Lacy* "Tell me what you saw." She said and smiled.

Brittany liked her. "I went out the back door and I saw Mr. Gardner getting into Mr. Maxxon's pickup truck. He had a gun in his hand. He pointed the gun at Mr. Maxxon. It scared me."

"Okay. That would scare me, too. How do you know Mr. Gardner?" Officer Lacy asked.

"He used to drive his fancy Mustang to start the races and if there was a crash he drove out to stop the cars," Brittany said.

"You mean, like the pace car?" Officer Lacy asked.

"That's it," Brittany shouted. "Yep, the pace car. Mr. Gardner drove the pace car. Me and Uncle Chuck rode around the track with him one time at the start of the race."

Officer Lacy pulled the microphone clipped to her epaulet and spoke into it. "Com. Seventy-one ... I've confirmed Kurt Maxxon left this location with the suspect in the Hightower homicide. They were seen driving north on Monroe. Suspect has a gun and appears to be threatening Kurt Maxxon."

"Copy, seventy-one. Did you copy unit three?"

"Unit Three copied."

Kimberly recognized Nick Boynton's voice as Unit Three.

Brittany stared at the lady police officer. "You've got to save Mr. Maxxon," she said, her voice breaking and worry lines creasing her forehead. "Please. You have to."

"We're going to," Officer Lacy promised as she stood up and adjusted her equipment belt. "I'm going to do that right now." She trotted back to the squad car and climbed in. The car sped off with its lights flashing and the siren blaring.

*   *   *

Kurt Maxxon

I stared at the muzzle of the pistol pointed at my chest. "What the hell are you doing, Boyd?"

"You're going to help me get out of town," Boyd said.

"What are you talking about?" I hoped my voice was stronger than it felt.

"You know the cops are after me," Boyd said. "You're always up to your ass into these things."

I had talked to this voice that Friday night—the voice that admitted he had killed Melvyn Hightower, and he would do in me if I tried to track him down. We sat in silence for a long time. "Where do you want to go?" I asked, my heart pounding in my ears.

"Get this rig moving," Boyd commanded. "You jump and run and I'll shoot you down."

"Then how would you get out of town?"

"Driving your truck. The tinted windows will hide me. Get going and we'll head north," he said, gesturing with the gun, "go north on Riverside Drive."

"Why don't you just give it up?" I asked.

"Yeah, sure, and spend the rest of my life in jail."

Boyd turned to look out the window. "Get to moving, or I'll blow you away now, and drive myself."

I pulled the gear shift into reverse to back out of the parking space. In the rearview mirror I thought I saw motion, but couldn't see anyone. If someone saw me leaving would they realize I was under duress?

"I was lucky," Boyd continued as I drove toward Monroe Street in front of the store. "When Nick and those cops showed up at my place a few minutes ago I was out back and got away without them seeing me. But I knew why they were there. I mean, Nick Boynton and six cops weren't there for my annual contribution to the police benevolent fund."

I waited to turn left across four lanes of traffic. "They'll track you down, Boyd. You won't get away with it." I tried to keep my voice conciliatory, smooth, and calming per the Marine Corps training programs I'd attended.

"Why should I have to spend the rest of my life in jail," Boyd droned. "Just because I did the world a favor by taking that lying, cheating, stealing sonabitch out of the world. I did the world a favor."

"Melvyn told you he'd sell the car to you and then backed out?" I asked.

"Yeah. Damn him," Boyd said. "Last year I had two other buyers for the car. Both times Shag backed out at the last minute. I tried to tell him this time we both could make some real money off this kid who had more money than sense. Once again, he backed out of the deal."

"You had a deal with Melvyn on the car?"

"Yeah, hell, we talked last Wednesday after I found out the kid was serious and had lots of money. Shag says, 'Yeah, I'll sell it for the right price.' I says, 'I'll give you seventy-five thousand for it.' Shag says, 'If you can get me seventy-five, it's yours.' Then that lying, cheating—he backed out again." Boyd swallowed hard. "Damn him. He wouldn't sell me that damn car of his."

"How did you get into Melvyn's garage Thursday night?" I asked.

"Shag went by and unlocked the padlocks," Boyd spoke as he surveyed the area. "I met the kid, who was late. When he finally got there, I took him over and showed him the car. He fell in love on the spot."

"Have you spent all the money he gave you?"

"No, dammit. It's all still in a safe in my secret hide-away. I was going to pay off some of the loans I have out, but hadn't done it yet. Obviously, I haven't had a chance to go get it."

"What kind of loans?"

"I bought those five Shelby Mustangs," Boyd said. "Remember, I used to run one of them as the Pace Car for all the races. I did that for over six years. Three of them were GT500 Shelbys models. Every time I bought a car I had to take out another loan. Like a damn fool, I kept buying those cars with money I didn't have. Then over the last three years, with the economy in the tank, I tried to sell the cars and was getting about half of what I paid for them."

"Where are you thinking of going?" I asked.

"I just want you to get me out of town. After that, I'll just fade away. I can lie low in my secret hide-a-way for a while, if I have to. Then get away for good. The cops won't be looking for me in your truck. I'll tell you where to go as we drive."

Boyd had let the gun float lower, but once again he brought it up pointing at me. Take Monroe up and get on Riverside Drive going north. I'll tell you when to turn."

I drove north on Monroe Street to the city limits where Monroe becomes Riverside Drive and started following the river on the bluff above. Boyd sat quietly letting the countryside fly by. "You won't get very far without a plan," I said.

"Oh, I've got a plan," Boyd said. "I've been preparing for this to happen."

"How far can you get? I mean, once I tell them where I left you, the cops will be all over the landscape."

"That can only happen if you're alive to tell them," Boyd sounded more menacing than he had before.

"Oh," I said. "This is my last trip out of town, right?"

"Well, think about it, Maxxon. If I let you live, my whole plan won't work, since I planned to lay low for several days before I try to get out of the valley." Boyd paused. "It'll take them awhile to find your truck, wherever I leave it. Then it'll take them some more time to find your body, wherever I leave it. In the meantime, I'll be waiting for the whole thing to cool. Some night I'll get into the motorboat I've got hidden on the river, and leave the valley, never to be seen again. By the way, the combination to my safe is my birthday plus my wedding date."

"I don't have a clue what either date is," I said.

"They're both easy enough to find out, if this doesn't go down like I plan."

"Where's your hide-away?"

"Yeah, right," Boyd grinned. "Like I want anyone to know. For your information, it's about a half mile from my motor boat."

We were winding along on Riverside Drive, climbing up toward the crest of the bluff when I spotted a helicopter about a mile behind us. I glanced at Boyd who was studying the countryside ahead and occasionally looking down at the river.

"You sure you want to go through with this?" I asked again. "It would be easier if you just give up and turn yourself in. You might be able to convince the DA Melvyn provoked you."

Boyd said. "I don't think my chances are real good with that one, Maxxon. You'll have to come up with something better than that."

I glanced at the weapon pointed at me. It looked about the same size as the weapon the drifter had pointed at me Friday morning. I looked in my side mirror. No chopper. Damn, maybe that chopper was just my imagination working overtime. We wound our way onto the top of the bluffs. When I looked again, the chopper was there. Tracking us. God, I hope so. I looked at Boyd out of the corner of my eye. He was still intent on the landscape flying by.

The chopper disappeared below the bluffs. Each time it reappeared, it was closer. I glanced at the chopper frequently in my rear view mirror. You've got to figure out how to take Boyd out. Watch the chopper.

"How much further?" I asked Boyd.

"Oh, we've got a little ways to go," he said. "I know about where I want to leave your body. I haven't figured out where to leave your truck. But, it'll all work out. At least, for me."

As I drove I watched my side mirrors. The chopper reappeared and I watched it move within a quarter mile us. It rocked the rotors. I touched the brake pedal lightly—just enough to light the brake lights—three times—watching Boyd out of my peripheral vision. Then I touched my brake pedal three long pauses, and then repeated the three short times. The chopper rocked its rotors three times. They had correctly interpreted my di-di-di; dah-dah-dah; di-di-di—Morse code for S-O-S. The chopper disappeared below the bluff. That'll keep the rotor noise from reaching us. I looked at Boyd. He was intently looking toward the river.

I saw a sharp curve coming about a half mile head. I drove into the curve too fast, then jammed on the brakes and swung the steering wheel hard to the left. Boyd slammed against the passenger-side door. The truck careened sideways, rocking violently. Boyd's gun fell to the floorboard. He scrambled to find it.

The truck stopped in a cloud of dust in the ditch on the opposite side of the road. Before it had fully stopped rocking, I leaped out and ran bent over back down the ditch toward a little dip caused by a washout. I had just about reached the washout when I saw a geyser of dirt shoot up just to my left. I ducked lower and kept running in a zig-zag pattern. I heard the report from Boyd's weapon as I scrambled down into the washout. Another geyser of dirt rose even closer to me this time. I looked back toward Boyd and saw him standing on the opposite side of my truck, resting his arms on the hood while he aimed the weapon. He knows how to shoot! I gave up the running and sprawled flat in the washout just as an explosion of rock flew into the air exactly where I would have been had I kept running. I lay on the ground gasping for air. It's all over unless that chopper gets back here—fast.

I heard the roar of the chopper as it came up over the bluff. I heard a bullhorn voice say, "Throw down your weapon, and put your hands straight up." I raised my head to look toward my truck. Boyd fired one more round at me. I heard the bullet whizzing by too close for comfort. I watched Boyd turn and point the weapon up at the chopper. Boyd's hand jerked as he fired a round at the chopper. Before I could even think "that isn't smart" an ear-shattering volley of automatic gunfire overwhelmed the noise of the chopper. Boyd's body jerked violently, stiffened and staggered backward. Stray slugs slammed into my truck shattering the passenger side window and leaving giant holes in a spider-webbed windshield and in the hood. Looking under my truck, I saw Boyd sit down on the ground his weapon still gripped by two hands, but resting on the ground between his legs. Both his sleeves had turned bright red.

The chopper landed up the road a few hundred yards, kicking up dust out of the ditches on both sides of the road. Two people in full desert camouflage body armor jumped out and slowly walked toward Boyd with their weapons trained on him. Boyd had not moved. I doubted he would ever move again.

*　　*　　*

"Let's go up to my office," Nick said, and led me to the elevator. Nick's desk was the usual mess and his visitor's chair held a leaning stack of file folders. Nick gathered two mismatched chairs from other desks and pulled them over. I sat down as Jeremy came walking into Nick's office.

"Are you alright?" Jeremy asked me.

"I'm fine," I said. "A little stiff and sore, and a few scratches, but I've had worse."

Nick dialed a phone number and asked someone to come to his office.

In a few minutes, Timothy Masterson came into the office and walked to me. As he shook my hand, he asked "How is Christina doing, Colonel?"

"She was doing great, Bat" I said. "I've got to get back out there. She's probably worried about me."

"I sent Officer Lacy over to tell her I'd asked you to help me out for a little while." Nick assumed a smug look. "Okay, tell me how it went down."

"I went to my store to meet Jason Tobias and Steve Cosburn. I was leaving and Boyd climbed into my truck with the gun. At first he was talking about me carrying him out of town. It didn't dawn on me he was planning that I never made it back into town."

"Good thing little Brittany saw you leaving your place," Nick said. "And then saw Boyd jump into your truck. Kimberly called me even as you were driving out of the parking lot. The chopper picked up your truck in about five minutes."

"I wondered—"

"That's a pretty smart little girl," Nick said.

"She's a brilliant young lady," I said. I looked at Jeremy. "Looks like you'll be getting your racecar."

"Thanks to you," he said.

"By the way," I said, looking at Jeremy. "Boyd gave me the combination to his safe. So we can go get your money." I handed Nick Boyd's card with a series of numbers scrawled on it. "Just as soon as Nick here locates Boyd's hide-away."

"Where's his hide-away?" Nick asked.

"I have no idea," I said, honestly. "I can give you a couple of clues, however."

"And what would they be?" Nick opened his notebook and grabbed a pen off his desk.

"Boyd told me he had a motorboat stashed somewhere on the river upstream from where we were when you took him out. And within a half mile of the boat is where he said his hide-away is."

"That narrows it down quite a bit, to about twenty square miles," Nick said as he jotted notes in his book. "We'll need to get the state boys in on this. Can you call Brad Langley?"

"I can do that," I said.

When we find the money, we'll have to put it into evidence. After we close the case we can get it back to Jeremy."

"Sounds fair to me," I said, glancing at Jeremy.

I dialed Enterprise Rent-A-Car and found out they had a few cars available. I told them I'd take it and be there in twenty minutes.

Against my better judgment, I decided to let Jeremy take me rather than have Enterprise pick me up. When he pulled out of the police parking lot, Jeremy said, "How soon before I should call that guy's wife and see if she will sell me the car?"

"Monday morning," I said.

The kid's dreams were going to come true after all. Well, at least the part about him owning a racecar. Becoming a racecar driver might take awhile—maybe even forever!

*   *   *

Jeremy dropped me off at Enterprise Rent-A-Car and in less than ten minutes I was cruising in a Caddy big enough to need a yacht berth at the marina. I drove home to take care of Beau and a quick shower. I thought about taking Beau with me to the hospital, but decided against it. I went to Christina's room. I hope she doesn't ask me where I've been. Lord, I hope she hasn't started watching TV—especially the local news.

When I arrived Christina had visitors. She said, "You know Mason. And this is his wife Mercedes."

I shook hands with both. "Welcome back to Centralia," I said. "Not the best circumstances to have to come home."

"Mom needed to meet Mercy anyhow," Mason said. "It's

not a bad drive. We took turns driving, and only stopped one night in a motel."

"Mason needs directions to our house," Christina said. "He's never been there. The guest bedroom is okay. There may be some junk on the bed, but just throw it in the closet."

As she spoke I realized that I had never really got to know Mason that well. He had left home long before Christina and I got together.

I gave Mason directions starting from Christina's old house about two miles from where we lived now. "I'm going to run by the track to return a folder I borrowed from Helen," I told Christina. "If you kids want to go to the house now, I'll give you my key."

"We'll probably spend an hour or so here with Mom and then head that way," Mason said. "If that's alright?"

"Sure," I said. "I'll be there in about thirty minutes."

"You need to take care of Beau," Christina said.

"I already did," I said. I ignored the questioning look Christina gave me.

*　　*　　*

I was nearly to my Cadillac when my cell phone vibrated. It was Christina's daughter, Tabetha. She had been to my house when Christina came over to visit Vicki, so she knew where it was. I gave her directions to the hospital and waited for her to arrive. I carried Isabella while Tabetha led the two boys. When we walked into Christina's room, she did a double take and her face wrinkled into the beginning of a cry as I handed Isabella to her. She fought down the tears and said, "My pretty baby come to see Namma."

The arrival of Mason and Mercedes had raised Christina's spirits several notches. Now her spirits soared as she cooed gibberish with Isabella with a boy snuggling on either side of her. I doubt she even remembered she was trussed up and wearing a cast—proving she could be a champion doting grandmother even with one hand tied behind her back.

On the drive home it dawned on me that we were going to be short a bedroom. I decided to lock the doll room and pick up the master bedroom for Tabetha and her kids to use. Mason and Mercedes could get by in the guest bedroom even thought it had two desks and a file cabinet taking up space.

Beau and I would be bunking on the sleeper sofa for the next few days.

The sun was setting into a purple western horizon and clouds were building. It would probably rain overnight. Beau had gone out through his door and returned quickly. He had taken a sip of water and was sitting calmly on Christina's recliner.

I thought over the visit with Christina. With my new respect for life, I was more sensitive to her new glow—a glow of inner peace and happiness. I know she will share her secret with me.

"Can we get by two more days without mom, Beau?" I asked. "And there's going to be a lot of company."

Beau swung his head to look at me; got up and jumped into my lap. He stood on his rear legs on my lap, put his front paws on my chest and wagging his tail he gave me one of his wet kisses. I'm sure he grinned and said "Yeah, we can get by."

"Life is good" I said, looking upward. "Thank you, Big Guy."

I was sure I heard Beau say he wanted pizza for supper again tonight. Beau and I should go share that pizza with the family of the brilliant young lady who saved my life. I owed that brilliant young lady a lot of pizzas.

THE END